THE DARK BROTHERS: BOOK 3

KEPT TO KILL

KYRA ALESSY

Copyright 2021 by Dark Realms Press

All rights reserved.

No part of this book may be reproduced in any form or by any electronic or mechanical means, including information storage and retrieval systems, without written permission from the author, except for the use of brief quotations in book reviews.

This work of fiction licensed for your enjoyment only. The story is the property of the author, in all media, both physical and digital, and no one except the author may copy or publish either all or part of this novel without the express permission of the author.

Credits:

Edited by Catherine Dunn

Cover by Deranged Doctor Designs

ALSO BY KYRA ALESSY

Sold to Serve:

Book 1 of the Dark Brothers Series

www.kyraalessy.com/sold2serve

One woman enslaved. Three callous masters. Secrets that could destroy them all ...

Bought to Break:

Book 2 of the Dark Brothers Series

www.kyraalessy.com/bought2break

A woman freed from chains. Three ruthless mercenaries redeemed. Intense attraction that won't be denied – no matter the cost.

For more details on these and the other forthcoming books in this series, please visit Kyra's website:

https://www.kyraalessy.com/bookstore/

IF YOU ARE IN ANY WAY RELATED TO ME

Seriously, I feel the need to put this in every book I write. If you are a part of my family, put this book down. Don't read it. Just burn it. It'll be better for everyone.

Granny, if you're reading this …. Ok, fine! But I did warn you, old woman.

To everyone else who's related to me: (Especially you, mom!) If you do not heed this page, never ever speak of it to me. I don't want to hear anything about this book from your lips. You will literally ruin my writing mojo if I know you read it. For real.

CHAPTER 1

LILY

There had been a fire. That much she knew from the shouts and screams, the scurrying people she had seen in the courtyard below the barred casement of her small room. The topmost bower; the highest and most inaccessible prison in the Collector's fortress. He'd never called it that, told her real prisons didn't have warmth, sunlight, food and all the books she could read from his library. But a prison it was, and it was where he had kept her since he'd brought her here from the north. She'd still been a child then.

The servants of Vineri's great estate had seen to her needs well enough; brought food, wood for the grate, and books. Couldn't have Vineri's prize possession going mad from boredom, could they?

Though sometimes she wondered if she'd gone mad anyway.

When she'd first come here, the room had been small and stifling. She'd longed for the sky. She'd hated this place. But now, after so long, she loathed accompanying Vineri on his journeys, his little displays of power where she was the main attraction – or deterrent. Without fail, she was immutably glad when she was returned to her room's stone confines. Hearing the lock sliding smoothly into place was like a balm on her spirit. Vineri was right. She'd never have survived without his generosity – though, like everything, it had its price.

She sighed as she craned her neck for some glimpse of what was happening below, but she couldn't see anything of merit. She threw herself down into her worn chair in front of the currently fireless grate and shivered as she wrapped her shawl closely around her, opening a book.

The wood had not been brought for two days. No food either. There had been yelling earlier, but it had stopped. Perhaps one of the servants would tell her about it later through the door.

Lily began to read, quickly losing herself in the new story.

The sun was high by the time she heard boots clomping up the stone stairs, echoing through the hall. She canted her head as she listened. They didn't sound like the—

A scraggly face appeared at the small window and she frowned. The bolt was thrown hard, making a loud bang that resonated through the tower. Still she didn't move as the door was flung open and a large man, unthinkably, *stepped inside her room.*

She was on her feet and shoving herself against the far wall by the time his eyes fell on her and he grinned – somewhat nastily, she decided – and started forward, *crossing the line.* Her eyes widened in shock. No one crossed the line! Not unless she was cloaked and gloved, and even then, only Vineri. By the gods, her food was usually pushed through the cracked door on a tray with a long stick!

'Stop!' she cried. 'Don't come any closer!'

He didn't listen.

'Read the sign!' she screeched desperately.

'Can't read, woman,' he snarled, looking her up and down

in a way that made her blood run cold. She'd never experienced a man *leering*. He didn't know. There were more men behind him, laughing and joking. None of them knew!

Lily screamed as he grabbed her, tearing off her shawl. She tried to bat him away with her arms, not touching her skin to his, but he grabbed her by the throat with his bare, meaty fingers and the contact felt like a brand.

He yelled immediately and dropped her. He jumped back, glaring at his palm and then at her.

She stared back in horror. 'You fool,' she whispered as he fell to his knees with a gurgle, his face turning an awful shade of purple as he gasped for breath.

He thudded to the floor. Already he was bleeding from his eyes, nose and ears as he twitched on the ground in front of her. Dimly she wondered if this was one of Vineri's diversions or, perhaps, a test. It had never happened so quickly before. He'd be delighted, she thought as she sank to her knees, feeling as though she might retch. At least there was nothing in her stomach, seeing as she hadn't been fed for days.

The soldier in front of her breathed his last and she gave the others behind him a level look even as she felt the prickle of tears that she forced back. He had been intending her harm, she reminded herself. He was probably a terrible person. But it didn't ease the guilt. She stood shakily, giving the other soldiers a wide berth. They'd all backed away at least.

'Get Vineri,' she ordered.

'Odd. I didn't think the Collector enjoyed women.'

A man cloaked in black pushed through the group of soldiers as they hastened to step out of his way. He was tall and broad, his hair a sable brown and his jaw square. His nose looked like it had been broken at least once and his ear was missing a piece at the top, she noted. He also had an intricate, winding tattoo that began on the side of his neck and disappeared beneath his tunic. She'd never seen such a man. Her breath hitched and she hoped that if her cheeks were coloring, he didn't notice.

She needn't have worried. He barely looked at her, his gaze flitting around the room, taking in the only home she'd ever really known and making her feel open, vulnerable. She didn't care for it. Not one bit.

'Your lover is dead.'

Her lover? She made a face at the thought. Wait, had he just said Vineri was dead? 'Dead?' she muttered aloud.

He finally glanced at her and then away again. 'Take her below to wait with the others.'

'But, sir, she killed Orinson.' One of them gestured to the man lying on the floor.

The man in black, their leader, sneered as he looked down. 'Doubtful. He was frequently seen overindulging in Faerie smoke. Looks like his body finally gave out.' He toed the corpse with his boot like a child checking an animal was dead, his condescending gaze falling on her again. Whatever he saw made him bark a laugh and descend the stairs without a backward glance.

Two of the soldiers advanced, but she could see in their faces that they knew their friend's death had been her doing.

'Please. You saw what happened,' she tried, ready to beg if necessary. 'I can't leave the room.'

But the nearest one shook his head. 'You're the camp's now. You'll soon learn that an order from the Commander is an order best followed for all involved,' he said, though he didn't touch her, and if there had been lust in his eyes before, all there was now was fear. But he drew his sword and used it to gesture to the door. The threat was clear. Their commander hadn't actually specified that she had to be alive when they took her below.

Lily took a step and then another, feeling as if she was walking to her death. Swallowing hard, she battled the dizziness that threatened to pitch her down the winding stairs. This couldn't be happening, could it? Where were they taking her? She reached the bottom and made herself loosen the death grip she had on the railing, walking over the threshold until she was outside, in the square she could see from her window. There were a few others sitting in the frozen mud, a couple she recognized from the kitchens, as they sometimes brought her meals.

She was prodded in the back with a sword and stepped forward, and the ones who knew who she was began to mutter to each other, their eyes wary.

She looked down as she walked, wishing she had some shoes or a cloak or her gloves, but Vineri always took them away when they got back from their *excursions* in case she got a 'stupid idea' into her head, he'd said. The man had been a permanent fixture in her life almost for as long as she could remember. Could he really be dead?

She was told to sit by the others, which she did, trying not to take it personally when they shuffled as far away as they could get. She was used to their fear. It hardly rankled, she told herself. The merest brush of her skin on someone else's was the touch of death itself. And whereas in the past it would have taken hours or days for her unlucky victim to die, now it seemed to be but a moment. Perhaps that was a good thing, though – less time for suffering.

'Who are these men?' she murmured to the older woman next to her.

'Don't speak to me, you fucking witch,' the cook spat so vehemently that Lily drew back with a gasp. The woman looked her up and down, the worry gone. 'At least these bastards will do what the Collector should have done: tie you to the pyre and burn that curse out of you. Your protector is gone!' she said with a cackle of glee.

Fighting a ridiculous urge to burst into tears, she conceded that Vineri must indeed be dead. No one would have spoken to the pride of his Collection thus unless he was cold in his grave. She let out a breath she didn't know she'd been holding. So what would happen to her now? she thought as she looked around. Part of the monastery was burnt black and still smoking in some places. There were soldiers everywhere and she finally saw what they were doing here. Looting. They were taking everything not bolted down. Even some things that were!

Her gaze moved upward and she took in the sky. It was so vast, so open. She took a long breath and closed her eyes, imagining she was still in her little room, closed off from the world. It would do no good to have an attack out here with everyone watching. It was just the sky. It was just outside. She'd been outside before. She was being silly, she told herself as she forced the panic down mercilessly.

A new soldier appeared and ordered them up and she got to her numb feet with a wince. She didn't even have her shawl to keep the bite of the wind off her shoulders.

They were led outside the fortress and Lily gasped at the sight. Gray tents everywhere, some gargantuan and some clearly meant for just one person.

There were rows and rows of them all around her. She wrapped her arms around herself as she followed behind the others, keeping her distance from them but hoping to the gods she didn't draw any attention. Thankfully, everyone out here seemed to be very busy, all rushing about with purpose to their strides and no time for errant gazing.

They were led into a warm tent and told to wait, and she let out a sigh as she began to defrost. It was mostly empty in here. At a lone table in the middle of the tent sat two more soldiers in gray. She couldn't hear what they were saying until she got closer, those in front being herded away. None of them protested, not even the cook who'd snapped at her.

She got to the table and the one in front of her glanced at her once and wrote something in a large book.

He said something she didn't catch, sounding bored as he motioned for her to be taken from the tent.

She was ushered outside again. No one touched her. She hoped that if she simply did what she was told quickly, no one would. Was the cook right? Would their Commander order her burned if he realized his men had been right? Best he didn't realize, she thought, which meant no killing anyone. Easier said than done.

She followed yet another soldier down a thoroughfare of sorts and into one of the larger tents. Inside, she gaped at the vibrant tones of the décor. Everything was bright and beautiful. Colored, sheer cloths hung from the ceiling, incense burned and there were cushions and – her eyes widened – *naked women.*

CHAPTER 2

BASTIAN

The wine here was more potent than he remembered. He wasn't sure if that was possible, but in the however many thousand years since he'd lived in the Mortal Realms, they'd definitely perfected the fermentation of their grapes. He took another drink. Yes, he was sure it was better than the swill he'd been drinking on the Mount recently, though he was in a – mostly – mortal body now, so perhaps it was just these primitive senses he now had.

The wind howled through the cloister as he made his way around the perimeter, through its hallowed, open halls. The places of worship had changed as well. This temple had lately been some dead mortal's fortress, but it had definitely been built for the gods originally. There must have been something more to the Collector who'd lived here, however. Gaila had told him that the man had been almost powerful enough to make it to the Mount, and normal mortals did not typically come to the God Realms. The last one he'd seen had only been there in spirit, and, after so long since one of them had visited, she had intrigued him enough to make him consider coming back here for a lifetime ... or several if it went well.

Bastian had intended on going straight back to his tent to spend the day sampling other wines from the dead mortal's cellars, but as he cut through the courtyard, he noticed a woman sitting on the ground. Her loose hair was the color of honey and she was dressed in a well-made gown of silk, but it wasn't her appearance that caught his eye. It was, for lack of a better word, her *aura*. It was black as coal. He'd never seen it's like – a glow of darkness that emanated from her, a smoke that hung around her like a beacon of death.

Frowning, he snuck back into the open hall to watch her at his leisure. She sat in the frozen mud with the others, but the other ten or so prisoners were staying well away from her. She leaned in and said something to one of her brethren. The matron sneered, saying something sharp that reverberated around the square; he couldn't pick up the words, but it must have been something nasty, seeing how the girl flinched back. After that she didn't speak again, just sat in the cold dirt shivering.

The prisoners were ordered up and began moving – being taken for sorting, probably. That was how the camp worked. Spoils were taken, all spoils. That included any person who wasn't dead. They were taken and assessed for their worth and if found to be useful, they would be taken to work for the betterment of the camp. If they weren't of use but weren't deemed completely use*less*, they were sold. Waste not, want not.

He followed, passing under the grand arch and back out into the mire where the Army had set up their traveling city. He observed her as they walked, her head down, trying to be invisible. She didn't walk too close to the others, he noted, wondering what it was she could do. Did she control some power or was the darkness he could see simply some minor aberration with no overt tendencies connected with it? No, he decided, she must be able to do something or else the others wouldn't be so afraid – unless it was she who was afraid of them, he mused.

The Army's captives were taken into a tent, each emerging one by one moments later, and each one in a shocked daze as if they couldn't believe how quickly their lives had been upended, their mundane paths so swiftly and completely diverted that they now traversed a different terrain altogether. One where the Dark Army was a permanent and overshadowing presence until the end.

The girl came out, head down and following another soldier. She did exactly as she was told as quickly as she could. He liked that. He enjoyed a woman that wanted to please. As he watched, she was led into one of the pleasure tents, one reserved for the Brothers, and he grinned. He'd known she was pretty enough for a pleasure tent, a good one, but some men's tastes were abysmal. He'd seen quite a few women doing jobs in the camp who would have been better suited to contributing on their backs, after all.

He smirked as she walked into her new world, and he took another drink from the bottle he carried. He'd see her later.

∼

Lily's eyes widened as she took in the lavish tent. What was this place?

'You!'

Her gaze snapped to a woman whose eyes were heavily painted. Her clothes, of sheer silk, made Lily's face heat as she averted her eyes. The woman strode forward, pointing at her.

'Yes, you. The timid mouse.'

Lily shrank back as the woman came too close, fearing a repeat of what had happened in the tower. Of course the women around her took it for fear. Some tittered and others looked sympathetic. But, thankfully, no one reached out to touch.

'Ever fucked before?'

Lily shook her head, almost laughing aloud at how ridiculous the odd question was. A man couldn't even kiss her hand in the courtly show of affection she'd read about, let alone do anything else. Barring what had happened in the tower and Vineri's orders, she hadn't touched her skin to anyone else's since ... She fled from the old memory. *No!* She mustn't think of that, never of that.

And then it dawned on her, no doubt more slowly than it should have. Was this a brothel? She opened her mouth to ask, but the woman had already flounced away. Another took her place and ushered her behind a sheer curtain and then another thicker one that couldn't be seen through.

That was when Lily saw the real tent past the gaudy façade. There were two rows of cots. Some had women lying on them reading, others were empty. There were many women, some by themselves, others in groups chatting in low voices. None of them looked surprised to see another enter. The one who'd brought her through pointed to a bed in the corner.

'That's yours,' she said curtly and then she was gone.

Lily made her way to the cot and sat down. It had no blankets, but then the tent was so warm, perhaps none were needed.

'What's your name?' asked a girl lying in the bed next to hers, staring at the vaulted ceiling.

'Lily.'

'I'm Susi.' She rolled over onto her side, facing Lily, surveying her. 'When they come, don't struggle,' she advised.

'Struggle?'

Susi gestured to something on the floor and Lily frowned as she noticed a set of irons attached to the frame of the bed.

'If you fight, they'll just chain you down. Well, unless they like a fighter,' she shrugged, 'but if you fight, whether they enjoy it or not, they'll beat you for it and be all the rougher. My advice, let whoever you get fuck you, give them a smile and you might even get a coin or two.'

'Do you mean to say that a man will come to … ravish me?'

'A man? Ravish?' The girl guffawed loudly. 'Where the fuck did you come from?'

Lily didn't answer. She couldn't stay here. What if she killed again? Another death would be bad enough morally speaking, but her curse had a sting in its tail. She'd be vulnerable if the fever took her here. She could already feel it beginning, but only one would be all right; she could deal with the effects of one. But not two or three. She broke out in a cold sweat.

'Gods, you aren't going to cry, are you?' the girl asked, looking vaguely disgusted at the thought.

'No,' she bit out, 'but I can't stay here.'

'See that old bitch over there?' The girl gestured with a flick of her head.

Lily looked to where she was pointing and saw the woman who'd met her when she'd first been brought in.

'That's the tent mistress. She's in charge here. I'm going to warn you, she's a nasty cunt. If you move from that bed, she will have you chained. Then she will strip you, take the largest phallus she can find from over there on yonder table …'

Lily's gaze swung to the table, which, as Susi said, was littered with phalluses … phalli?

'And she will "ravish" you with it while you scream and cry and beg her to stop hurting you.'

'Gods,' Lily breathed. 'Really?'

'Yes. I've seen her do it. See that pretty girl with the red hair over there with the vacant eyes? She's been like that since the mistress did it to her, and,' Susi dropped her voice, 'the fucking hag does it to her every day. Makes her beg for it or she does worse things to her. She's the example now. There's always one. At least until she's moved into one of the lower tents for the soldiers.' Susi gave her a pointed look. 'You don't want to be the next.'

'No, but you don't understand. I can't be touched.' Lily tried again.

The girl let out a biting laugh and shook her head. 'You haven't heard a fucking word I've said. Good luck. You're going to need it.' And with that, she turned her back on her, not bothering with Lily anymore.

Lily looked over at the tent mistress. The woman was watching her, her gaze traveling over her. She was waiting for Lily to do something so that she could punish her. Lily looked away, staying where she was for the moment. She didn't want to kill anyone else today if she could help it, if not for their sake, then for hers. Besides, her curse did not always work so fast. It could be hours before the person succumbed, and that was more than enough time for them to do her harm.

So she sat and she waited, hoping that a path would present itself.

Time passed and Lily noticed the other women in the tent getting twitchy. Some paced, others simply cried on their beds, and there were some who looked *excited*.

A gong rang and Susi sat up, unlaced her dress quickly and pulled it from her shoulders. She looked at Lily. 'It's starting now. It'll end at dawn.' She glanced at Lily's gown.

'You might want to take that off or there'll be naught left of it by morning,' she advised as the flaps at the back of the tent opened and men dressed in black streamed in. One of them made a beeline for her but stopped two beds away, grabbing the girl on the bed, who squealed – in fear or delight, Lily couldn't say.

And then there was one in front of her, staring down at her.

'You're new.' He leered and she shivered.

She didn't like it when they looked at her like this, she decided. It wasn't nice at all. He made a grab for her and she skittered away, throwing herself to the other side of the bed.

He laughed. 'I'm going to enjoy breaking you, whore, but I don't have time for a tussle just now.'

There was a gleam in his eye. He was going to hit her, she realized too late as his hand came hurtling at her face.

She felt it slam into her cheek and then she was falling, a man's yell piercing the air.

Her body bounced painfully on the hard floor of the tent, and she lay there, stunned. A moment later, he fell in front of her, his face purple and bleeding from his orifices.

She was in a haze, listening to the screams of women and the yells of men as if they were far away. Someone picked her up by her dress and threw her onto the bed, anchoring her arms over her head, and then he gurgled and died just as quickly. He was hauled off her and she half expected another one to try. They weren't the most intelligent bunch, these men.

It was like a joke. How many men would it take to understand that this woman couldn't be touched? The tent was silent except for the sound of someone giggling – and as her head began to clear, she realized the laughter was coming from her. She tried to stop but she couldn't. It was awful, yet she couldn't forget the joke.

The zing of a knife or sword pulled from its scabbard drifted through the air to her ears. They were going to kill her now. They'd finally seen the monster and they'd stop her for good. She found she wasn't afraid. Would she be free, she wondered? Would the curse be gone if she was dead? Would it leave her be in the afterlife?

A man stood over her, the one from the tower. The Commander of the Dark Army. He put the point of his knife to the middle of her chest. Still she laughed, but it was more of a chuckle now. Madness had finally taken her.

She stared into his eyes, and he into hers. He hadn't seen her before in the tower; not really. Fucking seeing her now though, wasn't he? It almost made the giggles start up again, but she made an effort to keep them at bay.

He was speaking to her, but she couldn't hear him properly, couldn't understand what he was asking her. He was handsome, she thought as the point of the sword pierced her skin. Her eyes closed and her lips curved up into a small smile.

∼

QUIN STARED down at the woman, seething.

He'd been called to one of the pleasure tents because one of the girls was killing Brothers. He'd thought it was a fucking jest, but here he was, looking down at *her*. The woman from the tower. The one who'd been in his thoughts all afternoon.

'How did you do it, girl?' he snapped. 'Some potion? Herbs? How have you killed three of my men?'

She looked at him like she couldn't understand him, staring at his moving lips with a puzzled little expression on her pretty face. Yes, she was pretty, he conceded, but she had killed three of his Brothers. How?

He looked over at the two on the floor. Blood pooled by their heads from their ears, noses, mouths, and eyes. What had she used?

'How long did it take for them to die?' he asked the nearest man.

'Moments, Commander, just moments. I don't know what the bitch did, but she did it quick.'

Quin nodded, his attention back on the girl. She hadn't moved a muscle, not even to pull her dress down. He couldn't help but glance at those creamy thighs. Perhaps, before he killed her, he'd punish her a little his own way.

That thought surprised him. How long had it been since he'd been interested in a woman enough to look at her twice? Before he'd made Commander, that was certain, and prior to that ... well, there had been one a few weeks ago. She'd been ... he didn't want to torture himself thinking of her. Lana wasn't his, she was Kane's, and that was for the best. He wasn't equipped for a woman, not in any way. He'd only just become the leader of the Dark Army, and that was a mountainous task in itself that left little time for anything else. The loss of Payn was still raw and his unit was still adjusting to Bastian, his new Brother, who ... well, to say it was early days was the kindest thing at present.

She closed her eyes and smiled just as he realized the point of his knife was drawing blood. She thought he was going to kill her. She wanted him to. He smiled coldly. Oh, she'd wish for death all right after he was through with her.

'Have her taken to my tent,' he ordered, 'but don't touch her any more than necessary and keep a guard on her until I arrive.'

With that, he turned on his heel and left, having no interest in the affairs of the tent. Some of the women, the ones who enjoyed being there, tried to entice him, but he ignored their efforts, exiting into the winter sunshine and finally feeling like he could breathe again.

He meant to meander, make the bitch wait upon him, let her mind twist and turn as it mulled over why she'd been taken to the Commander's tent. She should be scared. He'd have to make an example of her, after all. That was part of being the leader of the Brothers, a position he'd only held for a few weeks yet had worked towards all his life.

He was anticipating seeing her again and that annoyed him. He was usually a patient man, content to work quietly in the shadows to further his own agenda. So why was it that as soon as he'd met *her*, he couldn't help but want to be in her presence once more?

He found himself outside his tent already and sighed, conscious of the eyes that ever watched him. Anonymity was gone. That was the thing he disliked most, that and the tedious, never-ending politics.

He walked in as if he'd been planning to come straight here all along. His eyes found her immediately. She was standing in the middle, by the main beam that held up the high-top. Two guards stood close by, staring at her. She was staring back at them, the wisp of a smile on her face. Odd, but at least the maniacal laughter had stopped. He'd never admit it aloud, but the sight of her lying on that bed laughing with the bodies around her was not something he'd soon forget – and not all of what he felt was horror.

He waved the guards out. He could deal with some slip of a girl himself, that was certain. He grabbed a drink and sat at the Commander's great desk. His desk now. And he watched her in silence. In his experience, women always tried to fill the quiet with talk. His mother had been the same. He'd loved her dearly, but gods, she'd talked.

But this one didn't. She stared at him for a while and then, to his surprise, her eyes left him as she moved around the tent, looking at his possessions, *touching* his things. Not only did she ignore him, she turned her back to him. The girl was either very brave or very, very foolish. One did not take their eyes off a predator, and one certainly did not turn their back on one.

Deciding to teach her the first of many lessons, he moved out of his chair and stalked towards her in complete silence. Nothing gave him away, not a creak of the chair, not a shuffle of his boot on the thick woven floor nor on the thick furs as he moved across them.

'You shouldn't do that,' she murmured, not even deigning to turn around.

How had she known? Most of his best skills lay in stealth. He was sure he'd not made a sound to alert her.

'Don't feel bad.' She turned to him, her eyes fastening on his. 'I'm very good at knowing where everyone is in a room.'

He raised a brow. 'One of the detriments of being Vineri's woman?'

She canted her head. 'You said that before, in the tower. What makes you think I was his woman?'

He gestured to her dress. Slaves didn't wear silk, nor the latest fashions from the north.

'Ah, yes.' She looked down at herself, frowning. 'Well, you are right, I was his, but not in the way you think.'

'Go on.'

'I was merely an item in his Collection. He kept me separate from it, but part of it I was.'

'You?' Quin asked incredulously.

'I've killed three of your men. Two were full Brothers. Do you doubt it?'

'How?'

She looked away from him as if ashamed. 'My touch is death. It's a curse I've borne most of my life.'

Quin almost laughed at the absurdity. Did she think to

save herself from the pleasure tents by telling outlandish lies?

'And what do you hope to gain by telling me this?'

'If you were wise, you'd take me back to the tower and lock me in.'

He went back to his desk and sat down, taking his goblet in his hand. 'Vineri's fortress is to be destroyed once we've stripped it bare. There won't be a tower to imprison you in.'

So many emotions flashed across her face that he found himself riveted. Shock, sadness, desperation, fear, hope. She was an open book to him. She couldn't hide her feelings at all. How long had it been since he'd met such a person?

'Then,' she looked into his eyes and stepped closer, 'you should kill me.'

'You wish for death?'

'Not really. Sometimes,' she said truthfully, shocking him. 'But I'm a danger. You should do it.'

'Oh, I will.' He took a swig of his wine and was gratified to see her wince. She wasn't as unaffected by her situation as she seemed. 'But I think I'll make you suffer for what you did to my men first.'

'I see.' She let out a sigh and went back to exploring the tent, ignoring him once more.

'Are you not afraid?'

'You can't touch me,' she said simply. 'If you do, you'll die.'

Deciding to indulge her, he leant back, putting his muddy boots on the small portion of his predecessor's desk not covered in paper, which he did every chance he got because fuck the bastard. He and his power games were the reason his Brother Payn was dead.

'So if you touch your skin to another's, then that person dies. Is that right?'

'Yes. It used to take hours or days ... but its moments now.'

'And you can't control it?' he asked, watching her for signs of falsity.

'No. I just don't touch anyone.'

'Ever?' he teased. 'Not a kiss, not a caress, not a good hard fuck?'

He watched her cheeks color and chuckled.

'Never,' was all she said. 'Only …' She trailed off.

'Only?'

'Only when Vineri ordered it,' she said abruptly, turning away again.

So she hadn't liked being part of the Collector's collection, then. 'Have you killed many?' he enquired, wondering when she'd end this farce.

She was silent for such a long time that Quin wondered if she'd heard him before he received a very faint, almost inaudible 'yes.'

He clicked his fingers and a guard appeared. 'Have another bed brought,' he ordered, not taking his eyes off the girl.

'Am I staying in here?'

'I told you my aims, girl. That hasn't changed.'

She rolled her eyes, making his narrow at her arrogance. She had no idea what he was capable of, the many ways he could hurt her without laying a hand on her. He smiled as he thought about it.

'Though your tale was entertaining, I'm not quite convinced,' he said, watching to see when she'd begin to panic because she was a liar and he knew it, but there was nothing. If anything, she looked even more relaxed. 'What if I wanted a demonstration?'

'A demonstration?' she parroted faintly.

'Yes. Kill one of my guards.'

'No,' she said immediately. 'I won't do it anymore. If you must kill me, then do it, but I'll not execute anyone for you.

I'll not swap one evil master for another.'

'You'd compare me to Vineri? That fool?' he snarled, wondering why he cared what she thought.

'You're just another man who would use me. There isn't much difference,' she returned, not cowed in the least.

He jumped to his feet, infuriated by her. He'd show the little bitch just how easily she could be hurt, broken, without him touching his flesh to hers even once, he thought, grabbing his long knife.

She tensed immediately. 'Are you going to kill me now or do you think to scare me?'

He stood in front of her. She stepped back. He followed and she stepped again.

'Stop it,' she said, sounding more exasperated than scared. 'How else can I say it? The merest brush of my bare skin on yours will kill you. Don't you understand?'

Her back met the wall of the tent and he stood over her. It took the smallest, precise flicks of the blade for her gown to slide to the floor, ruined beyond repair.

She gasped in shock, looking down at her tattered dress, standing in front of him in just her chemise. Her eyes darted to his. They looked confused, as if she had no idea what she was supposed to say, how she was meant to act. No one had ever done anything like this to her, he realized in amusement. Whether that was because she'd enjoyed a certain power as Vineri's possession or because she actually had the touch of death remained to be seen.

She opened her mouth, but no sound came out.

'This is just the beginning,' he murmured. 'I can break you a thousand ways, girl, without touching you at all.'

Her terrified eyes closed and she let out a small sigh. 'But if I was valuable to you? If I proved it? Would that change things? Would I be treated better?'

'Perhaps.'

Her hazel eyes opened once more, staring into his for a long time. He heard the men bringing in the bed he'd ordered and he gestured to a corner at the back, not taking his eyes from hers.

'When I wake up, I will show you that what I say is true,' she said quietly, her voice breaking on the final words.

He steeled himself for her tears, but none fell. Instead she turned away from him and went to the bed. The two men who'd brought it were still here, gaping at the woman, he saw, annoyed that they were witnessing her in this state of undress. One quelling look was all it took for them to disappear from the tent as quickly as they could.

'I assume this is for me,' she said hesitantly.

He nodded once.

'Do I have your leave to move some things around?'

His brow furrowed. He wasn't sure if he should let her have any liberties, but curiosity won out and he nodded once more.

He went back to his desk, confident that, for the moment at least, the girl was appropriately subdued by fear. Tomorrow he'd have to do something else. She wasn't the type to roll over and take everything he meted out. Whatever she'd been to Vineri, he hadn't broken her. By all accounts, it seemed he'd treated her well. That in itself was at odds with everything he'd ever heard about the cunt.

He got to work tackling the piles of documents on the desk. He'd realized over the past days that Greygor hadn't sat at the gargantuan thing to make an impression; he just needed that much space for the sheer number of parchments that were piled on it daily. Every time he made a dent, he came back to higher mounds within half a day.

The woman cleared her throat daintily and he scowled at the interruption. Was the fear already dissipating? Did he already need to punish her further?

What?' he ground out, not bothering to look up.

'Is there water?'

'There's wine in the jug on the table,' he said absently.

'I need water.'

He finally looked up, ready to shout, to send her scurrying back to her bed, but he didn't.

She looked ill. Her skin was sallow and glistened with sweat, her eyes wide and fevered.

'Gods, you're not dying, are you, girl?' he asked callously and was surprised when she gave him a small smile.

'No, you may still have that to look forward to when this is done, but I need water.'

'I'll have some brought,' he found himself promising and frowned. Was he catering to her fucking whims now too? He opened his mouth to tell her that on second thoughts, the finest fucking wine in the region would have to do, but she was already turning away and making her way slowly and stiffly back to the bed.

'Please put the water close,' she asked quietly. 'When I wake, I'll prove my worth.'

He didn't answer.

'Commander?' she murmured faintly.

'Yes?' he asked, making himself sound impatient because in truth he didn't know what he was.

'I told them, you know. The ones I could. I warned them before I killed them.'

She sounded close to tears, but he didn't look up again.

CHAPTER 3

BASTIAN

It was long past dark by the time Quin's messenger found him in one of the pleasure tents the soldiers frequented. He was dozing with a couple of the girls who'd been only too willing to lie with him as soon as they saw the black of his tunic, hoping their fortunes would change and they'd be moved to the better tents if they pleased him.

That wouldn't happen. He liked them both well enough, but, in truth, the Brothers' whores were too haughty for his liking. He enjoyed women who didn't try to pretend to be something they weren't. The high pleasure tents were all smoke and mirrors, paint and proxy. It had been an age since he'd indulged so heavily, in women at least, and at first it had been a whirlwind of delights after so long without. But the enjoyment had waned after a few weeks and he found himself tired of it already. Perhaps Gaila had been right to laugh in his face when he'd told her he was leaving to live life in a mortal realm. She'd gleefully wagered he wouldn't last a full year – a wager he'd taken – even as she gave him a mission, seeing as she couldn't set foot here herself. Fuck her.

Ancient bitch. He'd show them all he still had what it took to be a mortal man.

He tried to focus on the words on the missive before him. He'd have to sober up before he met the holier-than-thou Quin or he wouldn't hear the end of it. Bad enough Bastian had passed all his tests easily, beaten all the men he'd been pitted against in combat to earn himself a place in the Brothers without having to earn his way through the ranks like many others did.

Chuckling, he remembered how he'd turned up as a stranger in the camp and announced he would be a Brother before the day was out – and then made good on his claim. Quin hadn't liked that one bit. But the look on his face when he'd announced that Bastian was to replace Quin and Mad Malkom's dead unit member – he'd remember that until the end of his very, very long life. In truth he'd been surprised that the Commander had actually done what the runes had told him to. Greygor had played fast and free with that aspect of his duties. He'd rarely done what the gods had wanted.

Bastian made his way to a horse trough, smashed the ice and dunked his head in, giving a whoop when he came back up a moment later, the freezing water making him at least appear well and truly lucid once more. He looked at the message properly. It simply summoned him as if he were some lowly mortal. A self-deprecating smile tugged at the corner of his mouth. Well, that was what he was now.

He stepped into Quin's tent on light feet, seeing the man at his ridiculously large desk as usual. Did he never imbibe? Never fuck a woman? Did he enjoy even a moment of his—?

He let out a low whistle as he noticed the extra bed and the delicious-looking woman upon it, dressed in just a thin chemise that was riding up very high indeed. Perhaps he should reevaluate his Brother. Quin's taste in female company was certainly on a par with his own.

'What's this, then?' He stepped closer and then he recognized her as the girl from the fortress – well, not her, perhaps, but that dark mist that hovered over her. He'd looked for her in the tents earlier but hadn't been able to find her.

'A woman,' came Quin's sardonic reply. 'Obviously.'

'I can see that,' he said amiably, not rising to Quin's baiting. 'Not seen you have one before. She must be special.'

Quin snorted from behind a tower of documents. 'She certainly thinks she is.'

'What's with all the …?' He gestured to the row of items around the bed in the corner, all in a line from wall to wall, creating a perfect little triangle of space.

'Her touch kills men, or so she says. Apparently, she'll give me a demonstration when she wakes.'

'Don't you mean if she wakes?' Quin asked, eyeing the girl, who was looking a little worse for wear.

She was drenched in sweat. At first Bastian had assumed she and Quin had just finished a frenzied marathon of fucking, but now he looked properly, he could see that she tossed and turned, writhed on the blanket-less bed. His gaze was riveted to that thin chemise, though, climbing ever higher. How long before he could properly see her—?

'Did you hear what I said?'

Bastian frowned, tearing his eyes away and shaking his head at Quin, who let out a long-suffering sigh.

'I wouldn't touch her. Her claims are absurd, but until I've proven that they're lies, she stays behind the line and no one crosses it.'

'What happens after that?' Bastian wondered aloud.

'You can have her if you like.' Quin took a drink from his goblet, 'When I'm finished with her.'

'What are you planning?'

'To punish her for thinking she could come here and dupe her way out of the pleasure tents, for assuming she could make me believe her deceits and for somehow killing three of my men. I aim to make an example of her to any other who'd think to gain power through trickery here.'

Bastian nodded. Quin was very angry about something, but he wasn't sure it was all to do with the girl.

A shadow moved into his periphery right next to him and Bastian jumped, only just stopping himself from screeching like a maid.

'By the gods, Mal. Fuck!'

Mad Malkom said nothing, as usual. Just materialized like a fucking specter and observed in silence before disappearing just as quietly. If Bastian didn't know better, he'd say Mal had some Dark Realm blood to pull off this level of stealth, but Quin was adamant that he was simply an assassin with skill. Bastian sneered at his unit Brother. If the fuck had ever seen Bastian in his previous godly form, he'd have shat himself.

He followed Mal's gaze to the woman and her shapely thighs and they simply watched together. It was oddly companionable even if he did think Mal was a prick. Two men who hardly knew each other bonding over an unconscious, fevered woman who was unknowingly giving them a show.

He heard Quin swear and stomp over. 'What are you two starin …?'

Quin trailed off as he stood with them, staring just as they did. Finally, Quin pulled on a black leather glove and stepped over the line of objects that separated her from the rest of the tent. Amid her writhing, he managed to pull her clothes down to a modest level, but before he could leave her, she opened her eyes and said something Bastian couldn't hear, but Quin only gave her a hard look before mouthing the word 'no.'

'What did she say to you?' Bastian asked as Quin came back.

He cut a glance at the girl, whose eyes were closed once more, her jaw locked as if she was trying not to make a noise.

'Stupid woman begged me to kill her.' He chuckled. 'As if I'd let her be free of us so easily with all the trouble she's causing.'

Bastian glanced down at her again. He almost felt sorry for her.

∽

MAL TRIED NOT to overtly scorn Bastian as the man walked away. His slovenly Brother was probably off to drown himself in more drink and whatever other vices he could find, which were around every corner in the camp.

He missed Payn. Gods knew the man had been a bastard, but he'd been someone Mal could count on to have his back. Bastian was – he let out a sigh – fucking useless. He'd tell him so if he cared to speak. But he didn't care to speak. Most assumed he couldn't, but why talk when there was so little worth saying? He'd spent the better part of his life not bothering, and he wasn't about to start now just to let Bastian know what he thought of him.

Mal looked at the girl. Her jaw was clamped shut and her knuckles were white. Her fists were clenched so tight, he'd bet her palms were bloody from her fingernails. He noticed that her clothes were riding up again. He stood and watched. Quin had gone back to his desk and Mal didn't care about preserving her modesty, that was for certain. A woman's nakedness rarely did anything for him. So why couldn't he rip his traitorous eyes away from where the white cloth was rising, giving him a tantalizing view of where her thighs met her arse?

His cock hardened and he looked down, surprised. What was it about this woman that made his body respond like a man when he'd not concerned himself with carnal pleasures in so long?

He suddenly despised her, lying there with her legs half spread, inviting any man to touch her, to fuck her. He turned away with a snarl to find Quin observing him with questioning eyes. His Brother was too perceptive. He threw himself into a chair in front of Quin's desk. Fucking thing took up half the tent. He was glad he had his own space down the row.

'Bastian left before I could tell him, but I've had a bird from Kitore.'

Mal inclined his head for his Brother to go on.

'There's dissent. Talk of war. Someone's stirring up bad blood against the Army. The king already sees us as a threat. He grows his army larger every season. I can't send many men there without drawing suspicion, but if we go and visit the palace, it will be seen as a gesture of respect. While we're there, we can take care of whoever is causing the problem at the same time.'

Mal frowned. It would have to be made to look like an accident.

'We'll have to make it look like general bad luck, a misadventure of fate,' Quin went on, as if reading Mal's mind. 'I'd say fire, but the city's wards prevent anything larger than a hearth flame from taking hold within its walls. Think on it and give me some options tomorrow.'

Mal nodded and jerked his head back in the direction of the woman. Quin would have to finish whatever plans he had in store for her before they left.

'Don't worry. My dealings with her will be short. Once

she's proved to be as useless as Bastian, I'll find a fitting place for her.'

Mal wished he'd do the same to Bastian, but he didn't let Quin know that. There was nothing Quin could do. The gods 'had spoken.' He scoffed inwardly. As if they cared what the lowly mortals did, what the Army did. If Mal knew anything, it was that if they existed at all, the gods didn't give a shit about him or anyone else and never had. Selfish fucks, the lot of them. And Mal had never seen a shred of evidence that they were real, save the wickedness men did in their names.

He left the tent without a backward glance. It was late and he decided to go back to his own bed for some rest. In a few days, they'd leave for the north. He let out a small sigh as he walked into his pitch-black tent, kicked off his boots, and threw himself onto his bed.

He closed his eyes, his thoughts drifting to the woman in Quin's tent, though why he should be thinking of her, he didn't know. He frowned in the dark, his cock hardening once more. Gods, he'd not be able to sleep like this. He took his rod from the confines of his breeches and began to move his hand over the length of it, trying not to think of the woman but not succeeding. He couldn't help but remember the way her chemise had ridden up and up, and he envisioned her writhing beneath him, responding to his touch, and, instead of clenching her jaw to keep herself silent, she'd whimper and moan under him while he took her. He imagined he'd be brutal. He hadn't bothered much with a woman since he'd first left the place of his birth, and that was only to see what all the fuss was about.

Nowadays he knew enough to realize he enjoyed the company of both sexes, though he rarely felt like indulging in either. No one and nothing brought him the peace he sought. No, that wasn't quite right. Slaughter did, battle did, stalking his prey down darkened corridors did. According to his sire, he'd never been good at much of anything, but he was a fine killer.

He imagined her in front of him and Bastian, Quin making her strip for them. The fear in her eyes, not because she wouldn't want them, but because she would. They'd make sure of that.

He found his pleasure with a grunt and lay on his back, sated for the moment, yet staring into the darkness in consternation. Why had he imagined both Quin and Bastian there with him, and why had the thought of her being with all of them sent him over the edge when he'd never shared before?

He pushed the thoughts away and closed his eyes, feeling a peace within himself that would probably dissipate with the dawn.

CHAPTER 4

LILY

As usual, after the fever had broken, Lily had woken in dire need of water. When she'd first opened her eyes, she'd started, having forgotten where she was. The reality of her situation had her lying still for a few moments, her chest tight as she fought for breath. Was her sanctuary really gone? Was Vineri really gone? Was she really lying on a cot in the Commander of the Dark Army's tent? Had he really cut off her dress? Panic swelled in her and she pushed it back. She had to keep herself calm, together.

She sat up gingerly, finding a jug of water next to the bed with a wooden cup. Thank the gods, he'd had water brought, she thought as she filled it and drank thirstily, replenishing the cup three times before her stomach felt so full that she dared not drink any more.

She could hear the furious strokes of someone writing at a frenzied pace and craned her neck to see if it was the Commander who sat behind the desk still.

'If I'd known it would take two nights for you to wake, I'd have given in to your request,' he said curtly.

'Request?' she rasped, her tongue still feeling swollen and dry.

'Your begging, actually.'

She couldn't see him but she knew he was smiling smugly behind all those parchments. She stuck said tongue out at him just as another man entered.

She grimaced, cheeks heating, as the new Brother saw what she was doing, his eyebrows lifting.

'Mal. Good. Have one of the Rats brought in. Whoever's next for the cull from last night's crimes.'

The Brother nodded. His unblinking eyes stayed fixed on her until he was gone. She shivered when he'd left, getting the distinct feeling that he would hurt her simply for the pleasure of it if he got the chance.

'So what did I beg for?' she asked, standing slowly and trying out her legs. 'I assume it wasn't for more of your pleasurable company.'

Lily wobbled slightly before she found her balance. Two days was longer than usual, but then, that bout had been an awful one. Killing three men in a day was not something she would repeat if she could possibly help it. She'd been in a fevered haze for most of it, but she remembered the pain. She hoped she hadn't cried out with it. She'd never told anyone about the agony she felt during the fever, afraid it would be used against her somehow. She wouldn't have put it past Vineri to apply it as a punishment when she hadn't done what he'd wanted instead of his other, usual tactics.

'Death,' he said simply, but she could hear a note of amusement in his voice that he was trying to hide. 'Your demonstration will be soon.'

'Demonstration?'

'Yes. You told me that in return for better treatment than meeting your end on the point of my sword – after I'd meted out the justice of the Dark Brothers, of course – you would prove to me you weren't lying about your gift.'

'It's not a gift,' she snapped.

'Curse, then.' He was unmoved by her outburst. 'There's food on the table. By the repulsive sounds your stomach has been making since the early hours, I'm guessing you're hungry.'

Lily's cheeks heated again as she turned to the table. Her mouth watered at the sight of it piled high with plates of meats and cheeses, bowls of nuts and fruits, baked apples filled with spiced raisins, and those were just the things she recognized.

She took one of the pewter plates and began to heap it with food, tasting a bit here and there and making noises of approval as she added spoonfuls of this and handfuls of that.

She sat down and stared at her plate in anticipation, a smile spreading across her face. She'd never had such an array of food in one sitting. Vineri had fed her, but nothing so fine as all this except sometimes on festival days when all the servants were eating well.

She tucked in with a sigh of contentment, eating until the plate was empty and wondering if it would be rude to go back for more. She looked up to ask the Commander and saw that he'd been joined by two other Brothers. One she hadn't seen before. He was attractive enough for her to have to force her eyes away from his strong jaw to take note of his long brown hair that was plaited away from his face. He was broad too and very tall, dwarfing the other two just a bit, though neither of them were small men. The other was the one from earlier who'd stared at her – much as he was doing now. He was just as good-looking, though in a different, slightly more *menacing* way. She sunk down in the chair slightly, as she was afraid she knew exactly what he was staring at. Her chemise was old, threadbare, and thin, and practically transparent in places.

'Gods, Brother,' the new one said, 'you'd better hope she *was* lying. If you leave her alive, she'll eat through our supplies in days!'

She looked down, feeling a flush creep over her skin. 'I hadn't eaten in a while,' she argued.

'Get up, girl,' Quin said impatiently.

She stood, crossing her arms over her chest so they couldn't see her dark nipples through the thinning cloth, but all three pairs of eyes moved downward and she knew there wasn't much left to the imagination down there either.

If she'd learned anything in Vineri's world, it was that weakness invited tyranny. She squared her shoulders and forced her hands down to her sides, pretending she didn't care that they could see her body. It wasn't as if they could touch her, was it?

'I thought she was Vineri's pet,' the new one remarked. 'Look at the state of that,' he drawled, referring to her ragged clothes. 'Not that I'm complaining, of course. Didn't Vineri like you very much, girl?'

She looked him in the eye. 'He was probably punishing me for something,' she conceded.

'For what?' the new one asked.

She shrugged, saying nothing.

'What else did he do to punish you?' Quin asked, clearly intrigued.

'I'm not giving you ideas.' She snorted, drawing a reluctant smile from him that had his Brothers looking stunned.

He recovered quickly, however, and beckoned her closer. 'Are you ready to prove yourself?'

'If there truly is no other way.'

'There isn't.' He smiled darkly.

He still thought she was lying. She sighed, wondering what poor sod would be brought in for their little test.

Just then a small boy entered the tent and she gasped, a rush of gut-wrenching images flooding her mind and making her rear back.

'I won't do it! Kill me, torture me. Do anything to me that you want.' She turned her horrified eyes to Quin's. 'I know the Brothers are cruel, but I'm not! Do you really think I'd kill a *child* to save myself?'

She couldn't help the tears that came to her eyes. She couldn't murder a little boy, she just couldn't. Memories of another boy assaulted her, his face just as innocent as this one's, and her heart squeezed, driving the air from her lungs. She couldn't do this.

∼

THE WOMAN TURNED hysterical within a moment. Quin regarded her, wondering what had wrought this sudden transformation. She'd been witty and halfway charming a moment ago … in her very thin chemise. How he hadn't noticed last night that he could see everything through it, he didn't know, but he found he couldn't stop looking however much he wanted to.

'Commander,' questioned a small voice from behind him.

'You're late.' He gestured to the papers on the desk that the messenger would deliver, his gaze not leaving the woman.

Her eyes flicked to the child and he realized what she'd assumed.

'No, not him,' he murmured.

'Not him?' she repeated, her chest heaving, hands clenching and unclenching at her sides. At least she was no longer yelling, but she was terrified he was going to make her kill the boy. Another thing he could use to his advantage even though she was probably mad and really thought she was cursed. Well, they'd know soon enough.

'No,' he reiterated, glad she was getting a hold of herself, 'but your test will be here soon, so I hope you're prepared,' he said coldly, still not able to help his eyes snapping down to take in those dark nipples. He eyed the ruined gown on the floor across the tent, wishing he hadn't been so impulsive as to cut it off her last night. It had had the desired effect of subduing his captive, but it wasn't worth what he was battling now.

A soldier stomped in, dragging one of the Rats that had been caught at some mischief in the camp the evening before. Quin didn't know what and he didn't care. The ragged man was thin and dirty. He looked frail and half starved, but his eyes were bright and sharp. No doubt he was memorizing the tent thoroughly in case he made it out of here alive so he could come back later and pilfer whatever he could.

Quin's lip curled into a sneer that had the girl stepping back. *Fucking Rats.* Would that they could be culled once and for all, but no matter how many the Army killed, others simply took their places to follow the camp around and devour its meager leavings.

'This is the one,' Quin said, turning back to her.

'Why him?'

'Why not?'

Her brow furrowed.

'If you want to confess to your lies now, you can,' he said, watching for her to finally crack and admit it.

'And if I did?'

'I will be spending some time showing you why little girls shouldn't lie to big soldiers. I know my Brothers – Mal at least – will want to educate you as well.'

The cruel gleam in Mal's eye wasn't missed, and she shivered under his overt perusal.

'Who is he?' she asked, looking at the Rat.

'He's one of many who follow the Army. Rats. They wait until we're finished a raid and they pick over the bones. They're ruthless and cunning. Now that he's seen the inside of my tent, if I let him go, he'll be back tonight with others to take whatever he can, won't you, my ragged little friend?'

The Rat knew enough not to speak, though Quin noticed that he was staring at the girl, a look in his eyes that Quin found he didn't like. The girl was his; no one should be looking at her save Bastian and Mal, and only because they were the Brothers of his unit.

'You want me to kill him because he's a thief?' she asked, her eyes wide.

'No, I want you to kill him to save your own life.'

He rolled his eyes, sick of this farce, and nodded at the soldier to release the Rat. 'Rat, touch the woman and you're free to go.'

The Rat was on the girl before Quin had even finished speaking, surprising even him, so the girl had definitely not seen the attack coming. She screamed as he fell on top of her, knocking them both to the ground. There was a loud tear and a feminine yip of pain before the Rat yelled and jumped away, holding his mouth. He dropped to his knees, blood beginning to drip from the corners of his eyes, then his nose. He let out a wheeze before he thudded to the floor.

The girl scrambled back, not stopping until she reached the wall of the tent and drew her knees up, curling into a ball and shaking like a leaf. Quin felt something that was almost like remorse for setting the Rat on her. It bubbled up from some long forgotten place in his soul, but he ignored it.

She'd been telling the truth. He could hardly believe it.

KEPT TO KILL

She could kill with one touch. Possibilities spanned out in front of him. With such a powerful weapon at his disposal ...

'I knew it!' Bastian guffawed. 'I knew she could do *something*! But, gods, that's some powerful gift.' Then he frowned, looking at the dead man on the floor. 'Hope it's not catching,' he muttered.

'Indeed,' Quin said, joining him. 'Girl, what if someone touches the body? Will the malady take them as well?'

'No,' she muttered, not looking at them. 'Nothing I hold that you then touch will hurt you. Not a cup, nor a plate, nor those killed by my hand.'

Quin gestured for the soldier to take the corpse away and he considered the girl thoughtfully. 'Congratulations, girl. You've earned yourself a place here.'

She said nothing, didn't look at him.

'Get up and come here,' he ordered forcefully and watched her flinch before she uncurled herself and wobbled to her feet. She turned to face them and he swore. Her nose was bloody and her shift ripped down the middle. He should have realized that dangling release in front of the Rat was a bad idea. He ignored another unwelcome pang of conscience.

She took an unsteady step towards them and another and another until she stood in front of him as he'd ordered. Her hands clenched the tattered sides of her clothes in a vain attempt to keep herself covered, and he had to stop himself from getting one of his cloaks to wrap her in. He wanted her to feel vulnerable, he reminded himself. She needed to know from the very beginning that though she may wield power, she didn't hold it here. He and his Brothers did.

'What is your name?' he asked her.

She still didn't meet his eyes, and he found himself wanting to put a finger under her chin to raise her head to look at him.

'Lilith,' she said and, almost as an afterthought, 'Lily.'

'Lilith,' he said, trying it out, 'go to the bed and I'll have someone attend to you. Will the fever come again tonight?'

Eyes on the ground, she shook her head. 'Not for just one,' she said softly, and then she did as she was told, going to the bed and sinking down on it, her back rigid.

He turned to Mal in triumph. If the girl could be tractable, she could be useful.

～

MAL'S GAZE flicked over the girl. Lily. She sat stiffly on the cot, staring straight ahead, her eyes vacant, and he suddenly needed to get out of the tent. He turned on his heel and fled, ignoring Quin's words that rang out behind him.

He emerged into the late winter sunshine and almost cursed aloud, his gaze finding the Rat who had thrown himself into her. Mal was angry. At the Rat. At Quin. But mostly at himself. Why hadn't he stopped the Rat from hurting her? The way she'd fallen under him, that shocked little cry as his face plowed into hers and he ripped her chemise with his pawing ... it had happened so quickly, but Mal could have stopped him regardless of what Quin had wanted. He let out a growl and kicked the dead Rat's corpse before practically running to the sanctuary of his tent.

But his mind was in a frenzy and there was only one thing that would quiet it. He took out one of his many knives and began to sharpen it. Tonight he would hunt some Rats.

The moon was high as Mad Mal made his way to the perimeter of the camp, easily passing through to the motley tents where the Rats lived, with the sentries none the wiser. The disorder of this part of the camp was in sharp contrast to the straight lines and uniform tents of the Brothers' side. He moved silently between their dwellings, watched them at their small fires from the dark, huddling together. Some of the luckier ones – or at least those better at stealing – had food or wine. Others skulked about, ready to slit a friend's throat for anything, everything.

He heard a thud and a cry and moved stealthily in the direction of the noises to find one of the larger ones on top of another, smaller one, his movements leaving little doubt as to what he was doing. The female or male on the receiving end fought him, or tried to at any rate, but was having little success.

Mal was unmoved by the little one's plight, but the larger suited his purposes, so he sprang forward, grabbed the man by his hair, and yanked his head back. He drew his blade across his neck from ear to ear, grinning in the darkness as he heard the Rat's gurgling. The one beneath him he left to either crawl out from beneath the corpse or not. He didn't care. Onward he went, a new spring in his stealthy step, resisting the urge to begin whistling.

Most of his night was spent thus. He didn't count how many he killed, but by the time the moon had sunk, he decided to make his way back to his tent. Feeling much less frantic now, he passed back, unnoticed once again, into the Brothers' side of the camp. As he went by Quin's tent, however, he paused and turned back, letting himself into his Brother's marquee.

There was a low light from the braziers, and he could make out Quin in his bed on one side of the tent and the girl in her little makeshift bower on the other. He was amused by her attempts to create a line. He'd been up to the tower they'd found her in, seen the sign that called her 'pestilence' outside the door, seen the line on the floor and an odd stick propped up outside by the wall.

Inside there had been little besides the usual bedchamber furnishings and books, and he'd found himself remembering his own little cell from when he was a boy. He'd been able to leave his, though he'd typically not done so unless they forced him out. Judging by the bolt on the door, she'd simply been locked up there for gods only knew how many years. He remembered how large the outside world looked when one had grown up in one so small.

He looked at her while she slept. Quin had given her a blanket, finally, though Mal found himself disappointed that he could no longer see her body. He eased forward through her little barrier of Quin's possessions to stand over her. What a small thing to have such power. His gloved finger grazed her jaw lightly, depositing a smear of blood on her cheek from his night's excursions, and he grinned, wondering what she'd make of that in the morning even as his cock hardened painfully.

She made a noise and he drew back silently in case she woke, but instead she simply rolled over with a sigh, one of her legs coming into view. He frowned in the low light. There were marks on her thigh; long thin lines. He hadn't noticed them the day before. Easing closer once more, he wondered what had made them.

Then he came to his senses and turned, making his way back into the pre-dawn light without a backward look. What did he care if she had scars? Most did. What made her seem so special in his eyes? He would destroy it, whatever it was.

∽

LILY WOKE WITH THE DAWN, blinking sleepily as she recalled what had happened yesterday. She'd killed another man. She sat up and looked down at her ruined chemise. No one had brought her anything else to wear. She recognized the power play from when Vineri had punished her similarly, though his first port of call was usually to take her books away, her only source of diversion, when she'd displeased him. How she hated it when he did that! But she'd learned to stuff one or two behind a loose stone in the wall so she always had something, even then.

Here, they took her clothes and let feral men attack her. There wasn't much she could do about that, she supposed. There wasn't a sneaky way to clothe herself and to ward off a man who thought he'd be rewarded for laying his hands on her.

Lily felt her nose gingerly and winced. It was sore from when that man, that stinking *Rat*, had leapt on her, his head smashing into her face. She'd fallen on her back, head reeling from the blow when he'd torn her chemise almost in half and then *bitten* her.

She glanced around the tent and saw that Quin was still abed, his eyes closed. She eased down the blanket that had been covering her and inspected the wound on her breast, unable to help a shiver. He'd gone right for it, as if that had been the first thing that came to his mind; not to grab her, not even to hit her, but to bite her *there*. What sort of man thought thus? She could see the outline of his teeth, the dark bruise contrasting with her pale skin.

After the quiet one, Mal, had rushed from the tent, Bastian, the one who seemed to enjoy the sound of his own voice more than anyone else's, had offered her wine, which she'd declined. Then he'd gone as well, leaving her to the darkness that was their Commander. Quin had ignored her for the rest of the day while she simply sat on the bed and tried not to let her turbulent emotions get the better of her. She didn't like crying in front of anyone, and it was threatening to happen with an alarming frequency since she'd been dragged out of her tower.

When the day waned, a soldier came in and stood guard

to ensure she didn't go wandering off, she expected, and Quin left, not returning until well into the night.

Lily had fallen asleep in the bed even though the unwavering gaze of the soldier unnerved her. Though the fever wouldn't take hold of her after just one death, she was always tired after a touch.

And now it was morning once more. She stood, pulling the blanket around her as she went to inspect the offerings on the food table. She grabbed a spiced bun and then another, taking them back with her to her bed to devour them in peace.

It wasn't until she heard him walking around the tent that she noticed that Quin was up. He ignored her, washing shirtless in a ewer of steaming water that someone had brought. She couldn't stop staring. The hot water, that's what she wanted, she told herself. It definitely wasn't his broad chest, the rippling muscles, or the shape of him that proclaimed the Dark Army Commander a warrior of the first degree – in case one was to forget. It wasn't that tattoo either, the one she'd caught glimpses of since she'd met him. She tried not to stare at it, memorize it's swirling, complex pattern that snaked from the bottom of his jaw down one side of his chest and past the waist of his breeches.

He dressed in his blacks under her surreptitious eye and ignored the food table in favor of the desk. He began his morning's work even as she sat on the bed, wondering if she would be allowed to wash or even relieve herself without being in the presence of a man. She'd had to piss in the pot last night while the soldier looked on, and it had been one of the most mortifyingly low points of her life since Vineri had brought her south – besides all the deaths she'd been made to cause, of course.

She approached the desk and waited for him to look up.

He didn't. She gave a small cough and he finally give her his attention.

'What is it?' he asked absently, as if he was still in the middle of something far more important than her wellbeing.

'Could I have some privacy to wash, please?'

He looked surprised, and she hoped to the gods he never got a pet or something. The poor thing would be dead inside a week with his lack of attentiveness to living things.

'There's a screen over there that you can put up,' he finally said, looking up at her. His jaw tightened and she drew back, wondering what he was angry about now.

'You didn't remind me.'

Her brow furrowed. 'Of what?'

'I was going to call someone to see to your face.'

She rolled her eyes. 'What for? What would they even do? Pass me a wet rag and ask me to do it myself?' She couldn't help the laugh that bubbled from her throat. Had he forgotten why he'd decided not to torture her, make an example of her?

He looked sheepish. 'They could wear gloves,' he muttered, and she shook her head.

'I can do it myself easily enough,' she said, pulling the blanket more tightly around herself and going in search of the screen. She found it behind his bed and dragged it out with difficulty, finding it much too heavy to stand up by herself. She was about to ask for help when he appeared by her side, making her jump back with a yelp.

He put the thick divider up as easily as if it were made of canvas and not oak and went back to his desk.

Lily found a chamber pot and saw to her morning needs before washing in Quin's now tepid water. When she had finished sponging away the dried blood from her nose and the grime from the rest of her, she eyed the ruined chemise she'd draped over the top of the screen. Was there much point in putting it back on? Her gaze shifted to the full-length looking glass. What an odd extravagance to have in a mercenary camp. She hadn't pegged Quin for being so … vain. Bastian, maybe; yes, he was definitely the type to primp in front of his own reflection. She looked past her own image and realized she could see Quin sitting at his desk. He was sitting back with his boots upon it, his eyes on the looking glass! Her eyes widened as they met his and she grabbed the chemise with a gasp. He'd been watching her!

She stormed out from behind the screen. 'You said I could have some privacy,' she accused.

He snorted. 'I said there was a screen you could put up. I didn't say that you could have privacy while you used it.'

Her mouth opened and closed, but she found she couldn't even form words. She turned away from him and his fucking smug, superior countenance, vowing to pay very close attention to what he said and how he said it from this moment on. *Tricky bastard!*

'Perhaps you'll forgive me if I have some clothes brought for you.'

Her eyes narrowed and she didn't get her hopes up. It was likely to be a ploy. He'd probably make her walk over hot coals or something equally awful to earn them.

'There's a pot by my bed. You can use it on your bruises and they'll heal more quickly.' He sounded absent again. Clearly the attention he'd paid to her was at an end. She told herself she was glad of it because she definitely didn't want the horrid spy's notice!

But she grabbed the pot and unscrewed it, sniffing at the greenish salve inside it in suspicion and sneezing at the cloying floral scent. But she put some on her nose and sat on her bed letting the chemise hang open so that she could attend to the bite.

'What is *that*?'

She gasped, dropping the pot of salve and covering herself in panic.

He loomed over her and she scowled at him. He hadn't been so quiet yesterday. He was employing extra stealth on purpose – probably to keep her from being able to relax.

'What is what?' she asked, eyes narrowing.

To her shock, she found that his hands were gloved as he took her wrists and pulled her arms to her sides. She let him, not sure what else to do. No one touched her, not even with covered hands. Even Vineri never had.

Her face must have shown her disbelief, but he didn't let her go. Instead his eyes traveled down to where her chemise gaped, her chest on full display. She simply stared at him, watching his jaw tic.

'He bit you,' he muttered. 'I thought it was just … I didn't see …' He sounded furious and she looked away, squirming under his stare that hadn't left her, unsure if it was unease she was feeling or something else, and not able to forget that his hands, though gloved, were touching her.

As she thought it, he let her go, and she felt the loss of his proximity with a keenness that made her want to burst into tears. Even with the leather between his skin and hers, he had felt warm. She hadn't felt another person in so long, and the loneliness that gripped her was worse than a punch to the gut.

She moved to cover herself.

'Leave your arms at your sides,' he ordered softly, and she stifled a sigh. Could he not just leave her be?

He picked up the pot of salve and dipped a gloved finger into it. He smeared it on the teeth marks, his finger tracing around her nipple as he rubbed it into her skin. Her breath hitched and she tried to hide her reaction, forcing her lungs to work. Her nipple hardened under his ministrations, and so did the other one. He wasn't even touching that one.

He looked up and caught her eye as he pinched her nipple gently, rolling it in his gloved fingers and making her gasp loudly. She couldn't take her gaze from his, wishing he would do more but not having much idea of what more actually was.

And then his hand left her and he straightened, smirking down at her. It was a game, she realized. Another performance designed to humiliate, to show her who was in charge. She blanked her face and stared past him as she slowly drew her chemise back together, willing her heart to slow. She wouldn't give him the satisfaction of a reaction to his cruelty. Gods knew she'd never given Vineri one.

She was seized by an impulse she knew she'd have to give in to if she wanted to feel better. She'd killed four men, after all. The curse had extracted its due and now her mind would take its own as well. She surveyed the tent past Quin, who still stood over her. She was glad he didn't lock his weapons away. She'd need a knife tonight.

~

As he gazed down at her blank expression, Quin felt a guilt that he couldn't push away this time. Why had he done that? Any of it? She could have dealt with the wound herself, but when he'd seen it, he'd been livid. The fucking Rat had bitten her and he'd let it happen. Nay, he'd made it happen. He remembered that cry of pain she'd given and his stomach churned. What would his mother have said if she'd seen any of his dealings with this girl?

He knew exactly what she'd have said, what she'd have thought. He could practically feel the cuff she'd give him around the ear. But what did it matter? She was long dead and she wouldn't have known the first thing about how to command an army of mercenaries, half of them vying for his position. No, his mother's sage advice would be useless in these circumstances. He needed to show strength, not weakness, if he was to lead the Brothers. Greygor, his predecessor, had been a prick, but even Quin had to admit the man had been very good at projecting strength.

He steeled his mind and turned away from the girl, ignoring her until he got back to his desk and peeked at her through the piles of papers. She still sat on the bed grasping her ruined clothes to her. His cock stirred as his gaze caught the mirror. That had been Greygor's as well, and to think Quin hadn't liked it at first. He'd meant to have it removed, but he was half glad now that he hadn't. He'd never have been able to watch her as he had, her defenses down as she sponged her body, if he'd remembered to tell one of his men to take it away. He gritted his teeth. Why did he want the woman so badly? Was it because he couldn't have her?

He got back to his work, shuffling documents around as he looked for this and that and vowing that he needed to find a Brother he could trust to sort out all the parchments for him. Half of it needed burning, but there was no time to organize it all.

He would have to sort something before they left for the north. And, now he was thinking on it, he knew of just the person – one of the few Brothers he could entrust with all of this.

He found the boy outside, the one Lilith had been afraid he was going to make her kill. He was usually lurking about when he knew Quin was in his tent. Quick lad. Motivated. He reminded Quin a little of himself when he was a boy after he'd been brought to the camp by his mother. He wouldn't be surprised if he became a full Brother when he was of age.

He gave the boy his tasks and disappeared back into the tent to wait. The girl still sat on the bed, staring at the tent wall.

He snapped his fingers to get her attention and she turned to him. Her face was still thoroughly clear, but he could see that she hated him all the same. It was better that she did, he thought, and yet ...

'There are some books in the trunk there,' he ground out, pointing at the wooden war chest behind his desk. 'They may not be what you're used to, but it's something to do, at least.'

She blinked at him. 'Before my next kill, you mean?'

'If you don't want them—'

'I do,' she said quickly. 'Thank you.'

Sitting back behind the desk, he watched her go to the chest, a blanket wrapped around her. He needed to have her clothed before they went north. Yet another thing to see to, he thought, adding it to his long mental list.

A woman's voice called his name – not 'Commander' as everyone else did now – from outside and he couldn't help a grin as she entered, her dark hair pulled back into a plait at the nape of her neck, dressed in the blacks of the Brothers.

'Maeve,' he greeted, and she inclined her head.

'Heard you've had a girl in here for days. Not usual for you,' she fished.

He rolled his eyes. 'Who'd have thought the Army of the Dark Brothers was no better than a gaggle of bored fishwives,' he muttered.

She shrugged. 'You're the Commander now,' she drawled. 'All the men want to be you and all the women want to fuck you, *sir*.'

He made a face and she laughed at him.

He cast a look at Lilith, still behind him looking at books, and was a little surprised that he'd turned his back on her. She could easily have snuck up behind him. It would only take one tiny touch, after all. He wasn't usually so trusting; *stupid*.

'This is the girl who's kept you entertained for so long?'

'It's not what you think,' he said stiffly, feeling Lilith's eyes on him.

'No?'

'No. She was Vineri's. She has a gift and I aim to keep her very close.'

'Aye?' Maeve's eyes surveyed Lilith as she skittered across the tent with a book in her hand, and she frowned. 'Any particular reason you're keeping her half naked, then?' Her tone was cold and Quin only just stopped himself from grimacing. Maeve didn't take kindly to women being mistreated. She wanted the pleasure tents taken down as well as other laws put in place. It had made her unpopular enough that several attempts had been made on her life since her return to the Army.

'Aye. I'm the Commander and I wish it,' he said sharply instead of admitting any wrongdoing.

She barked a laugh. 'Fuck off, Quin.'

He snorted. Maeve was one of the few Brothers who didn't treat him any differently now that he was in charge. That was one of the reasons he knew he could entrust her with this.

'I asked you here because soon we travel north.'

'Aye, to the capital, I hear.'

Quin raised a brow. Funny how everything that was meant to be secret traveled twice as fast through the camp. Could no one keep their mouths shut?

'Aye.' He sighed and gestured to his desk. 'I need a steward for while I'm gone. Greygor had that worm Morden do it, but, truth be told, I've never liked him and I'd trust him with fuck all. I need someone who is loyal to me. Someone organized.' He looked at Maeve meaningfully.

'Am I loyal to you?' she teased. Then she crossed her arms over her chest. 'You're taking me away from my unit, and you know how much time I spend in their company. What's in it for me?'

Quin's lips pursed as he thought. Maeve didn't want for much, and she would be taken away from Jax, Callan, and Seth. Their unit was extremely *close*. She'd want something special.

'A favor in the future?' he suggested.

'A favor from Quin, Commander of the Dark Army?' She sounded intrigued, and Quin could see that he finally had her undivided attention. 'Well, you don't give those away every day. I suppose it'll do,' she stated, 'but I'll need a document with your seal upon it. Morden, especially, won't believe you gave such a task to a woman without proof. And you know how they like to play at their intrigues whenever they can. Grown men turn into children with dangerous toys. They'll come out of the woodwork like vipers once your presence isn't forcing them into the darkness to do their shady deals.'

'Aye, I'll give you the authority, Maeve.' His eyes narrowed. 'But any power grabs and, friend or no, I'll kill you as I would anyone else.'

Maeve had the audacity to give him a cheeky wink and a smile. She knew he would do as he promised no matter how much it pained him; she was just fearless like that – always had been, he mused, except when it came to Callan, Jax, and Seth. She'd run from them like a frightened mouse and hidden herself for years. He still didn't know the whole story, but it was between her and her unit. Not his business.

'I have to meet the others,' he said, getting up and donning his cloak.

'I might as well start now,' she said absently as she began to shuffle papers around on the desk. 'How's Bastian getting on? I didn't much like Payn, but Bastian …' She shook her head.

'Fucking worthless,' he muttered as he began to walk off, and she snickered.

Quin glanced over at Lilith as he left the tent. She was sitting back on the bed reading one of his books, and he swung back on a whim. Just because she didn't seem dangerous, that didn't mean anything.

'Don't touch her,' he warned Maeve, and she gave him an odd look.

'I don't tend to fuck women, Quin. You know that.' Then she winked at Lilith, who was watching their exchange with wide eyes.

Quin shook his head at his incorrigible friend and went out into the rain. He would meet his Brothers in Mal's tent, away from the girl. He didn't want her knowing any more than was necessary about their plan and their movements over the next weeks. He trudged through the mud, pretending not to know that someone was following him. The fool would learn soon enough that he wouldn't be easily slain. As he neared Mal's tent, he heard an 'oof' and then silence. Bastian appeared at his side.

He didn't show it, but Quin was surprised. He'd expected Mal to get the would-be assassin, if he was honest.

'Who was it?' he asked in a murmur, unperturbed.

'A Rat.'

'They're getting bolder.'

'Aye. Heard quite a few were killed last night by a Brother, they say. They're trying to get your attention. Perhaps they want your protection,' Bastian drawled, sounding bored and half drunk as usual.

Quin grumbled an inaudible reply as they entered Mal's tent.

Bastian gave a high-pitched whistle at the sheer amount of weapons Mal had stored in here. The man favored knives, but he had an impressive collection that would put any castle armory to shame.

He was sitting at his table making an arrow when they entered. He didn't look up as they sat with him, only stabbed the back of Bastian's hand with the barbed tip when Bastian tried to touch it. Bastian simply licked his hand with a laugh, which made Mal's eyes promise future pain.

'Enough,' Quin ordered. 'We go north soon and we're taking the girl,' he said, his tone brooking no arguments. Best to just get it over with, though he knew at least one of them wouldn't like it.

He ignored Mal's surprised and then angry expression and Bastian's fascinated one.

'Why?' Bastian asked.

'Because she can be useful to us. She's practically a gift from the gods.' He grinned at his Brothers' expressions. He rarely invoked the gods to further his plans. 'She's traveling with us to the capital and she is going to quietly and efficiently kill our enemies with that gift of hers with no one the wiser that the Army had anything to do with it.'

'The north isn't a place for anyone who's different at the moment, or so I hear,' Bastian mused.

'As long as we get her there to do the deed, I don't give a fuck what happens to her after. If she's captured, we'll silence her before she tells anyone who sent her.'

'And if she's not captured?'

Quin shrugged. 'We may have uses for her afterwards. She's a powerful weapon, after all. But if we find the tiresome female to be a hindrance, we can rid ourselves of her easily enough before we return to the camp.'

CHAPTER 5

LILY

She watched the woman who was also, somehow, a Brother from behind her book, sneaking glances here and there while the woman reordered the papers on the desk. Lily was still reeling from what Quin had done to her earlier, but the woman was a welcome distraction. She wondered if she and Quin were lovers. They'd certainly seemed friendly.

She chanced another peek at the beautiful woman dressed in her Brothers' blacks and the woman's head whipped around to catch her spying. Lily looked back at her book quickly and the other woman let out a chuckle.

'Whatever Quin's said about me, I don't bite,' she said with a laugh.

Lily cringed, wondering if she'd said that because she'd heard the Rat had bitten her. Had Quin told everyone what he'd done and how her body had shamelessly responded to his touch as well?

Suddenly the woman was in front of her and Lily tensed, but she didn't cross the barrier, thank the gods.

'Did Quin do that?' she asked, gesturing to Lily's bruised nose.

Lily shook her head.

'What's your name?' the woman asked.

'Lily.'

'Lily.' She smiled and Lily was surprised at how kind she seemed. 'I'm Maeve.'

'Are you a Brother?' she blurted, putting down the book.

Maeve drew herself up. 'I am. One of the only females ever to get through the training, although I was bound to my unit before I became a Brother officially, in the end.'

'Bound?'

Maeve waved a hand. 'You don't need to worry about that,' she said. 'Boring Army nonsense. So you were Vineri's what? Slave? Pet?'

Lily looked down. 'I'm not sure what I was, but it doesn't matter now. He's dead.'

'You've killed a few people since you came to the camp,' Maeve observed.

Lily glanced up, wondering if the woman was going to turn on her. Perhaps she'd killed one of the woman's friends.

'Oh, don't worry. I didn't know any of them, if that's what you're afraid of, and I certainly didn't owe any of them enough loyalty to get on Quin's bad side.' She chuckled. 'He'd flay me alive if I killed you.'

'But,' she shifted, making sure the blanket covered her still, 'aren't you friends?'

Maeve pursed her lips. 'As good a friend as you can have here outside your unit. He and I grew up in the camp. We knew each other when we were just children running around, doing whatever we could to stay alive here.' Then she frowned, hesitating before she spoke. When she did, it was barely above a whisper. 'I don't know what Quin is planning, but if there is anything that you must remember about him, it's that growing up in the camp makes you hard and strong and very good at surviving. Becoming a Brother takes cunning, skill, and duplicity. Assuming command of the Dark Army takes a man who is stone cold and dark as fuck.'

Lily canted her head. 'What is it that you're trying to tell me?' she asked, just as softly.

'I suppose,' she shook her head, 'I just – don't turn your back on him, Lily, even if you think he cares for you. He doesn't. I doubt he even has the ability to, no matter what he pretends.' She looked behind her as if she expected him to appear. 'I don't know much about his life before he came here, but I do know that he was brought. Many of us were taken in raids or were simply born in the camp. But Quin's mother wanted him to be a Brother. She raised him for it and that's all he's ever worked for. In fact, all three of the Brothers in his unit appeared here of their own volition, drawn to the camp, to the death and the violence of this place.'

'If you hate it so much, why don't you leave?'

Maeve smiled. 'I did, but the fucking place dragged me back. There's one of my Brothers now,' she said, turning as a man Lily hadn't seen before entered the tent.

He was large like they all seemed to be, with long blond hair that was partly up in a knot on his head.

'I've been looking for you,' he said, grabbing her around the waist and pulling her to him.

Maeve smiled at him, taking his face in her hands and kissing him soundly as Lily watched, wide-eyed. She looked away, feeling very much an interloper as her cheeks heated with embarrassment. They finally pulled away from each other and Maeve gestured at her.

'This is Lily, Quin's new …'

'Weapon,' Lily finished for her.

'This is Callan, the leader of my unit.'

The man looked her up and down. 'I've heard the talk. So this is the girl with death's touch.' He raised his brows as he noticed she was wrapped only in a blanket, but he said nothing. 'Quin will be pleased if you can do half of what the rumors say.'

Maeve gave him a quelling look and he shrugged.

'Rumors?' Lily asked, not sure if she wanted to know the talk that followed her. She knew that even in Vineri's home, people must have told stories about her, but so few ever spoke to her that she'd never heard anything that was said behind her back until she was taken down to the square when Vineri was dead. In fact, the woman from the kitchens had spoken so nastily to her that she wondered how many of her meals had been gobbed in. Her nose wrinkled at the thought.

'Rumors follow everyone here,' Maeve said airily. 'Well, anyone interesting, that is.' She winked. 'Remember what I said. I'm sure you'll see me again.' And with that, she and Callan were gone.

For the first time, Lily was alone. She didn't tarry, bouncing up and grabbing a small knife, one of many that were strewn about. Watching the entrance of the tent, she unwound the blanket as she sat, baring her thighs, blemished with many thin, slightly shiny scars. Forty-one of them, to be exact, long and precise.

She let out a breath, feeling like she was going to burst from the feelings inside, emotions she knew not to examine too closely because if she did, she'd start to cry and wouldn't be able to stop. She found a space halfway down her right thigh and drew the knife over her flesh, cutting deep enough to bleed and to mark. She hissed, the pain bringing with it a sudden, palpable relief of the awful sensations that threatened to burst out of her. She cut herself again. Four deaths. Four lines.

Lily let her leg bleed, watching the blood run down and drip to the floor, almost mesmerized by the sudden release until she remembered that she was not in her tower now. Someone would notice the mess. She doubted they'd care, but it would raise questions she didn't want to answer. Ever.

Using strips of her ruined chemise, which was on the floor, she bandaged her leg and wiped up the blood, washing it away with the jug of water from the table. She studied the finished result. It looked as if she'd spilled some wine. Nothing amiss.

She picked up her book again, the welcome throbbing of her leg helping her to relax in a way that she hadn't been able to since she'd killed that first man in the tower. The price had been paid.

She was left alone for a long time. Two women came to replenish the table with food, taking the old away. Neither of them spoke to her, but they kept their suspicious eyes on her all the time. Camp rumors, Lily supposed.

The night came and still Quin didn't return. She lay in her bed in the dark, as no one had come to relight the braziers when they went out, and soon she began to shiver as the outside cold seeped in. The thin blanket wasn't enough, so she pilfered one from Quin's bed, as she couldn't find anything else.

Sometime later, she heard whispers and she was wide awake in an instant, frozen in fear until a candle was lit, flooding the tent with enough dim light to see by. Quin had returned and his two Brothers were with him. Quin cursed the cold, his eyes turning accusingly to her.

'Why did you let the braziers go out?' he ground out. 'We're going to fucking freeze tonight because of you.'

She blinked at him, opening her mouth to tell him that she had no idea how to keep a brazier lit, nor what fuel to feed it with, when Bastian, surprisingly, came to her rescue.

'It's hardly the girl's fault that the servants didn't keep the fires fed,' he said, sounding bored.

Quin sniffed the air. 'I smell blood.'

Lily hoped her face didn't give anything away. Surely he couldn't smell the cuts she'd made.

'The girl's probably on her monthly courses or something,' Bastian said casually.

Lily wrinkled her nose at him and he shrugged.

'Are you going to tell her before we go or just haul her out of bed in the morning and throw her up onto a horse?' he asked, directing his question at Quin.

Quin's eyes moved over her, narrowing when they noticed his blanket, though he said nothing about it. 'We travel north tomorrow, girl.'

'Tomorrow? Why?'

'So you can earn your keep. You didn't think I'd simply let you lounge around in my tent forever without paying your dues, did you?'

'You want me to kill for you,' she guessed and saw by his countenance that that was indeed what they meant. She nodded once and closed her eyes. It wasn't much different from being in Vineri's possession. She supposed that no matter where she went, as soon as her curse was found out about, she'd be used in such a fashion – or killed. Perhaps that was why she hadn't put any serious thought into trying to escape. She had no money, no skills, and sooner or later someone would touch her and she'd have to run from whatever paltry life she'd built. She let out a sigh. Was this the best someone like her could hope for? Killing to live? Was she such a coward that she couldn't choose death over this?

The next morning brought the same desolation, the only parting of the figurative clouds being the neat and quite large package that had been deposited next to the barrier around her little corner of the tent sometime while she'd slept. When she opened it, she found clothes that looked much like Maeve's, including a thick black cloak and sturdy boots.

With no one else around, she donned them quickly and gazed at herself in the looking glass. She looked like one of them. What would they say to that, she wondered? Though she found she didn't much care. If they'd wanted her to look different, Quin should have provided her with clothes himself instead of making her wander his tent half naked for days on end. Though Vineri had delighted in dressing her up in finery whenever she went anywhere in public – much like a child's doll, she'd always thought – and held things back when she displeased him, she'd never had to walk about her tower room with *nothing* on. She thought on this for a moment as she plaited her hair.

At the time, she'd never really thought about it, but he was known far and wide as a hard and ruthless man and he was feared for good reason. But though he'd made her kill for him, threatened sometimes, punished once in a while, he'd never had her beaten. She even remembered him coming to her tower with smiles on his long, weathered face. Then, she'd thought it was because he was taking her out to show the power he held, but perhaps he had looked upon her with a fondness. Or maybe that was just wishful thinking. Regardless, her time in that tower could have been much worse, that was certain.

She missed him. That shouldn't shock her. He was the only person she'd spoken to for weeks sometimes, after all. But she was surprised. He hadn't been her friend. She knew that. And yet ...

Someone walked into the tent as she tied off her hair with a piece of leather twine she'd found in Quin's things. It was Bastian.

'He sent me in here to ...' He trailed off as his eyes moved over her and she turned to him, ignoring his roving gaze.

Out here, all men seemed to think she was simply a prize to be ogled.

'To …?'

He seem to recover himself. 'To tell you to gather your things. It's time to leave.'

She looked around the room and wondered if he was trying to be funny. He must know she had nothing save the clothes she now wore. 'And we're going north?'

'Yes.' He drew a flask out from under his cloak and took a gulp.

Gods, the man couldn't go a moment without imbibing. Why? 'You seem like such a jolly fellow,' she mused aloud and then shut her mouth as his eyes flashed.

'You don't know me,' he said harshly, his cold eyes boring into her.

She looked away from him, not answering and cursing herself for making another enemy. She'd be traveling with these men for gods only knew how long. It would be far less enjoyable to journey with men who hated her before they'd even left the camp.

'I'm sorry,' she whispered as he stalked from the tent, not giving her any indication that he'd heard her.

She donned the warm cloak and two black things fell to the floor. She grabbed them up and tears swelled in her eyes. *Gloves.* She wouldn't have to be so careful about every person around her if she had these. Hoping she'd see Maeve again to thank her, she put them on and left the tent, blinking in the bright sunshine.

The three Brothers were there, already astride their massive black horses, and if Quin noticed her clothes, he didn't show it. One of the soldiers had one for her as well, an enormous thing that snorted and pawed at the earth. Vineri had only ever had her ride small ponies. This was a *real* horse. She walked up to the steps that were by the side of him, glad they didn't expect her to be able to simply jump up onto his back, which stood almost as high as the top of her head. She climbed up and swung her leg over the saddle, hoping she wouldn't make a fool of herself by slipping off the other side. That would be mortifying, she thought; dressed in her Brothers' clothes only to fall into the stinking mud as soon as she got outside. A chuckle left her at the idea and she bit her lip to keep any others from escaping.

Once she was on the horse and quite sure she wasn't going to simply slide off, she looked up at the others. Quin and the quiet one looked impatient. Bastian still looked angry, but at least he wasn't directing it at her. Perhaps she should apologize again, though she didn't really know what for. What she did know was that she was in these men's hands, and she didn't want them to be any angrier at her than they already seemed to be.

'Are you ready?' Quin ground out in a pretense of patience.

When she nodded, they immediately began to move. She grabbed the reins and squeezed with her thighs, swallowing hard and trying not to show fear as her massive horse took a great step forward. The Brothers were leading, eight soldiers on horses in front of her and two more behind her. She was relegated to the back of their Brotherly procession, which didn't bother her. She wasn't one of them, after all, despite how she was dressed.

They left the tents of the Brothers' camp, heading towards the snow-covered mountains that she'd stared at from her casement for so many years. At the beginning, she'd dreamed of traveling to them, exploring them and going further. Now, she turned, looking back at the camp and Vineri's fortress, which was already some way away down the open road.

So open. She looked up at the sky. Vast. Her chest seized.

It was so *big* out here. She gasped for breath, feeling dizzy and lightheaded, threading her fingers through the horse's mane to ground her mind. She leant forward and took a shallow breath though her nose and another. It was calming, she thought, looking down at the ground as it moved slowly past them. She was all right. She just couldn't look up. She had to pretend, just as she had on her outings with Vineri. Except this time there would be no tower sanctuary after she'd done the only thing she was good at. Perhaps they'd kill her once she'd been of use.

She didn't find the prospect as frightening as it should be.

'She doesn't look like much.'

'Heard she killed two Brothers.'

'Sounds like horseshit to me. Look at her. How the fuck would a slip of a girl kill two of *them?*'

She glanced up, her cheeks coloring. The two soldiers, one on each side, were talking about her. She didn't look at them, remembering how vicious the woman was to her in the square. She supposed she'd have to get used to it. She was out in the world now, and if she remembered anything at all from *before*, it was that most people were cruel. But before any of those memories could materialize, she focused on the present. She promised herself that one day she would think of that time, but not enough of it had passed. It was still too raw, even ten winters later.

So she did the only thing she could. She rode and listened to the two soldiers talking about her as if she couldn't hear them, growing smaller and smaller with their comments about her, the barbs, their licentious comments about her hair, her mouth, her legs even. When one of them saw her crimson face that she tried to hide, it made them both worse. When one of them leaned over and put a hand on her leg, she froze, pulling hard on the reins to stop her horse in its tracks. She could take anything else, but that was too much.

She gaped at him, her heart thudding in her chest. Was this what her life would be now? Would keeping herself covered not be enough? There was thick material between their bodies. It wasn't a danger to him. But what about later? One of them would touch her hand or her face unless she made them understand. She had to make them understand.

'Have you not heard the rumors, you fool?' She didn't let him answer. 'I am the touch of death. Even a brush of your flesh against mine will make your lungs bleed, your brain melt like ice over a fire in your skull. Your blood will flow out of your orifices while you lie on the ground and gasp in agony. I don't want to kill you, but I will.'

The soldier paled, but his friend laughed, causing the first one to chuckle at her warning. Once his friend turned away, though, his mirth died and he looked at her with a bit more respect.

'Why have you stopped?' came Quin's impatient voice from up ahead, and she saw that the rest of the party were some way up the road. She clicked her horse back into its slow plod, not trusting herself with a canter or a trot on the first day. The Brothers would simply have to wait. As she looked ahead and saw Quin's piercing eyes, she gave a little snort. It would do that man good to realize that the whole world was not under his command, her included.

~

AS THEY TRAVELED to the next town of Westport, nestled at the foot of the mountains that separated the north from the south, Bastian couldn't help but steal glimpses of the girl. She lagged behind their little party with the two soldiers who'd been assigned to keep her close. She'd seemed quite bright as they left the camp. No doubt excited to leave the site of her captivity for however long, but once they were on the open road, she'd kept her eyes lowered. She hadn't looked up at the mountains, nor towards the sea as they neared the coast. She rode in silence, ignoring all but the road as it passed beneath her. Her eyes only rose once they were within the town limits.

They entered the main street. It was a small town but bustling at this time of year, with it being the last port before the mountains, which couldn't be crossed until the spring thaw. The town was set in a small bay with deep waters, so the ships could come quite close to the docks that were built out into it. They passed impressive stone buildings built to stand up to the salty air and the storms that sometimes battered this line of coast. The inn came into view.

Bastian had already sent a messenger ahead to procure the only two rooms for his Brothers and the girl, so they were able to simply leave their horses for the soldiers to take to the nearby stables, where they'd be making their own beds for the night. He envied them. They had a camaraderie that he did not share with Quin and that silent prick Mal.

He took a small gulp from his flask and then scowled as he remembered the censure in the girl's eyes when she'd seen him do similar this morning. Who the fuck was she to judge the way he wanted to live this mortal existence? He'd put her in her place sooner or later, regardless of the impressive power she had. The touch of death was a sizable gift, one mortals rarely harbored. Usually that sort of power was relegated to beasts far into the Dark Realms where those from here rarely ventured and, if they did, they weren't making it home to their families, that was certain.

He watched her slide from the horse, her cloak billowing for a moment and giving him a tantalizing view of her figure in those blacks she'd appeared in. He couldn't believe that Quin had found her something like that to wear, and he was sure Mal wouldn't have bothered with her at all. He watched her a moment longer before dismounting and grabbing his pack.

Inside, the inn was typical. It had a small tap room and an annex for private dining. Up the creaking wooden stairs, the two rooms he'd taken for the night were serviceable and clean. Each had a small tub for bathing, a hearth, table and chairs, and a bed, of course.

Quin had already given him his orders regarding the woman. They'd take turns watching her at night while they traveled, as she wouldn't be under lock and key all of the time. What was her name again? Lizy? Bastian had drawn the short straw, so he'd be in her room tonight.

He rolled his eyes. She'd probably be a handful. Women in general, from mortals to goddesses, were very much the same in that regard, he'd found in his experience.

In truth, until he'd come back to this realm, he hadn't actually remembered much about mortals in general. He hadn't bothered with them on the Mount unless one of them found his or her way into his presence, and he didn't obsessively watch them as he knew Gaila did from her tragic window, barred from this realm as she was. She argued that it was because she needed to keep an eye on things, but he suspected it was more a case of wanting what she couldn't have. Bastian didn't know the particulars, but the ancient goddess had let it slip once that she had made a deal with someone or something and her end was that she wasn't allowed here.

Luckily he suffered no such affliction. Since a woman had appeared to them and behaved in a most non-pious fashion, he'd ached to see what this world was like after so long away from it.

He'd been a bit disappointed when he got here and found it not much changed. The people were still the same, squabbling over trinkets, warring, lying, thieving. Bastian enjoyed those things, of course, but he supposed he'd just assumed they'd have grown somehow. But no, they still made the exact same mistakes as their forefathers.

He made his inspection of the room and met the innkeeper downstairs to order refreshments and hot water to wash the road dust away. He watched as Mal quickly herded the woman up the stairs as if she were a sheep that had strayed from the flock. He goaded her, got close enough to make her panic as he went, the ghost of a smile playing on his lips as he tormented her.

But when they got to the room, she whirled around and slammed the door closed in his face, bolting it quickly, and Bastian couldn't help the loud laugh that exploded from his chest. Mal gazed down at him, his eyes narrowing as Bastian snickered at his expense. Bastian made a rude gesture at him and watched as his Brother descended the stairs, somehow in complete silence despite the creaking planks, and disappeared out into the street.

Bastian grinned, taking a cup of wine from the innkeeper, and climbed back up and knocked on the door to his room.

'Go away,' came a haughty voice from inside and he shook his head. Yes, there it was, that female entitlement. It was so hard being right all the time.

'It's Bastian. I bring refreshments,' he coaxed, and the door opened a crack just as he'd known it would.

He entered and watched as she moved back towards the wall, not the bed. Curious. It wasn't as if anyone could rape her, so why? Was it something she did with purpose or randomly?

He put one of the goblets he carried on the table and surveyed her, much as he had the room when he'd first come up here a few moments ago. She looked drawn and was breathing heavily from Mal driving her up the stairs.

'Are you all right?'

He wondered why he'd bothered asking. It wasn't as if he cared.

But she nodded as if he should of course ask after her welfare as she unclasped her cloak and hung it over the back of one of the high-backed wooden chairs on the other side of the table. Tentatively, she reached forward, her hands now gloved, he noticed.

'Where did you get the clothes?' he asked, automatically moving back so that she wouldn't feel crowded.

'Maeve,' she said and took a long drink, making a face when she realized it was wine.

'Ah, of course.' He'd only met the woman once or twice since he'd joined up with the Army. Her unit was very protective of her, though from what he'd seen of her fighting skills, they didn't need to be. She was a vicious and savage bitch when she fought.

Odd that they'd formed a bond, but then women were as likely to bond as sisters as they were to hate each other to the bitter end. Bastian much preferred the former. Catfights tended to get loud rather quickly from his experience on the Mount.

She drank some of the wine before turning her back on him and going to the casement. She opened it wide and stared out of it at the view of the mountains, now much closer after their day's trek.

She stared out at the scene for ages, and Bastian found he was content to stare at her backside while she did so.

When she turned abruptly and caught him ogling, she didn't react past a roll of her ordinary hazel eyes, though he saw how her shoulders tensed once more.

'What are you afraid of?' he asked abruptly. 'That I'll throw you on the bed and fuck you?'

Her eyes widened at his crude words, but when she

opened her mouth, her voice didn't waver. 'Yes, I am often afraid of such a thing out here.'

'Why?' he scoffed. 'You're not so beautiful that I'd forget what would happen if I stuck it in you.'

'I've killed four men since I was found in my tower,' she reminded him. 'I'd rather not make it a fifth.'

He snorted. 'I feel sorry for you,' he confessed coldly. 'No man able to touch you. You must be so unsatisfied. Gods, you poor girl, your quim is probably a shriveled thing.'

He thought that would make her angry, but instead she seemed to battle a smile. 'Don't feel too bad,' she said, obviously trying to control her amusement. 'I got quite good at doing it myself.'

'I'm sorry?' he squeaked and cleared his throat, his heart hammering in his chest as a picture of her doing what she described appeared in his mind.

'Pleasuring myself. I'm very good at it, so you needn't worry about my quim withering like a dried-up husk,' she explained with a straight face, though she was clearly mocking him. 'Did you not realize women could do it? Don't worry. I'm quite well satisfied. Thank you for your concern, though.'

He felt his cheeks heat as if he were a boy of fifteen summers trying to kiss his first girl. He couldn't even remember being that young, but he would guess it felt like this.

She thought to embarrass *him*?

He let his eyes wander over her, lingering over her form-fitting tunic and the breeches that hugged her hips. 'That's something I'd like to see,' he said softly and watched her lips part in a tiny gasp.

Her cheeks reddened, but she didn't back down. 'I'm sure you would,' she said sultrily. Then she tipped her head back and gulped down the rest of her wine as he stared at the alluring curve of her throat. He wanted to taste her, lick that hollow at the base of her neck. His cock, already well and truly hard, bobbed painfully in his breeches and he stifled a groan. Why was he torturing himself? He couldn't touch her.

She reached to put the goblet on the table, not stepping any closer to him. 'But, sadly, the only show I'll be giving you ends with someone bleeding from their eyes on the floor.'

Without another word, she turned her back to him and returned to the window, leaving him surprised and aroused in a way that he hadn't been in a long, long time. There was more to Lily than he'd first suspected. Much more.

'How long will it take to get to wherever it is we're going?' she asked, not turning around.

'I've got no fucking idea,' he muttered. 'All I know is that we take a ship from here. You'll have to ask Quin.'

He left the room, willing his aching cock to settle down as he ordered the girl's dinner from the innkeeper and left to find a different ale-house to get drunk in. With any luck, he'd find another woman to quell his sexual appetites so that he'd actually be able to sleep in the same room as Lily tonight.

CHAPTER 6

LILY

Only after she heard the door click closed behind Bastian did Lily put her hands to her hot cheeks. What had possessed her to speak to him so brazenly? She'd just been so annoyed with his condescending pity, making her feel as if she were truly missing out on something simply because men couldn't bring her pleasure. She let out an angry noise. What a prick, she thought, even as she remembered how he'd stared at her. She hadn't liked the way men looked at her since she left the tower, but, gods, she found she very much enjoyed the way that he had. She didn't know what the difference was, but there definitely was one. It couldn't only be because he was handsome, could it? There had to be more to it than that, didn't there? Granted, she hadn't met many handsome men in her life. Was she just being seduced by his good looks?

She stared up at the mountains, the scene almost identical to the one from her tower room, though the mountains looked bigger, of course, now that they were so much closer. She found it calmed her frayed nerves, and if she just looked from the window, she could pretend she was still in her safe little room. She knew it wasn't helpful to pretend in the long run. Sooner or later she was going to have to face the fact that her old life was gone, that that room was no more. She had to make this new one better any way she could, and perhaps that had to begin by turning this unit of Brothers she traveled with into her allies. She had no notion of how to do that really, of course – well, except for following their orders and killing whoever they wanted her to.

Someone opened the door and she started as she was abruptly brought out of her thoughts. It was the quiet one, Mal, who'd rushed her up the stairs by putting out his hand and pretending to touch her. She put her hand to her chest, where her heart was already starting to beat faster. What was the tyrant going to inflict on her now? After a tiring and fearful day in the open, on the road, in the company of those two nasty soldiers with their horrible words, and then what this one had done as soon as they'd arrived here, followed by her conversation with Bastian, Lily was strung tight as a bowstring. If this one tried anything, she might just use her curse voluntarily for once.

He stopped in the middle of the room and watched her. She drew herself up and adopted the pose Vineri always used; a sort of conceited nonchalance. It had always worked for him well enough and everyone had feared *him* nicely.

Mal cocked a brow at her, looking smug as he took a step forward. What was he doing? She took a step back and felt the wall at her heel as he took another step towards her. His narrow eyes never left her and he still had a look on his face as if he was playing some sort of twisted game. Anger bloomed inside her. If he wanted to kill himself, why should she stop him? She straightened and looked him dead in the eye as she took a large step forward. He didn't falter even a tad, his step matching hers until they were so close that she could feel his breath on her face. The feel of it wasn't altogether unpleasant. Her heart began to speed up in her chest. It wasn't just from fear; it was anticipation as well. What would it be like to touch someone and for them not to simply die? For them to want her to do it, to not be afraid? What would it be like to reach out and touch his handsome face, for him to touch her back? Her breath caught in her throat as she stared at him.

It struck her what an odd sensation it was to be so close to another person, so close that she could feel their body though they weren't touching her. She realized he was looking down at her face, his smug countenance having been replaced by something akin to respect. She frowned. Had this been a test of some kind?

Then his bare hand rose, stopping just shy of her cheek. She froze, not even daring to breathe. Would he do it? Would he use her to end his life? She closed her eyes and waited, refusing to flee from him and his silly game. And then she heard the door click and opened her eyes. She was alone.

Lily let out a long breath and staggered, weak-kneed, over to the bed, sinking down on it with a sigh of relief. She was very far out of her depth out here in the world, that was certain. Very little over the past decade had prepared her for this, and she had a feeling it would make or break her. She had to make sure it was the former. She wanted to survive, she realized with surprise. There had been times in the tower that she wouldn't have cared if one of Vineri's men had barged in and cut her down where she stood, but something was different now. She was changed after only a few days out here.

There was yet another knock at the door and she sighed. Which one was it now – Quin to come in and manhandle her with his gloved hands, perhaps? At that thought she felt a tingle between her legs and she shivered. No! She would not think about any of them that way. If nothing else, wanting these men – who were basically her captors – would set her down a disastrous path. She couldn't let those sorts of notions in because there would be no fulfillment, only a hollow, lonely road. She almost laughed as she imagined it. Them all traveling together, her secretly wanting them while they gave her the orders of whom to kill for them and her doing what they wanted because she loved them. Her sitting in her rooms at the inns or in Quin's tent, waiting for one of them to notice the cursed girl, give her a morsel of attention to keep her sweet.

She shuddered. What a pathetic existence. That was definitely not the life she wanted. She had to ensure she didn't come to want them or even like them. So far as they'd behaved to her, liking them wouldn't be a problem, though, so at least there was that. But she couldn't be seduced by their stupid fucking beautiful-as-the-gods bodies either.

The door creaked open and a girl in an apron brought in a supper tray, thankfully not lingering except to tell her that hot water would be brought afterwards for bathing.

As soon as the girl was gone, Lily fell upon the food like a ravenous beast, not bothering with the manners that Vineri had made her learn, though she'd never really had to use them. She'd only eaten with others once or twice the entire time she'd been with him; the rest of the time had been trays brought to her room, pushed in with a stick. She felt annoyed now, remembering it. She'd not really minded before that they'd been so terrified of her. Would it have been nice for someone to tarry and speak to her, ask her how she was, learn her name? Of course, but it had simply been a fact of life that she was almost completely alone, and she'd told herself it was better so that there weren't any more accidents.

But now she'd got to thinking. None of the men around her seemed afraid. The soldiers she put down to ignorance. As soon as they saw her in action, so to speak, with their own eyes, they'd find their fear. But Quin, Mal, and Bastian had seen what she could do and they hadn't treated her much differently. She didn't see fear or hatred in their eyes when they looked at her or spoke to her. She supposed it was because they were big bad Dark Brothers who weren't afraid of anything, least of all death. But for her it was like a breath of fresh air not taking her cues from other people's reactions. Even Vineri had never got very close to her, and he'd certainly never let his guard down.

It was quite nice not to have to be so scared just because everyone else seemed to be, and while the Brothers hadn't been exactly kind to her, they hadn't been as cruel as they could have been. Lily was under no illusions. Vineri had made sure of that in order to keep her from ever trying to run. If people found her out, even down here in the south, and there was no one to protect her, she'd be killed and probably set on fire wherever she fell. What was left of her would be burned again until there was nothing left but ash. And from what he had told her, it would be worse in the north.

She ate until all the food was gone, taking her goblet of water over to the casement to look over the darkening mountains she'd see from a ship tomorrow, she supposed. She'd never been on a boat before. When Vineri had brought her from Kitore, they'd traveled through the mountains, as it had been summertime, her only a girl of about nine or ten, she guessed. She had no way of knowing exactly, as if anyone in her home city had had any inkling of her exact age, they certainly hadn't told her before Vineri had carted her away.

She watched for a long time as the sun set and the sky darkened until the room was too black to see much at all. She lit the candles from the small fire in the grate and sat on the bed, wishing she'd brought some books now.

She heard someone climbing the stairs and assumed

correctly that it was the water for the small tub, which was just large enough for her to squeeze herself into. The innkeeper and the girl from earlier carried a massive copper bucket through the door and carefully filled the tub to halfway.

The maid asked if she needed help bathing, and she shook her head and waved them out as she'd seen Vineri do many times. They left her and, after hearing them descend the stairs, she shed her new clothes and stepped into the hot water. Sinking down to sit, she used her goblet to scoop water from the copper bucket they'd left, which still had some water left in it to wet her hair. She lathered herself with the lavender soap she found on the side and rinsed with the goblet before stepping out into the cold room and wrapping herself in a blanket from the bed. She sat by the fire for a while so her hair could dry. And then she lay on the bed, still wrapped in the blanket, and closed her eyes just for a moment.

The door slammed shut and she sat upright with a small scream, trying to remember where she was. She saw movement and was up and pressing herself into the wall before she was fully awake. It was Bastian, swaying drunkenly as he removed his cloak and his sword belt.

His eyes turned to her, practically guileless in his bibulous state. He didn't speak, just started undressing in front of her. Her eyes widening, she lay back in the bed, looking away but keeping watch in case he came any closer. She heard him washing in the tub, swearing at the now-cold water as he splashed it all over the floor, and then he was standing over her, looking a bit more sober after his cold bath.

'Are you going to take the bed and all the blankets?' he asked, his very naked body dripping yet more water all over the place. She shook her head, trying and failing not to notice the way the water rolled off his broad chest, the glistening of his large arms. Gods, there wasn't an ounce of flab on the man. It looked like he'd been carved out of rock. And that V that led down ... She swallowed hard as she fumbled for one of the blankets off the bed and practically threw it at him.

She heard him chuckle knowingly and turned in the bed. If he was going to touch her, he probably would have tried already. She closed her eyes and tried to go back to sleep.

She heard him sit on one of the chairs and felt a twinge of guilt. The bed was large enough for him as well, but it wasn't safe, of course.

She turned back to him and opened her eyes, grateful that he at least had wrapped that blanket around his waist so she only had to contend with his upper half. He had poured himself a wine and was sitting at the table, his head propped up by his elbow on the table. It made him look normal, almost vulnerable, she thought. She didn't know his age. He looked to be a bit older than her, perhaps. But this was the first time his eyes were youthful. From what she'd seen of him, he typically looked like he was trying very hard to act like a young man, but he never actually seemed to be one.

'If you want, I could sleep in the chair,' she offered.

The goblet on the way to his mouth froze and he turned to stare. He looked surprised that she'd offered.

'Won't you be uncomfortable in the chair all night?' he finally asked, his eyes narrowing as if he were trying to find a plot or a machination in her offering and was confused that he could see none.

She shrugged. 'I've slept a bit already,' she said. 'It's unfair if I have it all to myself all night. The other two are probably sharing, but,' her cheeks heated and she cast her eyes to the floor, '*we* can't, of course.'

'Of course,' he murmured, still watching her. He took a drink of his wine and seemed to consider. 'I'll be fine here,' he said after a few moments. 'You get some rest. You look like you need it.'

'Are you certain? I don't mind.'

His gaze on her sharpened. 'I'm sure, unless you'd like to give me that little show we talked about earlier.'

She successfully halted the gasp before it could give away her shock at his words. Instead she gave him what she hoped was a long-suffering roll of her eyes as she lay back down and turned her back to him, closing her eyes.

She ignored his chuckle behind her and tried not to imagine what he wanted her to do in front of him. Did people really do such things? And she definitely ignored the way her lower region pulsed as she *didn't* think about it as well.

In the morning, she was woken by a bang on the door and Bastian telling whoever it was to fuck off. The door clicked open anyway and Quin entered, taking in Bastian in the chair and her wrapped tightly in the blanket on the bed.

'The ship sails in an hour. Get a move on or we'll miss the tide,' he ordered, kicking Bastian's booted foot. The Brother snarled at him, not even bothering to open his eyes, but Quin was already gone, slamming the door behind him.

Lily sat up, keeping the blanket around her as she squatted over the chamber pot quietly and hoped Bastian wasn't fully awake. That done, she washed her face in the cold, clean water from the copper bucket and then looked at her clothes, wondering how she was going to get dressed with Bastian just sitting there. She surveyed him. He looked asleep. He had come in very late last night and quite drunk.

Deciding to chance it, she got all her clothes ready on the bed and, with her back to him, dropped the blanket and got dressed as fast and as silently as she could.

'I've seen naked women before, you know,' came his bored-sounding drawl from behind her and she whirled with a yelp, holding her shirt in front of her and thanking the gods her breeches were already on.

'I thought you were asleep,' she accused.

'Not since Quin came in,' he admitted with a grin, not in the least sorry for watching. He waved a hand as he poured himself another wine from the jug, not taking his eyes from her. 'Continue, by all means. Pretend I'm not here.'

He was goading her, calling her bluff, and she wasn't sure what to do. Part of her wanted to drop the shirt and show him that she didn't care what he saw and the other half thought that was a ridiculous idea because that was clearly what *he wanted*. She chose the latter and turned away from him, putting her black shirt on quickly and the tunic over it, donning her cloak for good measure. She heard his quiet laugh and she scowled. And to think she'd tried to be friendly last night.

She ignored Bastian as he hefted himself out of the chair with a grunt and washed his face. Then he put on his sword belt and opened the door, gesturing with a flourish for her to go first. She did, inching past him carefully despite the fact that she was once again wearing gloves and the only part of her that wasn't safely covered was her face. But it was always important to be careful … She shook herself free of dark thoughts and made her way down the stairs slowly, wincing as they creaked at the early hour.

She found Mal waiting for them in the deserted tap room, looking impatient.

Bastian immediately waved a hand in her direction. 'It's her fault. Took an age getting dressed.'

She scowled at him but didn't dignify what he'd said with a reply. Mal simply rolled his eyes and walked out. Bastian followed with a grin and she let them lead her outside. The morning sun made the snow on the mountains glisten. As the panic of being unconfined reared up,

Lily forced herself to think of it as if she were simply looking out of the casement. Tried to forget she was outdoors at all.

She walked down the busy street with the Brothers and their men. She was in the middle of their formation in her own little space, and she breathed a sigh of relief. Not only did being in the center of them mean no one could jostle her or, you know, accidentally die horribly, but it actually helped with the panic that was trying to claw its way to the surface. She wondered how long it would be before it all became too much. It would happen. It always did sooner or later. After every trip with Vineri, she'd had an attack within days of being back in the tower. Being safe didn't seem to matter. She'd have dreams about it, awful, vivid nightmares until she woke drenched in sweat and gasping for breath, her heart beating wildly in her chest as she lay in her bed, dizzy and disoriented.

She hoped it didn't happen in front of them. Gods only knew how they'd take that sort of weakness. Vineri had seen it just once and had made sport of her with his men forever after. He'd brought it up whenever he decided she needed putting in her place and had made sure she knew how pathetic she was.

She'd detested that man, yet the thought of him lying dead made her feel sad. She wasn't sure if it was because she'd cared about him or not. And if she had, she didn't understand if it was because he'd been her savior or it was simply that she'd had no one else in the world who'd cared about her – even though he probably hadn't.

Staring at the ground and lost in her musings, she was surprised when the Brothers in front of her stopped. She looked up and gasped at the sight. So many ships! There were small ones by the long docks that went out into the water and much larger ones anchored in the bay. She wondered which one they'd be taking, finding herself excited by the prospect of the adventure.

Would she have a cabin? She hoped so. Would there be a galley and would they let her look around if the crew were elsewhere? Brightening at the idea, she felt lighter as they began to move again and she found herself walking on the wooden slats of the docks themselves. She looked down and could see the dark water sloshing beneath her feet, making her feel a bit unsteady. Lily focused instead on the ships they were passing. No one marked their presence at all. She supposed the people here must be used to seeing all sorts of travelers, Brothers included.

They walked all the way to the end of the docks, where a largish ship was tied up and a gangplank was attached ready for boarding. She looked up at it in awe. It was an impressive ship. She'd seen drawings of them in books before and this one was definitely nice. The three masts were so tall she had to crane her neck to see the crow's nest at the top and the sails – well, they were all folded away until they reached the open sea, she guessed.

She watched as Quin hailed one of the men onboard and they were moving again, this time across the gangplank and onto the ship's main deck. She tried not to gape, sure they'd poke fun at her, but she couldn't help but swing her head this way and that, not wanting to miss anything.

'... girl. Lilith?'

She turned, finding Quin in front of her, telling her something.

'Sorry?' she asked.

He rolled his eyes at her. 'When you are in my presence, you will keep your attention on me, girl,' he barked and she frowned.

From the corner of her eye, she saw that they'd drawn the crew's attention. He'd done that on purpose, but she wasn't sure why. Vineri had sometimes shouted at her when they were with new people to ensure that everyone knew that he was the one in charge, that he pulled her strings, so to speak. Perhaps Quin was doing the same. But whereas with Vineri she always acquiesced, she decided that she wouldn't be doing that anymore. She was not a puppet, not a trained beast. So she looked him in the eye, her expression stony, not letting the anger she saw in his eyes deter her, though she knew she'd probably be punished for showing him up in front of the other men later.

'Take her below,' he ordered Mal, and she noticed how he ignored that some of the crew were smirking. He observed it, though, and inwardly she cringed. Yes, she'd be paying for that little show of defiance later. Men like him didn't like being questioned in front of other men, especially not by those they thought of as lesser.

She followed Mal into the ship and down a steep flight of steps. It was gloomy despite the lamps that were strategically placed so that nowhere was in complete darkness. She followed him down a narrow corridor and down another set of steps and then another ladder. They must be in the deepest bowels of the ship now. Surely not where the cabins would be, she thought as she descended lower and felt the floor under her foot. She turned and saw where he'd brought her and her heart sank before she could stop it. Iron bars, a dank smell, a large lock, a small wooden bench.

'The brig?' she squeaked.

He simply shrugged and opened the barred door of the cell. She stood dumbly as the metal hinges screeched, feeling very disappointed. Looked like she'd be enjoying the voyage from a cage.

She forced her face into a neutral mask and couldn't help but wonder if this was her punishment for not toeing the line on deck with Quin just now or if Mal would have brought her down here regardless. She supposed she should count herself lucky that she was the only occupant.

She stepped inside, not looking at Mal as the door creaked shut and she heard him lock it with a finality that made her spirits sink.

He stood there watching her for a while, perhaps willing her to turn around to face him, but she didn't. She simply stared at the wall with her back to him until she heard him leave, the hatch above booming closed behind him.

She sank down onto the wooden bench, which also creaked beneath her relatively insignificant weight compared to the sailors who probably found themselves down here from time to time, but it held.

Lily let out a sigh. How long would it be until they got to Kitore? Would they keep her down here the entire journey in the gloom without a porthole? Gods, there wasn't even a bucket to piss in. Resting her head against the solid planks of the wall, she closed her eyes and settled in to wait. If she had learned anything from her time in that tower, it was how to be bored for long stretches of time. She wouldn't go mad down here, but if Quin thought that this was treating her well, she'd disabuse him of that notion the next time she saw the bastard. The deal was that she would kill for them and that would treat her well in return. Putting her in a cage in the dark was not *well*.

Sometime later, when the lamps were burning low and threatening to wink out and leave her completely in the pitch black, she heard the hatch open. She didn't move as two shady figures slid down the ladder one after the other so adeptly that she knew at once they must be crewmen. They stayed in the shadows, whispering to each other, and she was glad that they were out there and she was under lock and key in here.

Finally, they drew nearer, and she tensed as she heard the

word 'witch'. They stood in front of the door and both of them simply stared.

'Are you sure?' the taller one asked. 'She doesn't look the way the stories say.'

The shorter glanced at his friend. 'Well, she isn't going to wear a fucking sign, is she? And I'm sure. Heard them talking in the town. She's a killer.'

'Pretty, though,' Tall said. 'I dunno. I think witches are meant to be wrinkled old hags. What if ye're wrong?'

'I'm not,' Short insisted. 'And if I am, we throw her over the side, leave the cage open and they'll think she escaped.'

Tall sighed. 'Open the door,' he said, pulling a long, sharp-looking knife from his belt.

Lily's eyes widened as Short pulled a set of keys from his pocket. The same set of keys that Mal had used. 'Wait!' she said. 'I don't know what you've heard, but I'm not a witch. I'm merely one of the Brothers.'

'Then why are you locked up down here while your friends enjoy the hospitality of the upper decks?' the short one scoffed, trying another of the keys.

'A jest,' she tried, and they both chuckled.

'Don't listen to her,' Tall muttered to his friend. 'Witches are tricky.'

The lock opened and Lily jumped to her feet, looking this way and that for somewhere to go, but of course there was no escape except through the cage door. Should she take her gloves off, she wondered? Was she prepared to kill them? She should be. They clearly meant to kill her.

'Why are you doing this?' she asked.

Tall slunk into the cage and she put her hands behind her, slowly pulling off a glove.

'It's our duty, as good citizens, to kill any witches that we come across.'

'But, as I say, I'm not a witch,' she said, letting her glove fall to the bench before slowly working off the other one.

Neither of them replied as Tall came closer, brandishing his knife.

'The Brothers will know I was killed if you do it here,' she cried desperately. 'I'm valuable to them and they'll gut every last man on this fucking ship if you don't turn around and leave!'

Tall paused and looked back at the ringleader. 'We could take her to the aft hold. No one will be anywhere near there until we get to Kitore, and by the time they find what's left of her, we'll already have our reward money.'

'Reward money? Kitore?' Lily felt sick.

'Aye, we'll get gold for your pretty head in the capital, witch.'

'Come on.' Tall pointed with his knife and she slipped past him out of the cell.

Short turned on his heel and she was prodded in the back, so she followed him as he opened a door to another room filled with produce and supplies. She walked slowly. Would she know when her moment was? Which one should she kill first? They were both armed, but Tall had his blade out, so maybe him? She wished that she'd been taught some sort of defense, but she'd never needed to know. Vineri would simply have his men take hold of his unlucky enemy and tell her to touch him or her. It had always been as simple as that. He'd rarely drawn it out and certainly never put her in the position to be in any actual danger from her target.

They walked through another door and she knew that her time was running out. They'd take her to a dark recess, run her through, and then cut off her head to prove they'd killed a witch. How they expected *that* to verify to whoever was going to give them their reward that she wasn't simply some hapless wench they'd slain, she didn't know. Perhaps there was some sort of test for witchery.

They passed through another room and into a much darker one, and Lily sent a silent prayer to the gods as she pretended to stumble, whirled around and grabbed for Tall's hand, which held the sword, except she missed entirely and caught his covered arm.

He jumped back and swore as she mumbled an apology and turned back towards Short. She wasn't cut out for all this, she thought. She was a clumsy idiot and she was going to die. She picked up her pace, getting closer to Short, but Tall was on his guard now and she felt the knife digging into the middle of her back.

Short slowed. 'Here,' he said as he turned to face her, keeping well away. 'On your knees, witch.'

Lily shook as she knelt on the ground in front of the two sailors. One of them made a crack about how he loved to see a woman on her knees and they gave each other a look that made her glance between them in confusion. One shrugged.

'I'm willing to chance it if you are, but you go first.' Tall laughed.

Short grinned and, to Lily's horror, he began to unlace his breeches.

'Open your mouth, witch. If you pleasure us well, we might even let you live.' He guffawed.

Lily shook her head. 'Please,' she pleaded. 'I don't know what you want of me, but if I touch you anywhere at all, you'll die.'

He ignored her, probably assuming she was telling stories to get out of whatever he wanted her to do as he drew his hardening staff from his trousers, stroking it with a dirty hand and watching her as he did so. His tongue flicked out to moisten his lower lip and he stepped forward, putting his cock in her face.

She shuffled back with a cry, her head hitting the bulkhead with a low thud.

'Looks like she'd rather die than suck your cock,' his friend commented behind him with another laugh.

Short didn't laugh; in fact, he looked very angry as he loomed over her and she shrank back. It was too much, all of this was too much, she thought, knowing she should do something. She should just touch him. Gods, she could touch his cock and he'd go down like a felled tree. Yet she was frozen, her hands gripping her own thighs as he came closer and closer.

She shrank back further, staring at him. Inside, her mind screamed at her to reach out and touch him, but she didn't, just stared at him.

She saw a movement beside them in the shadows, but they were so intent on her that they didn't notice the man in black that was moving slowly towards them like some Dark Realm creature from the old stories. Tall let out a small cry, falling to his knees and then onto his side with nothing more than a gurgle. Short spun around to find nothing and no one. He whirled back to her.

'You killed him, you fucking killed him. I knew you were a—'

She heard a crack and he fell to the ground on top of his friend in a macabre little pile. Behind him stood Mal, an excitement in his eyes that she'd seen once or twice before, like when he'd tormented her at the inn. This man liked to hurt and kill; nay, he loved it.

He gazed down at her and she met his eyes defiantly as she tried to still her quivering lip.

'Should have killed them,' he rasped in a voice that sounded gravelly and unused.

'I know,' she said softly. 'I …' She trailed off, not sure how to explain it to him in a way that didn't make her sound like a fool. Perhaps she simply was a fool, she thought. 'I wanted to, but I ... I just couldn't.'

She looked up at him, expecting to see censure in his eyes, judgment. But they showed nothing at all. He dropped something in front of her. Her gloves. Gratefully, she snatched them up and dragged them on quickly.

'Thank you.'

He motioned for her to get up and she stood slowly, holding onto the wall.

'Hurt?' he asked, and she wondered why he cared. It wasn't as if she was mortally wounded, and they'd made it quite clear that they didn't care much for her comfort.

'No, they hadn't got to the killing part yet. They wanted ...' Her brow furrowed. Until today she hadn't known people did that. If there was a word for it, she had no idea what it was called. She must have seen that sort of thing before she wound up with Vineri, but so many of the specifics of that time were vague.

Mal's eyebrow raised and she thought he looked a bit angry for a moment, but then it was gone and she looked back down at the bodies.

'Are you going to just leave them here?'

He shook his head and waved her back the way the sailors had brought her, his attention now on the dead men. He didn't look at her again. She might as well not exist, she thought as she made her way back through the cargo holds to the brig. She opened the cell door and went back inside, sinking down onto the bench with a sigh and putting her head in her hands.

A tap on the bars had her head snapping up, fearing more sailors. But it was Mal. He surveyed the cell and then opened the door, gesturing with his head for her to come out. So she did.

He beckoned her as he turned and climbed up the ladder

to the next level, and she followed. Where was he taking her now, she questioned wearily? Perhaps he'd realized he shouldn't have gone to the trouble of saving her and he was going to rectify his mistake by flinging her over the side of the boat. If the gentle rocking was anything to go by, they'd left the port while she'd been in the brig, so they'd be in the deeps now.

He led her down a corridor to a closed door that he knocked on three times before opening. She followed him into a spacious cabin that housed a large table and chairs as well as two sets of narrow beds. The other Brothers sat around the table enjoying an afternoon meal, it looked like. How lovely for them while she'd been cooling her heels in a cell and being assaulted by the crew.

'I told you to keep her stowed below,' Quin said to Mal, sitting back and looking at her. Whatever he saw as his eyes reached her face made his eyes narrow. 'What happened?' he asked her.

She matched his expression. *Stowed below.* As if she was a piece of cargo. To him she guessed she was. Instead of answering, she sat at the table with Bastian and Quin. She'd have taken some of the food for herself, but actually, now that she thought about it, her interlude with the sailors and their subsequent deaths had made her lose her appetite.

She stared at Quin for a few moments. 'Two sailors took me from the brig to kill me,' she said matter-of-factly, and Quin's countenance darkened.

'Why?'

'They said something about a reward for my head in Kitore.'

'Did you kill them?' he asked, his voice low.

'No, I— they ... Mal did.'

Quin and Mal shared a look and suddenly Lily was no longer in the mood to sit at this table and speak to anyone.

She stood up abruptly and went to one of the bunks, lay down facing away from them, and closed her eyes. She didn't want to sleep either, but it was better than having all their eyes on her. Perhaps she should request to go back to the brig, but that idea held even less appeal. It wasn't safe. What if there were others who would do what Tall and Short had? She shivered and wrapped her arms around herself, hoping that they'd let her stay, because, stupidly, she felt much safer here with them.

~

Lily's back was to them. Quin watched as she curled up in the bunk and he frowned.

'Did you leave them where they fell?'

Mal gave him a single nod and he stood.

'Watch her,' he said to Bastian, not sparing him a look as he followed Mal out of their cabin and down to the brig. When he saw the large iron cage, he felt uncomfortable that he'd had her put down here alone. He tried to push the feeling away, but it was there, ruminating in the back of his mind.

Something he'd seen in her face was bothering him. A lingering fear that she shouldn't have, not with the power she possessed.

He followed Mal to the hold and through several rooms before he stopped and looked down. Two men lay in a heap on the floor. He hefted the first one up and turned him over, his brow furrowing when he saw the cock protruding from the crewman's breeches.

'Why is his …?' He looked at his Brother, wondering at first if Mal had decided to desecrate the bodies somehow. Quin had watched him do worse over the years, that was certain. But Mal simply gave him a meaningful look and bent down to turn the other one over. Quin's lip curled as he imagined what they'd tried to do to her, but surely she wasn't afraid of that. Perhaps she'd never seen a cock before. He'd heard that innocent maids were sometimes terrified the first time they saw one, but even so ...

'Why didn't she simply kill them?' he wondered aloud.

Mal didn't answer him, of course, just helped him drag the bodies over behind some boxes so they wouldn't be found. Sailors were a close-knit bunch and Quin didn't fancy having to watch his back every moment they were on the ship in case someone tried to put a knife in it. He'd send a message to the captain after they disembarked to let him know where his men were. Until then, Quin hoped he just assumed they'd missed the boat.

He went back to the cabin, Mal melting away into the shadows as he always did in a new place. His Brother liked to get the lie of the land before he settled in. He'd turn up later for food. Much like a feline, Quin mused as he opened the door and stepped inside their cabin.

The girl was still in the bed, but she was turned towards Bastian and her eyes were open.

'Are you going to tell us the rest?' he questioned.

'The rest?' She feigned confusion.

'Of what happened with the sailors.'

'It's as I said. They took me from the cell, made me go with them to a darker spot. So they could hide my body better, they said. I suppose there's a lot of blood when you cut off someone's head,' she muttered.

'Then what happened?' Quin pressed, not sure why he cared but finding that he absolutely did.

She wouldn't meet his eyes. 'They had me get on my knees and ...'

Quin made an impatient sound.

'... one of them said something I didn't really understand

and then he unlaced his breeches and …' She trailed off, not looking at either of them.

'Gods, woman, why didn't you just put your hand out and touch them?' he exploded and she flinched.

'I— I tried, but I missed and then when I was on m-my knees,' she stuttered, 'I wanted to, but I just couldn't. I was … afraid.' She said the last word in a whisper.

He let out a long sigh. 'Next time, grasp the fucker's cock and kill him.'

She gave a small jerk of her head. 'Don't worry, I won't die before I can kill for you,' she muttered, and he almost told her the truth, that he'd been concerned for her safety.

But he didn't. Instead he forced out a biting laugh and watched her turn away. She drew her knees up into a ball again while he sat at the table and poured himself a large goblet of wine, keeping up with Bastian for once and feeling like a bastard.

～

SOMETHING WAS GOING on between Quin and Lily, Bastian was sure of it, but gods only knew what. He didn't really understand a lot of the social nuances these days, or perhaps he'd just forgotten. He interacted with the other gods on the Mount quite differently, after all. He'd hadn't known *new* people for a very long time.

He was angered by the girl's tale of what the men had done to her. She was clearly terrified, though, like Quin, he didn't understand why she hadn't simply killed them. She had tremendous power. Why not use it?

'Why do you think she didn't kill them?' he whispered to Quin.

Quin took a very long drink before he answered just as quietly. 'She froze.'

'But why?'

'You heard what she said. They made her get on her knees and one of them got his cock out. Surely you can guess what they told her to do.'

'Yes, but why didn't she just …?'

'She was scared, Brother. She's not used to being outside that room Vineri had her locked in. She's not used to men.' Quin made a derisive sound in the back of his throat. 'Probably never even seen a cock before.'

Bastian nodded. He'd noticed the look she got on her face when she was outside, the panic she tried to hide. In some ways they were similar, he suspected. Both of them were learning about this world and about the people in it. But she hadn't seemed to mind when she'd seen him undressed last night at the inn. Granted, she'd tried not to look, but he didn't think she'd been afraid.

Then he realized what Quin had called him. It was the first time he'd called Bastian 'Brother'. He almost smiled at the absurd sense of belonging. It had certainly been a while since he'd felt that.

He opened his mouth, wanting to speak with Quin for once, have a conversation that wasn't simply talking about plans and receiving orders. They didn't really know each other. He'd thought him a strait-laced cunt at first, but he was thinking now that though he was undeniably strait-laced, perhaps the Commander of the Dark Brothers wasn't so much of a cunt as he'd first suspected.

As he looked over at Quin's demeanor, however, he saw that of a man who only wanted to drink himself into numbness. That he understood, so instead of talking, he stood, poured himself another goblet of wine for the road, and left the cabin. He decided to wander and found himself in the brig before he'd realized where he was going. It smelled musty and dank, and he eyed the cell behind the iron bars with distaste. This was where Quin had ordered she stay for their entire six-day voyage.

Bastian had been alive for a very long time. He'd seen things, dark things that would make a grown man scream himself hoarse. Perhaps it was because all of those things had happened so long ago, but none of those memories left as nasty a taste in his mouth as the idea of Lily in that cell alone when those two crewmen had come for her. She was powerful, but she was still a mortal girl with more feelings than she'd let on to him, he suspected.

He left the brig and traveled through the hold until he found the spot where the men had threatened her and Mal had killed them. Mal. He really *was* a cunt. But at least he'd saved Lily.

Feeling oddly ill at ease standing in the dark confines of the ship, he climbed quickly up the ladders to the main deck, one hand still clutching his goblet, of course. When he reached the outside air, he allowed himself a small sigh of relief.

The sun was setting, casting pink and purple hues over the clear skies. He gazed out over the coast. They were already past the highest of the mountains, all covered in deep snow that made them impassable for at least another sennight. This was the quick part of the journey. Once they reached the curve of the coast, the ship would be battered by the edges of the winter storms that raged perpetually in the far north. That was the longest and most dangerous part of the journey, taking about four days before they rounded the northern cliffs and came into the more sheltered channel that led to the north coast and, subsequently, the capital, Kitore.

He wondered what Kitore would be like now. Last time he'd been there, it hadn't been much more than a village, and the 'king' had been merely a warring chieftain who'd won a few battles. A hard fellow, if Bastian remembered correctly. The current king did not take after his family line in that respect, according to the stories he'd heard.

Leaning on the rail, he finished the last of his wine and was just contemplating finding the galley for a refill when a disturbance off the port bow caught his eye. The water whirled and frothed into a maelstrom. Dark waves churned, slapping against the hull of the ship, and Bastian's eyes widened. Gods, they couldn't be that unlucky, surely!

He turned, yelling up to the crow's nest and pointing to what he saw, as the sailor on watch hadn't rung the bell. He needed to ring the fucking bell because if this was what it looked like, the sea was going to get much rougher before it got better. The man yelled something and the chiming began in earnest as the waves began to climb higher, tilting the boat so quickly that Bastian was knocked off balance and slid head-first across the deck and into the starboard side railing. He grabbed it before he could be thrown over, but he heard yells quickly followed by splashes and knew that some of the crew hadn't been so lucky. The boat pitched back the other way and Bastian used the momentum to run for the door in the middle, practically hurling himself down the steep steps.

He was stuck at the bottom as he waited for the ship to roll back, the corridor in front of him one moment a mountain and the next, a slippery slope down. He slid, catching hold of whatever he could until he reached their cabin, pushing the door open with one arm as he braced his legs on either side of the threshold to keep his body from falling back the way he'd come as the boat bobbed back like a child's toy.

Inside, Quin was holding onto one of the beds, which were, thankfully, bolted down, and Lily was struggling to keep herself wrapped around another on the other side.

'What the fuck is happening?' Quin yelled as the ship

creaked and moaned. 'A storm couldn't have come upon us this quickly!'

'It's not a storm!' Bastian let out an *oomph* and almost lost his precarious foothold as the door flew back and slammed into him. 'It's a breach on the seabed!'

'Fuck!' Quin said as the boat tipped again like a pendulum, throwing Lily into the wall next to the bed she was gripping on to, her head hitting with a thump that made him wince.

But it was lessening, Bastian thought. Yes, it was definitely slowing. He kept his grip on the doorframe, hearing bangs and crashes as the cargo thudded around in the hold.

'Keep holding on,' he called into the room. 'The waves aren't crashing against us anymore. The portal is closed. It will stop soon.'

A few moments later, they saw he spoke the truth as the ship began to even out. It was still pitching as if in choppy seas, but no longer with the violence of the past few minutes.

'Are you all right?' Quin asked Lily as she sat up and rubbed the back of her head. She nodded.

'What was that?' she asked shakily.

'A breach,' Quin muttered.

At her blank stare, he rolled his eyes. 'You've heard of portals, yes?'

The girl frowned at him. 'Yes, of course I've "heard of portals",' she said scathingly, not flinching at the menacing look Quin gave her. Bastian's brows rose. It was true he didn't know his Brother well, but if the girl wasn't careful, Bastian was quite sure Quin would be stinging her backside with the lash. From his expression, it was practically a certainty – when, not if.

Bastian swallowed hard as an image of her stripped and her wrists tied with long rope to a high tree bough entered his mind. He hadn't done *that* with a woman in a while, he thought, his cock stirring to life as he imagined her trapped there, stretched taut and at his mercy.

He tried to bring himself back into the moment. Quin was still staring at her with that impatient look on his face.

Finally he spoke through clenched teeth, but she didn't seem to notice Quin was angry, close to losing his temper, it looked like, for whatever reason. 'Well, the bridges don't only appear on land.'

Her mouth opened and closed again. 'Oh,' she said. 'You mean a portal opened *under the sea*?'

'Aye.'

'I— I've never heard of that before,' she murmured as she sat on the bed, her hand over her chest as if that alone would calm her racing heart.

'Shocking,' he said under his breath, and she stiffened but didn't say anything more.

Bastian sauntered in, intending to get himself some more wine now that the little adventure was over, but before he could even close the door, they heard yells from the deck.

'Gods, now what?' Quin snarled and pushed past him into the corridor. 'Stay with the girl,' he ordered Bastian.

Bastian snorted. It wasn't as if she was going anywhere. But he sat at the table and poured himself a drink anyway, avoiding her gaze in case she was going to mention his drinking habits again. But she said nothing, just walked over to the porthole and peered out into the darkening sky.

'Do you know anything about the portals?' she asked quietly from behind him, and he peered over his shoulder.

'As much as the next person,' he half lied. He wasn't an authority on them, but he did know more than mortals did.

'I heard once that Dark Realm creatures can come through into our realm,' she said.

He chuckled at the notion. 'Impossible,' he told her. 'There are wards in place to prevent such things.

'I heard—'

Whatever Lily was about to say was drowned out by the bang of the cabin door being thrown open, Quin's form obscuring the threshold. He was breathing heavily. 'Grab what you can,' he ordered. 'We're leaving.'

'What?' Lily said, her eyes like saucers. 'To go where? We're on a boat!'

'So help me, woman, do not test me now,' he snarled so vehemently that this time she did recoil. 'Mal is making sure they don't leave without us.'

Bastian moved quickly, gathering up their packs while Lily fumbled to put on her cloak.

'Move!' Quin yelled at her when she hesitated.

'I need my gloves!' she spat at him angrily.

'By the gods! Leave them and come!'

Bastian was already halfway up the steps to the deck when he heard another sharp rebuke and a whimper from the girl. He turned back to see her cowering before Quin, his gloved hand around her throat.

'Thought you were in a hurry,' he called over his shoulder, pretending he didn't care that she was receiving any kind of punishment, though he wanted nothing more than to turn back and push Quin away from her.

He heard Quin swear and then they were both behind him, the girl first and then his Brother.

When Bastian got outside, he scanned the ship in the low light and turned back to Quin in query. Nothing seemed amiss.

'What's the prob—?'

Look out!' someone yelled as a great thick tentacle smashed down only a few paces from them, tearing through the planks as if they were parchment.

'Fuck!' Bastian jumped back, following Quin and Lily as

they ran for the last boat hanging beside the ship, waiting to fulfill its purpose as they heard the ship groan and crack.

Mal stood inside it already, his knife brandished. It wasn't until Bastian got closer that he saw five crewmen sitting in it, all looking murderously at Mal. They would have taken the last boat if Mal hadn't stopped them, Bastian could see.

He chucked in the bags he carried and they clambered over the side. As soon as they were in, Mal drew his knife and cut the rope that held the small boat. Next to him, Lily screamed as they fell, landing hard in the water with a jolt that sent her backwards.

For a moment, he saw her terrified face and then she was gone, the dark sea swallowing her up in an instant.

'Lily!' he yelled and rushed to the side to throw himself in. He could see her just there, if only he could reach ... he felt her hand and grabbed it, hauling her up and out of the water. Coughing and spluttering, she landed in the bottom of the boat with a soft moan and he breathed a sigh of relief as the men began to row them towards the shore.

He looked back at the ship, seeing the last of the mast sinking beneath the waves. Then he looked down at Lily. She was shaking with cold, staring at him – no, not at him, at his bare hand. She looked stricken as she peered down at her own, the one he'd grabbed when he'd pulled her from beneath the surface of the freezing water. She wasn't wearing her gloves.

He held her gaze for a moment before giving her a little shake of his head when she opened her mouth to say – what? That he was going to die? He rubbed his cold fingers together. Shouldn't he be bleeding from his eyes by now? He felt fine, but perhaps his mortal life would be over before it had really begun.

He frowned as he imagined Gaila's face when he appeared back on the Mount a mere few weeks after he'd come back here. She was practically unbearable to live with as it was, thinking herself better than the rest of them simply because she was their elder. She'd be impossible if he died now without finding out any of the information she'd asked for.

He looked back at where bits of the ship now floated, and his jaw set. One thing was for certain. If the wards were still in place, that great sea beast would not have been able to enter this realm. Something was seriously wrong, though he'd had his doubts when Gaila had told him about her suspicions. There had been stories for a long while now near to the most-used portals. Those used for trade had the most traffic and the most gossip; tales of dangerous creatures being found in realms where they hadn't existed before. Bastian hadn't given them much credence. Dark Realms were Dark Realms. They were dangerous places. Who cared if the creatures mixed? But was Gaila right about the problem being in this realm as well? If so, what did that mean?

They reached the shore and Quin jumped out with the others to pull the boat in. Lily was still huddled in the bottom, her face drawn as she snuck peeks at him every once in a while – to see if he was dying yet, he supposed.

What was left of the crew went to join their shipmates who'd already made it to shore and were setting up camp down the beach to await rescue. Bastian picked up their bags and made to follow, but Quin stopped him. 'We keep to ourselves. On land, without their captain, they're little better than pirates.'

Quin looked meaningfully at the boat, where Lily still cowered, and Bastian nodded. If they decided to try anything like their friends on the ship, at best she'd kill them all; at worst, they'd run her through when men started to die.

'Time to get out of the boat,' he called softly.

She didn't move, nor did she give any indication that she'd heard him. He walked back to the craft.

'Come,' he said, and she raised her head.

She was shaking, her gaze focused on something behind him. He looked over his shoulder, but all he could see was the sky. Looking back at her, he stepped closer.

'Lily?'

She huddled further into the bottom of the boat.

'What is it? Are you hurt?'

'No,' she said so quietly he almost didn't hear her. Her hand was on the wood of one of the benches, clasping at it. She was saying something under her breath as well, the same inaudible phrase over and over.

He leant even closer and strained to listen. It sounded like 'only a little journey' and 'just for a little while'. She began to tap at the wood of the bench in sequences of five, and he simply watched her in fascination, trying to fathom what could be wrong with the little mortal.

Her breath, which had been coming in short, quick bursts, began to ease. Not taking her eyes from him, she uncurled slowly and stepped gingerly onto the sand, but she didn't approach him until he beckoned.

'Are you all right?' he asked her again.

She didn't look up from the beach. 'It's just so ... *big* out here.'

All at once, he understood. She'd lived in such a small place for such a long time. The sky, the vastness of the outside was something she would have to get used to again.

'Will being under the trees help?'

She nodded.

'Come on, then. Let's get into the forest.'

Another nod.

Quin had already trudged up into the treeline where the beach ended. Mal had disappeared altogether.

'Ladies first,' Bastian murmured, and she began to walk unsteadily in front of him, her arms wrapped around herself.

'Where is your cloak?' he asked, only just noticing it was gone.

'Lost it in the water,' she said quietly. Then she turned on him, still looking at the sand. 'I'm so sorry,' she said brokenly, the anguish she clearly felt at odds with their relationship – or lack thereof. Why did she even care if he died? It wasn't as if he'd even been particularly kind to her. 'I couldn't find my gloves before we left.'

'It's no matter,' he said quietly, not sure what platitudes to offer that she'd believe. Don't worry, if I die here, I'll probably just be reborn on the Mount? She'd probably think his brain was turning to mush on the road to Deathstown.

'No matter?' she asked incredulously, finally looking up at him. 'Just because you didn't die outright like the others means nothing. It could still happen. It will.'

'Has everyone you've touched died thus?'

'Yes,' she whispered, turning away and beginning to follow Quin's footsteps into the dark trees, once more looking at the ground. 'Every single one within two nights without fail since I was a small child.'

Intrigued, he ran to catch her up. 'What about before then?'

'Before then I don't remember,' she said after a long hesitation that made Bastian think she was lying, either to herself or to him.

They walked only a few moments before they came upon a small clearing under the evergreens next to what he could just make out in the low light was a small stream.

He could see the two figures of Mal and Quin in the center, starting a fire and setting up a small shelter.

'Sit close by,' he told Lily and took the pack she carried from her, putting it carefully on the ground.

She nodded dully and simply sat down where she stood, teeth chattering.

'Do you have some clothes in your pack?' he asked her, knowing how cold she must be.

She shook her head. 'I don't have a pack,' she murmured.

'Maeve gave me spares,' Quin said, throwing his pack over to Bastian.

'Good,' he said. 'The girl's going to catch her death if she stays in these soggy ones for much longer.'

Rooting through the bag, he found a small bundle and handed it to her. 'Put these on,' he ordered, dropping it into her waiting hands and watching intently as she got to her feet and walked into the trees. He followed and she stopped.

'What are you doing?'

'You're not going alone,' he stated. 'You've no idea what could be lurking around us. I'd urge you to just do it quickly here in the clearing.'

'No,' she said stiffly.

He shrugged. 'Go, then, but I'm coming with you. I won't be able to see anything, don't worry. It's too dark,' he added when she didn't move.

Finally, she heaved a sigh and went to the side of the clearing, ducking behind a tree. He went with her, stopping a few steps away and keeping his eye on her as her shadow peeled off the sodden clothes. Gods, he'd give just about anything to see her in the light right about now. Shaking his head, he gave her a few more moments and then she came towards him.

'Better?' he inquired.

'Yes,' she said in a small voice, 'thank you.'

'How long did you say I had? Two days?'

'At most,' she replied, her shoulders slumping.

'It wasn't your fault.' He grasped her shoulders and she gasped, trying to pull away.

'Don't,' she pleaded.

'I'm not going to touch,' he promised with a sigh, 'but truly, I don't blame you. If I die, I don't want you taking on guilt for it.' He gave her shoulder a pat. 'Because I can see that you will. It weighs heavily on you, your gift.'

'Curse,' she corrected.

He grinned in the dark. 'Perhaps.'

He urged her ahead of him, ignoring her gasp as his hand moved to the small of her back. 'Did no one ever touch you while you were with Vineri,' he asked, 'not even when they were sure that both you and they were covered?'

'Never,' she said and he gaped, glad no one could see his ungodly expression. How many years had she gone without a hug, an embrace, any touch at all save when she was killing? Ten? Twelve? Even a god would probably go mad. It was a wonder she hadn't hurled herself from the window of her tower, he thought, a surge of compassion flowing through him. He blinked. When had he last felt sympathy for anyone, god or mortal? He didn't know, but it had been a very, very long time.

They emerged from the trees to a small fire and two rabbits roasting. Where the fuck had those come from so quickly?

As if reading his thoughts, Mal appeared next to them, making him jump and curse his Brother to the darkest realms imaginable. Mal ignored him, of course, though his eyes lingered on the woman, Bastian noticed, while pretending not to.

If Lily observed Mal's prolonged gaze, she didn't let on, however, sitting down close to the fire and murmuring her thanks to Quin for the clothes.

He sat close by, the heat welcome in the cold winter air. 'How far have we come?' he asked Quin, knowing the man had made this journey several times in the past.

'We're past the mountains. It's not ideal, but there may be a half day's trek tomorrow before we make the forest. After that, two or three more days on foot to the nearest sizable town.'

Bastian nodded absently, rooting around in his pack for a wineskin. Not finding one, he made a sound of disgust and, when he saw Lily watching from the corner of her eye, pulled out his bedroll instead and pretended that was what he'd been looking for all along.

'Is no one going to say anything about what happened?' she asked.

'What do you want us to say?' Quin asked her, his eyes fixing on hers.

She held his unwavering gaze 'Well, Bastian told us there had been a portal breach beneath the sea and then the ship got attacked by that— that *creature*. It was Dark Realm. It came across the bridge.' She turned to Bastian. 'You told me that was impossible. You said there are wards to stop that from happening.'

'It should be impossible,' he ground out, not wanting to talk to any of them about this.

To his surprise, Quin interjected. 'It *was* impossible. There *were* wards. But everyone who's ready to see the truth knows that they are failing and have been since the first gate collapse – what, six, seven winters ago?'

Across the fire, Mal nodded.

'But why?' Lily asked. 'What's making them fail?'

Quin shrugged. 'The king has scholars devoted to the task of finding out. But the truth is, the portals have existed since before records began. No one knows where they came from, only that someone or something is destroying them and they need someone to blame.'

Lily looked confused. 'Someone to blame?'

Bastian cocked a brow. 'Why do you think everyone keeps going on about witches? Killing anyone accused?'

Quin looked grim and he gave Lily a pointed look. 'Now that we're in the north, we're too far from the Army for it to be any use to us. You don't speak about what you can do with anyone. Do you understand, girl? If anyone suspects anything, they'll have your head cleaved from your shoulders before you can scream or you'll be thrown in the king's dungeon to await death.'

~

Lily shivered. 'I understand,' she muttered, staring at the ground. 'I touched Bastian,' she blurted, and he turned to look at her with a growl that made her cringe.

'What?' If Quin's cutting tone could wound, it would have.

'It was an accident,' she whispered, hating the way the Brothers looked at her; with a mix of disbelief and, in Quin's case, unbridled fury.

'You stupid little harpy,' he snarled, and she wrapped her arms around herself in misery.

'It was my fault,' Bastian said calmly, and she shot him a look.

It was as if he didn't even care that he was going to die. Perhaps he still didn't believe that he would. She'd briefly met those sorts of people in her travels with Vineri, the ones who didn't believe *they* were going to die – until they fell on the ground, incredulity etched on their lifeless faces.

'It was my fault,' Bastian said again. 'It was when I pulled her from the sea.' He showed his hand, wiggling his fingers, a sort of *rueful* expression on his ridiculously handsome face that would soon be gray and dead.

Lily's face contorted in sadness. He should have let her

drown. Why had he bothered to save her? So she could kill some more people? She stared at the fire in agony, knowing Quin's eyes were still trained on her.

'Why aren't you dead, then?'

'Before … it would take a day or two so …' She trailed off and drew her knees up to her chest.

'So you'll be dead in less than two days?'

Bastian shrugged. 'Perhaps. Perhaps not. Maybe because our hands were wet it didn't work. Maybe I'll keel over in the snow tomorrow. Who can say but the fates?'

'Fuck! Should have brought the soldiers,' Quin said half to himself.

'Why didn't you?' Lily asked.

He waved a hand. 'Because I'm the Commander of the Dark Army. Less people traveling with me means my movements are not as remarked upon,' he answered absently.

Lily said nothing more. In truth she was still reeling from the panic she'd felt on the boat after Bastian had dragged her out of the water. There was no boat, no inn, nowhere to close herself into. It was a nightmare come to life. She was trapped in the open. She'd been able to hide it on the boat, waiting until everyone had disembarked before her heart had begun to hammer and she'd begun to sweat as she'd huddled in the bottom. She'd concentrated on the small things; the feel of the boat, the wet of the clothes on her back, the sound of her tapping her fingers on the wooden bench.

She'd been surprised that Bastian had been so kind, especially after what she had done. She buried her head in her hands. Another was going to die and she couldn't do anything to stop it.

CHAPTER 7

MAL

They all ate the rabbits Mal had caught in silence, and he was glad they'd stopped their incessant chatter. He realized he was staring at Lily again and stood up with a scowl, taking his bedroll from his pack and remembering he had hers as well. Why Quin hadn't given the girl her own bag to carry, he didn't know. It was probably so she wouldn't have any provisions should she try to escape them.

She was lucky he'd been on deck when the creature had attacked or she'd be floating face-down in the waves about now. They all would be. The sailors had run for the boats to escape the sinking ship like rats, and it was only because Mal had threatened the last of them that they hadn't cut the ropes and been long gone by the time Lily, Quin, and Bastian were able to get topside. As it was, one of them had rushed him. He'd had to slit the prick's stomach open and throw him over the side. After that, the ones left had been more reasonable.

He unrolled Lily's bed and put it close to the fire. Then he put his on the outside of hers so that she wouldn't be able to rise and sneak off without him knowing about it.

She looked surprised that she even had a bed, murmuring

her thanks to him and even offering him a tentative smile that had him turning his back on her, pretending to ignore her.

He bedded down and closed his eyes, hearing the rest of them doing the same. As always, he would take first watch and Quin would relieve him later. Bastian was meant to be after that, but when it was his turn, Mal would be awake. He didn't trust the man. They still had no idea where he'd even come from. They had men who appeared sometimes, fancying themselves good enough fighters to be Brothers. They almost always died during the combat trials. But Bastian had done very well. Too well, in Mal's opinion. There was something more to the man than wine, jokes, and women, and Mal didn't mean the *gifts* that some of the Brothers had. There was something about Bastian. He had secrets, and a Brother shouldn't have secrets from his unit. It made them weak.

Quin should have refused the bond with Bastian in the first place. It might be rare for a Commander to go against the wishes of the gods, but it wasn't unheard of. Mal had read the runes himself and knew Greygor had ignored their outcomes countless times. He'd gotten Brothers killed because of it, including their own unit's third before Bastian had joined them, in his pursuit of power, it was true. But he wished Quin would simply ignore what those fucking stones said, if only this once. Even if the gods on the Mount were real, their wrath would be better than this fractured unit they now had. Quin wouldn't keep his command of the Army long if they didn't mend it. Unless, of course, Bastian succumbed to Lily's death touch. Mal hoped the bastard did. Perhaps then they'd get a better third; stronger, more in command of himself.

Mal breathed out slowly. But if he did survive, Mal would likely have to swallow his pride and try to abide the fellow, he supposed, even if he had shown himself to be mostly incompetent. They had no wine with them now. It would be water from the mountain streams for at least two days. Mal wondered if Bastian would crack without his vices. He grinned nastily. That would be something to watch.

He lay for an age, listening to the breathing of Lily and the others and the sounds around them, but no one ventured near. The sailors would likely stay on the beach and try to signal a passing ship rather than make the journey inland. They knew the sea best, not the land's terrain, after all. But Mal doubted another ship would come this way for at least a week. It was faster to go on foot.

At some point, he heard Quin stir and let himself drift into sleep.

The morning brought a fair day and Mal woke to the sound of hard biscuits being unwrapped for breakfast and was surprised that, firstly, it was Bastian who was up and about and, secondly, that he hadn't woken when it was that idiot's turn to keep watch. Mal didn't like that they'd been vulnerable, that Bastian has been their one and only line of defense for the latter part of the night – especially as he could theoretically die at any moment. But he caught the biscuit that was thrown at him and ate it, kicking Lily awake gently and finding that he liked the little moan she made when he did.

'Not dead yet?' Quin inquired and Bastian snorted.

'Sorry to disappoint you, Brother.'

Mal noted that Lily looked relieved that he hadn't succumbed. Why should she care if Bastian, or indeed any of them, died? They were her jailers, and if Quin had his way, she'd be dead after she did the job they'd brought her north to do. But, then, she didn't know that. Perhaps she thought Quin would let her go when it was done.

They smothered the fire, packed up and left, Mal taking a piss behind a tree as the others went on ahead.

As they left the coast, the winter became more pronounced. They weren't quite out of the mountains yet and would have to ascend at least one or two large hills before the land began to flatten off.

He kept an eye out for any threats as he knew Quin would also be, but there was nothing and no one out here. Not that he was surprised. No one would venture this way until the thaw when spring arrived in a few weeks. The mountain paths would be impassable before then.

They trekked until the sun was high. Then, without warning, Lily stumbled in the snow and fell to her knees. Quin called a stop, offering her some water, and they rested. Mal scanned the vicinity, ensuring there was nothing waiting to pounce. He glanced back from where they'd come and could just see the sea on the horizon. They were making good time despite the woman needing rest. If they didn't tarry, they'd make the mountain inn at the very edge of the ranges before nightfall.

The girl got to her feet and they carried on. The rest of the afternoon was spent descending, and it looked like the thaw had already begun when the snow began to fizzle out, making way for the first greens of the new season as well as the sounds of waterfalls and rising streams now that the winter's ice had begun to melt.

Lily stumbled again, falling hard to the ground with a low cry, and before Mal knew it, he was helping her to her feet – gloved, of course – and she *didn't* pull away from him. He glared at her. Just because he'd stopped those sailors, it didn't mean anything. He'd have to make her remember he was not her friend.

He let out a menacing snarl and let his fingers bite into her arm until she let out a noise of discomfort. He let her go abruptly so she stumbled again and he gestured at her to keep going. Quin gave him a questioning look but said nothing. Bastian, however, stepped in front of him in challenge.

'Leave her be. She tires.'

Mal stepped closer and pushed Bastian hard in the chest, looking him up and down with a belittling snort of disdain that would not be misconstrued as anything other than what it was – not even to that idiot. Bastian's face contorted in anger and he let out a growl as he attacked, not going for Mal's face as he'd assumed he would but straight for his side with two quick punches that would more or less guarantee that he'd be pissing blood for the next few days. Mal backhanded him hard across his annoying face with a smile creasing his own, bruising Bastian's cheek as well as insulting him by hitting him as he would a female.

Bastian let out a bellow of fury but was hauled away by Quin.

'Enough!' the Commander barked. 'We need to make the first inn by nightfall unless you two fools want to spend another night out here freezing your bollocks off.'

Without waiting for answers or reactions to his words, he ushered Lily down the path with him. Mal gave her a smirk as she glanced back at them over her shoulder, trying to ignore the upset he saw in her eyes.

Bastian didn't give him the satisfaction of rubbing his cheek. Instead he gave Mal a narrow look that promised a reckoning before turning to follow the others down the hill. Once the bastard was gone, Mal let himself press the area that Bastian had hit. He had to hand it to him, his Brother was a formidable fighter from the little he'd seen. Bastian was easy to underestimate with his drinking and his fucking jests at all hours of the day. Mal needed to remember that, he thought as he tried to quash the sudden and very tiny spark of admiration that appeared, but he found that he couldn't quite extinguish it.

They arrived at a dilapidated inn just before sunset, all of them bone weary and in need of a hot meal. Thankfully the place was dead because who the fuck else would be traveling now? Once the large, aproned woman had discerned that they did indeed have coin, she hustled and bustled to get a hearty stew cooking over the great hearth in the tap room and, in her words, 'give the rooms a bit of an airing'. Mal assumed she meant that no one had stayed here since the passes had become obstructed after the first heavy snows.

The woman was probably living on the dregs of her income. He'd have to keep an eye on her lest she get greedy and decide no one would miss them if they disappeared. Easy to poison the stew and let them die in their beds later before hauling their bodies back up into the hills a ways. She wouldn't even have to cart them very far. When they were found in spring, it would be assumed that they'd succumbed to the elements in the mountains and their bodies had been dragged down the mountain by the flowing streams.

So he kept an eye on every ingredient she added to that pot as she chatted away to put them all at ease. He caught Quin doing the same, and finally she hurried off to sort out their accommodation for the night while they ate their supper in relative peace.

He watched Lily practically falling asleep in her stew and couldn't seem to tear his eyes away from her. What he wouldn't give to touch her, he thought and felt his traitorous cock begin to harden. When was the last time a woman had affected him so? Gods, when had a man? His eyes found Bastian of their own accord, roving over his broad shoulders for a moment, and he immediately looked away from the idiot. His Brother got one or two lucky strikes in and Mal was suddenly lost?

He let out a growl and ignored both Lily and Bastian as they looked up at him. Finishing his food, he got up quietly and made his way up to the second level where the woman had disappeared.

She gave him a great smile and a look that lingered just a bit too long as she told him the room on the right was ready and if he needed anything, anything at all, then to ring the bell just inside the door. He nodded once and slipped into the room, shutting himself inside before sinking into one the chairs by the crackling fire and rubbing his face with a calloused hand. What was wrong with him?

He sat there for a long time, mulling over the past few days. Quin and Bastian came in, falling quickly asleep in the two beds behind him. He was exhausted, but sleep eluded him. Quietly, he got up and slipped from their room. The inn was silent and the lamps extinguished. The only light came from the fire in the hearth, but he didn't even need that really. He'd mapped the place out as soon as they'd arrived here.

He got to Lily's room and eased the door open silently. She hadn't locked it. Stupid girl.

He stepped into the room, finding her predictably asleep on one of the beds and dead to the world. She'd removed her clothes and – he sniffed the air – washed with some of the lavender soap he'd noticed in their own room. He thought of her under the coverlet, divested of every shred of clothing. Unable to stop himself, he stepped stealthily closer.

Her eyes remained closed, the lids moving slightly as she dreamed. She was in a deep sleep, he thought as he loomed over her small form. He should leave, whispered the voice of a conscience he hadn't heard in a very long time, but he snuffed it out as he took hold of the blanket and eased it off her.

She didn't move an inch as he looked his fill. Her breasts

were the first things he saw, larger than he'd thought, her nipples beading in the chill that still lingered in the unused room despite the heat of the newly built fire. Her slightly rounded hips and stomach, a testament to the time she'd sat in the tower room, led to a thatch of blonde curls that were fairer than the ones on her head, he noted. Her voluptuous thighs led to long legs that would be wound around him if he had his way.

He canted his head as he stared at her legs. He'd noticed before that there were long, shining scars. He'd not given them much thought before, but now that he could look at his leisure, he could see that they'd been made methodically, with a blade; lines and lines like a delicate tattoo. His brow creased as he noticed four that looked newly scabbed over. They'd been cut deep enough to bleed and scar, but not so hard as to carve into the muscle. His fists clenched. Had Vineri done that? He hadn't noticed them when he'd seen her at the camp, but that meant nothing. He hadn't really been looking at her properly then.

Unable to help himself, he put out a finger and traced the air just above one, playing a dangerous game with himself, he knew, as he let his hand drift closer and closer. One touch and he would be dead before he could even taste her. The gods and their sense of humor. Giving himself a mental shake, he straightened. What the fuck did he care what Vineri had done to her?

Tomorrow or the next day they'd come across what was left of the place where he had started out in this life. A part of him wanted to see it, if only to prove to himself that that cursed place held no sway over him. Regardless, he doubted he'd be good company while they were in this part of the land – if he ever was, he thought self-deprecatingly.

He looked down at her, his gaze cold now. Her eyes fluttered.

When she opened her eyes, she was sure she was going to see someone there, but there was no one. She shivered in the cool air and rose, padding quietly across the room to put a piece of wood on the fire before hopping back under the covers.

She peered around the chamber. The hairs on the back of her neck were standing up. But she could see the whole room and there was clearly no one in here. She looked at the door. She hadn't locked it, assuming that the Brothers would simply knock the door off its hinges if they wanted to come in for any reason, and she didn't think the proprietress of the inn would have any need to come in. Those were the only people here, after all, but perhaps it would be better to bolt the door ... just in case.

She got out of bed again and eased the bolt across, the sound much louder than she would have expected, and she cringed, hoping she didn't wake anyone. They must be tired as well, she thought.

Her thoughts went to Bastian and she couldn't help the sadness that permeated her being, though she knew he'd never feel anything for her if their roles were reversed. If not tonight, then tomorrow he would die. She hung her head, leaning against the door as she let the guilt she'd been keeping at bay envelop her. She should never have taken those gloves off. She was a fool and her stupidity had cost another person their life.

She looked down at her flesh. It was a rarity to be so completely uncovered. Well, except since leaving her tower, of course. She'd seen more of her own body than she ever had before. One of Vineri's rules was that she usually remained as covered as possible so that there weren't any mishaps. She stared at her hands. So innocuous. Just like anyone else's that you'd pass on the street, yet she'd killed forty-five people. Forty-six tomorrow.

Heaving a great sigh, she wandered over to the table and poured herself a large goblet of wine that she gulped down in its entirely before getting back into bed, even though she could hardly abide the taste. Hopefully the wine would do its job quickly and help her sleep. She assumed there would be another long walk tomorrow and she wasn't looking forward to it. Her muscles weren't used to all the exercise.

She let out a small sound of horror. She was worrying about aches and pains when Bastian was going to die. What an awful person she was. She deserved whatever happened to her.

If she was caught and killed for being a witch, then so be it. It would be better that way. Then she wouldn't murder anyone else, accident or no. She felt the four long scabs on her thigh. She'd have to cut another tomorrow, she thought, closing her eyes as the wine did its work.

The next day, they left the inn early after a small breakfast, Bastian included. He looked as hearty and hale as ever, but Lily knew that the curse could strike without warning.

He came up to her and she kept walking, finding she couldn't look at him knowing that he would shortly be dead.

'Are you in pain?' He fell into step beside her. 'You're walking oddly,' he elaborated at her questioning glance.

'My legs ache from yesterday,' she muttered, though in truth her body burned or hurt in a multitude of places. She let out a breath. 'Is there anything that you'd like ... you know, after you ... after your body ...'

'You mean when I'm dead? Last rites and such?'

'Yes.' Her voice broke on the word and he grabbed her elbow, turning her so roughly to face him that she gasped, but when he spoke, he sounded puzzled, not angry.

'You really would care if I died, wouldn't you?'

'Of course.'

If anything, he looked even more confused by her reply. 'I had assumed you enjoyed it.'

Now it was her turn to feel bewildered. 'Enjoyed what?'

'The power you have.'

'Enjoyed it?' She practically shrieked in his face. She took a quick step back, wrenching her arm from his fingers. 'How could you think such a thing?' she asked in a whisper.

He opened his mouth to speak, but no words came out. He seemed completely unsure of what to say as she just stood in front of him and stared in anger and upset. How could anyone think she *wanted* this?

'Move,' Mal's gravelly voice said from behind her, and she turned away from Bastian, quickening her step to escape him and his horrible assumptions about her. Out of the corner of her eye she saw Quin's mouth hanging open, but he wasn't looking at her, so she ignored him and simply led the way down the path.

She looked into the distance. They were still quite high but descending rapidly now. She guessed they'd make the plains later today, and she'd heard talk of another inn, so she wouldn't have to spend the night out in the open. The forest that first night hadn't been too bad. The trees had blocked out much of the sky and she'd not been frightened, but as she gazed over all that open land, her heart began to hammer in her chest. It would be days of journeying out there in the immense terrain. Exposed.

She could make out one discerning feature in the distance, and that was a mound with a large walled fortress built on the top. She could vaguely make out birds flying around its towers, but that was all she could see at this distance, especially with the haze that made the horizon appear somewhat wavy.

They walked the rest of the way down the hill in silence,

and the trees gave way to smaller shrubs and then nothing but the remnants of the grasses that covered the plains in green but at this time of year were merely tufts of brown sticking out of the boggy earth like macabre little graves. The idea made her shiver. She knew that venturing off the path was dangerous in many parts of the plains near to the thaw. The ground got so wet that people easily became trapped in the mire and sank to their deaths, or so she'd read.

As if he knew her thoughts, Quin came up behind her and said in a low voice, 'Keep to the path no matter what.'

She looked over her shoulder at him and nodded gravely. Yet another place where dying was so much easier than living.

~

Mal walked behind the others, staring out at the lone hill that rose so high and stark against the flats. He'd thought it would appear smaller, less intimidating now that he was no longer a boy, but, if anything, the vice that tightened in his chest was worse now. There was nothing to be afraid of. He knew that. He'd made sure of that long ago. And yet here it was, still dominating the landscape as if it still had a right to be there. As if it ever had.

'It's an old temple, isn't it?' Bastian said from just in front of him to no one in particular, but Mal found himself nodding absently as he stared at it.

They walked along the wide path, the only way that was guaranteed to always be safe across this large area. The land stretched further than they could see in all directions save the one they'd just come from.

Though Mal saw Quin hardly look at the fortress, the others' gazes flitted to it frequently, and for some reason it made him furious. Furious that they were looking at it, furious that it was still there at all. Why had the bogs not swallowed the cursed thing up? He pushed at his side, the one Bastian had hurt yesterday, as he seethed. These people weren't his Brothers. Not like Quin was, not like Payn had been, curse the bastard. He'd thought he'd be rid of them soon, that she'd get herself killed in Kitore in a few days and that Bastian would die today, but the prick seemed fine. He wished he could help him along to his reward, but it was against the most important of the Army's laws. You didn't kill the members of your own unit. He doubted he'd even be able to raise a hand to the man if his intent was to mortally wound. The wards that were invoked during the binding ritual, ancient blood magick, would probably spring to life and stop him somehow. He spat in the dirt. Pity.

They arrived at yet another inn. Unlike the practically derelict one they'd stayed in at the edge of the mountains, this one was busier with a few merchant travelers who'd arrived early and were eagerly waiting for the passes to become accessible again so they could take the trade routes south.

More than a few turned and gaped when they were noticed traveling from the wrong direction.

'Are the passes thawed already?' one brave soul inquired, and Quin shook his head.

'No. We were shipwrecked off the coast and had to trek the final hills. Be a few weeks yet,' he replied as he went indoors to get them a room for the night amidst audible groans from the many peddlers who'd been hoping it was time to move on.

Next to him, Lily stifled a yawn, looking dead on her feet, and he rolled his eyes. How did this tiny, weak girl have so much power flowing through her veins? Bastian caught his eye and gave him a dark look that promised something that made Mal shiver inwardly. He gave Bastian a cold smile as he followed Quin, bashing his shoulder into Lily hard enough to send her sprawling in the mud as he passed her, ignoring them both.

Inside there were only a few people in the tap room, but enough that there was a hum of conversation that became discernibly quieter as the black of their clothing was noted.

Mal thought perhaps some fool would ask them their business. It was rare, but it did happen, and then they'd be forced to teach the hapless idiot or two a lesson. He found for once, though, that he was in no mood to mete out any abuse.

Then the door opened and closed behind him. He turned to find Lily, now covered in mud, scowling at his back, and his lips curled into a tight grin. Perhaps he was in the mood after all. The anticipation of punishing her and, in fact, Bastian simply for harassing him with their continued presence in the unit made him feel lighter somehow. He didn't know how he was going to make them suffer, but it would either be very petty or very dark indeed. His eyes narrowed. And it would very much depend on his mood in the moment.

There was only one room and they were lucky to get that. Quin had been half afraid they'd have to camp out in the stables, and though he knew that wouldn't bother Mal or Bastian, he could see that the journey was taking its toll on Lily. Not only could she clearly use a hot meal and a warm bed, but she must have slipped over in the stable yard, because she was covered in mud.

He frowned at her. It wouldn't do if she sickened and died before she could be of use. That was the only reason he was ensuring her wellbeing. He paid extra for their meals to be brought to the room he'd procured for the night. There were too many people in the tap room wanting to chat for his liking, and none of them seemed to be scared enough of Dark Brothers. All of them looked like they'd engage him in unwanted conversation if he sat down. Clearly it had been too long since the Army had been camped in the north. People had forgotten that it was best to give Brothers a wide berth.

He gestured for Lily to go upstairs and he followed behind her slowly, showing her to the room and giving it a once-over before she entered. She looked at him curiously but didn't say anything about his behavior – even if she did notice anything odd about it.

'Food will be up in a bit,' he told her as the other two traipsed into the room, throwing their bags down and each taking a chair at the table.

Quin supposed they were all tired. It had been a long few days since they'd left the Army. He knew he hadn't truly let his guard down even for a moment in that time, and his Brothers hadn't either. Not even Bastian, who, since they'd left, had shown himself to be much more useful than he'd anticipated.

And it wasn't just Bastian who was different. Mal had spoken. He'd heard him clear as day. Only one word, but, as far as Quin knew, his Brother had never spoken, not since joining the Army, at any rate. What had made him do so now? His gaze locked on the woman who traveled with them and his eyes narrowed.

Lily stood in the middle of the room, eyeing the men and seeming not to know what to do with herself. Mal was watching her with disdain as usual and Bastian with something else in his face that Quin didn't want to look too closely at. He had enough problems to deal with at present. The biggest being, was Bastian going to die tonight? It was the second day, after all. He felt a pang as he thought about losing another Brother. It happened, of course it did. It was the reality of their lives, but that didn't make losing family any easier. Payn had been the first Brother from his own unit that he'd ever lost. The thought of losing another so soon, or indeed ever again, left him feeling hollow and sick. It didn't matter that he hardly knew Bastian. A Brother was a Brother.

And he noticed the dark looks that Mal and Bastian were giving each other. There was something going on, something more than petty rivalry, that had something to do with their fight on the road, and he'd bet anything the woman was right in the middle of that too.

He knew, looking at Mal, that if Bastian didn't die today, Mal would find a way to do it. Not directly – the power of the wards wouldn't allow it – but Mal wouldn't think twice about engineering an accident. And, knowing him, he wouldn't feel a modicum of guilt afterwards. Likely he'd not even think about it again. That was how Mal was when someone got in his way. Quin knew it had been him that killed all those Rats in the camp before they left, though he couldn't fathom why. Perhaps he'd just felt the need to kill. Mal had joined the Brothers not because he'd wanted to be part of the Army, but because he was a wanted man.

Mal was a murderer and, in truth, had the Army not taken him, he'd have been hunted and put down like a beast. That he had excelled in his training and become a Brother wasn't surprising. He'd been a stone-cold killer before he'd joined. The Army had honed his skills, made him even more formidable, but also given him the purpose he'd needed not to descend into madness ... well, not *complete* madness, anyway. Though the way he was eying Bastian and Lily, Quin wasn't sure anymore. He needed to speak to him, but gods only knew what he'd say.

He rubbed his stubbly jaw. His unit was ripping itself apart at the seams and he hadn't even noticed until now. He was meant to be the leader. Gods, Greygor had been a massive cunt, but he'd made being Commander look easy all while keeping his unit strong – at least it had appeared that way from the outside. The reality hadn't been quite so clear-cut, or so he'd found out when he and the others had strung up the previous commander for his betrayal of the Dark Army and the other two men he called Brother hadn't raised a hand to stop them. But no one had known their bond was weak. If he, Mal, and Bastian were in the camp right now, everyone would be able to see the rifts between them.

What had happened with Greygor's unit still haunted him, if he was honest with himself. From the outside they'd been a steadfast group, but they'd all hated each other behind the veneer. Was that what his unit would be like, all at each other's throats for the rest of their lives? He shook his head slightly.

'By the gods, woman, would you just sit down?' he thundered and watched Lily tense. She didn't look at him, just sat down hard on a chair and stared at her lap.

There was a bang on their door and he answered it. A woman and two younger girls stood outside, each carrying a large copper kettle of hot water, which they deposited into the greenish copper bath in the corner. They left immediately, promising to bring more to fill it and that their supper would also be ready shortly.

He dug Lily's spare clothes from his pack and put them on the table.

'You can have the bath first,' he told her, and she blinked up at him as if unsure of whether he was being kind or if it was a trick of some sort.

He waved a hand at her, turning away as she stood and walked, a bit unsteadily, he thought, to the bath.

'There's no screen,' she said, not turning around.

'Check under the beds,' he said absently as he noticed Bastian and Mal watching her.

'Ah, here's one,' he heard her say, and he listened as she dragged it out and put it up, the cloth obscuring the bathing corner.

Soon he heard her clothes falling to the floor and pulled at the collar of his tunic, feeling very warm as he heard her get in. Her audible sigh as she lay back in the hot water made his shoulders abruptly relax when he hadn't even known they were tense.

The other two were looking around the room now, basically anywhere but at each other.

'You both need to get a handle on yourselves,' he hissed in a low voice, not knowing if he meant their in-fighting or their obsessions with Lily. Both were liable to get them killed.

Mal tossed Bastian a look, his eyes lingering on the screen, and Quin threw up his hands.

'You can't even touch her!' he snarled in a whisper. 'Why are you letting yourselves be led around by your cocks?' He looked at Mal. 'Gods, I heard you speak today. To *her*. Years we've been Brothers and I didn't even know you could.'

Mal looked furious and then surprised, even sympathetic for a moment, and Quin realized he'd let more slip than he'd meant to regarding how his Brother keeping secrets had made him feel, and inwardly, he cursed.

'Don't speak much,' Mal rasped.

Bastian rolled his eyes. 'That's a fucking understatement, you prick.'

'You'll be dead soon,' said Mal, swiping a thumb across his neck as he spoke.

'Is that a threat?' Bastian's smile didn't falter.

Mal didn't say anything, just gestured with his head towards the girl in the bath.

There was a knock at the door. Probably more water, Quin thought, getting up to answer and letting the women deposit the full kettles just inside the room.

Bastian smirked. 'I think we all know that if I was going to die, I would have already,' he said after the servants had left.

'Aye,' Quin agreed thoughtfully. 'And you're sure you touched her skin? There was nothing between you?'

'Nothing. I'm certain. Only water.'

Quin sat back in the chair. 'How?'

Bastian shrugged. 'Many of the Brothers have gifts. I've always been resilient when it comes to poisons and venoms. Got bit by an adder once. It didn't even swell. Perhaps I'm immune to her ... curse.'

'Perhaps, but the others were killed when she was fearful. Perhaps her curse is more potent when she's scared. I say you touch her again to be sure, but this time,' he looked Bastian in the eye, 'you make her afraid when you do it. If you don't die immediately like the Rat did, then we'll say you're immune.'

∼

BASTIAN ALMOST FLINCHED at Quin's command. He glanced at the wooden frame with the dark green cloth draped over it and then back at his Brothers. Mal now had a gleam in his eye that made Bastian want to hit the bastard. Quin just sat impassively and then gave one of his imperious waves that had Bastian gritting his teeth as he stood.

'I was a fucking *god*,' he wanted to scream, but he stayed silent as he grabbed one of the kettles of water, walked quietly over to the screen, and peered around it.

'Make sure you touch dry skin,' Quin whispered in his wake.

Lily lay in the water, facing away from him, her long hair not yet wet. He silently edged closer and saw that her eyes were closed. Was she asleep?

He took another step, and then he could see her. He swallowed hard. She was as beautiful in reality as she had been in his dreams since he met her. Long legs, nice-sized tits, an arse and thighs that he could see had some substance to them despite the water obscuring her.

'Get on with it,' he heard Quin whisper and he grimaced at the order. He didn't want her to be afraid of him. Now that he realized at least one or two of his godly powers hadn't dissipated completely, he wanted her to let him touch her; he wanted …

He let out a growl and her eyes snapped open, widening as she took in his hulking form standing over her. She started, flailing and trying to cover herself, the fear in her eyes palpable when his hand shot out and gripped the dry skin of her throat. She let out a ragged cry, throwing her body back into the hard copper of the bath. There was nowhere to go.

He released her as quickly as he could, after letting enough time pass so that there could be no error.

Her arm came up to cover her breasts as she drew her knees up to her chest. Her face showed everything and, shockingly, it cut him to the quick. He staggered back a step, the kettle thudding to the floor. She looked horrified, frightened, and perhaps worst of all, betrayed.

He turned and left her, donning his mask of indolence as he stepped out into the room.

'Well, I'm not dead,' he said lazily and forced a yawn, sitting back down next to Mal, who, oddly, looked like he felt, his eyes not straying from the curtain. He almost looked disturbed by what Bastian had done, but that couldn't be right. The man was devoid of emotion. Bastian had met enough of them in his long life to know that any feelings Mal showed merely demonstrated that he was a good mimic of his fellow mortals. His Brother lived to kill – deserving, undeserving, in the wrong place at the wrong time, it made no odds to him; he'd kill anyone, everyone. Bastian's eyes narrowed. He'd be the one to kill Lily when they were finished with her if Quin ordered it. He'd murder Bastian if he could … but he couldn't. An idea began to take shape in his head, a way that might keep her alive when all this was done.

'Just because I'm safe, doesn't mean you are,' he murmured.

Quin frowned. 'So?'

Bastian gave him a relaxed glance. 'Well, we saw how quickly things can go wrong in the heat of the moment. If I wasn't immune to her, I'd be dead by now. If it had been either of you …' He trailed off. 'It was only luck that it wasn't.'

'And what do you propose we do to mitigate the risk?'

'Bind her to us,' Bastian said simply.

A strangled sound came from Mal.

'Unusual to make a Fourth in such a circumstance,' Quin said, clearly gauging his reaction.

'No better circumstance than survival,' Bastian said with a frosty smile, as if he truly didn't care. But if Lily was bound, Mal wouldn't be able to hurt her easily and Quin might even be able to stop him entirely.

He heard Lily clamber out of the water. She stood unmoving, it sounded like, for ages before Bastian realized the problem.

'She doesn't have anything to dry herself with,' Bastian murmured, hoping she wouldn't hear him. He'd done enough. He didn't want to humiliate her as well.

Quin cursed, grabbed one of the large folded cloths from

the stand by the casement and, not looking, handed it to her from the other side of the divider.

A moment later she teetered across the room and sat heavily on one of the beds, staring at the floor, her arms wrapped tightly around herself. She was shaking, Bastian saw. His fault. He'd done his share of vile things in his life, but he'd never felt like such a cold-hearted bastard as he did at this moment.

Quin took a fresh cloth and disappeared behind the curtain next while Bastian and Mal glowered across the table at each other.

Bastian sneered at him and Mal stared darkly back, neither of them willing to be the first to look away.

'I didn't know you could talk,' Bastian said conversationally.

Mal shrugged.

'Why did you decide to start?'

Mal didn't say anything, but, for a split second, his eyes darted to Lily before coming back to Bastian. *He wants to speak to her. Interesting.*

Then Mal spoke quietly through his clenched teeth. 'Wanted to call you a cunt out loud,' he growled low.

Bastian guffawed loudly; he couldn't help it. 'Fuck you too.' He chuckled and laughed harder at the look of furious disbelief on Mad Mal's face. He was sure this was the first real emotion he'd seen from his silent Brother during all these weeks. Perhaps Mal wouldn't conspire to get around the wards and kill him after all. Stranger things had happened ... or *not* happened as the case may be.

There was a knock on the door and the woman from earlier entered bringing their dinner, one of her girls trailing behind her with the second tray. The older one glanced at Lily sitting on the bed and Bastian noticed a concerned look that she quickly wiped from her face when she looked at the men at the table.

She crossed the room in silence and put their suppers out on the table. The girl left quickly, but the elder stayed, approaching Lily, who, when she noticed, tensed.

'Can I have your clothes laundered for you? Perhaps bring you up a nightgown to wear?' she asked. Then, drifting closer, she murmured something too soft for Bastian to hear.

Lily nodded, then her gaze locked with theirs for a moment before she shook her head.

'Very well. If you're sure. I'll have it brought up. Or, if you'd like, you could sleep downstairs with my daughters in their room. Might be a bit more,' she gave a delicate cough, 'proper.'

'She stays here,' said Quin, his booming voice resonating through the room as he emerged from behind the curtain.

The woman stepped back with a small shriek and a hand on her chest, but Bastian noticed that Lily's eyes drifted over their commander's broad arms and chest and down lower to where the cloth was wrapped around his waist and his large tattoo disappeared. She looked away quickly, her cheeks coloring, but she was interested, that was certain.

'Oh, sir!' the woman gasped. 'Forgive me! I didn't know you were there.'

'The woman stays with us,' Quin said again, thrusting Lily's soiled clothes that she'd left on the floor before her bath into the woman's hands. She took them without comment, giving Lily a look that Bastian couldn't discern, before leaving quickly and shutting the door quietly behind her.

'What did she say to you?' Quin said coldly.

Lily stared up at him, looking defiant. 'Surely you heard our exchange. It's not as if we left the room to speak privately,' she said without fear.

'Tell us.' Quin stepped closer, letting out a sound that spoke of punishment if she didn't answer truthfully. 'Or do I call her back and tell her that you'll sleep in her daughters' bed with them after all? How far into the night do you think they'd last before you killed them?'

Bastian watched Lily's resolve crumple. 'You're such a bastard.' she whispered brokenly. 'Gods, she just asked me if I was all right, if you must know.'

'All right?'

'Yes, because I'm a lone woman here with three Dark Brothers. Obviously I look like I'm in some sort of distress.' She looked down at the floor again. 'Perhaps she's right,' she said very softly.

Quin made a sound of amusement. 'Distress? Trust me, Lily, I could show you what distress actually looks like.' He stopped right in front of her so she had to crane her neck and lean back to see his face. 'Would you like me to "distress" you?' he growled.

She held his gaze, her jaw trembling, hatred in her eyes. She wasn't going to concede, Bastian thought, and he'd give her the lash for her insubordination.

Bastian stood up. 'Enough of this,' he said sharply. 'The night grows late and our food, cold.'

Quin grunted but backed away from Lily. There was yet another knock at the door, which he answered, snatched something, and closed the door hard. He turned and threw something at Lily, which she caught. The nightgown the woman had promised. He watched as she immediately draped the thick winter nightie over her head and stood, the hem falling almost to the floor. She looked so prim and proper, not like a killer with the power of death running through her veins at all. His cock grew uncomfortable in his trousers and he shifted slightly. His eyes narrowed knowingly as Mal did the same. Gods, did they all want her?

Perhaps he shouldn't have suggested binding her to the unit after all.

Frowning, he watched her cross to the table and sit next to him, hunger winning out over fear. If they did bind her, both Mal and Quin would be able to touch her with no ill effects. Would she be safe with them after that? Bastian didn't hold with rape personally, but he knew many Brothers did or, at the very least, didn't care one way or the other, and there were no specific laws against it in the camp. He glanced surreptitiously at Mal. What if Mal hurt her in other ways once she was bound to them? A Brother could hurt another Brother. The wards didn't stop that. The idea he'd put into Quin's head would do her more harm than good. He was a fool.

∼

SHE CHOKED DOWN HER MEAL, trying not to let any of them know how rattled she was. Dinner was chicken and potatoes and brussels. It looked and smelled delicious, but in her mouth it might as well have been ash.

As soon as she was finished, she pushed her chair away from the table and practically ran for the furthest bed. She tried to sort through her turbulent emotions. The day's exertions had left her weary. Traveling with these awful men made her weary too. She rubbed her shoulder, where a dark bruise had formed. When Mal had pushed her down in the muddy yard, she'd hit it on a stone or something that had been beneath the mud.

She curled into a ball beneath the coverlet as she went through the rest of the evening. Why had Bastian attacked her like that? She shivered. She'd been so afraid, not just of what she could do to him, but actually of him. It was obvious now that, for some reason, he was immune to the darkness in her. She'd put that to one side for now, though. She just didn't know what to make of such a thing.

She moved on to Quin's threats. She had no doubt that callous man could and would – how had he put it? – *distress* her. Her mind was running rampant with all the ways he could do that without touching her. Between his threats and Bastian and Mal's attacks on her person, it was sinking in how dangerous these men really were. She'd known it before, of course, but the way a person knows a wolf is dangerous without ever meeting one. If they did, they knew they were in danger, but really it was no different than a big fluffy dog until it snapped its jaws.

She closed her eyes, trying to relax. She was exhausted. She needed to sleep. But the thoughts just kept running through her mind, over and over, giving her no respite.

'Are you awake?'

The sudden voice behind her made her jolt. Turning her head, she saw that Bastian was sitting on the bed and that the other two were already asleep in the other one. How long had she been lying here?

She didn't answer his now moot question.

Unthinkably, he kicked off his boots and lay next to her. With a gasp, she rolled away until her back was to the wall and she was as far away from him as she could get.

'What are you doing?' she hissed.

He turned towards her and wriggled about, clearly getting more comfortable, and she frowned. 'There's a chair over there by the fire.'

He looked over to where she pointed. 'So there is. Would you like one of the blankets?'

She opened and closed her mouth several times. Wasn't it bad enough that they were being … how they were being? Did they have to torture her with sleep deprivation as well?

Feeling like crying, she began to edge down to the foot of the bed. 'No.'

He gave her a look and reached out a hand that made her throw herself back from instinct. 'Don't be ridiculous,' he said. 'The bed is more than big enough for us both and it's obvious that you can't kill me.' He grinned. 'At least not with your usual methods.'

Her eyes narrowed at him. 'Perhaps that's a problem. Did you ever think of that?'

He gave a low chuckle. 'Don't tell me you think yourself so alluring that you believe I can't control my baser urges.'

Her cheeks heated. That was what she had feared – well, not that she was alluring. She wasn't sure she knew how to be *that*, but she was afraid that he would attack her again. She had no way of fighting back if her touch didn't kill him, after all.

'Why did you—?' She broke off and began to scramble, freezing when she felt his hand take hers in a gentle hold.

She looked down at it, almost unable to comprehend that someone's touch was *lingering*. She could feel his skin on hers, the warmth of it not fleeting or terrifying. He said something, but she didn't hear what, too wrapped up in the feeling of it.

She stroked his hand with her thumb and tears welled in her eyes. She couldn't hold them back. She would have if she could. She already felt more vulnerable than she had since she was a child. She didn't want to cry in front of him too.

She looked up at him and saw that his head was cocked to one side, a peculiar look on his face as if he was shocked yet mesmerized by her state of awe.

'Do you know how often I wished for this?' she asked brokenly. 'To be able to touch someone – anyone at all – to feel the warmth of their skin and not hurt them?' She looked back down at his hand and hers, their fingers now inexplicably intertwined. It looked ... right. It was so surreal. 'Why did it have to be someone like you?' she whispered.

That realization broke her out of the moment and she snatched her hand away with a small cry.

He laid his hand in his lap, looking like she'd just slapped him, and she wondered why she cared after what he'd done earlier.

'Just lie down in the bed, Lily,' he coaxed. 'You're tired and you'll not get a moment's rest on that flea-bitten monstrosity.' He gestured to the old, faded chair that looked like it had seen many a traveler's backside over the years.

'You won't touch me?' she questioned, even knowing he could just lie, but she hoped he had at least a shred of honor.

'Not unless you want me to.' He winked.

She drew back, hesitated, and then lay back under the coverlet to face him, pointless though that was. What would she do if he did make a lunge for her? What if he did let his 'baser urges' take over and ravish her? Would the others stop him or would they simply – she swallowed hard, but not in fear – *watch*?

Shivering, she drew the covers up to her neck and saw him grin as if he knew what she was thinking. It didn't matter that they were all three of them beautiful, she reminded herself. They were Dark Brothers. All they knew was how to take whatever pleasures they could from life while robbing everyone else of theirs. The Army was a scourge; she'd heard that often enough from Vineri and his friends – a very powerful scourge whom everyone was in bed with. Though at the moment that was a literal thing in her case. The absurdity of everything that had happened to her since she'd been taken from the tower was enough to make anyone question their sanity.

'Go to sleep,' Bastian murmured from the edge of the bed, not making any move to come closer to her.

Unwilling and unable to keep up the fight, she let her eyes close.

When she woke it was still dark and she found she desperately needed to piss. Slowly, not making any noise, she made her way to the bottom of the bed and out of it, careful not to wake Bastian, who still slept on the edge and outside the covers like a gentleman sentinel, the idea of which almost made her laugh aloud.

Getting a handle on herself, she went behind the curtain, where she'd noticed a chamber pot close to the bath earlier. She bent down, feeling around for it in the dark, when she felt someone behind her, standing just a hair's breadth away. She felt fingers skim over her arse and straightened with a gasp as she whirled around to where the shadow stood. But before she could even take breath enough to scream, she found herself pushed hard against the wall just to the side of the curtain, her mouth covered with a gloved hand and a cold blade biting into her throat.

From here she couldn't be seen by whichever men were still in the beds, and the light from the embers of the fire gave out enough light for her to see that the shadow ... was Mal. Her heart skipped a beat and her stomach felt like it was rising into her chest. What did he want? His eyes bore into hers. Expressionless pits. And then he seemed to decide something.

He kicked her legs wider and she made a sound of distress. *Distress.* This was what Quin had promised. Had he told Mal to do this to her or was this just how Mal amused himself at her expense? Her eyes found his again, pleading silently for him to let her go. She breathed a sigh of relief as the knife left her neck only to gasp anew as she felt him hiking the long nightgown all the way up to her waist. She began to struggle, but he effortlessly held her with that one hand over her lips, the rest of his forearm pushing hard on her chest to keep her on the wall.

He tucked the swathes of cloth he'd pulled up into the fingers holding her face, the knife glinting menacingly near her eyes, where his other hand held it. She felt something cold between her legs and jerked, trying to close them, but he stood between them, keeping her at his mercy as he pushed at the hole she'd explored herself once or twice before. She was terrified, but there was something more as well, something that made her clench in excitement that she wished she could deny. She shouldn't want this. Had she been denied so much human contact that she would accept it from the likes of this man, from his Brothers? *Yes.* The answer came unbidden and made her despair even as she ached for what Mal was forcing upon her.

A muffled sound exploded from behind his hand and his hard eyes snapped to hers again. The emotion she now saw in them made her even more terrified than the void had before. Lust. Even as she thought it, the thick hilt of his dagger popped into her *easily* and she whimpered as he pushed it, more gently than she would have thought a man who was fucking a woman with a weapon of steel capable. She didn't know what he was trying to do, but it wasn't hurt her, she realized, confusion marring her features for a moment before he eased it out and filled her again slowly and her eyes closed as she moaned behind his hand.

This time, after he pulled it from her, he took it out entirely and she felt her hips straining for it without her permission. Seeing his very surprised expression that she had enjoyed something that was clearly meant to be some sort of punishment, she looked at the knife he held in mortification. It was practically dripping with the evidence of her arousal. Her eyes widened as he *licked* it, letting out a small hum of appreciation. And then she was leaning against the wall alone, Mal having disappeared as instantly as he came. She sank to the floor, breathing hard but trying to be as quiet as possible. What had just happened? What had he done? What had she done?

The place between her legs tingled as she relived his actions for a moment and she shivered in pleasure simply from the memory of Mal taking her with a *knife*. What was wrong with her? How could she have liked what he'd done? How could she hope that he did it again? Somehow getting her legs beneath her once more, she stood, found the chamber pot, and finally did what she'd come here to do.ABs, even the sensation of weeing made her want to finish what Mal had started.

She made her way back to the bed, half afraid and half hoping Mal was lying in wait for her in the main part of the room, but then she saw his form lying in the bed next to Quin and she sighed, not really sure if it was relief or longing that she felt. She climbed into the bed carefully and got beneath the covers. Only then did she pull up the nightgown herself and let her fingers drift to the thatch of curls at the apex of her thighs. She slipped them into her folds, aching for release. She spread her knees and did the things that she knew would relieve the throbbing of her sex, if only for a short time; she touched herself in the ways she'd only ever done in the dead of night, high in her tower when no one else could see or hear her. Except now she did it in the same room as three deadly mercenaries who she almost wished would hear her muffled breaths, wake, and finish what Mal had begun, even though she knew it was impossible and that the reality would definitely not be the girlish notions that danced in her head.

The force of her release stunned her and she bit down on her knuckles as her body shuddered beneath her fingers. Sated, she withdrew them and hesitated only a moment before she did what she'd never done before. She tasted herself.

The next morning brought with it an itch much different than she'd felt in the night, though just as unwelcome. As soon as she became aware, her skin began to burn and tickle almost unbearably. She sat up and scratched her arms, but the sensation only worsened. Her face and neck, her hands. At first she wondered if there were perhaps fleas in the nightgown she'd been given, but the skin that had been covered by it was fine. The bed, then. She wrinkled her nose in distaste and looked around the room, intending to ask Bastian if he was the same, but she was alone.

She got out of bed and went behind the screen, taking off the nightgown and washing in the now-cold bath while trying not to remember what Mal had done with her in this very spot in the night ... and her reaction to the dangerous killer. She shivered and told herself it was just the freezing water she was sluicing her arms and face with. When she was finished, she dried herself off, but the itching hadn't abated. In fact, it was worse. She tried not to scratch, but it was impossible; her skin felt like there were insects crawling all over it. Noticing her freshly laundered clothes folded neatly on the table, she donned them hurriedly. The Brothers' belongings were gone, and she entertained the idea for a moment that they'd left without her and she was free to go where she willed now, but she found that instead of happiness, dread coursed through her. Would they abandon her up here in the north with no money, no gloves, and very little idea of the outside world? If she was no longer any use to them, of course they would.

Her breath quickened as she left the room, imagining navigating herself to Kitore, and for what? So someone could brush by her on a busy street, die horribly, and she be labeled a witch and killed? Now that she'd seen some of the outside,

Lily was even more aware that she was woefully ill prepared for life here. She doubted she'd last a day without the Brothers' protection, though their price was steep.

She practically ran down the stairs and through the door into the tap room, belatedly realizing that it was heaving with people, shoulder to shoulder on benches around tables; more than she'd ever seen so packed-in together. She gasped and leapt backwards, feeling the wall behind her as she edged along it, away from the groups, who, thankfully hadn't seemed to notice her or her odd behavior.

She slid down the wall in the corner, trying to formulate a plan that was more than simply to wait here. Her escape route back to the other room was now cut off by more people, and she saw that one or two had seen her and were casting questing glances in her general direction.

And then the most terrible thing that she could imagine happening in her worst nightmares happened. One of the daughters of the proprietress approached her. Lily froze. She couldn't move, couldn't force any intelligible words from her lips. The girl was asking her if she was all right, but all Lily could do was try to nod – unconvincingly, it seemed, because the girl, who couldn't be much more than fourteen winters, stepped closer and her bare hand rose towards hers.

Lily could only watch in mute horror as it slowly got closer and closer, and though it seemed like she had so much time, she couldn't … she shrank away, praying to the useless fucking gods that this girl would just back away and go off to find her mother instead of trying to help a monster.

CHAPTER 8

MAL

Mal ate slowly, not to savor, but because he couldn't countenance going back into that room where *she* was, not even to see the aftermath of his revenge. The revenge that was meant to start and stop last night with the powdered velvet bean he'd bought off one of the many peddlers waiting for the mountain passes to open. He hadn't meant to do any of the rest of it, but when he'd seen her get up, he'd seen his chance to put the powder in her sheets, even throwing some on Bastian's sleeping form for good measure, though the bastard seemed fine this morning; no itching and no chafed skin at all.

He briefly thought about finding that no-good charlatan of a merchant and carving him a new gullet, but after a brief look around, he realized they all looked the fucking same to him and he had no idea who he'd bought it from. Even he couldn't kill an entire room of people in broad daylight and get away with it. Well, he could so long as he made sure he got every single one of them, but he doubted Quin would approve.

Oddly, his usual thirst for death seemed muted. In fact, he

hadn't murdered anyone since ... the ship ... That had to be several days ago now. He stared at his plate, deep in thought. He hadn't gone more than one or two nights without killing in a very long time.

'Go and see if she's up,' Quin drawled in his general direction and he gritted his teeth as he stood, shoving the last piece of bread from his plate into his mouth and making his way to the door. It took all of his discipline to be calm and not simply throw men out of his way, but by the time he got to the door, his patience was wearing thin. People were fucking idiots.

He was just about to slip out of the room when he heard a snippet of conversation that made him stop dead. *A girl ... corner ... looks distraught ...* He craned his neck and saw her. She was huddled by the wall, trying to make herself small like she did whenever she was afraid. One of those fucking children was in front of her, trying to help. Little fool. Didn't she know that helping anyone was liable to get you killed in this world?

He strode towards them, and just as the girl was about to meet her doom, he pulled her away, more gently than he would have if Lily hadn't been in front of him looking horrified.

He got between them and the girl drew back when she saw his blacks and his face. She paled, and whatever she'd opened her mouth to say died before it left her lips.

'She is unwell,' he forced himself to grind out, wondering why, in less than a day, he'd found himself speaking aloud to people when he hadn't felt the need to in so long.

The girl nodded and turned away, but the determination he saw in her face made him sigh. She was going to her mam, and that woman was a force of nature. She already thought Lily was with them against her will, which wasn't exactly an untruth, but she clearly thought they were hurting her as well. He canted his head. Not an untruth either, actually. If they didn't need her, if she wasn't a walking plague, he might consider trying to convince Quin to leave her in these women's capable hands.

He turned to Lily, who was still looking upset, her hands trembling, though she tried to hide them. She was staring at him oddly, and he realized it was because there was no fear in her face when she looked at him now. Strange. First, only his Brothers weren't afraid of him. Second, he would have thought that after last night, she'd be even more afeared.

She got a hold of herself and stood up, holding the wall for support.

He made a path through the people to the door and led her out into the quiet hallway.

He snarled at her as soon as the door to the tap room was closed and was annoyed when she didn't even cringe in the face of his anger. After what he'd done with that knife, any sane woman would flee. But not this one.

The memory of her back against the wall in the dark, his hand over her mouth to stop her from alerting the others and from escaping as he pulled up that horrible nightdress and fucked her with his knife, his ears filled with her muffled moans ... His cock hardened in an instant and he swallowed a groan. Why did he want a woman he couldn't have? He was going mad with it. It was why he hadn't simply gone back to bed after doing his dark deed with the itching powder. He'd had to touch her, even if it was with gloves on. And he hadn't been disappointed. Gods, she'd been so wet from his rough handling. He'd never known a woman enjoy ... Her reply to his anger pulled him from his reverie.

'When I woke and you all weren't there, and all your things were gone ... I thought you might have ... left me here.'

'Coming to tell the women that you're captive?' he asked, his anger rising.

'No.' She looked up at him, shaking her head. 'I was afraid that you had decided to abandon me.'

He frowned, not quite understanding. '*Want* to stay with us?'

To his surprise, she gave him a small smile, much like the one he'd had from her when he'd killed those men on the ship. 'It's not a question of want,' she said pragmatically. 'The fact is that I think I want to live, and if you all aren't with me, the chances of that are very slim.'

He snorted. That was the truth.

The door opened and, thankfully, it was Bastian and Quin who exited.

When Quin saw them he nodded. 'You're ready. Good.' He handed Lily half a bacon sandwich and Mal was stunned when he realized Quin had saved it from his own meal for her. Since when was Quin so concerned over anyone's wellbeing?

'Let's go,' Quin ordered, leading them out into the muddy yard where only last evening Mal had pushed Lily down in the filth with a laugh. He didn't like that he'd done that now he thought on it. He cast a quick glance and frowned as he saw her scratching her neck, noticing how red and inflamed her skin looked – what little he could see of it.

Steeling himself, he turned away. He wasn't Quin. He cared little for the wench's comfort, he told himself as they mounted the horses he'd procured for them from various merchants. They had further to go today and they'd never make it to the next inn on foot. And it was definitely nothing to do with the fact that the girl was looking more and more tired every day that they were on this cursed journey.

'Only three?' Bastian asked.

Mal shrugged. Three horses were all he could get. No one would part with even one more.

'Guess you're riding with me,' he gloated to Lily, and Mal noticed a moment of trepidation in her eyes before the bastard – who *could* touch her – plucked her off the muddy ground and settled her in front of him.

Mal's jaw clenched.

The day passed slowly, for Mal at any rate. Between Bastian murmuring softly to Lily while she sat between his legs and the fortress of his past looming ever closer, by the time they stopped to rest the horses, Mal's mood was dark and he was no longer feeling any guilt whenever he saw Lily scratching at her raw flesh, though she was trying not to.

He jumped off his horse with a barely suppressed snarl and left the path, foraying into the thick undergrowth that grew in clusters all over the flats. He didn't look back, just kept going until he could no longer see the road. He stood in a small clearing with a few boulders here and there, breathing hard as he tried to make sense of the turmoil within. He gripped his knife, the one that had been inside Lily, and clenched the blade with his other hand until his blood began to drip to the ground. He embraced the pain of it, what little there was, hoping it would stave off the worst of his impulses until he could do something more.

'Quin sent me for you,' said a voice from behind him. *Bastian.* His lip curled as he turned and was pleased when Bastian's face morphed into an expression of shock – only to realize a moment later that Bastian was staring at his bloody hand.

And then Bastian looked disappointed, as if Mal had somehow let him down.

Fury took hold of him and he leapt at Bastian, taking his Brother by surprise. He couldn't kill the prick, but he could do some damage. He hit him hard across his smug fucking face with the back of his hand, making Bastian's head snap back, but before he could dance away, Bastian's fist connected with his cheek in retaliation, the force sending Mal backwards over one of the boulders. He used his own momentum to roll and push himself away, but before he could get up, he felt Bastian at his back. He thrust his head back with a growl, trying to catch Bastian in the face, but the quick bastard dodged, laughing low in his ear in a way that, Mal was surprised to find, made his blood heat.

Mal struggled, trying to twist out of Bastian's grasp, but he found himself bent forwards over the large stone and his arms locked behind his back. He kicked back, aiming for Bastian's knees but only able to catch his shin. Bastian swore in pain, pulled him off the rock, and flung him back into it hard. Mal hit his head on the stone as he was propelled forward and groaned as a wave of dizziness made him sway.

He recovered quickly, however, and let out a snarl as he struggled anew, but Bastian kicked his legs apart and pushed his body between them, taking away his leverage. Mal was effectively trapped between him and the boulder.

He cursed himself for underestimating Bastian. He'd seen him fight, knew how fast he was. If Bastian had a gift other than the obvious one, then it was speed as Mal's was stealth.

Bastian stood frozen behind him for a few moments. Mal didn't bother with entreaties to let him up. He'd never beg, not ever. Then his brow furrowed as he felt a hardness at his back that could only be one thing, but, for some reason, he wasn't surprised or shocked as he felt Bastian reach around him and deftly unbuckle his sword belt. It fell to the ground with a clatter and Bastian palmed him through his breeches, a small growl reverberating in his chest when he felt Mal's quickly hardening cock. He couldn't really be ...

Mal bucked in one last-ditch effort to throw Bastian off, but it was no use. He was outweighed and had been deftly outmaneuvered. His head ached where it had hit the stone. He'd lost the fight, he thought, relaxing slightly against the rock in defeat. He wondered what Bastian was going to do, how painful it would be. Gods knew he deserved whatever punishment he was going to get, but it irked him that fucking Bastian had bested him. He let out a huff.

Bastian kept him immobile and bent over the boulder. The larger man didn't say a word as he unbuttoned Mal's breeches and, with one hand, eased them down to his thighs. Mal's breath hitched. He knew what came next.

A cold breeze blew through the air, rustling the leaves and branches around them and making Mal shiver as Bastian fumbled with his own clothes. And then Bastian spat into his hand and his hard staff slipped between Mal's cheeks, prodding at his entrance, slipping in just enough to burn and stretch.

Mal swallowed back a moan, resting his forehead on the cold stone as Bastian eased himself in slowly. Mal's cock pulsed at the intrusion, and he admitted to himself that he was surprised that Bastian wasn't rutting him hard or trying to cause him undue pain. He had thought about this, just not knowingly. He had, on some level, yearned for Bastian, even if he was a fucking prick.

And then Bastian began to move slowly, easily, letting Mal become accustomed to the intrusion, for which he was grateful. It had been a while since he'd indulged with anyone, whether man or woman, and Bastian was not small. His hot breath tickled Mal's neck and he liked it. There was something intimate about it that he hadn't experienced before.

Behind him, Bastian moaned and finally let go of Mal's arms and took hold of his hips. Mal braced himself on the rock, holding himself steady for Bastian's increasingly powerful thrusts, making his legs go weak, his cock ready to burst. As

Bastian's hot, thick staff filled him, he had no thoughts of fighting, didn't want to get away, didn't want Bastian to stop. His body felt as if it was overheating even in the cold breeze, and he irrelevantly wondered if Bastian was feeling the same.

He heard another moan and realized it had been him, and he clenched his jaw, grunting with the force of Bastian plunging into him, faster and faster, erratic and unbridled. Mal's release was hard and brutal, making him throw his head back in an ecstasy he'd never felt before with anyone.

Bastian took hold of his hair and pulled him up with a snarl, pulling his head to the side and kissing his neck, biting him hard enough to bruise, to mark him. And then he shuddered and buried his face in Mal's shoulder as he came, some of his seed falling to the earth as he pulled out, leaving Mal feeling equal parts bereft and strangely content, the impulses of only moments ago now having dissolved into the background once more.

Mal stood still, breathing hard, trying to get his head around what had just happened. He and Bastian hated each other, didn't they? He pulled up his trousers and retrieved his sword belt from the ground. Then he turned. He expected Bastian to have gone, but, shockingly, he was still there. To Mal's embarrassment, he felt his cheeks heat as if he were some callow youth. He couldn't discern from Bastian's uncharacteristically guarded expression what the man was thinking; whether or not he regretted what had just transpired.

Finally, he met Mal's eyes and spoke. 'Well— I—' He broke off and looked away again.

'Unexpected,' Mal said, putting the other man out of his misery.

Bastian's playful countenance returned in an instant and he winked at Mal. 'You'll find I enjoy being unexpected,

Brother, and count yourself lucky that I was, or that could have gone a bit differently.'

Mal snorted and walked past him, back to the road, finding Lily and Quin waiting for them impatiently.

'Where the fuck is Bastian?' Quin barked and Mal shrugged just as the man himself appeared and mounted up behind a shivering, miserable-looking Lily once more, her skin redder than before, if that was possible.

Mal couldn't look away from her, remorse hitting him like a punch to the gut as he took her in. She hung her head, looking cold, unhappy, and sore, both from the saddle, it looked like, and the trick he'd played on her. Seeing her like this didn't satisfy him as he'd thought it would. Not at all.

They continued on, the rest of the day uneventful, and as the sun began to set, they came upon the next inn where they'd rest for the night … in the shadow of the hill, the fortress.

Mal gazed up at it, feeling the fear of times long past. The imprint of that place was on his soul, he thought as he gazed at it.

'What happened to that place?' Lily asked from next to him, staring up at the black shell that had once been Mal's whole world with an awe that it didn't deserve.

He didn't answer, ignoring her red face as he went inside, this time not feeling any need to push her or hurt her. In fact, he didn't feel the need to hurt anyone at all. Perhaps he had just needed a good hard fuck. Who'd have thought Bastian would have been the one to give it to him? His eyes narrowed as he walked up the steps to their rooms. He couldn't wait to return the favor, he thought as he hid in Lily's room.

He heard the door go and he watched from his vantage point in the half-closed wardrobe as she sat heavily in a chair and pulled off her boots. He watched her undress and frowned at the state of her skin. It was worse that he'd imagined it would be. Her hands, arms, and neck were the worst, the skin red and raw, bleeding in places where she hadn't been able to stop herself from scratching at her flesh. He muttered a curse and she froze, listening for more sounds, but then continued to disrobe when she heard nothing else.

He'd have to show her to check a new room before she started taking her clothes off, he thought. It was easy enough for someone to hide in a woman's closet to spy on her with her none the wiser.

She peeled off her shirt and went to the bath, already full with steaming water. He watched her step in and wince as she lowered herself down, hissing when the water reached her chafed skin. She picked up the soap nearby and began to wash herself before letting it fall from her hands. Then, as he watched, she burst into tears, great, heaving sobs that she somehow made almost silent. He stared in an almost fascinated horror as she drew up her knees and let the tears fall into the water.

Before he realized it, he was beside the bath, though he felt like the worst kind of voyeur. Somehow this was more intimate than watching her undress. More personal. More terrible. Now that he was closer, he noticed a dark bruise on her shoulder where he'd pushed her down in the mud as well. He grimaced at it. She was close to breaking. He'd thought he wanted that, but now that it was imminent, he didn't want to see her that way and he didn't want to be the cause of it.

He leant down. So close. If she moved ... Gods, he almost hoped she would. He poured the small packet of powder into the water; the antidote to the itching plant he'd put in her covers. He threw a pot of salve on the bed and then he left.

He didn't go to their room at all, instead leaving the inn, climbing up the old stone steps that led to the back entrance of the old fortress and letting his demons loose in the place they'd been formed.

~

By the time Lily's tears finally abated, she was feeling a little more herself. She sniffed as she found the soap she'd dropped and began to clean the scratches and abrasions she'd made with her constant itching all day. She'd thought it had been last night's bed, but Bastian had slept in it as well and he hadn't come down with any peculiar maladies. Should she tell Quin? She snorted. As if he would care. What would he do about it? Probably laugh in her face.

She stepped out of the water and dried herself, noticing a small pot on the coverlet of the bed that hadn't been there when she had got in the bath. She opened it, finding some of the salve that Quin had used on her in the camp.

She didn't like that one of them had been sneaking around her room, but she'd also learned in Vineri's care not to look a gift horse in the mouth. Her skin had finally stopped its incessant and unbearable itching, thankfully, and the balm felt cool against her overheated skin. She dried her hair and put on her spare breeches and shirt from the pack that Quin had given her this morning to stow her own meager belongings in. The dusty clothes from the day's travel she washed in the bath and left to dry by the fire.

A knock at the door brought a dinner of roast pheasant, sprouts, potatoes, and parsnips, which, with no one to watch her, she gobbled up as if she hadn't seen food in days. She'd never realized before how hungry traveling could make a person, even if they were on horseback, it seemed.

She thought back over the odd day. It had begun normally enough after they'd left the inn, she supposed, though she'd ridden with Bastian. She'd been afraid he'd be a difficult travel companion, but riding with him had actually been quite enjoyable. He'd told her tales, asked her about herself. He'd seemed to want to get to know her, and she wasn't sure what to make of it.

After she did the job they wanted her to do, what would they do with her? Would they take her back to the camp? Somewhere else?

She resolved to ask Quin. She wasn't their slave. Surely she was entitled to know what was going to happen afterwards. She deserved that, didn't she?

She lay on her bed and wished for the hundredth time that she'd brought a book or two with her. The nights spent in her own company with nothing to do were tedious and boring. Perhaps she should see what the men were doing.

Throwing on her tunic, she left her room, going down to the next door and pressing her ear to it. She heard talking inside, a man and a woman. Not that one. She walked back the way she'd come and went to the room on the other side. This time she could make out Bastian's booming voice and Quin's quieter one. She was just about to knock on the door when a shadow fell on her. She gasped as she turned to find Mal, a haunted look in his eyes that had her reeling. What could make a man like Mal afraid?

'Are you all right?' she asked.

He finally looked down at her as if only just noticing she was there. He scowled. 'What are you doing out here?' he said in that rasping voice of his that was sounding more normal every time he used it.

'I was bored,' she admitted, looking away from him and wondering if he'd order her back to her room just to be spiteful to her. But, to her surprise, he didn't. Instead, he reached around her and practically pushed her into the room. The voices inside ceased as they stepped inside, Mal shutting the door behind them.

She looked around. Their room was identical to hers, except that they had one large bed and a second smaller one where she only had the one large. She wondered why Bastian wasn't sharing it with her as he had last night but pushed the thought away as her cheeks began to heat. Riding with him all day had left her feeling as wound-up as she had been last night.

It made her think again of what Mal had done, as she had a thousand times over the day, and she shivered. Would he sneak into her room and do it again? Mortified, she shook her head, trying to get rid of these unwanted thoughts. Gods, if they knew about these sordid imaginings that were going through her mind ... What was wrong with her? She'd never had such thoughts about any men before, not Vineri's soldiers, nor even his massive gladiators who dwarfed even the Brothers with their hulking arms and chests. Why now? Why *them*?

'... Lily?' she blinked at Quin, belatedly realizing he was speaking to her. 'Is something amiss in your room?' he asked again.

'N-no,' she stuttered, feeling like a fool for coming here. Then she remembered she still held the pot of salve. 'Here! I was just bringing this back.'

'Listening,' Mal said from just behind her, glancing at her, then at Quin and jerking his head towards the door.

Eyes widening in denial, she gave the Brother a look. 'I wasn't—'

'How much did you hear?'

'I— nothing! I was only there for a moment,' she said, taking an uncertain step back and bumping into Mal, whose gloved hands settled on her shoulders, hemming her in. Her heart began to pound in her chest. 'Please! I didn't hear anything,' she whispered, staring at Quin with frightened eyes as he stalked towards her.

'We can't take the chance,' he said to her and then to the others, 'We do it now. Are we in agreement?'

'Aye,' Mal growled next to her ear.

Bastian stood apart from them, looking tense and uncertain, then his shoulders dropped under his Brothers' scrutiny.

'Yes,' he said, his eyes closing in something that looked like regret.

Mal's grip tightened on her painfully, but when she cried out, he loosened his hold.

'What are you going to do?' she asked Quin, hating the way her voice wavered and wishing she had just stayed in her dull room. She'd give anything for boredom now. Why had she thought coming to the lair of the beasts was a good idea?

Quin didn't answer her, instead speaking to the others as if she wasn't there. 'Ours first and then hers. We don't know if her blood will do the same as her touch.'

He produced a knife and cut his hand, dropping the blood into a goblet. Bastian did the same, not meeting her eyes as he added his. When it was Mal's turn, he thrust her at Bastian, who turned her around to face them, his arms encircling her waist in more of a lover's caress than the hold of an enemy.

Quin splashed some wine into the cup from the earthenware jug on the table, swirling it around to combine the ingredients, all the while watching her.

'What are you doing?' she asked again, pulling against Bastian ineffectively even as the large man attempted to calm her by hushing her as if she were nothing more an unruly horse. Anger reared up in her and she stamped hard on his toes, broke free and ran for the door.

Mal grabbed her, subdued her, and pushed her back to Bastian in the space of a moment, but his hold on her compared with how he'd manhandled her in the past was gentle – almost as if he didn't want to hurt her unduly, which she knew couldn't be so.

Bastian grabbed her again, easily pinning her arms to her sides as she thrashed.

'I'm not drinking that!' she shrieked.

Quin stepped closer.

'Hold her still,' he ordered, pinching her nose closed with a gloved hand as she wriggled and writhed. Her hair was grabbed in a punishing hold, used to keep her head still. Tears came to her eyes as her scalp smarted and, finally, when she couldn't leave it any longer, she opened her mouth to take a breath and the liquid was poured down her throat. Her mouth was forced closed so she couldn't spit it out as she spluttered and screamed, wondering if anyone would come to find out what was happening to her. Someone would have in the last inn, but here, no one cared, she thought as her body went limp.

'What's wrong with her?'

'I put a sleeping draft in the cup with the ... rest of it.'

'You drugged her as well?'

'I didn't want her hurting herself for the next bit. It's just to keep her calm.'

What was the next bit, she wondered dully, unable to conjure up much of anything except tiredness, though she knew in the back of her mind that she should be trying to fight.

'Do it, then.'

She felt a sting on her finger and jerked in Bastian's arms.

'Make certain to get enough for all of us.'

Her finger was squeezed and she yelped. Bastian's arm tightened around her, holding her up now that her legs had turned to jelly. She watched as Quin added more wine to the cup and took a gulp, handing it to Mal, who did the same.

When Bastian had drunk of the cup as well, all three of them looked at each other.

'Did it work?'

'Binding her to the unit should make it impossible for her to kill us.'

'Should?'

Quin approached her, his hand raised, and she realized what he meant to do. She tried, sluggishly, to move away. *No!* She didn't want to kill anyone. She didn't want to kill him, even if he did hate her. She let out a small cry of anguish as his hand settled on her cheek, caressing it, the look in his eyes almost compassionate. Then his expression turned blank, his hand moving to the back of her neck and tightening as he brandished the knife and put it to her throat.

She whimpered, fighting feebly to be free of Bastian as the knife bit into her skin.

'Enough,' came Bastian's quiet growl, which sounded so menacing that Quin looked up at him in surprise as he took the knife away and his touch gentled once more.

'I had to be certain,' he said softly. 'Now we know it worked.'

Lily's eyes fluttered closed, even as she tried to make sense of what they had just done. She had an odd feeling that it was something important and life-changing. But she couldn't seem to hold onto any thoughts as she sank into oblivion.

～

LILY'S EYES closed and her body sagged, finally succumbing to the sleeping potion he'd put in the cup. Bastian still held her and didn't seem to be in a hurry to put her down, which he could understand.

Quin disliked all of this, if he was honest with himself,

but it was necessary. Bastian had made him see that, and if he hadn't drugged her, she would have got herself into such a state that she could have been hurt. She was a slight thing, after all.

Now, as he looked down at her, knowing that her power could no longer hurt him, he wanted to touch her with his bare hands. He imagined running them over her, as he had wanted to for days.

He shouldn't fuck her. Even if he made her want it, they were on a mission. He had to keep a clear head. His fingers trailed down the curve of her throat and he swallowed hard, biting back a curse as he turned away.

'Put her back in her room,' he said to Bastian, who was looking vaguely disgusted. Quin stepped away, trying to get some distance from Lily in more ways than one. 'What's the matter with you?'

'We shouldn't have done this,' Bastian muttered. 'We should have told her at least – explained it. This was wrong.'

'Right or wrong,' Quin snapped, 'what's done is done. For now at any rate.'

'What do you mean?' Bastian's eyes narrowed.

Quin walked back to the table in what he hoped was a casual manner and filled a new cup with wine, thinking that he hadn't seen Bastian drink himself into a stupor since the ship, though he'd had ample opportunities since then. His eyes cut to Mal, who was still standing in the same spot, still as a statue. He frowned. There hadn't been any disappearances to explain away, either. With Mal there always was, but not since the ship … Both men seemed to have found some new way of fighting their demons. He glanced between them, gathering by the way that Bastian and Mal were eyeing each other when they thought he wasn't looking that there was something more going on here that he wasn't privy to.

'I mean that I'm the Commander,' he finally said. 'I can break a bond if I need to. When I need to,' he corrected.

Bastian snarled. 'You'd bind her and then cast her aside?'

Quin shrugged. 'It won't be long before we reach Kitore and she does what we brought her to do. It's a dangerous task that she probably won't survive anyway, so I won't have to do anything,' he said callously. 'This discussion is pointless.'

Bastian turned away without another word and left the room with Lily in his arms.

When Quin turned back to Mal, his Brother was looking at him strangely.

He ignored him and went back to his wine. By the time Bastian came back, slamming the door in his wake and throwing himself on one of the beds like a petulant child, Mal had disappeared again. Quin went to Lily's room. He slipped inside, finding her in the bed, still sleeping off the effects of the drug.

He settled down in her room to wait. When she woke, he was going to talk to her. He skimmed a hand over the bulge in his breeches, allowing himself a moment to indulge, looking her over as she slept, wondering whether she'd be pliant or if she was a fighter. He'd put good money on the latter. He could always tell when she didn't agree with something. Her jaw would set mulishly and her eyes would flash for just a moment.

Her first instinct was to fight, and he knew that drive well enough. But so much of her life had been controlled by Vineri – and now by the Brothers – that she swallowed that spirit down and pretended obedience. He wondered what she'd do if she were free, who she would become if given the chance to step out of the shadows of everyone else's selfish needs and live her life as she willed.

She gave a groan and he shook himself free of his

thoughts. Her future didn't matter; she didn't matter past the part she would play in Kitore. He had to remember that or they would not succeed. Failure wasn't an option. He'd worked too hard for too long to become the Commander to only be remembered as the Brother who'd held the title the shortest amount of time.

He stood, pouring some water into a cup. He knew she preferred it, so that was what he'd started ordering them to bring at every inn they stayed in. A tiny part of him wondered if she'd noticed. An even smaller part wanted her to.

He growled audibly at his errant thoughts and she sat up in the bed with a gasp, looking at him like he was her enemy. He was, he reminded himself, and it was a good thing that she had remembered.

Lately she had not seemed particularly afraid of any of them, and that blasé arrogance would get her killed, if not by the other Brothers, then by the overzealous witch hunters who seemed to be so much more abundant in the north thanks to the rewards offered by the king. She was safer with them. Most of those sort wouldn't tangle with a unit of Brothers, but alone? She'd probably be dead already.

She was looking around the room, her eyes falling on him at close intervals as if she thought he would attack her.

He held the cup out to her, but she made no move to take it, looking at it as if it were a snake set to strike.

'It's just water,' he said to her. 'I won't drug you again.' *Probably.*

She didn't look convinced, but she took the cup from him gingerly, not letting her fingers touch his. Losing patience with her, he grabbed her wrist with his hand tightly and held on as she tried to pull away.

'Let me go!' she wailed in a tone he hadn't heard from her before, but which just about broke him.

'No,' he told her, stepping closer, trying to intimidate by looming over her as he fought to push his sudden reactions away. Her eyes flashed, boring into him with that defiance he liked to see from her.

'Get. The. Fuck. Off. Me,' she ordered, the command losing much of its power as he noticed how her body shook with fear. But it wasn't him she was afraid of, he realized; it was herself.

'When was the last time you could touch anyone without killing them?' he asked her, gentling his grasp on her wrist and sitting on the bed beside her.

She drew back and he let her, but her searching eyes never left his. 'Before Bastian, you mean?'

Quin rolled his eyes at his Brother's name on her lips, a feeling he didn't like forming in the pit of his stomach. Gods, was he *jealous* of that prick?

'Yes, before Bastian,' he said tersely.

'Never.'

'Never?' he asked incredulously. 'So you killed the midwife as you entered the world, your mother as she held you to her breast?'

'I ...' She looked away and shrugged. 'I don't remember.'

'You're lying.'

Lily refused to meet his gaze. 'What did you do to me? Why did you make me drink your blood? Is that how you're still alive?'

'I – *we* bound you to our unit.'

'I thought Brothers came in threes, not fours.'

'You met Maeve. She's a Fourth,' he pointed out.

'Why?'

He looked down to where his hand was still wrapped around her bare wrist and squeezed it to remind her that it was there. 'Brothers in a unit cannot kill each other, not even with the gifts they possess.'

He watched her face, wondering if she would be afraid now that she had no power over them, but all he saw was utter relief in her countenance. Either she didn't care that she was helpless when it came to them or she was too naïve to understand that that put her in a certain amount of danger from the men she traveled with.

'I don't understand. Why do it now? It's been days since we left your army.' She was staring at where their flesh touched as if she couldn't believe that it was happening.

He let her go. 'Now that we are in the north, it would be safer if we don't have to worry about accidentally brushing against you all the time. There may be occasions where we have to touch you to save your life, and hesitation can mean death in perilous situations.'

'So all three of you can touch me and you won't … succumb?'

He nodded.

'And I – I can …'

'You can touch us with no ill effects,' he confirmed.

Tentatively and very slowly, she nudged her hand towards him. He didn't move, didn't want her to startle and stop what she was going to do. Quin didn't know if she'd initiated anything with Bastian or if he had been the one to touch her first, but if she hadn't, Quin wanted to be the first man she touched not to kill, not because she'd been told to, but because she wanted to.

He made himself stay still, though his very being screamed at him to lean in closer as she reached her hand up to his face and, very lightly, traced two of her fingers over his brow. Lily's movements were precise, and the look on her face as she moved down his stubbly cheek to where his tattoo started on his neck was one of intense concentration. He let his eyes drift shut.

Her fingers stopped, staying where they were as if she too

were frozen now. He looked at her and found her staring at him, a look of wonder on her face that she quickly shuttered when she noticed him watching. She pulled her hand away and looked at her fingers.

'Is this the first time you've ever done that? Touched someone, I mean?' he fumbled, cheeks heating. He hoped she didn't notice. He was a Dark Brother and he'd had his share of women. He knew he was considered charming when he wanted to be. So why did this girl leave him feeling like a foolish, green lad with no experience whatsoever?

But she hadn't seen. She was touching him again! A finger skimmed his lips and then stroked his jaw more boldly.

He couldn't stand it any longer. He surged forward and captured her lips with his roughly. She made a sound of surprise and tried to break the kiss, but he didn't let her, moving with her until her head was on the pillow and he was practically on top of her. Her arms came up hesitantly, as if that long-inured part of her had already forgotten that she couldn't kill him. Then her hands were on his tunic and he expected her to push him away, knowing that he would let her.

He had no interest in forcing her to do this. She'd had enough of that in her life, and he didn't want to add any more to it than he absolutely had to. But she didn't push him away. Her fingers gripped his clothes and drew him closer, making a sound of such utter satisfaction that he deepened the kiss, his tongue slipping past her lips to tease hers in long strokes in a promise of what was to come.

He opened his eyes for a moment and saw hers were open too, wide with her astonishment and something else. She was looking past him.

The door slammed and he pulled away with a suddenness that had his body yearning to return to her arms for more.

He turned his head, already knowing it would be one of

his Brothers, but which one would he be punishing later for interrupting?

Mal. *Fucking spy.*

He stood by the door, simply watching. His expression was blank, but Quin knew his Brother well, and he was anything but unmoved. Quin had been afraid that Mal wouldn't be able to stop himself from killing her before she could perform her task, and he knew that Bastian had believed the same.

Bastian had thought he was clever by bringing up the binding the way he had, but Quin knew what he was trying to do from the beginning. He'd developed an attachment, however tenuous, to their little prisoner – who was still under him, breathing hard with her eyes locked on Mal. And his eyes, in turn, were on her. Binding her had suited Quin's purposes for safety's sake and to soothe Mal's more murderous urges when it came to her.

But Mal didn't want to *kill* her, he wanted to *fuck* her, and by the way he was looking at her, he'd already whetted his appetite somehow. How could Quin have been so blind? Bastian and Mal were both interested in her, and, he readily admitted, he was as well. And in binding her to their unit, he had made it so they could all indulge themselves with her, a girl so starved for the warmth of another's skin on hers that it would be so, so easy to make her acquiesce. Muttering a curse, he scrambled off her, ignoring the look of hurt in her eyes that was there one moment and gone the next.

She sat up and put herself to rights, touching her lips, which were swollen from his kisses. Her unfocused eyes weren't on him, and he wanted them to be more than anything in that moment. He turned away from her and strode to Mal.

'We need to talk,' he barked, striding from the room and not bothering to check if Mal was following.

He barged into their chamber down the hall, finding Bastian sitting up in the bed as if waiting for them.

'No one touches her,' he announced without preamble, making his voice loud enough that he knew she'd be able to hear through the wall in the next room as well.

'What are you talking about?' Bastian drawled, making Quin want to break his nose.

'Lily. No one touches her. Even though we can, we don't. Understand?'

'No,' Mal bit out from behind him and he turned.

'No, you don't understand?'

Mal threw one of his knives at the wall, embedding it almost to the hilt with the force of it. 'No, Brother.' He smiled that mad grin of his that made his enemies wither under his gaze. 'You bound her. She's ours. *Mine.*'

And then he was gone.

'Fuck!' Quin swore.

Bastian was on his feet and making for the door when Quin stopped him.

'You'll never find him if he doesn't want to be found, Brother.'

'We can't just let him go.' Bastian tapped the side of his head. 'He's not right. You know he's not.'

'Aye, I know. It makes him one of the best in the Army.'

'He'll hurt her. He'll *enjoy* it.'

Quin sat down heavily and didn't answer. Mal had never gone against his orders before. He wanted Lily badly. How far would he go to have her? Mal dealt in pain. That was all he knew.

'We shouldn't have bound her. Undo it!'

'It's not as simple as that, you fool! If we were at the camp, then perhaps, but I can't just wave my hand for it to be so. This was your idea. If Mal hurts her, be it on your head.'

The larger man pulled him from the chair by his tunic

and shook him. 'You were going to do it anyway. Do you think I haven't seen how you look at her? You bound her for yourself, Quin, not for the protection of the unit.'

Quin butted him in the head and Bastian let him go with a grunt, staggering away and sitting hard on the bed.

'I did it so that she wouldn't accidentally murder us with a power she can't begin to control, you selfish cunt! It was only a matter of time. Her not being able to kill only you was hardly the solution,' he hissed.

'And I wanted to ensure Mal couldn't kill her whenever it entered his head to do so,' Bastian fired back. 'How was I to know he wanted her? Fuck!'

'You couldn't have foreseen, just as I didn't,' Quin muttered. 'He rarely visits the pleasure tents. His urges are always satisfied … elsewhere.'

Quin took off his tunic and threw it at one of the chairs. 'You should check to see if she's in need of anything. If you can keep your hands off her, stay with her tonight. From now on, she's never to be without one of us.'

Bastian nodded, leaving their room without a word, but he was gone for just a moment before he rushed back in.

'She's gone.'

CHAPTER 9

LILY

The fortress loomed high on the hill in front of her, many of the wide stone steps that led up broken and cracked. She shivered as she stared up at the burned-out shell. It still dominated the landscape here, even like this. It must have been a grand place once.

She glanced behind her, knowing she wasn't meant to be here. They hadn't expressly told her she couldn't leave her room, but she assumed they wouldn't be happy that she was roaming about by herself when the sun would soon set. She wasn't even sure why she had come, but when she'd seen the path up from the casement in the inn, she'd been drawn to it.

Still reeling from what they'd done to her, holding her, making her drink their *blood*, she'd had to get out of that room. She wasn't safe there. She wasn't safe anywhere. Yet a part of her was glad that she couldn't kill them now. She thought back to Quin sitting on her bed, how she'd touched him. The experience had been … sublime. And his kiss … She'd never felt anything so intoxicating. She hadn't wanted it to stop.

In truth, she wasn't sure what she thought about what the

Brothers had done, binding her into their unit, as well as how they'd gone about it. She wasn't surprised they hadn't asked her, or even told her what they had planned. She was long inured to having most decisions made for her, from what she wore to what she would eat, from being little more than Vineri's instrument. No one had ever asked her what she wanted before, so it stood to reason that she wouldn't expect it now, but maybe she should. She was more than a tool. She needed to begin acting like it.

She began to ascend the stone steps, tilting her head up. Birds circled crumbling towers that wouldn't be safe to climb, though she wanted to explore them. It was an ominous building, but it reminded her a little of Vineri's fortress. It had once been a monastery as well before he'd turned it into his home ... and hers.

She was breathing hard by the time she reached the top of the steps, finding what remained of the main door blackened and half off its hinges. Steps not faltering, she walked into the structure slowly. It looked like no one had been here in a very long time. She'd overheard someone in the tavern mention that the fire had killed almost everyone in their beds while they slept. No one had sounded an alarm until the whole place was ablaze and the inferno was too hot for anyone to get close enough.

Inside, there was just blackened stone in the main hall, dust and ash on the floor, and lots of cobwebs. It still smelled faintly of smoke. She walked around, unafraid and in complete silence. Finding an opening, she was led down a level towards the back of the keep and found herself in the kitchens, still largely intact. She opened a cupboard here and there but found little of significance.

Lily's curiosity began to wane and she turned to go, but a noise echoed down a corridor. She followed it, finding rooms, probably larders and the like, she thought, coming to a small door that looked like it had hardly been touched by flames. It was ajar and she peered inside, finding, to her surprise, a candle flickering on an old wooden crate and a small bed.

Creeping in, she looked around. Someone had been here, or they still were. Feeling as if she'd outstayed her welcome, she turned to leave, only to be confronted by a shadow. She gasped, lurching away. He reached for her at the same time as she realized it was Mal.

If anything, it made her fear more acute. She shouldn't be alone with this man. She knew that instinctively. He was a hunter, a killer, a bully. Yet a traitorous voice in her head asked if he was going to do again what he'd done to her the other night. Unbidden, her eyes flicked to the knife on his belt and back to his face. She wet her dry lips.

He didn't say anything, didn't move, as if he was in shock that she was here.

And then he pushed her hard and she staggered back, her head thudding against the stone wall. He pinned her there with his body, a hand at her throat, on her bare skin. Her breath hitched as she felt his fingers like a brand, but whereas in the past the feeling would be followed by his harrowing death, now it simply made her tingle low in her stomach.

She searched his face for any sign of humanity, but he was blank, his dark eyes pitiless as he squeezed.

She clawed at his hand, but it was useless. He was just too strong. But just when she started to see spots, his grip eased and she could breathe again. She sank against the wall, her body going limp, wondering what he was going to do with her, knowing that she could do nothing to stop him now. She was helpless and she found that although she was terrified that she was completely in his power to do with whatever he willed, she also felt free in a strange way.

His hand stayed around her throat, but his thumb began to trace the welts left from the rash that were well on their way to healing. She saw something flicker in his expression but didn't know what to make of it. Shame?

Her hand fluttered up to his where he held her, but instead of trying to pull him away, she laid her hand on his wrist, lightly caressing, thinking of how his skin felt under her fingers. She loved the texture, the warmth of him.

His other hand flew to her core, roughly pushing up at the apex of her thighs and making her gasp as she rose to her toes to escape his forceful fingers that would have pressed into her if not for the barrier of her breeches.

Her eyes pleaded with him, but in that moment she wasn't sure if she was silently begging him to stop or keep going. The pressure on her core eased as if he couldn't make up his mind what he wanted to do.

'Why?' He leant in, whispering into her ear.

She shuddered at his closeness, feeling his breath on her cheek and knowing she'd never been as close to anyone before leaving that tower, and now she had been with three men who definitely didn't have her best interests at heart. Yet she was so lured in by them; their looks, their hands on her, the peril of being in their presence. She was a fool. This wouldn't end well for her. She knew it, and yet...

His fingers popped one of the buttons on her breeches and then another, and she felt her body heating.

'Why am I here?' she asked, her voice unnaturally high.

'Aye,' he breathed.

'I saw this place from the casement.'

She gasped as he unfastened the last button and felt a need to try anything to keep him talking, coward that she was.

'I've been watching it get closer and closer since we left

the mountains,' she yammered on, 'and I needed to see it.' Her eyes fell on the bed. 'You've been sleeping here.'

He didn't reply to her unspoken question, but his hand stopped its advance. Instead his fingers stroked her abdomen lightly, making her quiver.

He nodded once.

'Why?'

'Born here.'

She gaped at him. 'Here?' She looked around again and then she understood. 'This was your room.'

'Aye.'

'But what happened here?'

His features darkened and his fingers began to descend slowly. But as they brushed against her skin, a laugh bubbled up from her throat that she couldn't suppress.

He startled, looking puzzled. And then he did it again, watching her closely as she giggled once more, using one of her hands to push at him feebly as she tried to writhe away from the maddeningly tickly sensations.

'Stop!' she laughed. 'Please!'

He ignored her, of course. His fingers became bolder, moving over her stomach and to her sides ruthlessly, and she squealed for mercy. By the time he stopped, she was on the floor, wriggling this way and that as he crouched over her. When she was finally in control of herself again, she found him standing before her, a look on his face that she'd never seen. Lighter, almost as if it might produce a smile of actual enjoyment.

But then it was gone, the moment was over, and his usual menacing countenance settled over him like a shroud. All laughter fled under his perusal and she scrambled back as he grabbed her, hauling her to her feet and pushing her back against the wall, her wrists held fast above her head.

This time there was no slowness to his actions, his hand

plunging into her open breeches and then between her thighs. He kicked her legs apart as he had done before, but this time his bare fingers slipped between her folds, feeling her. More than one entered her shallowly and she gave a small cry as he shoved them into her, pulled them out and thrust them in again. She gasped and panted, whimpered, and her hips began to move of their own accord, her body needing more contact than he was giving her.

'Please,' she whispered, and this time it *was* for him to continue.

Her legs felt like jelly, small cries exploding from her lips as his strong, calloused fingers fucked her hard. It felt so much better than anything she'd done to herself, even though it hurt, and she would have told him so if she was capable of any words other than those begging him not to stop.

Another finger entered her, stretching her, pushing deep, and his thumb found the other, higher place, circling it fast and then pressing it. She screamed as her body tightened, legs shaking as pleasure enveloped her, cascaded over her, made little lights dance in her vision, and he kept going, his fingers moving and scissoring until he'd wrung every little bit of enjoyment from her.

As she was gradually coming back to herself, he let her go, jumping back as if her curse could still hurt him. She slid down the wall to the ground, her knees not able to support her, and glanced up at him, feeling bashful. She'd never done that with another person before, after all. What happened now? Whatever people usually did after engaging in such a thing, she had a feeling Mal wouldn't follow the precedent, if that was the right word for it.

She was right. After staring at her in a heap on the floor for a moment, he stepped closer and put his fingers in his mouth, sucking them as he watched her eyes widen in surprise. Heat smoldered in his own for a moment ... and then he was simply gone and she was alone in his childhood room. Her gaze fell on the door, noticing the bolt on the outside. Cell.

What had happened to him here? The stories said that no one had survived the fire, but if he had, then ... Had he done it? Had he started the inferno that had killed everyone who'd lived here? *Yes.* She knew it with the same certainty she did of needing air to breathe.

She picked herself up as she followed that train of thought, finding her legs would hold her now, though she felt a bit wobbly. She'd let a madman do those things to her ... and she'd liked it.

Shaking her head at her stupid self, she left the room as she tried to sort through the mess in her head. Would Mal come back here again before they journeyed on tomorrow? What had made him torch his home and then flee? How had he ended up joining the Army, becoming a trained killer ... liking being a trained killer? Because he did like it. She'd seen it when he'd killed the men on the ship, when he'd thought about hurting her ... when he had. But she'd also seen the uncertainty in him. He'd never met anyone who liked it before. But why did she? She didn't know. She didn't understand how she could like the things he did. *That knife ...* she shivered. Truth be told, she was disappointed that he hadn't done it again, she thought as she left the fortress and slowly descended the steps to the bottom of the hill. It was so wrong, but she couldn't deny that she enjoyed it, mind and body.

What would Quin say if he knew what Mal had done with her tonight? She'd heard him order both Mal and Bastian to stay away from her earlier and she'd assumed that meant she must respond in kind. He was the Commander ... and she was a Fourth like Maeve. Did that mean he was her commander now too?

∼

Mal watched Lily enter the inn just as he'd been watching from the moment she'd left his boyhood room. He didn't fully comprehend what had just transpired between them, but he had an urge to make sure she was safe. He didn't understand that either. He had urges to kill all the time, but protect? Help? Never that he could recall.

He glanced up at the towering fortress so close behind him, just able to make out the silhouette of it against the light of the full moon. Dark memories rushed over him, the ones he'd denied purchase in his mind for so long that it was usually very easy to keep them at bay, but not tonight. He remembered the high priest's face as he'd stabbed him in his own bedchamber with the knife he'd pilfered from the kitchen. Recalled the exact hue of the curtains that he'd lit on fire before he'd turned and calmly left, leaving the casements and the door wide open for the through breeze to feed the flames well. He'd killed the few who weren't abed though the hour was late so they wouldn't raise the alarm.

While the place burned, he sat on the roof of this very inn and viewed the carnage he'd caused with a smile on his face, laughing as the towers fell in on each other. Then he had gone, left this place and all its darkness behind him. So why he'd felt the need to go back to lie in his old, rotten bed, he didn't know. That room hadn't granted him even a moment of the solace that it had when he was a child. Well, not until she had appeared. He'd been furious that Lily would trespass here at first; trampling all over his past, his secrets, with her naïve looks and annoying... presence.

He was going to give in to his darker impulses and teach her a lesson. He'd already decided to ignore Quin's order to keep away from her. He would touch her if he liked, when he liked, where he liked. But when he'd noticed all those little scratches and welts left over from what he'd done to her, he'd felt sick to his stomach. Then she'd *stroked* his hand of her own volition, such an innocuous touch – because she'd *chosen* to.

As he'd stood there with his hand around her throat, the wards stopping him from squeezing hard enough to kill her, the need to harm her had been rapidly and largely replaced by a different need altogether. But then he'd shocked himself further by not giving in to those urges either. Instead of shoving her to the floor and fucking her like he'd wanted to, *he'd* pleasured *her* instead. And now he didn't know what he wanted from her. He let out a breath. Things used to be simple – kill, eat, sleep, kill – but since Lily, everything seemed much more complicated.

Deciding that enough time had passed since she had entered, he followed, slipping in and up the stairs like a ghost, no one hearing or seeing him unless he wished them to. He opened her door silently and went into her room, shutting it just as quietly as he took in her form on the bed under the coverlet – and another next to her.

Mal frowned. *Bastian.* There was another thorn in his side that was quickly turning into something else, he thought as his cock began to harden. He wanted both of them, he realized in shock. But that wasn't the problem. It wasn't even unusual – not for other Brothers, at any rate. What was disturbing him was that only yesterday he'd still been fantasizing about killing both of them. Now he wanted to climb into bed between them and definitely *not* to sleep. How could his desires have changed so drastically in one day?

He sat in the chair by the fire to think. He and Quin were close in many ways, though they'd obviously never shared conversations, but he wondered if perhaps he should get some advice from his Brother. Quin knew what Mal enjoyed, after all. They'd trained together, learned to fight and kill together. And even before they were unit Brothers, Mal had considered him a friend. Now that he thought on it, it was odd that they'd never talked, that Quin had never even heard him speak. Perhaps it was time to change some things, try harder to act as others did – in some ways at least.

Lily made a small sound and he went over to where she lay asleep, drawing his knife on impulse, the whisper of it leaving the sheath only just audible, but, in her sleep, Lily whimpered, and he thought it was in fear until he heard her moan 'Mal'.

His breath caught. She was dreaming of him? And not a bad dream either; he was doing something she liked.

Bringing the knife close, he sliced off a piece of her hair from the back, underneath, where she wouldn't notice, before stepping away and melting into the darkness.

The next day, Mal awoke in the bed in the next room, still fully clothed as per usual and thinking about Lily. Quin was next to him in the other small bed, still sleeping. Mal almost woke him – to talk – but luckily came to his senses and left the inn. He always scouted early before they left a place. He liked to know what was coming.

At about midmorning, he came upon the large river they'd have to cross to leave the flats and make it to Kitore's city gates, but to his dismay, the ferry wasn't on either bank.

Another traveler approached him.

'If you're wanting the ferry, it broke its moorings last night. They won't have it back running again till tomorrow, they said.'

Mal nodded his thanks and made his way back to the inn to tell the others they'd be stuck here until tomorrow. There was no point in journeying on. The ferry was the only way across unless they wanted to go three days out of their way to the nearest bridge.

He arrived back in their room, finding Quin and Bastian sitting at the table, looking irate.

'Fucking finally!' Bastian exploded. 'Where the fuck have you been?'

'Scouting,' he said calmly, unperturbed. Deciding to try what he'd decided last night, he continued. 'Ferry broke free last night. Won't be running until tomorrow.'

Neither of them said anything, so he sat at the table and poured himself some wine, knowing it would annoy them further. He sipped it as he waited for them to tell him what their problem was.

'What did you do to her?' Bastian ground out, jaw clenched, and Mal had an almost overwhelming inclination to caress it to relieve the tension.

He fought against it, however, and instead he shrugged.

'You weren't to touch her,' Quin snarled, the anger in his tone taking Mal aback slightly.

Quin didn't lose his temper often, but when he did, it was certainly a sight to behold. Mal leaned back in the chair, listening to it creak as he pondered what he was going to say. Finally he decided on the least of the incendiary comments going through his mind, which was to say nothing. He shrugged again.

'She has bruises on her neck. She wouldn't tell me if there are others anywhere else.' Bastian stood abruptly, his chair crashing over behind him as he reached over the table and grabbed Mal's tunic.

Mal grinned at his Brother as he was wrenched forward.

'What did you do to her?'

Mal pulled one of Bastian's fingers back in a practiced move, making him let go of the tunic or risk a break.

'Whatever I did, she *liked* it,' he teased, chuckling as Bastian's face darkened with rage.

'She's—'

'—not yours,' Quin finished for Bastian.

Mal bared his teeth at them both, making a noise of anger. Why did they care what he did with the woman? 'You bound her. She *is* mine. *Ours* to take.'

'What if she doesn't want to be taken?' Quin asked softly.

Mal snorted. Where had the Commander of the Dark Army gone and who was this soft waif who'd taken his place? 'She does,' he said with conviction.

'How do you know?'

'Just do.' His eyes narrowed. 'I'll prove it.'

'You know the price if you don't follow my orders, Brother.' Quin sighed, looking tired all of a sudden. 'She's still abed. Leave her to waken on her own. Clearly she needs more rest than we do.'

Mal gave another shrug, a small smile playing on his lips as he thought of what he was going to do with her next.

Bastian and Quin stayed in the room with him, Bastian sharpening his sword while Quin sat at the table, writing missives to send south when they got to Kitore. He was still the Commander even if he wasn't acting like it, Mal mused. He conceded that he was probably being unfair. There was something about this girl. She was different from the others who'd been brought to the camp. He didn't know why it had taken him so long to see it. The others must have noticed it too. They were both being strange. Bastian hadn't touched a drop of wine since the ship. Quin was acting like he had a smaller stick shoved up his arse than usual. Mal's needs had changed, at least for the moment.

He still wanted to hurt her. It was in his nature, but he also wanted to turn that pain into pleasure as he had last night. Without a word to the others, he slipped from the room quietly. Both Brothers were turned away from him and engrossed in their tasks. He smiled, shaking his head at how easy it was to elude them as he moved down the hall to Lily's room.

He went inside, not even bothering to be overly quiet, and found her dressed and lying on her front, reading.

She looked up as he closed the door and scrambled up. He noted the black bruises on her neck from his fingers and scowled, not taking any enjoyment in seeing the proof of his misuse of her.

'W-what are you doing here?' she stammered.

He moved closer, eyeing her neck. 'Those the only ones?'

'What?'

'On your neck. Are there others?'

She didn't reply, but her tell-tale flush confirmed that she was in pain in other places, and he could guess where.

He stepped closer, noting that her breathing was already quickening. He'd bet it wasn't simply from fear. To test his theory, he unsheathed his knife, his eyes not leaving her face. And when her mouth opened in a tiny gasp and her pupils dilated, he had his answer. He could practically see her clenching her thighs together at the very thought of what he might do with the weapon he held in his hands. He advanced slowly, prowling towards her. She stood her ground, daring him to notice how much she wanted his hands on her.

It wasn't until he stood in front of her, towering over her, that her eyes lowered in a show of submission that made him even harder if that was possible.

Using the knife, he raised her chin to look at him. 'Strip.'

Her eyes pleaded, but she didn't say a word as she began to undo the toggles of her tunic with shaky fingers. She shrugged it off and he found she wasn't wearing a shirt or chemise beneath it.

At his questioning look, her cheeks reddened.

'I washed them,' she murmured.

He took the tunic from her fingers without a word and let

it fall to the ground. He was mesmerized by her breasts. They were round and plump, and so soft and heavy in his hands. He ran his hand over a small, mostly healed wound near one of her rapidly pebbling nipples and she shivered.

His eyes narrowed as an anger rose in him at the evidence that someone had hurt her other than him, even though whoever it was must be dead by now. 'Who?'

'Th-the Rat back at the camp.'

Of course. He was even more glad he'd killed so many of them that night in retaliation.

'The rest,' he ordered and she rushed to comply, divesting herself of her breeches so quickly that it took effort for him not to grin at her eagerness.

When she was completely bared to him, he stepped back and looked his fill. Her shortness emphasized her round figure, large tits, and plump arse. He moved his finger in a circle to make her turn, and she did, though her cheeks were looking more and more crimson in her embarrassment.

He frowned as in addition to the bruises on her neck, he noticed there were some on her back and shoulder from the stone wall he'd ground her into the night before.

While her back was to him, he bent her at the waist.

She braced herself with her hands with a cry as she fell on the bed.

'Open your legs,' he ordered softly.

She did as he said and he almost groaned at her obedience. He'd never have expected that from her.

His fingers delved into her slit, already wet, but when he stroked her, she let out a small sound, though he was being gentle.

'It hurts?'

'A little,' she whispered.

'On your back,' he commanded, taking off his belt and removing all his weapons and pouches from it. When he was finished, he looped it around her wrists and then the wooden slats of the headboard, anchoring her in place.

She made a sound of distress when she realized what he'd done, pulling at the bonds fruitlessly.

He hushed her as he moved between her knees and opened them gently, her pink folds coming into view. His countenance darkened as he found the evidence of his roughness with his fingers. He eased her apart, revealing her slick core for his assessment too.

She whimpered but still didn't speak, nor plead for mercy as he left the bed to find another pot of salve in the pouch he kept on his belt – the last one. Good thing they'd reach Kitore's cache soon to stock up on their dwindling supplies.

He joined her on the bed again and opened the tub. Coating his fingers, he leant over her and started with the bruises on her neck, covering the marks deftly. Then he moved down to her breast and put some on the bite mark as well, pinching both her nipples to hard peaks for good measure. Then he dipped to her mound, rubbing her softly, trying to make her feel better instead of bringing about more pain. She gasped as his thumb worked inside her.

He grinned deviously as an idea came to him and he went across the room to the small writing desk and took one of the quills from the inkwell. He returned to her, not missing the trepidation on her face. He liked that she was scared, that she didn't know what he was going to do. He gathered that she liked that too. And there was another side to that coin anyway. He never knew how she was going to react either, and he enjoyed that as well.

First, he took the quill and wrote his name in ink on the underside of her breast, drawing back and taking a moment to appreciate how she looked with his name on her. He imagined her getting it marked on her permanently with black ink. Perhaps he would have her name put on him as well. Yes, he liked that idea. Then Quin and Bastian would know that she belonged to him first every time they fucked her without him.

What was he thinking? Permanence? Would they all return to the camp together after their mission in Kitore, with Lily in tow as their Fourth, following them into battle, journeying with them on long campaigns, being thoroughly pleasured by them every night? He shuddered at the thought, but not in revulsion. Perhaps, somehow, there could be a future for them, but he couldn't imagine Lily being happy with that particular arrangement. She wouldn't enjoy the life of a Brother, he didn't think, but then it hardly mattered. Surely life with them was better than no life at all.

Lily craned her neck to see what he'd written on her. He pushed her down with a tut and ran the feather lightly over her chest and down her side. She shivered deliciously as he did the same to the other side before tickling her neck with it, grinning as she giggled. Last night, her fit of laughter had unnerved him. He'd never made a woman laugh before, never made anyone laugh before, now he thought on it.

Except for Quin, he was a solitary creature, and he and Quin certainly didn't have the sort of friendship where they'd joke together. That was more Bastian than him.

He used the feather for a little while longer, making her squirm and beg for mercy. Then he put it down and took up the other item he'd placed there. Her eyes widened as she took in the knife he held as it glinted in the morning light that shone through the cracks in the closed casement shutters.

'I don't think I—' she began, a tremor in her voice, though Mal could see she was also aroused simply by the sight of it.

'Will stop if you ask.' He put a finger to her lips. 'Won't hurt you,' he murmured. 'Not unless you want.'

If it was possible, she looked even more anxious, but she didn't tell him to stop, thank the gods.

He pushed the blade to her throat for a moment, just enough for her breathing to quicken, before grazing it down to her breast, not hard enough to break the skin, just leaving a little red line in its wake. She gasped as he circled her nipple where the bite mark was.

'I killed them,' he said offhandedly. At her inquiring look, he went on, 'After the Rat, I slaughtered many.'

'Why?' she asked, her voice barely above a whisper.

'Angry,' he said after a moment, moving to the other nipple and digging the blade in sharply.

She cried out, more in pleasure than pain, her back arching so suddenly that he had to snatch the knife away so as not to cut her.

'Angry with them?' she somehow found the presence of mind to say breathily, though he could see she was already almost lost to the sensations he was giving her.

'With myself.' If he'd known then what the Rat had done to her, he might well have killed many more, but he didn't tell her that.

He drew the knife down her belly, watching as she tried in vain to keep still, chuckling as her hips surged up to his hand. He shook his head and pushed her down, giving her mound a little slap with the flat of the blade. She whimpered, biting her lip and silently begging him for more.

He flipped the knife into the air and caught it by the opposite end, dragging the metal hilt down her slit, listening to her husky moan as he did so. Then, with a wink, he coated the handle in salve.

∼

LILY'S BREATHING was quick and shallow, that much he heard as he opened the door. Then he saw her, arms over her head, bound by a belt, naked with Mal leaning over her. She whimpered as he murmured something Bastian couldn't hear.

'What are you doing to her?' Bastian growled, slamming the door and practically leaping across the room to Lily's side. He pulled Mal away from her. 'What the fuck are you doing?'

'Nothing she doesn't want.' Mal smirked.

Bastian turned back to Lily, trussed up on the bed. She was curled up on her side now, trying to hide herself from him, her cheeks crimson.

He cupped her face, making her look at him. She met his eyes, and though she was clearly embarrassed, she didn't look afraid or hurt. His eyes tracked a thin red welt that went from her neck down to her breast. Without thinking, he traced it with his finger and she shuddered. Bastian looked back at Mal, who was watching him touching Lily, his eyes beginning to smolder.

'She enjoys what I do.'

Bastian looked down at Lily once more. He could see Mal was right. Whatever he'd been doing, Lily loved it. He pinched her nipple gently, rolling it between his fingers as she closed her eyes and let out a mewl.

'Please,' she begged and Mal immediately sat on the bed next to her, taking the dagger he usually carried at his belt and drawing the sharp point down the inside of her thigh. Bastian watched her shudder and she sobbed, her body needing more.

'If it's too much, tell me,' he ordered and she gave a frenzied nod.

Mal took the sharp end in his hand and plunged the hilt between her legs. She let out a loud cry as he pounded it into her mercilessly, her hips rising to meet the thrusts of the object he was using on her. It didn't take long for her to climax, her arms pulling at the bonds around her wrists as the rest of her body tightened in pleasure. Her breathing stuttered and she screamed Mal's name, arching clean off the bed as he pushed the handle of the knife deep into her.

Afterwards, she went limp, her eyes lidded as she locked eyes with Mal and watched him let the knife fall to the coverlet as he eyed her core.

Bastian knew what Mal would do next, but he stopped him.

'My turn,' he said darkly, watching Lily's eyes spark in fear for a moment and wondering why she would be afraid of him and not Mal.

His Brother got off the bed with a flourish. Bastian took his place and descended on her core, licking her folds gently.

Then he heard Mal behind him. 'My turn as well,' he said softly, a sharpness to his tone that made Bastian shiver. After what had happened between them on the road – whatever it had been – the old tension between them had gone, but a new sort had taken its place.

Bastian hadn't even meant to do what he had. He still wasn't sure that Mal had wanted it, despite the sounds of pleasure he'd made during the act. But Bastian had hardly been able to help himself. Now it seemed that Mal was intent on evening the score, and he shivered in anticipation. Bastian had a feeling that this would be a very enjoyable experience.

His tongue didn't stop feasting on Lily as she pulled at her bonds fruitlessly, making little moans and whining unintelligibly. Mal unbuttoned Bastian's breeches and eased them down his legs to his knees and he let him. Bastian stayed where he was, though he couldn't remember ever feeling so vulnerable. He wasn't sure what Mal would do in retaliation for fucking him over that rock on the flats, though knowing his mad Brother, it could be anything short of death, he thought as he pushed Lily's knees further apart and felt Mal caress his bared arse cheek before delivering a stinging slap that made him growl into Lily's core.

Three more came in hard and he breathed through the pain of it, not wanting Mal to hear him beg for mercy. Then he heard Mal spit into his hand in an odd imitation of what he'd done to Mal the day before. But instead of Mal's cock, it was his fingers that drilled into his arse, making him grunt as his knuckles pushed past Bastian's outer ring with a pop.

This wasn't the first time he'd had a man's fingers inside him, not by a long way. He'd taken them many times in the past, in fact, both on the Mount and well before, when he'd lived in this realm and others. Like most gods, he'd partaken of all the carnal pleasures possible as much as he was able. But in that moment, he couldn't remember a single time that had felt as right as this one. Gods only knew why it was a lunatic like Mal that elicited such a visceral response in both his mind and his body, and as he tore his mouth away from Lily for a moment and saw her staring with large – and very aroused – eyes at what Mal was doing to him, he knew how she'd felt when Mal was working her over with that knife.

Mal began to pump two of his fingers in and out of him, making him squirm as his mouth returned to between Lily's legs, taking that sensitive pearl between his lips and sucking gently. He was rewarded by her fevered cry, her legs trying to close as she attempted to squirm away from him.

Mal chose that moment to slap him again. Once. Twice. Thrice. Each one hard enough to propel him harder into Lily, each one tearing a pleasured cry from her.

Then Mal's fingers pulled out. Bastian heard him spit again and then it was his thick cock that thrust into his readied passage. Unable to help himself, Bastian let out a guttural moan as his own cock pulsed and he ached to push it into Lily's dripping channel. The image of her beneath him, taking his cock as he took Mal's, sent him spiraling over the edge, his seed jetting from his staff onto the coverlet. Lily found her release again a moment later, crying out his name.

At her cries, Bastian felt Mal's cock throb inside him, and Mal gripped Bastian's hips as he drove in hard once more, letting out a moan of his own as he spilled himself inside Bastian. He pulled out, giving Bastian a caress that surprised him.

The floor creaked. Bastian's gaze shot to the door to find Quin there. Gods only knew how long he'd been standing in the room, staring at the three of them, the cold, unblinking eyes of the Commander watching them all. His face was devoid of emotion, but Bastian knew him well enough to assume there would be a reckoning for them for disregarding his order.

He looked down at Lily, hoping that she'd be spared. Surely Quin wouldn't punish her for this.

~

MAL FREED Lily's wrists from the bed as she shrank away from Quin's hard gaze. He wasn't showing much, but she could tell by his fists, clenched at his sides, that he was very angry – with all of them.

She shivered as she felt Mal caress her cheek with something akin to affection, though when she tilted her chin up to look into his eyes, they were as black and pitiless as always. His hand fell away and she curled up under the coverlet to await Quin's wrath, but instead, not looking at her, he spoke.

'Get dressed. The ferry is running.'

Bastian, still rebuttoning his breeches, grunted a response. Mal had already disappeared out the door.

Once the men had left her alone, she gathered her clothes, got dressed, and packed her small bag. Not wanting to be the focus of Quin's anger further, she left the room as soon as she was ready and made her way outside to await them.

That was where she found Mal, in the middle of the muddy yard with the saddled horses, staring up at the imposing fortress.

She stopped and looked with him. 'You burned it, didn't you? Why?' she asked softly.

At his silence, she glanced over at him and found such an abhorrent look on his face that she took a step back, realizing it had been a mistake to assume any closeness with him even after all he'd done to her, the things he'd made her feel. His hand whipped out and caught her elbow in a bruising grip that made her wince. Her eyes searched his as she tried to pull away.

'Let me go,' she demanded and, to her everlasting surprise, he did.

Then he shocked her further by actually answering her question with more words than she'd ever heard him utter together.

'My father was high priest here. My mother, a kitchen slave, died giving me life. Didn't know he was my da until the day I left.' He stared at the burned-out ruin once more before spitting in the mud at his feet. 'This place is pain and hatred. They got what they deserved.'

Not sure of what to say, Lily didn't reply. His hand went back to her arms and rubbed gently where he'd hurt her. He looked at her again.

'I'm not good. Don't know what you want, need. I'll fuck you. Give you pleasure, hurt you ... whether you like it or not.'

Lily's cheeks heated, his words sending a shiver down her back. She wasn't sure if he was trying to entice her or warn her away, didn't think he knew either.

She heard the other two arrive and Mal mounted his

horse. He hesitated and then held out his hand to hoist her up on his horse's back when an arm snaked around her waist from behind and she shrieked as she was pulled up into Quin's lap.

He quirked a brow at Mal. 'Probably best if she rides with me today.'

Mal smirked in response and clicked his horse into a gallop immediately, riding ahead of them to scout as usual.

Quin and Bastian kept their horses at a canter for most of the afternoon. They'd left later than usual, so they didn't stop for an afternoon meal, and by the time the day was starting to wane, she realized she hadn't eaten anything.

At her stomach's incessant growling, Quin finally produced one of the hard biscuits from his saddlebag and handed it to her without a word. She nibbled it slowly.

'You seem to need more food than anyone I've ever known,' he muttered next to her ear.

She was aware that this was probably the first time Quin had ever begun a conversation with her. 'The first few months I was with Vineri, I was very thin,' she began. 'One day, after a few weeks had passed, he came to my tower – to have a look at his acquisition, I suppose. He was furious when he saw. Thought they weren't feeding me. I think he had some of his kitchen staff taken to the hole ... His lowest dungeon,' she clarified. 'He had them bring me twice as many meals after that.'

'I thought he would have mistreated you,' he murmured to himself.

She looked back at him, giving him a weak smile. 'I suppose there are many ways to mistreat someone. I was useful to him. Part of his ever-growing collection of powerful artifacts. He needed me hale, but I'm under no illusions that he saw me as much more than a tool for his own ends.' She left it at that, the correlation between Vineri and the Brothers whose power she was now in, unspoken.

Quin didn't say anything more and, as they traveled on, she began to notice the land around them slowly changing until the foothills appeared in the distance. Kitore waited for them on the other side.

'How long will it take to get through to Kitore now?' she asked Quin

'Tomorrow, perhaps early the morning after.'

She nodded, trying to still her heart, which had begun to quicken. What would they want her to do there? Who would they want her to kill? She hadn't really allowed herself to think about it properly. It had seemed a long way off, but now here they were, within a day of the largest of the northern cities. The city she was from.

Would she remember it, she wondered? Would she recognize streets, gutters where she and the others had played? Would she see the places where they'd cuddled up to survive the cold? She swallowed hard, willing herself not to cry as she thrust those memories away. They were from another life, another person entirely, and she didn't want to think of them.

But now they were here, it would be impossible not to. She'd remember little Toman's blond hair tickling her nose as he slept in her arms. She'd think of— *No!*

She wrenched her thoughts away, thinking of the hills, how they were already almost upon them. That her fears of the open seemed to have waned as they'd traveled, or perhaps as she'd begun to feel safe with these dangerous sellswords.

They ascended the winding paths slowly, the horses seeming to already know their way somehow. Mal appeared in front of them for the first time since they'd left the inn and nodded, leading them off the path and into a small copse sheltered by trees. Here, a fire already crackled merrily and there was meat cooking on a makeshift spit. Mal had been busy. She could hear water close by as well.

'Stay here,' Quin said to her as she slid off the horse. She watched him and Bastian dismount and, as if by some unspoken command, all three of them left her with the horses to walk silently from the clearing. She watched them go, unsure of whether or not she should follow, but Quin had told her to stay and she didn't want to go against another of his orders …

She took the bags off the horses and unbuckled their harnesses, unpacked the bedrolls and put them out on the dry ground around the fire.

Sometime later, after the sun had set and she was beginning to worry, the three men emerged from the trees. She drew in a quick breath as they came closer and she saw that Bastian and Mal had been beaten. Bastian had a split lip and was favoring his right side. Mal's left eye was swelling and he was dabbing at his bleeding nose with the sleeve of his tunic.

'What happened?' she gasped.

All three of them looked surprised that she'd asked, or perhaps it was that she seemed to be worried.

Bastian grinned at her, even throwing her shocked face a wink and settling on his bedroll by the fire to pick at the meat, which was smelling done.

Mal didn't look at her, just sat close to Bastian and began to eat as well.

'They ignored my orders,' Quin said from just behind her and she whirled.

'You did that to them?' she asked, her mouth falling open in disbelief.

'It is the Brothers' way. When the punishment is needed, the unit gives it. They'd do the same for me if I'd done wrong.'

'Bu-but ...' she stuttered.

Clearly finished talking, Quin walked past her and sat down.

'Eat,' was all he said, and she did as she was told, plonking herself down ungracefully near to the fire just as they had and pulling her cloak around her.

As was their typical custom now, one of them gave her a portion of food, though she noticed that she seemed to have more than the others; not a lot more, but enough to notice. She gazed at Quin questioningly across the fire, remembering what she'd told him earlier, but he ignored her.

Tonight there were some peculiar stone-cooked flatbreads that she assumed Mal had made when he'd set up camp. She watched the men pull their meat from the bones and wrap it in their breads, so she did the same. She couldn't help the moan of surprise that escaped her as she took her first bite and wondered why they'd never made this before! All three men's eyes swung to her and she looked down in chagrin, focusing on her meal and trying to forget their stares.

When she'd eaten every morsel of her meal, she looked up to see that Mal and Bastian had gone.

Quin, still sitting across from her, jerked his head towards the trees to the left, where the bubbling of the stream seemed to come from.

'They've gone to get water.' He rolled his eyes. 'Probably to do other things as well,' he muttered, taking a swig from his wineskin. He held it out to her and she got up and walked over to take it, but he pulled it back and gestured for her to sit down next to him.

Once she was seated, only then did he hand it over, and she took a long pull, grimacing when she realized it was wine.

'You don't like wine,' he noted, staring into the fire.

'Never liked the taste. I prefer water.'

He let out a sigh. 'You should drink a little more this evening,' he said, finally turning his head to look at her. 'It'll make this next part easier for you.'

Her brow furrowed. 'What next part?' she asked as he stood.

Her mouth turned dry as he took off his belt slowly, watching her all the while as he loomed over her. The threat clear, the wineskin dropped from her fingers and landed with a soft thud on the mossy ground in front of her.

Giving a small cry, she scrambled back as he doubled the leather in his hand and pulled it taut with a crack. He followed slowly, stalking her like the predator he was.

'You're going to punish me as well? Like you did the others?' she asked, her voice high and squeaky.

'Not like the others. I won't hit you like I did them. But you defied my order. I must be obeyed. Your life may one day depend on it. So you'll learn your lesson a different way,' he said ominously. He crouched down in front of her, his hand flicking out to unclasp her cloak. It fell from her shoulders immediately and he watched her, his eyes taking in all the ways she was showing her fear, from her quivering lip to her shaking hands.

'W-what will you do?' she whispered.

'That depends on you, Lilith. Are you going to take your punishment like a good girl or are you going to run?' His hand raised to stay her reply as he continued. 'If you want to run, I'll give you a head start, but when I catch you – and I will – my lashes will be harsher.'

Her eyes swung to the side, staring into the darkness, and before she'd even made the decision, she was running through the dark wood, darting between trees and scrambling over the large rocks that, despite the change of terrain, still littered the ground in many places.

She was vaguely aware that the sound of the stream was closer and that she shouldn't have fled. She wasn't used to this and was already tiring. She slowed, trying to catch her breath as she picked her way through the brush in the twilight. Why had she bolted? He was going to catch her, of course he was! She should have just stayed there in the clearing and endured her penance. It would probably be finished by now if she had!

Miserably, she stopped behind a wide tree trunk and doubled over, panting. She heard a twig snap close by and startled like a rabbit, flitting from her hiding place and looking behind her. She ran slap bang into something hard and then his arms were around her, stopping her from rushing in the opposite direction. She screamed loudly and his hand clapped over her lips.

'Do you want to advertise our location to all and sundry?' Quin growled in her ear.

She shook her head and his hand dropped from her mouth.

'You shouldn't have run, girl,' he said softly in her ear and she shuddered in fear but also that other thing that she was beginning to learn well. Anticipation.

'I'm sorry—' she began, but he hushed her, tutting.

'It's too late for sorrys,' he said, taking her shoulder in a firm grip and marching her back the way she'd come. 'You shouldn't have let the fear of it get the better of you. I thought you would have had more restraint.'

'Where are we going?' she breathed.

'Back to the camp. It's too dark to do it out here now. Gods only know what I'd hit in the dark, and I intend to concentrate on one particular area,' he said cryptically.

'You don't have to keep going on,' she snapped. 'I'm already afraid. You don't have to make it worse.' She felt tears coming to her eyes and was glad it was dark and he couldn't see them.

'You're the one who made it worse by running. I did warn you,' he pointed out as they re-entered the camp.

The other two were still absent, she noted gratefully. She didn't want them to witness whatever Quin was going to do.

'Why did you take them away for their punishment?' she asked.

He chuckled. 'Don't try to stall the inevitable.' Then he sighed. 'I thought it might scare you if you saw me beating them and thought you'd get the same.'

'Yet you seek to scare me anyway.'

He shrugged. 'Take off your breeches.'

'No!'

'Do it or I'll do it for you.'

She held his unwavering gaze for a moment and then let out a shaky sigh as she unbuttoned her breeches and eased them down her legs.

'That should be enough,' he said tightly, something strange entering his tone that she didn't understand.

He sat on the ground, legs in front of him, and drew her front-ways over them. He pushed her down so she was lying across his thighs. Without preamble, he drew her tunic up, exposing her arse to him.

'Fight me,' he said softly, 'and it'll be all the worse for you, Fourth.'

With that, the leather of the belt came down hard on her backside and she cried out, biting her knuckles to contain the sound of her pain. His arm snaked across her back and held her tightly as he hit her again, and she screamed into her fist, tears already blinding her.

Again the belt cracked on her flesh and, to her shame, she squirmed and writhed, trying to escape its sting, but he held her down, not letting her move as he swung his belt into her again.

She was openly crying now, not bothering to hide her tears, past caring if he or the others saw.

Lily was begging as well, she realized, little sobbing pleas coming out of her as her body, which she'd always thought was strong, betrayed her. She was weak and her power had been a crutch easily kicked out from under her. She saw that now. She shouldn't be out here with these men. Someone like her belonged in a tower where she and everyone else was safe. Out here, she was going to die and none of them would care. She was as much a tool to them as she had been to Vineri.

Quin ceased his discipline.

She felt his hand on her arse cheeks, rubbing lightly in small circles.

Abruptly her tears dried and she wiped them from her face, sniffling, a hollowness enveloping her. These mercenaries didn't care about her, a voice inside her reminded her cruelly. She was naught but what she could do for them. As she had been to everyone save the two boys she'd called family. But they were gone now and she had no one.

She could pretend in that tower, make believe that Vineri cared about her because he made sure she was clothed and fed and had a roof over her head. But there was no room for girlish fancies here. The truth was that she was worth nothing to them without her curse.

'Is it done?' she asked in a small voice, carefully keeping it emotionless, though she felt like her heart was going to leap out of her chest and throw itself into the fire simply for some respite from the bottomless sorrow in it. The sadness had been there a long time, but she'd pushed it down and forgotten it. Now, perhaps because of Quin or the others or her proximity to Kitore after so long, it was there again, in the open for anyone to see. Perhaps it was a good thing that no one cared enough to look.

'Aye,' he said gruffly, letting her go as she rose.

Refusing to look at him, she pulled up her breeches with a wince she couldn't quite hide and averted her face, noticing the other two standing at the edge of the clearing and quickly turning away from them as well.

Had they seen? she wondered, feeling a dullness pervading her mind. Had they watched Quin take his belt to her, seen her tears, heard her pitiful entreaties for mercy? Did they see how pathetic she was now? Tears came to her eyes anew and she willed them away. Did she want them to have even less respect for her than they already did?

Unable to stomach their eyes on her, she made herself walk slowly to her bedroll and slip into it, closing her eyes and barely stopping herself from hiding her face under the cover like a frightened child. Her arse was on fire and she yearned to soothe it, but Quin hadn't offered her their magick salve, so this must be part of it too, she reasoned. Not much of a punishment if she could take the pulsing soreness away as soon as it was done. She closed her eyes and, luckily, sleep came quickly.

∽

QUIN SAT ON THE GROUND, his mind racing. He could hear his Brothers' angry whispers. What had he done? He'd lost control of himself, that was what he had done. When had such a thing last happened? He'd been angry with her since he'd found them all together that morning, he realized. He'd thought it was because they'd all gone against his orders, but it wasn't simply that. He was furious that she seemed to welcome their advances, even Mal's. Gods, before they'd bound her into the unit, his Brother would have killed her as soon as look at her, but how quickly she'd welcomed him into her bed despite his predilections. Though after what he'd seen this morning, it might well be because of them.

He'd wanted to show her what real pain was, show her that Mal was merely playing games with her. For whatever reason, he didn't seem to want to hurt their little Fourth, not really. Quin had needed her to see how weak she was without her power keeping them at bay. He'd wanted to prove how easily he could hold her down and cause her pain. Now that her body couldn't hurt him, he'd wanted his to hurt her.

The look in her eyes when she'd struggled away from him, averting her face in shame from him and the others. They'd seen everything and he knew she realized that because he'd planned it that way as part of his discipline.

They had gone to get water, that much was true, but he had ordered them away. Although his Brothers had already been dealt with, he knew they'd hear Lily's cries and return, yet be unable to do anything to prevent Lily's punishment. More penance for them as well as her humiliation in understanding that they'd seen her break.

He shook his head and got slowly to his feet, throwing the belt from him, the sight of it disgusting him. What had he done?

'Fuck,' he growled as he turned to find her huddled in her covers like a disgraced child.

His Brothers hadn't approached. Both pairs of eyes swung from him to Lily and back again. They didn't say anything to him, but he could sense their anger, their fury.

Quin turned and pushed his way through the undergrowth until he came to the stream. He fell to his knees on the gravelly bank and put a hand in the cold water. He drew it over his face. His Brothers were coming ... for him. He didn't bother to stand as they melted out of the trees close by, the two of them for once not at cross purposes.

'You hurt her,' Mal snarled menacingly, the tone making Quin's skin prickle.

'So did you,' Quin retorted, though he knew he'd done wrong.

'Different when I do it. She didn't like *that*.'

Quin sighed, getting to his feet to meet them head on. 'No, she didn't,' he agreed.

'She shouldn't have been punished for what *we* did,' Bastian spoke up. 'And punishment isn't personal. It's meant to be as fair as it can be.' He sounded calm, but there was an anger simmering under his cool expression that Quin hadn't seen in him before. 'But you took your wrath out on her, Brother. I saw the look on your face as you did it. That's not how you treat members of your unit, *Commander*.'

Quin inclined his head and stood his ground. There was nothing to say.

Surprisingly, it was Bastian who stepped forward to deliver the first blow. He'd have put money on it being Mal. It made him see that he didn't know the man Bastian truly was.

His huge Brother's strike to his cheek sent him staggering back and, dizzily, he fell to one knee. Struggling up, he regained his footing only to be winded by Mal's well-placed fist to his stomach. Bending over in pain, he tried to recover and straighten, take his punishment as a Brother should, without complaint. But he had trained for this, passed trials by combat and tests of his endurance. Lily hadn't, and he'd treated her as a Fourth the way that Maeve was a Fourth, he realized. Callan, Jax, and Seth loved Maeve with everything they had, but they would punish her as a Brother because she'd grown up in the camp, passed the same trials that he himself had.

Lily had spent years alone in a room. Her endurance was of the mind, not of the body. And tonight, he'd taken even that from her. How could he have done such a thing? He'd never thought of himself as an overly callous man, but he'd been crueler to her than Vineri ever had been. That thought sent him to his knees as Mal hit him in the face.

He vaguely felt the water as he fell into the stream, clogging his nose and mouth for what seemed like an eternity before one of them dragged him out and laid him out on the bank on his front to come back to his senses.

After that, they left him there in the darkness and the cold to make his own way back when his head began to work properly again.

It was still dark when Quin was able to stand, grunting in pain as he washed off the blood he could feel caked over his nose and cheek. He made his way back to the camp, threw some wood on the fire, and got under his blankets. Lily was in his line of sight. Her eyes were open and she was staring at him. Where he might have expected gloating at his own punishment at the hands of his Brothers, he saw only sadness in her eyes as she looked over his injuries. Her eyes widened slightly, so it must look bad, he thought, but she said nothing, closing her eyes again after a few moments of staring into his. The intimacy of it made him want to go to her. And do what, a voice in his head jeered, cuddle her? Tell her he was sorry for losing his temper? Too little. Too late.

He let his head fall back and stared up at the clear night sky, letting his eyes close.

The next morning came quickly and he awoke to the sun streaming through the trees as it came up over the rise of the adjacent hill. The others were just stirring as he was rubbing the sleep from his eyes. He stifled a grunt as he sat up slowly, his body protesting after the beating he'd received last night. Next to him, Lily had clearly forgotten what had befallen her as she rolled onto her back and didn't hold back the whimper that bubbled up from her throat when she put weight on the welts he'd covered her arse with.

He watched her from the corner of his eye as she bit her lip in an effort to keep silent. She got to her feet, not looking at any of them, and walked from the camp in the direction of the stream, her gait stiff.

The other two were still under their blankets, so after waiting until she was gone, Quin got up, grabbed the last of the salve from Mal's pack, and followed her. He wasn't sure what he intended, but he didn't like her wandering off by herself.

When he got to the stream, he stayed in the trees close by, watching silently as she cupped her hands in the clear water and drank deeply. She took off her tunic and washed her face.

He looked away as she took down her breeches and saw to her morning needs, but his eyes were drawn back to her as her hands lightly traced the welts his belt had left before she pulled them back up. She turned as if to go back to the camp, and he did as well. But out of the corner of his eye, he saw her stagger to the side blindly, bracing herself on a large boulder by the bank. He watched as he sank to her knees and began to cry quietly. Alone.

Whatever there was left of his heart broke in that moment. He had done this. And he had not the first idea of how to undo it. He turned his back on her, leaning against a tree and putting his head in his hands.

If she knew that he had seen, it would make things worse. She kept her thoughts and her feelings to herself. He left her by the water, making the short journey back to camp at a run and finding the others there.

They eyed him warily, though the anger he'd seen in their countenances last evening had been greatly diminished. That was the reason Army discipline was usually carried out within the unit. Everyone felt better after it ... almost everyone.

'She's by the river,' he said to Bastian, throwing him the salve. 'She doesn't want to see me this morning.'

Bastian gave him a hard look as he caught the pot. 'Fucking astonishing.' He walked silently into the underbrush, disappearing from sight.

Quin gathered his possessions, finding his belt that he'd thrown down last night and buckling it around his waist. He packed Lily's things as well.

'What do we have to eat?' he asked Mal.

'Fuck all.'

'Find something for her,' Quin ordered. 'You know she needs more than she lets on.'

Mal mumbled his assent and found some hard biscuits in the bottom of one of the packs just as Bastian returned, Lily walking behind him.

Quin noticed Bastian frowning as they drew near. His Brother looked pointedly back at her and Quin followed his gaze. Her eyes were cast to the ground. She didn't look up even when Mal handed her the breakfast he'd found, though she mumbled her thanks.

They smothered the fire and mounted their horses, Bastian settling Lily up with him. She didn't make a sound, though Quin knew how her wounds must be smarting. She still didn't look at any of them, holding herself stiff and straight as she rode with Bastian. They all shared a look as they began the last leg of their journey, slowly traveling up the final crest.

As the white spires of the king's residence and the Great Library came into view, he heard Lily gasp at the sight below them. The city was larger by far than all the others in their realm, a sprawling behemoth of whitewashed state buildings, the rest the color of golden sand.

They descended the last of the winding paths and reached the end of the hills, the trees thinning out as they rode, unencumbered, to the practically empty southern gate. A soldier leaned just inside the stone gatehouse, whittling a stick to nothing out of boredom. When he saw them, he stood to attention and shouted something through a doorway.

Another soldier came out, the black stripes adorning his red uniform indicating his higher rank.

'The pass opened, then?' he asked cordially.

'Not yet,' Quin answered, his tone just as friendly. 'We were ship-bound, but we wrecked off the coast. Came over the last of the mounts and through the flats.'

'Oh, aye? Lost a few ships this season, I hear. So what's a unit of Brothers doing up here, then?' The soldier hid any suspicions well under his mask of amiability, but Quin was anything but fooled. A whiff of anything untoward and they'd be in the deepest of the king's dungeons before they could blink. And they'd spend months there awaiting trial.

'We have business with the king,' Quin said. It was half true.

'At your service,' the soldier said with a flourish so nicely performed that Quin was hard pressed to determine if the man was taking the piss or not.

He nodded once as the soldier let them pass with a recommendation of a good inn – which they would definitely *not* be staying at. Once they were out of the man's sight, they veered off the main road and into the winding, cobbled backstreets, Quin taking a roundabout route and doubling back as Mal went in another direction, looping around behind them to ensure they weren't being followed.

They arrived at a nondescript door that looked just like all the others in the neighborhood. Quin got off his horse and knocked twice in quick succession and the door opened. An old woman poked her head out and he grinned in disbelief.

'You're here,' she croaked with a smile.

'I didn't think it would be you,' he said, surprised, and pulled her in close for a hug.

'Enough, boy, enough. You'll crush me old bones.' She chuckled as he squeezed her. 'When we got the bird that you were coming, I thought I'd sort things for you myself. I wanted to see you. It's been an age, boy, an age.'

'Aye, it has.'

'And who do you bring with you? I heard about Payn. I'm sorry.' She squinted behind him. 'Mal,' she greeted coldly. She'd never liked him, Quin recalled.

'This is Bastian. And Lilith.' He gestured to the old woman. 'This is Del, my mother's aunt.'

Del grinned at them. 'Come, come, I'll have one of the others see to your horses. Just leave them there for now. Probably get a fine for it, but,' she waved a hand as he turned and hobbled inside, 'get fines for everything in this city these days. Can't piss in the gutter without someone reporting it.' She made a sound of disgust from inside. Quin turned back to the others and watched Bastian help Lily down from his horse. She was looking around with trepidation.

He turned his back on them as he followed Del into the dark hall of the house. The front rooms were mostly for appearances. It was a small, sparse parlor in the back that Del led them to, with a few comfy chairs and a couple of tables.

'This is a safe house,' Bastian murmured to Lily from behind him.

Thinking about how worried Lily had looked, Quin felt the need to elaborate to put her mind at rest. She was safe within these walls and it was important to him that she know that. He'd chosen the house and not one of the other, more secure locations available to them in the city because of Lily. After last night, after their journey here and with the reason they'd journeyed north, he wanted to see to her comfort.

'The Army has safe houses in some of the larger towns and cities, much like the caches where we resupply ourselves when we're away from the Army itself. There are caretakers that look after them, get them ready for when we arrive. That's why Del is here.'

'Why?' she asked.

'When we're far from the main force of the Brothers, its best to have options,' Quin answered. 'There are other places we could go besides the houses that would be more secure, but,' he gave her a slow perusal,' this is the most comfortable.'

Quin sat, Bastian following suit. Mal ignored the chairs, instead prowling around the room, looking at everything as if he'd never been inside a safe house before. Lily eyed the chairs but stayed as she was, moving away from their group to stare out of the casement overlooking a small enclosed garden.

Quin frowned. He knew why she wasn't sitting down, but she hadn't shown any pain on her face since this morning either. She looked strained. Tired.

'Perhaps you could show Lily to her room,' he suggested to his aunt, and Del nodded.

'The boy will bring food and drink in a moment. Then, Quin, we must talk about the reasons you're here.'

He nodded and watched Del lead a more and more subdued-looking Lily out of the room to the bedchambers that were located up a narrow flight of stairs, if he remembered rightly. All three of them marked her leaving. She didn't look at them once.

Bastian sighed heavily. 'She isn't right.'

Mal snorted from the corner, where he leant against the wall, cleaning his nails with his knife, but said nothing.

'You talk to her,' Quin said to Bastian. 'After what I saw at the stream, I doubt she wants to be anywhere near me.'

'I tried earlier. She'll have none of it. Wouldn't say a word to me.'

'Mal?'

Mal frowned. He pushed himself off the wall, looking like a deer caught in the forest unawares. 'No,' he finally said, pacing to the other side of the room.

'You were the one who did it,' Bastian said to Quin. 'You must make amends.'

Quin threw up his hands in frustration. 'How?' he hissed. 'The reason we're here is to put her in a room with our enemies so that they die with no one being able to prove it wasn't an accident. Perhaps it's better if she's like this. We can distance ourselves.'

Mal made a noise from where he still paced and left the room, his feet not making a sound. Bastian was sitting back in the chair and looking thoughtful.

'No,' he said finally.

'No? No what?'

'No, we aren't putting our Fourth in danger like that. We need to find another way.'

Before Quin could reply, the door opened and a young lad brought a tray of refreshments. He put them on the table while Quin quietly seethed at Bastian, and as soon as the door closed again, he leapt up.

'You don't give the orders here,' he said sharply. 'She's not even a true Fourth. We only bound her for safety, and as soon as we're back with the Army, I will break it.'

'She was *Fourth* enough last night for your belt.' Bastian sneered. 'Do you truly believe I will let you unbind her? Do you think Mal will?' His tone was colder and more ominous than Quin had heard before from his usually jovial Brother.

But Quin barked a short laugh. 'I don't know what you

believe Mal feels for you, but he would as soon slit your throat if he could. Don't think to turn him against me. He and I have been Brothers much longer than you have been part of the Army ... wherever the fuck you came from,' he ground out.

Bastian stood, his presence making the room feel much smaller. 'I don't need to turn him against you, Brother. You do that on your own.'

And with that, he too was gone, leaving Quin alone to flounder, his unit fracturing at a time when it needed more than ever to be strong.

CHAPTER 10

LILY

The woman, Del, led her up a narrow flight of stairs, yammering on about this and that, the walls of the city crumbling on the north side because of winter storms, the taxation on seal pelts and blubber coming from the far north ice sheets. But Lily was only half listening, most of her energy going into staying upright after their morning of riding. She was in pain, she was tired, and, most of all, she was afraid.

As soon as Kitore had come into view, those great white spires shooting up from the ground like jagged blades that would pierce her soul, all she'd felt was panic. She was afraid she would retch. In fact, as soon as the woman left her alone, she feared she would lose what little was in her stomach.

All she could see in her mind's eye was that last day she'd spent in the city, when her sad little world on the streets had come to an even more tragic end. She'd tried to forget, spent years not thinking about them. But now she couldn't help but remember. Everything here reminded her of those days before she had changed.

The Brothers had asked her if she could remember

touching anyone before and not killing them. The truth was, she could. The day everything altered was seared into her mind with the clarity of a child whose life was destroyed in a moment, when the city was wreathed in bright decorations for some festival or another to some arsehole deity who didn't give a shit about any of them. And she remembered with that same clearness the first of many men she had killed. Except that he had been her friend, one of her little family. And he hadn't been a man at all.

'Did you hear me?'

Del was speaking to her, her brow creased.

'I'm sorry,' she said, trying for a rueful grin even as she wanted to burst into tears. 'It's been a long journey. What did you say?'

'I asked if you're their Fourth, child,' Del said quietly as she opened the door to a small, bright bedchamber with a comfortable-looking bed with an ivory bedspread embroidered with pink flowers.

'Yes. I think so,' she answered, entering the room fully and feeling a little more at ease.

'You *think* so?'

'I— well, it's a long story,' she stammered.

Del didn't look convinced. 'Well, I'll leave you to get settled. The lad, Jona, will bring you some water up to wash the road off you and some clothes to make you look like you belong in the city.'

She was gone before Lily could thank her, but she was grateful the woman had left her alone. She sat gingerly on the bed, winced and got up again. Bastian had brought her their salve this morning, but her backside was still bruised and sore, the raised welts she felt this morning sensitive and throbbing after their ride.

There was a tentative knock on the door and a boy of no more than twelve, Jona, she presumed, shuffled in slowly when she opened it, carrying a large steaming jug in one hand and a bundle of clothes in the other.

He left quickly, not saying much and seeming to be embarrassed in her presence if his flaming red face was anything to go by. When she'd made sure the door was closed behind him, she took off her clothes and washed the grime of travel from her skin, hissing as she pressed the hot cloth onto her arse cheeks, though the heat did at least loosen her saddle-sore muscles some.

She turned to don the clothes the boy had left and shrieked loudly as she caught sight of Mal leaning on the wall, watching her with a detached expression. She grabbed the dress and clasped it to her chest with a gasp, glowering at him.

'Can't you fucking knock?' she asked angrily.

He took a step closer and she stood her ground, furious that she couldn't even have a moment without one of them appearing to watch her or to touch her or to *beat* her.

Then he reached her, his arms came out slowly, and he touched her shoulders tentatively. He turned her gently – so he could look at the marks Quin had made, she realized belatedly. She made a sound of anguish, trying to twist away so he couldn't see, but he wouldn't let her go. She could feel his eyes on her and she looked away from him, feeling so pathetic, so ashamed that he could see what she was.

She tensed, afraid he would use her injuries to hurt her further. That was what he did, after all; he hurt her and she liked it. Except she didn't think she would at the moment, and even if she didn't like it, she was afraid he wouldn't care, that he'd do it anyway because he could, because that was what Dark Brothers did. She'd simply forgotten.

But he didn't grab her or stroke her or even touch her. He just looked, and when he was finished looking, he turned her back to face him slowly. He lifted her chin to look into her face and the anger she saw in his made her recoil.

Noting her reaction, his face softened. 'Won't let him do that again,' he said quietly, brushing his fingers over her cheek in a caress that, she was ashamed to say, had her leaning into him despite what he was.

He produced one of those pots they always seemed to have from his pocket and nudged her towards the bed. She went without a fight, letting him lay her down on her front. She gasped as she felt the cool balm on her skin as he applied it, being more gentle than she'd ever known him to be, than she'd ever expected him to be with her. She closed her eyes as the lids became heavy, his ministrations lulling her almost to sleep. Almost.

When his hand left her, she opened her eyes drowsily to find him sitting next to her, just watching her with a strange look upon his face, a calmness she hadn't seen before.

'Thank you,' she said quietly.

'Last night—' he began and she turned away in shame, curling into a ball with her back to him.

But he carefully pulled her back. 'My father had me beaten many times.'

She looked up at Mal, wondering at the kind of monster his father had been. But she let him continue, afraid he'd stop if she said anything or looked at him in pity.

'I know the shame of being broken.'

He picked her up in his arms and cuddled her. She gaped at him. She'd never have expected him to do this, not even in one of her fevered dreams after she killed.

'Quin didn't break *you*.' Mal smirked. 'You're strong.'

She looked down. 'But you saw ...'

'Hush,' he said quietly, gripping her chin gently and making her look at him again.

'Perhaps we're all broken,' she whispered, heaving a great sigh.

She leaned her head on his chest, listening to his heart. Until just now, she wouldn't have believed he had one, but he did. He wasn't deceiving her. At least she didn't think he was. Besides, what would be the point, she mused. She wrapped an arm around his neck and pulled his head down, hesitating for just a moment as his eyes widened as if he didn't quite understand what she was doing.

She put her lips to his gently, savoring their softness against her own. They were different from Quin's, but she liked doing this very much. This was one of the things she'd always wondered about ever since she'd seen two servants embracing in the square from her window once. They'd looked so happy.

She could have done it if she'd wanted, she reasoned. Killing men with kisses did sound wonderfully dramatic. However, most of Vineri's enemies had been the unsavory sort of characters a girl didn't want to kiss at the best of times.

To her surprise, Mal didn't seem very adept at it either. She drew back just enough to look into his eyes, which were open and watching her intently as usual.

'First one?'

He nodded hesitantly and she gave a small grin.

He didn't smile back, but his eyes were warmer than she'd ever seen them as he bridged the gap between them and put his lips back on hers. His tongue licked her lips and she drew in a sharp breath that had him invading her mouth shallowly. She met his tongue with hers, touched it and drew back with a laugh that bordered on embarrassment.

'I thought you hadn't done this before,' she said, feeling shy.

'Seen others do it,' he murmured, pulling her towards him more forcefully and kissing her again.

'Whenever you disappear, I find you two together,' Bastian drawled from the door.

Lily's eyes opened and she watched him, Mal's lips leaving hers to kiss down her neck, making her groan. Her cheeks heated, her eyes following his as he came closer. For some reason she felt even more vulnerable than she had when he'd walked in on her and Mal the other day when she'd been tied to the bed.

'Whenever we're together, you appear,' she parried and he gave a small laugh.

'Perhaps I know instinctively when you're having a good time without me,' he replied, pulling Mal's head back by his cropped black hair and kissing him as he'd been kissing Lily.

Mal gave a strangled sound and pulled away, his panicked eyes meeting Lily's.

Bastian frowned and, all at once, his expression changed to one of chagrin and then to wonder. 'There is more to you than meets the eye, Brother,' he said softly. Then he kissed Lily and smiled at her obvious inexperience as well.

'You two,' he gently mocked with a chuckle and a roll of his eyes.

Mal was looking at Bastian strangely, fear in the depths of his eyes that he was trying to hide. Taking Mal's hand, Lily interlaced her fingers with his in comfort. He looked mildly surprised at the gesture as he gazed down at their hands.

Then Bastian's finger tipped Mal's face up towards him as he stood over them still sitting on the bed. This time, he kissed him more gently, his hand caressing his stubbled cheek as he did so, calming him. By the time he pulled away, Lily could see that Mal's eyes were heavy as he lazily looked Bastian over.

Mal gave Lily another quick kiss and deposited her on the

bed gently before standing and prowling towards Bastian with purpose. Looking as if his prior uncertainty had melted away, he unbuttoned Bastian's breeches, slipping his hand inside to touch him.

Now it was Bastian's turn to look unsure as his eye met Lily's over Mal's shoulder. Mal looked up from his purpose, turned his head to gaze at her still sitting on the bed where he'd left her.

'What about Lily?' Bastian asked, still seeming to be a shadow of his typical confident self.

Mal smirked back at her. 'She likes to watch.'

Lily found herself nodding her head, eyes widening at the prospect of what Mal and Bastian might do. She had enjoyed it the other night when Mal had … done what he'd done to Bastian while Bastian's head had been buried between her thighs.

She liked to see that they were enjoying themselves with each other. She suspected that neither of them had felt much real happiness in their lives. Neither had she, in point of fact, but in the past few days, though she had been at times confused, they had both given her an intimacy and closeness that she'd not had with anyone. She cared about these men, she realized.

She watched as Mal eased Bastian's trousers down and commanded him to strip. To Lily's surprise, the bigger man did as he was told, his cock bouncing with every biting command that Mal uttered to him.

Lily gasped as Mal sank to his knees and licked the tip of Bastian's staff, making Bastian moan. His eyes closed and his head fell back as his fingers intertwined in Mal's hair, trying to direct his mouth to where Bastian wanted it. But Mal tutted and slapped his cock instead, making Bastian gasp just a little, though he tried to stifle it by biting his lip. Mal looked up knowingly and licked him again.

'Lily,' Bastian ground out, 'what you said to me that day at the inn about what you used to do in your lonely tower at night ...' His eyes moved meaningfully over her body, still bared from her earlier wash. 'Show me,' he half begged, half ordered.

'But ... what about Quin?' she asked, not wanting any of them to receive another punishment.

Bastian just rolled his eyes. 'Let us worry about Quin.'

She bit her lip and, wondering what she was doing – because she couldn't believe she was going to do this in front of them, notwithstanding her bold talk that night with him – she opened her legs so he could see her pink center.

With deliberate slowness, her eyes never leaving his, she ran her fingers over the folds of her core lightly, the sensation making her shiver. How many nights had she lain in her tower bed alone, yearning for something she couldn't name, a connection to another that she couldn't begin to understand, let alone describe? Had she found it, she wondered? Just because she could touch them and vice versa, did that mean she was destined for these men, even Quin? Or was it simply because they needed her to help them, and this – whatever this was – was just a benefit that meant nothing?

She widened her legs and caught Mal's eye. He'd turned them to the side so that he too could watch what she was doing as his head bobbed up and down in front of Bastian.

Emboldened, she shoved all thoughts of doubt from her mind and opened herself with the fingers of one hand, her other moving down slowly to circle the aching part of her that didn't want to be touched, not yet. She teased herself, watching the men as they watched her, Mal not wavering in his worship of Bastian's cock. And it was worship. The expression on his face was serene, calm, and with just a hint of determination.

Bastian's fingers were intertwined in Mal's hair, stroking

the strands, playing with them. No longer did he try to control Mal's direction but let the other man do as he willed. His breath was quick and shallow, his eyes locked on Lily's core.

Her fingers began to rub, just touching that still too-sensitive part, and she shuddered, easing a finger inside herself and then two, moving them in and out at her own pace. She heard both men groan and a small smile settled on her lips for a moment, knowing they were observing her, needing her to continue. Despite the strength of her curse, this type of power was much more heady, she realized. She'd never felt so strong as she did in this moment.

Her fingers quickened and she moaned as she felt her body tightening. She looked up to find both men watching her, Mal's mouth matching her pace so exactly that she shivered as she imagined what Bastian was thinking.

He threw his head back and roared his release, the sight of his pleasure and of Mal swallowing his seed thirstily sending her over the edge herself. She let out a cry as her muscles tightened and waves of pleasure washed over her abruptly, making her shake and wriggle. Her fingers left her and she fell back on the bed, panting and still, and feeling even more sated than she had in her tower after she'd done this simply because they were here to share that pleasure with her.

But not Mal. She frowned and made herself sit up. Bastian was pulling up his breeches and Mal was getting to his feet slowly.

She got off the bed on shaky legs and went to stand in front of him. She sank to her knees as she'd watched him do in front of Bastian, her eyes not leaving his.

He didn't move and her gaze flicked down to the bulge in his trousers uncertainly. She'd not taken control like this before. What if she did something wrong?

Hesitantly, she unbuttoned his breeches and delved in with her small hand the way she'd seen him do. She'd never felt a cock before and was surprised at its silken texture. She tugged his clothes down quickly and felt his body shudder. Alarmed, she looked up to find him chuckling. He was laughing at her. Holding back a wince, she drew back only to have him lunge forward and grab her head, forcing her back to stare at his cock.

'Lick it,' he ordered, dominating her as he had with Bastian, though his role was now reversed. He pulled her hair hard, making her whimper and wonder if she might not enjoy this at all.

But she did as he said, her tongue darting out to lick the tip of him and finding it salty. She leant back to look at him. Did he want her to continue? Should she stop?

With an impatient growl, he looped her plaited hair around his fist and pulled her back so that her lips were on his staff. 'Do what you saw,' he said softly, and she got the impression he was fighting his nature to be gentler with her.

She took him into her mouth, locking her lips around him, and moved down as far as she could, gagging when she could take him no further.

He pulled her head back gently and thrust himself back in. She braced her hands on his thighs, understanding that he had been in control when he had done this to Bastian and he had not relinquished it. In this room at the moment, he was lord and master.

She spluttered and choked as he pushed more deeply into her mouth and towards the back of her throat, her eyes beginning to water. She couldn't breathe!

She heard a rustle as Bastian moved on the bed, where he was watching from.

'Mal,' he said in a warning tone.

Immediately, the grip on her hair gentled and Mal's

thrusts became softer. She let out a relieved sigh, using her tongue on him and sucking gently as Mal moved in and out of her mouth. His breath stilled for a moment and his body tensed. And then he shoved into her erratically, his hand on her head not letting her move away as she looked up at him in trepidation.

'Take it,' he growled at her and she did, swallowing the seed that invaded her mouth as he himself had done only a few moments earlier.

Afterwards he let her go abruptly, his cock falling from her mouth. He rebuttoned his breeches and took a step back, his face unreadable. He didn't look pleased. She looked down, feeling exposed as she knelt naked on the floor.

She struggled to stand, wrapping her arms around herself, and heard Mal curse. And then he swung her up into his arms and his lips were on hers as he cuddled her like a babe.

'Thank you,' he said quietly into her ear and she grinned, her hesitation vanishing in an instant as he took her to the bed and laid her gently next to Bastian before climbing up to lie on her other side so she was in the middle of them.

Bastian's hands immediately began to massage her shoulders gently, and she groaned as he worked the knots from them. Mal's hand rested on her hip, doing nothing. When she looked into his face, he was simply regarding her with a blank look.

'What is it?' she murmured.

'Never known anyone like you,' he said quietly.

She barked a laugh that seemed to surprise him. 'I've never known anyone like you either, but I was stuck in a tower for a very long time, so perhaps you aren't unique at all,' she teased, and he looked startled.

She supposed most wouldn't mock a man who could easily kill her, but she found that she knew beyond any doubt that Mal would never hurt her now, not really, no more than these interludes where he knew she liked what he did to her.

'What were you thinking,' she asked, 'when I was on my knees and doing ... that?'

Fingers moved over her cheek. 'Can't wait to fuck you properly.' His other hand skimmed her bare belly as they traveled to her mound, but here they stopped, going no further.

'Why haven't you?' she asked, fighting the urge to shiver at his ominous tone.

Mal said nothing and instead it was Bastian who answered, still kneading her shoulders and back.

'The old laws say that a female Fourth is to be claimed by the leader of the unit first, then by the others. It strengthens the binding, the blood magick, especially if the Fourth is ... untouched.'

She thought about that for a moment. 'Females? Are there male Fourths too?'

'Sometimes. In the case of a male, it's slightly different, though. The unit can decide not to claim him that way, as it is only really necessary for females.' He made a face. 'Old laws,' he said by way of explanation.

She twisted around to look at him. 'So Quin would have to claim me? But what if I don't want ... what if *he* doesn't? He hates me.'

'If he doesn't, then we don't.' Bastian shrugged. '*If* we adhere to the old laws.'

Mal snarled at her side. 'Laws of the Army are followed,' he said darkly, 'or she could be taken.'

'Taken?' asked Lily, drawing back and looking from one to the other in unease.

'In the camp itself, other Brothers can take an unclaimed woman as spoils because the binding isn't strictly complete.' Bastian shrugged. 'But only if the Commander allows it.

Quin won't. It would fracture us, and he knows he won't last a day in the camp without a strong unit.'

Mal snorted and then murmured in her ear, 'Rest.'

～

Bastian rolled his eyes. He wouldn't have thought Mal would have such traditional ideas. Yet here he was spouting about the old laws. His gaze landed on Lily's arse and he found his brow furrowing. What had Quin been thinking? She was such a slight thing compared to them, yet his Brother had not drawn his blows if the marred flesh and bruises were anything to go by.

Mal saw where he was looking and caught his eye. His countenance was grim.

'He deserved more of a reckoning,' Bastian said.

Mal gave him a quick nod and then slid out of the bed.

'Going to find out the plan.' He sneered.

Bastian let his eyes drift over Mal. He was an unusual man, his Brother. Quiet and angry, but there was much more beneath the surface, and Bastian vowed that he would explore the many facets of his Brother. All he needed was time. Remembering the kiss they'd shared, he smiled slightly.

Mal might have fucked before, but he'd never shared affection or intimacy with anyone, woman or man, Bastian would wager. The man's lips had been as inexperienced as Lily's. He couldn't wait to show them more of the delights he'd taken for granted for so long.

His brow furrowed. The more time he spent in this realm, the more perspective he seemed to have on the mortals of it. He didn't remember being drawn to them so completely when he'd been here in his youth except for the occasional dalliance with the more beautiful ones. He'd spent much of his time in battle with other gods, beasts and mortals alike.

He thought on that for a sentimental moment. Simpler times. He'd been flightier then, though, and prone to letting his emotions get the better of him like many gods in those darker days.

Mal left the room and Bastian watched him go. He looked down at Lily, who'd closed her eyes, though he could tell she wasn't asleep.

'Did you like seeing Mal and me like that?' he asked.

'Yes,' she murmured.

'Why?'

Her lips turned up in a faint, sleepy smile. 'I like to see you both enjoying yourselves. I thought at first that you didn't like each other much.' She wrinkled her nose and looked up at him. 'That sounds ridiculous, doesn't it? We've only been traveling together for a few days and yet I feel as if I know you well.'

'Perhaps you do,' he said in spite of himself.

But Bastian didn't want to look too closely at whatever this connection was that the three of them seemed to have. He had come here with the intention of staying for a lifetime at least, but since they'd crossed the mountains to the north, he had begun to hear things in the inns they'd visited; stories of portal collapses, mortals suffering terrible afflictions when close to the open bridges. People vanishing, strange lights, dangerous creatures appearing where they'd never been before from realms much darker than this one.

He'd have put down at least some of the talk to gossip and scaremongering, but after what had happened on the ship, when that portal had opened under the sea and *that thing* had destroyed the boat … It shouldn't have been able to cross the breach if the wards were still in place. And there were so many tales of the same that Bastian was beginning to wonder how long this realm would last before it was overrun. Who would save it? Was Gaila powerful enough?

There had been twelve bridge collapses or outright disappearances in this realm alone in the past two years, he'd found out. Information that, oddly, had never made it to the Mount. What could possibly make the portals start to fade after so long? Why did the problems seem to be worse in the north? How could he protect his unit?

He glanced at Lily. He wouldn't be surprised if her curse was related in some way to these odd happenings. There was no way of knowing when they'd begun to occur, after all. The portals were the bedrock of the realms, as fundamental as the very air. Even the Gods didn't know where they'd come from. They'd existed since time was time, and the mere idea that they'd begun to fail … Bastian shuddered slightly. He couldn't even imagine what that would mean for this realm and the others. Without the portals, even the gods would be stuck in their realm on the Mount.

Gaila had wanted him to find out what was going on and why, as she hadn't been able to, but he had little idea of where to begin and, in truth, he'd expected the problem to be little more than some small oddity that was easily repaired. It was clearly much bigger than either he or Gaila had anticipated. He wondered if he should speak with Quin about it. As the Commander, he would surely have more knowledge.

There had been a stack of missives from that woman, Maeve, waiting for him when they arrived in Kitore. But, he reasoned, if he spoke to Quin, he would have to tell him the rest, and he wasn't sure he was ready to tell his Brother, his Commander, that he was in fact a god. He gave a small shake of his head. What would they make of that? What would Mal say? He got the impression that Mal did not look kindly upon the gods. And that was fair enough. It was rare for them to directly involve themselves in most matters. And when they did, it typically didn't end very well for the mortals involved.

He looked down at the woman next to him who, once more, had closed her eyes. He hoped that wouldn't be the case this time. He cared for her. It had been so long since he'd formed an attachment to another being, yet there was something about Lily that called to him.

He loved her smile, loved that light that shone within her. He loved her touch. He loved that she loved his touch. His cock began to harden as his thoughts diverged to more carnal imaginings. He hoped Quin would take her soon, otherwise he would definitely ignore the old laws and get there first.

He slid his legs over the bed.

'Something wrong?' she asked, not moving at all.

'No. Nothing,' he replied. 'But, you were brought to the north for a reason. Get dressed and then join us downstairs if you want to know why we've come.'

He donned his shirt that he'd left in a heap on the floor, taking one last look at Lily's bruised arse before leaving her alone and slinking quietly down the stairs back to the parlor where he'd last seen Quin.

Inside, he found both his Brothers sitting in silence as if they'd been awaiting him. There were refreshments on the table. He chose a small bun that looked like it had raisins or currants in it and bit into it, savoring the taste while outwardly pretending indifference.

That was something he'd missed in all the time he'd been on the Mount; not being in this realm of foods. Of course they had all manner of foodstuffs in the God Realm, every bit of it fit for the gods. But here ... perhaps it was because the mortals had such short lives. They were always inventing new tastes, new combinations.

The fayre available on the Mount was fine enough, he supposed. But the gods were set in their ways. They ate the same breads, the same cheeses, the same fruits and nuts. But mortals in this realm were artisans. Everything tasted unique in different regions, in separate towns and cities. Even within the Brothers' camp. There were men from all different corners of this realm and others, and the many dishes available there reflected that.

'Lily will be here soon,' he said between mouthfuls. 'Is there anything that we need to talk about before she comes down? We don't want to frighten her.'

Quin regarded him for a moment. 'No. She should know everything that we do. She's our Fourth, after all,' he said without a hint of irony. 'Besides, whether it scares her or not, it's safer for her to understand the importance of her role here.'

Mal's eyes narrowed. 'You consider her our Fourth now?'

Quin sat back in his chair. 'Yes,' he finally said. 'I do. What I said before …' He trailed off. 'I want her to be as safe as possible.'

'And if it's too dangerous?'

Quin threw up his hands. 'What is too dangerous, Brother? She's a Fourth with power of her own. She has us at her back. That's more than most who survive in this world have.'

'Mal and I, she has,' Bastian corrected. 'Does she truly have you?'

'She is my Fourth as well as yours.'

'A Fourth you considered expendable. What's changed, Brother?' Bastian countered.

'I—' Quin stopped. 'I don't want her to be harmed and I would only break the bond if necessary.'

From his place by the wall, Mal uttered a low growl, his intense gaze on Quin. 'You would unbind her from us?' He sounded almost frightened.

Quin nodded. 'If she wills it.'

Mal's jaw snapped closed and he looked away as if he was afraid of what he might do if Quin stayed in his line of sight.

'And what if she doesn't want to perform her tricks for us?' Bastian asked.

Quin's lips drew into a grim line. 'She must. What choice is there? It must be done and she is the only one who can do it.'

'Why can't we?' Mal snarled.

'We have spoken about this, Brother,' Quin said, looking tired as he drew a hand over his eyes. 'Kitore only stands because of the spells that protect it, ancient wards that prevent fire, floods, natural calamities. They've even repelled armies that have marched on its walls.'

Quin stood, directing his full attention to Mal. 'The king already knows we're here. No doubt we'll be invited to the palace tonight or tomorrow. If our enemies die in unnatural happenstance, we'll be the first to be thrown into the dungeons. Use your head. Lily's gift is the best way. The only way. No one will even suspect it's anything more than one of the maladies brought in on the ships from time to time.'

When they'd left the camp, Bastian had had no thoughts either way about putting Lily in danger. She'd simply been a prisoner with a use. How he could have thought such a thing was laughable, but now ... he looked over at Mal. His Brother agreed with him that Lily should not be put in danger, but, unless Quin changed his mind, there was little they could do at the moment. Some Brothers laws couldn't be cast aside.

'What do we know about them? This enemy?' Bastian asked.

'They're wealthy merchants of some sort who have influence in the palace and a driving force behind the witch killings as well. Between them, the king, and the Great Library, this city and half the realm is whipped up into a frenzy. They are throwing a celebration of some sort tomorrow night. I'll get more information from the unit we have in the city already, but that's all we have for now. That and our contacts here have made it clear that they're concerned by the dogma regarding the Army as well as secret talks with the king's representatives.'

'What is their dogma?'

'They want the Army disbanded and the Brothers executed,' Quin replied concisely.

'To what end?' Bastian took another bun from the table as Quin shrugged.

'We don't know the why of it.'

'You say there's a unit already here?' Bastian asked.

'Aye. They were seconded to the Great Library after they finished their education at its academy. Something Greygor put in place years ago to have eyes and ears here as well as access to the knowledge of the library itself.'

'Much good it did him,' Bastian snorted. 'Do we know nothing more? Who they are? Their numbers?'

'There are three of them.'

Mal, sharpening his knife on a whetting stone in the corner, choked. 'Three?' he asked incredulously.

'Three men who lead many more. Enough to be a problem for us if they join the king's forces,' Quin snapped, breaking off as the door opened quietly and Lily entered, dressed in the typical garb of a young woman of the city.

Her dress was a light green with white embroidered flowers along the collar, and her long hair was plaited down her back. She looked quaint and as innocent and beguiling as Bastian knew her to be. All their eyes roamed over her.

'Well, at least you no longer look out of place,' Quin commented, sounding bored and looking away from her.

Bastian almost laughed aloud as he noticed the bulge in Quin's breeches that he tried to hide. Quin wasn't as unmoved by her as he claimed. Bastian hoped that perhaps that would stay Quin's hand the next time he meted out a punishment to her. Discipline was a necessary evil in a unit and within the Army, but regardless of the Army's views on such things, Bastian wasn't sure he could stand the sight of Lily under the belt again.

Even Mal, with his passion for it, would not stand for it either. He seemed to only relish hurting her when she also enjoyed it, which, for a man with his reputation, Bastian found unusual. Gods, the man went on killing sprees. He murdered without conscience or thought whenever the mood took him, yet he seemed protective of Lily – and of him, now he thought on it. Perhaps he now saw Bastian and Lily as he saw Quin, that they were all indeed one unit – solid when their bonds with each other were strong.

Quin ushered Lily in and Bastian took her a goblet of water. She accepted it from him with a small smile before sitting down and looking at Quin expectantly.

She didn't speak and neither did Quin. He seemed to be at a loss for words now that she was here.

'When will I be needed?' she finally asked quietly, despondently, and Bastian watched Quin cringe almost imperceptibly at her tone.

'Tomorrow,' he answered, finding his voice. 'Three men.'

'If we cut off the heads of the snake, won't they just grow back?' Bastian interjected.

'There are no others fit to take their places, so I'm told.'

'Who are they?'

'Dangerous men who want to make trouble for the Army.'

'And you need me because of the city's wards so that it doesn't look like they were assassinated by you,' Lily guessed.

She was clever, Bastian thought. Quin underestimated her.

His Brother walked to the window looking out over the small garden at the back of the property. 'Yes.'

'And there are ...' She faltered before a look of determination came over her features. 'There are just three of them?'

'Only three.' Quin looked back at Lily, quietly surveying her. 'These are not good men, Lily.'

'Neither are you,' she fired back, and even Mal seemed surprised at the vehemence in her tone.

'I don't string people up and burn them alive,' he growled. 'Mal can take you to the northern wall and show you what they have caused, if that would make it easier for you to do what must be done.'

'You would do anything if you were paid to do it,' she countered.

'There are three men,' he said again, his voice hard. 'You need to kill them. There is a celebration tomorrow night in the city. All of them will be in attendance. You'll be disguised as a courtesan to gain entrance.'

Lily choked on her water at his words and he smirked.

'I'll be dressed as what?' she asked at the same time as Bastian and Mal exclaimed, 'She'll be dressed as a what?'

'What do courtesans wear?' she inquired faintly after a moment.

'Not enough,' Bastian said dryly, his eyes narrowing on Quin. 'What if someone touches her unexpectedly?' He turned to her. 'How many can you kill at once?'

'I— I don't know. Three was the most I ever— the day I was brought to the camp ... and afterwards, I was ill for days.'

'Don't like this,' Mal hissed while continuing to sharpen his knife.

Quin snorted. 'We'll have people loyal to the Brothers in attendance as well. They'll keep you safe while you do what you were brought here to do. Our concern is to kill the men that threaten the Army and our relations with the king, the men behind the burnings of the women outside the city walls.'

Bastian rolled his eyes at Quin's words, designed to appeal to Lily's goodness.

She set her cup down on the table. 'How will I know these men?'

'Likenesses of them will be delivered so you will know them by sight. There won't be more than twenty men there tomorrow, and they'll be away from the others, so you'll be able to find them easily.' Quin sighed. 'I know you're afraid, but their followers are of a number that, if they join forces with the king, the war will wipe out the Dark Brothers. If that happens,' he explained, 'the balance of power will shift to the north.'

At her blank stare, he continued. 'The portals up here are closing more quickly. Nine of twelve were north of the mountains. The king has his eye on the south, and the Dark Army is the only thing that stops him. We are two equally matched forces.'

Lily frowned. 'But he's the king. Can't he just ... buy the Dark Brothers?'

Quin shook his head. 'Believe it or not, the Dark Army has some scruples. If the king used us to take the south, it would be bad for business. Besides,' he added with a cold smile, 'the poor bastard can't afford us.'

'And if I do this for you, for the Army, what happens to me after?'

Quin glanced at the others, clearly not sure what to say.

Bastian cleared his throat. 'You are bound to us,' he reminded Lily. 'Where we go, you go.'

Quin frowned at him and then looked at Lily once more. 'I will give you enough gold to disappear, to be safe, and ...' he didn't look at his Brothers, 'I'll break the bond. You would be free.'

The knife Mal had been sharpening clattered to the floor.

Bastian's mouth opened and closed, but he said nothing, stunned into silence.

'I thought it was unbreakable.'

'Not by me,' Quin said softly.

Lily's expression gave nothing away for once.

'Very well,' she said, standing up and going to the door, her voice flat. 'Tomorrow, then.'

And she was gone.

As soon as the door closed, Quin turned to look out of the window again, heaving a sigh.

'You will not break the bond,' Mal snarled, pushing himself from the wall and advancing on Quin menacingly.

'She's stubborn as an ass. If that is what it takes for her to do this, I will,' Quin said, unmoved by his Brother's threats.

'You don't like any of this any more than we do, Brother. Why are we following this plan?' Bastian ground out.

'I can see no other way for the good of the Army … and for the many who are being killed here. Have you seen the outside of the north wall? Have you seen how many charred, shriveled bodies hang on the gibbets, their limbs cut away, their heads hacked off?'

'Many,' Mal said quietly.

'How long before this madness spreads more than it already has? There's already talk of it in the south, wise women being hanged in the forests, crones being burned in their houses by mobs of townsfolk.'

'What of Lily? If anyone suspects that she killed them, she'll be taken to the dungeons beneath the palace, tortured and killed. They'll hang her on the walls with the rest.'

Quin didn't answer.

'You may not care for her, but we do,' Bastian said in disgust.

Quin struck the table hard with his fist. 'I am the Commander for a reason. I must put any feelings I have aside for the good of the Army – and for all our futures now as well. Who else but us could keep the balance of this realm? You've been with our unit since midwinter. It's time you understood that your decisions aren't just yours.' Quin sneered. 'Perhaps we should have a talk about where exactly you came from, Brother. How you know so much about things that you shouldn't?'

'What do I know about?' Bastian airily scoffed, drawing back, not ready to spill his secrets just yet.

Perhaps he never would. It wasn't that he didn't trust them. But he feared the look on Mal's face when he discovered the truth – and Lily's as well, for that matter. How differently would they treat him if they knew from whence he came and what sort of a being he was?

Most worshipped the gods, after all, but out of fear more than anything else. Few had any real liking for them. What if they turned away from him? Would he go back to the Mount? Would he be satisfied with that existence now that he had had a taste of this mortal one, so much more vibrant and real than anything he had felt in so long?

He was changing, he realized. He was no longer a god of the Mount, but neither was he a mortal man. He was some curiosity, an in-between thing that had no place. He could pretend, if no one else knew, but as soon as they did, he feared that the bubble he had put around himself would burst, leaving him adrift in a sea of uncertainty, never able to find a home. He would have to leave this realm and roam the others, searching for an imitation of what he had lost here.

He shook his head. Had this life really become so important to him already? Before Lily, he had not had any ties here. And now he cared for her, and he cared for Mal as well. He looked at Quin. Even Quin, who was, in truth, part of his family even if they didn't share the blood of kinship.

'I've heard you asking about the portals at the inns we

visit. You soak up all the tales you're told,' Quin answered. 'Why?'

'Interested is all. Stop changing the subject. Lily doesn't want to do this. We should not force it on her,' Bastian said. 'Have you not noticed how hard she takes every death she causes?'

Quin leant back in his chair. 'We must all do things we don't like. She simply needs to realize that these men are not good men.'

Mal made a sound of derision. 'Neither are we,' he rumbled, mimicking what Lily had said earlier.

Quin shrugged. 'And that's true enough, I suppose, but since when have you cared? When did you develop this strong moral compass?'

'She likes me.' Mal didn't looked up from his task. He'd picked up his knife at some point and was rubbing it against the whetting stone again, though it was probably as sharp as it was ever going to get. 'Likes you too, Brother,' Mal drawled, finally leveling a look at Quin. 'Why she's sad you beat her.'

Quin looked surprised, whether it was at his Brother's previously unperceived depth of emotional knowledge or that he truly hadn't realized why Lily may have felt so betrayed, Bastian didn't know. His Brother said nothing.

'If you're truly going to go ahead with this plan,' Bastian interjected, 'then we must ensure she understands exactly what she must do, what these men look like, who would be best to kill first, where the guards are stationed, how she will escape. She must know where she must go after, which of us will meet her, and where she will go from there in case he is delayed or not there. She must know her way back to this house or the closest safe place.'

'Agreed,' Quin said.

'Where has she gone?' Mal asked.

Quin gestured out the window. 'She sits in the garden, safe for now.'

Bastian looked to where he pointed, approaching the casement so he could see outside. Lily was there, sitting on a stone bench, calm, and as serene as he had ever seen her. Birds tweeted. Flowers bloomed. It was quiet and peaceful. A part of him wished to join her, but he knew that if any of them intruded on her reverie, they would bring her anything but calm at the moment.

He cursed the fact that he had no powers of his own anymore, save his odd little quirks. If he could kill those men for her, he would. If he could make it look like an accident, he would. But he could not. 'Would that we could destroy the wards.'

'They're worked into every stone of Kitore. Such a thing would be impossible.'

There was a tentative knock at the door, and it opened slowly as Jona entered.

'This arrived at the Brothers' cache in the city. I was told to bring it here,' he said quietly, putting a sealed missive on the table in front of Quin. 'I wasn't followed,' he added before bowing slightly and retreating, closing the door quietly again as if he'd never entered in the first place.

Quin cracked the wax with his thumbnail and looked over the elegant scrawl.

'As expected, we are summoned this evening for an audience with the king.'

'Why does he want to see us?' Bastian muttered.

'It isn't an odd request for the king to want to see the Commander of the Brothers, especially given the unrest between us,' Quin replied. 'Make sure your clothes are clean at least. We don't want to insult the cunt.'

Mal growled from the corner. 'Fuck this,' he barked, and then he was gone from the room.

Quin rolled his eyes. 'I think I liked it better when that bastard didn't talk.'

Bastian chuckled in spite of himself, turning away from the casement and his perusal of Lily in the garden to watch Quin reread the missive from the palace.

They'd tried to change his mind, but their Brother still wasn't listening.

He turned and left the room, no longer wanting to argue so fruitlessly. Quin could see little but his own ambition. As he climbed the stairs, he wondered if Quin had always been thus. He suspected so. Quin was the youngest Commander the Army had seen in many, many years, and there was a reason for that. Quin was single-minded in his pursuit of the Army's agenda, and Bastian feared that anyone who crossed him, even if that was Lily, would pay a steep price.

In that moment, Bastian vowed that, if it came to it, he would find a way to get around the wards and kill Quin before he let that happen.

But for now he had to primp and preen to be ready to see a king.

～

They arrived at the palace without the pomp and ceremony they'd been afraid of, Quin taking the lead with Mal and Bastian following closely behind him. They'd unanimously decided that Lily should stay out of sight at the safe house to avoid scrutiny during their visit.

They wore the usual blacks of the Dark Army, but both their clothes and their persons were clean enough at least to pretend an air of respectability. The white palace gleamed in the twilight in front of them, the many torches resting in the sconces that lined the outer gate illuminating the open archways that had no portcullis. There was little ritual on their arrival, one guard appearing to take them into the inner court that, surprisingly, was deserted. Instead, they were ushered through a curtain at the back of the hall to a smaller, more intimate sitting room, where the king, a man in his late forties with thinning hair and a portly belly, sat alone. His two guards, posted at the nearest door, were the only other people in the room.

'Greetings, Commander,' the king said easily, not rising from his chair as they entered.

Although Quin had not expected the patriarch to show him such an honor considering the strained relations between them over the past few years, he would have expected, at the very least, some show of strength.

'Greetings to you, Your Majesty,' Quin said with a respectful bow of his head. He was Commander of the Dark Army and he groveled to no man, not even the king of the realm. 'Thank you for your invitation.'

'Think nothing of it, my friend. Please sit down. Partake of some refreshments. We have the finest wines brought in from the islands no matter the time of year.'

Quin sat in the one chair across from the king that had been provided. The other two stood behind him on either side. The room was tastefully decorated, the walls as white as the rest of the palace with accents of red, the king's color. The décor was quite sparse, which was most probably by design. The king sought to put them at ease, hence no display of force. Why?

'I was surprised to learn you'd come to Kitore. You're most welcome, of course, but what brings you to my city, Commander?' the king asked.

Quin waved his hand nonchalantly. 'Merely some business in the Ice Plains. After our ship was wrecked, coming through to Kitore was the best option before we travel on,' he lied.

'Nothing too pressing, I hope.' The king sat back in his chair and frowned when it creaked. 'A ship from Kitore's fair shores will, of course, get you there quicker than traversing the wilds north of the city.'

Quin nodded. 'Indeed, but we're in no hurry. We're simply tying up loose ends from Greygor's time.'

'Ah, yes. Greygor. My condolences on the death of your leader, though in truth I'd often wondered how much longer that old fool would stay alive. I'm amazed he lasted as long as he did. I had heard he was killed by his own. Is that true?'

Quin nodded again, as if it were perfectly natural that the king would know so much about the internal goings-on within the Dark Army. Someone was telling tales about Brothers' business. 'Unfortunately, Greygor was found not to be acting in the best interests of the Army. He was dealt with according to our laws.'

The king gestured to Mal and Bastian behind him. 'And who are these Brothers you've brought with you? Your unit, I assume?'

'This is Mal and Bastian.'

'My guards said you had a beautiful woman with you as well who was dressed as one of you. I was most intrigued.'

Inwardly, Quin cursed. This was the sort of interest they didn't need. 'Yes, our Fourth.'

'A female Brother?' The king looked astounded.

'The Army has a few,' Quin explained, straining to remain outwardly calm.

The king made a surprised face. 'Well, to each his own, I suppose. Though here in the north, we like to ensure that a woman keeps to her place. You didn't bring her this evening?'

'Regrettably, she wasn't feeling well after our travels,' Quin replied, keeping his expression pleasant. He knew well what places this man would have a woman. Slaving in his palace, bearing his children, in his bed, or dead on the gibbets outside.

The king shrugged. 'Ah well, that's to be expected, I suppose. But as to these two. That one.' He pointed at Mal. 'Hear he's unhinged. A mad killer, they say.'

Quin shrugged, a small smile playing on his lips for effect, but really he wished he could grab this cunt by his graying beard and snap his weak royal neck. 'Mal enjoys his work. He's one of the best in the Army.'

'And this other? Bastian, did you say?'

'Bastian took my former Brother Payn's place some weeks ago,' Quin said, inwardly rolling his eyes. As if the king hadn't found out as much as he could before they'd set foot in his palace. He knew their names and he must have had them looked into. If he had a spy in the Brothers, how much did he know about them? How much did he know about Lily? They hadn't revealed her power, but there had been rumors about her before they'd left. How recent was the king's information?

'And where are you from?' the king asked Bastian directly.

Bastian cleared his throat and Quin tensed, afraid Bastian would tell the king to mind his own fucking business just as he wanted to do.

'I was born in an obscure Dark Realm, Your Majesty. I journeyed to this one via the trade portals to join the Army as many do.'

'Indeed,' the king murmured. 'Interesting. Which realm did you come from?'

Bastian waved a hand casually. 'Just a tiny backwater sort of place.'

'Well.' The king stood abruptly, so Quin did too. 'I suppose I should let you get back to the beautiful companion I've heard about.'

Quin bowed his head once more. 'Thank you for your invitation to the palace this evening.'

'Of course. Of course. I do hope we can put the past behind us and step forward together. As you know, tensions between your army and mine have been strained as of late.'

'Yes,' Quin said, 'that is my hope as well.'

'Good, good,' said the king, gesturing to one of his soldiers standing at attention by the door. 'Have the Brothers shown to the main gate. Good evening.'

And then the king flounced from the room. They'd clearly been dismissed. They followed the guard through the great hall and out the main gate, the small door closing behind them with a bang and sealing them out of the palace.

'What a waste of time,' Bastian murmured, glancing back at the wall behind them.

'Prick,' Mal said.

'Lower your voice,' Bastian snapped.

'Why did he want to see us?' Quin muttered to himself. 'There was no point to any of that.'

'Perhaps it was simply to get the lie of the land, so to speak,' Bastian volunteered.

'Perhaps,' Quin agreed outwardly, yet he wondered if he had more to worry about from the king.

They went back through the city to the safe house, doubling back on themselves, looping around and walking in opposite directions to ensure they weren't followed. Quin did not want the king to specifically know where they were staying, especially not after his questions about Lily. He had seemed oddly fascinated by their Fourth and Quin didn't like it.

The city was quiet as they walked through the streets, though the hour was not late. They passed near the north wall. Quin could smell the many corpses that lined them on the outside, all those who'd been accused of sorcery and burned outside the walls. He'd asked Del about it, but she'd simply shrugged as if it was merely a fact of life, telling him she hadn't known any of the women herself.

But she had to have. According to Mal, there were hundreds hanging from the parapets, and no one in the city seemed to speak of it. There were no rumors, no tales of the people. Quin might have put it down to fear of the king, but it was more that no one cared enough to even speak of it except to say that they were witches who'd gotten what they'd deserved.

He glanced back at his two Brothers, their faces set and grim. There had been a time when Mal wouldn't have thought twice about what had happened here, yet it seemed to affect him in some way now. It had to be Lily, didn't it? She had changed him or awoken something in him that had been dormant before. She had taken some of his darkness from him – made him more human.

Quin didn't think for a moment that Mal couldn't still kill without remorse, but it seemed to him that his Brother was more able to resist his impulses than before. And Bastian had changed completely as well. Since they'd begun their journey, Quin hadn't seen the man pick up more than a glass of wine per sitting, whereas before that he'd hardly seen the man sober.

He also realized that he'd not seen Bastian with any women save Lily since the camp. Previously, he'd rarely been without one, different each time, sampling them like fine wines.

Quin frowned as he thought about Lily. He needed to speak to her privately about what had happened. He wanted to apologize. He should have before, but he was a coward where she was concerned. Perhaps he had no business being Commander if he couldn't even tell a girl that he was sorry for losing his temper. He had not looked upon her injuries since he had inflicted them, but considering how gingerly she sat, they must still be painful.

When they got back to the safe house and went inside, a box awaited them on the table.

'What's this?' Bastian asked.

'Lily's disguise,' Quin said.

Bastian pulled the lid off the box and whistled low as he pulled out a flimsy white transparent— could one even call that a dress? Quin's brows rose. He'd seen his share of brothels, but he hadn't realized quite what the courtesans in Kitore wore ... or didn't wear.

'She needs to look like all the others,' Quin muttered, more for himself than the others.

'Yes, but look at it.'

'Not clothes,' Mal said from behind them.

'She won't wear this,' Bastian muttered. 'She always covers herself when she's around others.'

'Gets upset otherwise,' Mal ground out.

'She's afraid of people touching her and you're sending her into the belly of the beast dressed like that? You may as well make her go in there naked,' Bastian said to Quin. 'If she's touched at the wrong time, she'll be captured and killed before she can even get to the men she's actually there to slay.'

'What do you expect me to do about it?' Quin snapped.

'We need to find a different way,' Bastian stated yet again, sitting heavily in one of the chairs. 'This. Will. Not. Work, Quin.' He emphasized every word with a fist, pounding on the table.

Quin threw his hands up in frustration. 'There is no other way. Why don't you understand?'

'We do understand, but you forget that Lily is not a Brother, not Maeve. She is a girl with a gift for death but no skill in it.

For this to work, we must have someone on the inside, someone that can let her in later, after the festivities have already begun. Perhaps then she'll have a fucking chance of actually getting to the ones she needs to kill,' Bastian growled.

Quin let out a frustrated sigh, but an idea began to take form in his mind. 'The unit we have in Kitore is coming here in the morning. They might know someone who can get inside to help.'

'They know where the safe house is?' Bastian asked.

'They're Brothers, aren't they?' Quin replied impatiently.

'Can we trust them?'

'If we can't, it's already too late,' Quin replied sardonically, turning to Mal. 'I want Lily there as well.'

His Brother nodded.

Quin scowled. 'Where is she, anyway?'

'Abed,' Mal grunted, and Quin heard him take out his knife and begin to sharpen it anew.

His brother seemed very tense. It wasn't like Mal not to be able to relax. Usually he was calm and collected, but at the moment he seemed worried, Quin mused as he left the room and walked up the narrow stairs. He paused on the landing, hesitating at Lily's door before knocking lightly.

'Come in,' floated Lily's soft voice from the other side, and he opened the door.

Inside, she was sitting on the bed, propped up and reading a book. When she saw it was him, he saw her shoulders tense.

'You need not be afraid every time I walk in the room,' he said. 'If I'm going to punish you, you'll know.'

Her expression became even more shuttered and he belatedly grasped that she feared being alone with him. He cursed himself for being the Commander. He hated that he had had to be the one to do it, knowing that she would despise him for it, yet it had been his fault that he had not reined himself in.

'I'm sorry,' he blurted out to her.

'What did you say?' she asked, putting the book down.

'I said "I'm sorry."'

'For what, exactly?' she inquired.

'I don't apologize for the punishment,' he clarified. 'It was necessary and the way of the Brothers, the way of the unit. If I make such a mistake in the future, I would hope that you will do the same for me to correct my behavior.'

Her brow furrowed. 'Then what are you apologizing for?'

'For losing control,' he answered. 'I don't know why I did. I was angry.'

'Angry?' she asked.

'Yes.'

'Because— because of what you saw at the inn,' she guessed. 'Because I was with Mal and Bastian.'

'Yes,' he said again.

Lily frowned. 'I don't understand. You don't even like me.'

'That's not true,' he said, his voice barely above a whisper.

'Isn't it?'

'No.' He rubbed a hand over his face in tiredness. 'I warned them away from you because I knew that I would not be able to … the truth is I don't know what I feel. But I must feel nothing. I'm the Commander. I cannot let anything cloud my judgment. I have a duty to my Brothers and to my unit that does not include—'

'Me?' she finished for him.

'That's not what I said. Don't twist my words.'

'I'm not twisting them,' she said, getting off the bed, 'but you're not making any sense. Ever since you found me in that tower, you have been harsh and cruel. I know that you don't like me, and it seems to me that you wish your Brothers didn't either.'

'I'm sorry that I've been hard with you,' he said quietly. 'I do like you. More than I should.'

His eyes moved over her before he could stop them. He took the box out from under his arm abruptly. 'This is for you for tomorrow,' he said, trying to change the subject.

'What is it?'

'I doubt you'll like it, but it's necessary.'

She looked at it in trepidation. 'It's my disguise, isn't it?'

'Indeed,' he said.

'Let me see,' she practically ordered.

He opened the box and took the garment out. She gasped, her eyes widening, putting her hand over her mouth.

'I can't wear that!' she exclaimed. 'Anyone could touch me. Anyone could ... and you'll be able to see all of me through it. It ... it's like spider silk!'

Quin grimaced. 'It's what they wear.' But the excuse seemed hollow in the wake of her shock.

'There must be another way,' she said, her words echoing the others'.

Quin exhaled deeply. He couldn't have this argument again.

'There is no other way,' he said, 'but I am meeting with the other unit tomorrow to see if you can enter the celebration later, after the revelries are starting. You cannot go in with the other courtesans. That much is clear. But there may be another way so as not to draw much attention to you.'

Her eyes did not stray from the garment he held and ... he couldn't help but imagine her wearing it. He watched her shudder. Was she afraid he was going to take his belt to her backside again in anger for making him want her?

'You need to try it on,' he said, his eyes moving boldly over her.

'Try it on?' she parroted.

'Yes. It must fit properly or the jig is up before we've even begun. Courtesans in Kitore are highly paid for a reason. They pride themselves on their appearances.'

'How will I know if it fits? I have no idea what it's meant to look like,' she said, grimacing at the offending gauze.

'Try it on. I'll make sure it looks how it's meant to.'

Her mouth opened and closed several times. In the end, he turned around, amused at her artless expressions. Though he hoped she could pretend better than that tomorrow.

Tearing the nightgown over her head, she practically ripped the sheer garment from his fingers.

'It's so soft,' she exclaimed a moment later, and he turned to find her running her hands over herself.

When she looked up and found him watching, her eyes widened. The gossamer of the long garment made her glow in the candlelight, the gold threads sparkling, yet that was not what riveted his gaze. It was the silhouette of her body, clearly visible through the silk; her breasts, her dusky nipples, her rounded hips, and the thatch of curls between her thighs.

'Turn,' he ordered, wondering if she'd do as he said.

She yelped, only just realizing what he could see. She covered herself with her hands, turning on impulse to shield herself from his gaze rather than because he'd ordered it.

His eyes roamed over her back to the base of her spine to her rounded arse, and he frowned as he saw the mottled bruises left over from his belt. He started forward, quietly moving towards her. When he stood directly behind, he put his hand on the globe of her cheek and heard her sharp intake of breath.

'What are you doing?' she gasped.

'Hush,' was his only response as he lifted the silk to get a better look at his handiwork. 'I'm sorry,' he muttered. 'I was very heavy-handed. I promise you that I will never punish you thus again.'

She moved away from him, not making a sound and not turning to face him.

'Please go,' she pleaded.

He took one of their salve pots from the pouch at his belt. 'Here,' he said. 'I'm sure you've used it since, but put it on again tonight.'

She nodded and he went back to his own chamber, disrobing at once. He sat on his bed, a goblet of wine in his hand and resting his head in the other. He felt such *guilt*. If he could take back what he had done, he would. He would have punished her a different way. There were many ways he could have done it, yet he had chosen the lash because it was easiest.

He shook his head, taking a long drink and wondering if she would ever forgive him, though he knew he did not deserve it. He had been weak, let his emotions get the better of him. He was a shit Commander.

Perhaps it was best that she didn't absolve him. He was making her do something she didn't want to do. It was him who was putting her in danger, and he could see no other way. For the first time, he didn't want to be the Commander. For the first time, he wished he hadn't worked toward this and that he could simply walk away. But he couldn't. There was no one to take his place. He was a fool, he thought, and, depending on what happened tomorrow, they might all pay the price for it. Especially Lily.

CHAPTER 11

LILY

Lily heard Quin leave the room and then she was alone. She stared at herself in the looking glass and unwrapped her hands from her body. She gaped anew at what she saw. The garment she was expected to wear truly had no modesty about it. How could she walk into that place in such clothes knowing that not only could everyone see everything but also that such a sight would make men *want* to touch her? She didn't consider herself vain, but the Brothers seemed enthralled enough by her form. Other men might be as well.

She thought back to what had happened in the pleasure tent in the Brothers' camp. Had that only been a fortnight ago? Her gaze locked on the door where Quin had exited. The way he had looked at her … It was the same expression that she'd seen on his face when he'd caught her in the forest before he had taken the strap to her. Would he do it again, she wondered, or would he do something else instead? He wanted her. She could see it in his eyes. But he hated her regardless of what he said to the contrary, didn't he?

She gave a sigh. She was so confused. How could a man

KEPT TO KILL

hate her and yet still find her appealing enough for *that*? She continued to gaze at herself in the mirror, trying to see what he saw. All three of the men seemed to enjoy her appearance. She'd never thought much upon it herself. No one had ever remarked upon her looks while she'd been kept in the tower. And when she was paraded out, most refused to look at her because they feared her power. So Vineri was the only one who had ever met her eyes when he spoke to her. And he – she snorted – he'd not been interested in women anyway, so he had never watched her with any hunger in his eyes.

But these three Brothers; they seemed to stare into her. It was as if she truly was important to them – not just her power, but *her* – and she didn't understand it. There was nothing to her. There was nothing important about her save the power they needed, save what she could do for them. And yet ... she looked down at the floor. Perhaps it *was* just convenience. They'd been on a journey. There hadn't been many women at the inns they'd stayed at. Perhaps she merely scratched an itch.

She frowned, staring into her own eyes. The thought sent her spirits plummeting. Why she should be concerned what these three men thought of her she didn't know. But she did care. How pathetic she was.

You threw yourself at the first three men you could, she thought. *Yes, because they could touch you*, the other side of her said. *You've never had that before. It's new and exciting.*

She thought about Mal and Bastian's hands on her, the way they made her feel. Her stomach fluttered and she wished they were here. She wondered what they would think of this disguise she was meant to wear on the morrow. Would they like it, she wondered? Or would they see her as little more than a woman whose services were bought and paid for? She grimaced. That was what Quin had offered, wasn't it? She killed these three men and he released her from the binding and let her live out her life in peace ... with gold. Couldn't forget the gold. She was little better than a mercenary. Perhaps she really was one of them. Perhaps she was meant to be their Fourth.

Glancing back towards the door, she ran her hands down the flimsy silk once more. If it wasn't for being so completely transparent, she would quite enjoy it. She'd never felt something so soft next to her skin. The way it glided across her body, she liked it. So had Quin.

She had thought that perhaps Quin might not leave when she asked. She'd wanted him to, of course. But there was another part of her that had sort of wished he had stayed, perhaps pushed her down on the bed and done some of the things with her that Bastian and Mal had already done.

What was it Bastian had said – that they couldn't take her properly unless Quin did first? She wondered if he would. She wondered if she would try to stop him if he did. She wouldn't, she realized, for she was as drawn to him as she was the other two. She just hadn't wanted to admit it because of how he'd treated her.

She remembered those first hours in his tent when he had invited that man, that Rat, to attack her. Bite her. Then she thought of what he'd done afterwards, rubbing the salve into the wound, and she shivered. Though he had humiliated her in that moment, she had wanted him to do more then as well.

What sort of lover would Quin be? What sort did she want? When she'd naïvely thought of such things in her tower late at night, she had never imagined she would enjoy a man hurting her as Mal did, being so forceful with her, tying her up, making her spread her legs and holding her immobile as he did whatever he liked. Her breathing quickened. She did like these things. She didn't know why she liked them, but she did. The thoughts she used to have back in her tower of sensuous, courtly, gentle lovers had been all but abandoned. Those thoughts did not make her feel the same pleasures, the same flutterings, as her memories of Bastian and Mal did.

Before she knew what she was doing, her hand was on the latch and she opened the door. She knew where Quin's room was. She stole through the hall, bare feet making nary a sound on the floorboards, to Quin's bedchamber. She didn't knock and was grateful that he had not locked the door when it opened easily and she slipped inside his room.

She let the door close with a small sound and saw that he was sitting on his bed, his head in his hands, drinking wine. He looked up when she came in, and his eyes widened.

'What are you doing here?' he asked.

'I don't really know,' she said, moving towards him slowly.

'You should leave,' he said aloud, yet his eyes pleaded with her to stay.

'I know that I should,' she replied, 'but I don't think that I can.'

She came to a stop in front of him and he looked up into her eyes.

'Do you understand what will happen if you don't leave?' he said quietly, his voice containing just a hint of steel, as if he battled himself not to simply grab her. He put his goblet down slowly, his hands shaking slightly, she noticed, but he did not make a move to touch her. 'This is your last chance,' he said.

'What will you do?' she asked, fearing and anticipating his answer in equal measure.

'What I've been wanting to do since I saw you in that tower,' he replied smoothly.

Her breath caught. Perhaps he didn't hate her after all.

'What if I try to stop you?'

He snorted. 'As if you could.'

In one swift motion, he grabbed the garment she wore and drew it over her head. She stifled a gasp at his sudden movements but raised her arms so he could take it off her, forcing herself not to back away. His hands moved up her arms and came to rest on her shoulders. He caressed her neck lightly, tilting her head up, and then his lips met hers so gently that she wondered if perhaps he would be a slow and sensual lover after all.

But then his fingers entwined in her hair, keeping her head still for him as he began to ravage her lips harder. She whimpered as his stubble grazed her face and he growled low in his throat as his tongue slipped past hers. She mimicked what he did, touching her tongue to his and enjoying the taste of him.

She was on her back on his bed before she knew quite what had happened and he crouched over her, continuing to kiss her mouth and then her cheek and then her neck, moving down and down until he took her breasts in his hands, kneading them gently, twisting her nipples just enough to make her cry out and arch into him.

'You want this, don't you?' he whispered. 'You've known you were mine since the beginning.'

'Yes,' she cried.

'Why do you want me?'

She cupped his face with her hands. 'Perhaps it's the bond,' she said, and his eyes flashed with something. Unease?

'Perhaps.'

He lowered his head and drew his tongue in a circle around her nipple before nipping it gently, and she shivered. He bent down to her navel, licking it and making her squirm as he chuckled. And then his mouth was on her core, her thighs in his grip as he opened her to him fully. He licked her folds with the flat of his tongue, drawing whimpers from her that she tried to smother with her hand.

KEPT TO KILL

She wasn't sure why she wanted to keep quiet. Perhaps she was afraid the others would hear. She didn't want them to come, she realized. Not for this. This was just between her and Quin, and she wanted them to be alone for it. Whatever it was. He spread her thighs wider, his tongue dipping into her channel, and she bit back a cry, aching for more.

'Is this not enough for you?' he taunted from between her legs.

She met his eyes and shook her head, her body hot and feverish and growing increasingly frustrated.

'What is it that you want?' he growled low.

'You,' she said simply.

'Would you beg for it?' he asked. His eyes were hard, but she also saw fear in them. He was trying to make her pull away. He was afraid.

'I will beg if you wish me to,' she said breathlessly, not above pleading for what she needed from him.

He looked surprised before his head descended once more and he began to draw his tongue over the apex of her thighs. Over and over again he licked it, laved it until she was writhing and moaning, unable to keep still beneath him, unable to form a coherent thought. He made a noise of contentment as he drew back.

'Don't stop,' she snarled and he laughed.

'I'm the Commander here,' he said quietly, his smoldering eyes surveying her beneath him. 'You're but the girl in the village about to be ravaged. And when I'm finished, you'll beg me for more.'

Her eyes met his in challenge. 'Do you think so?'

He moved over her, capturing her wrists and putting them over her head.

'Yes,' he growled, positioning himself at her entrance.

She stared into his dark eyes, afraid as she felt him *there*. But instead of the harsh deflowering that she had anticipated, he moved slowly. A bit at a time, he let her tight channel become accustomed to the intrusion of what she thought must be the largest cock ever felt by a woman in the history of the realm. Although, considering that she had never felt a cock there before, perhaps it only felt that way, she conceded.

She panted, already feeling full, though he seemed as if he was hardly in at all. She recoiled slightly. He was still watching her face, she realized, and she looked back at him. His lips met hers and he thrust forward.

She cried out as he buried himself in her to the hilt and then he stilled, propping himself up on his hands over her. In his eyes, she could see a mixture of awe and something else she couldn't name.

She felt embarrassed and wanted to look away, but he wouldn't let her.

'Have you ever done this before?' she whispered. She thought he might laugh at her, but he remained somber.

'No,' he said. 'Not with a maid.'

She swallowed hard, biting her lip to keep it from quivering, all at once feeling as if she might cry, though she didn't know why. An unexpected tenderness appeared in his expression.

'What is it?' he asked. 'Already wishing you'd left when you had the chance?'

'I don't know,' she said. 'I thought you hated me and now … I don't know.'

'I don't hate you,' he said.

He kissed her again slowly as he pulled out of her, and she took a breath as he eased himself back in again, her channel conforming to his size, though it felt uncomfortable still. But she found if she thought about the hurt that Mal enjoyed inflicting on her, it made her pulse beat wildly and made what Quin was doing feel more enjoyable.

Each thrust began to make her keen in pleasure, made her clench and tingle.

'You like that,' he whispered, and she nodded. He drove into her harder, making her brace herself against the headboard so that she didn't hit her head upon it with the force his body moved against hers.

'On your knees,' he ordered, pulling out of her, and when she turned to do as he bid, he pushed her down on her haunches.

She cried out as he entered her from behind, grasping her hips, and he moved harder, faster. He didn't hurt her, not really, but his actions were animalistic, carnal – as if he could no longer hold back his need for her body. She whimpered and moaned with every thrust as he filled her completely. He spread her legs wider, giving him more access to her. His hand reached around to the bud that longed for his touch. He was not gentle as he began to play with her as if she were an instrument, and considering the noises he was eliciting from her, perhaps that was somewhere near the truth.

The pleasure that had been building cascaded through her so intensely that she found she could not make a sound, her breath frozen in her chest. Her mouth open, she struggled through the sensations his body was giving hers.

And then he grabbed her hips and dragged her to him. One. Final. Hard. Thrust. He emptied himself inside her with a howl that sounded more wolf than man.

He rolled off Lily to lie beside her, breathing heavily. She watched him, wondering what would happen now. Would he make her leave? Would he turn on her now that she had given him what he had wanted, what they'd both wanted?

In truth, she was afraid that he would pull away from her. He said he didn't hate her, but that meant little. She'd asked for no assurances and he'd given her none. Perhaps she should simply be glad that they had been able to give each other some moment of respite and pleasure. Perhaps that was all any of them could hope for.

She made to get up, but he grabbed her wrist and pulled her back.

'Stay here,' he growled and got off the bed, walking over to the washbasin on the other side of the room.

He came back to the bed a moment later with a small square of damp muslin. In slow, methodical movements, he drew it between her thighs, his ministrations gentling as she gasped.

'Thank you,' she said.

He said nothing, continuing his attentions until he had wiped away all traces of his seed before lying down beside her.

'What happens now?' she asked.

'Sleep,' he said, drawing the coverlet over her.

'In here with you?'

'Yes.'

He took her in his arms, cuddling her, and she realized her fingers were drifting over the muscles of his chest, his broad shoulders and his thick arms, tracing that intricate tattoo he bore. Somehow, this felt even more intimate. She felt a tear slip from her closed eyelid. She hoped he didn't notice. But then she felt his fingertip follow the tear's trail. She didn't look at him.

'Do you regret it already?' he asked.

'No,' she murmured. 'It's just that I've never had this. I've never felt this before.'

'You've never been held.' It was a statement, not a question.

'Who would hold me?' she asked.

'Not your mother?'

'I don't remember my mother,' she said. 'My earliest memories are of this city.'

'Kitore?' He sounded surprised.

'Yes. Vineri took me from here when I was a child. Before that tower, my home was on these streets with the others.'

'Others?'

'The other children,' she elaborated. 'Did you know your mother?'

'Yes.'

'Where is she?'

'Dead now,' he replied without emotion.

'And your father?'

'I never knew him. He was a lowly soldier in the Dark Army. They met when he traveled through her village, and they fell in love, but by the time I was born, he was dead. She joined the camp when I was still a child.'

'What did she do in the camp?'

'She was a seamstress and a wise woman who was good with herbs.'

Lily frowned. 'I didn't realize people ... just joined.'

'Yes,' Quin said. 'It happens all the time. If they prove themselves to be useful, they are taken in. The Army can always use a healer, so she was welcomed gladly and I grew up in the camp. I became a soldier and then I went through the trials to become a Brother.'

'And then you became the Commander,' she said.

'Yes. I worked towards it for most of my life.'

'But why did you want it?' she questioned. 'What little I heard of the Army made me believe that you're all bloodthirsty mercenaries, a plague on the land.'

'A necessary one,' he said amusedly, 'I think you'll find.'

'Why? Do you do anything else?'

'We help to keep the balance of power.'

'I thought that's what the Brothers used to do, but surely now you're just a group of mercenaries trading coin for services.'

'Sometimes,' he said. 'There are many of us and we must eat.'

'But once the Dark Brothers had a different purpose, didn't they?' she asked.

'How do you know that?'

'Vineri had a library of books and all I had was time to read. I know many things about the history of our realm.'

Quin looked at her with a newfound respect. 'There's more to you than meets the eye.'

'Thank you. I think.' She chuckled.

'We were once considered to be sentinels of our realm and the others.'

'Why no longer?'

'Things change. Sentinels were needed no more.' He shrugged.

'And your mother? What did she think of your plans?' she asked him.

'It was her idea at first. She joined the camp in order for me to have a chance.'

'Do you miss her?'

He nodded. 'She was a good woman. A hard woman, but a good one. Much like Del,' he clarified. 'She and two of her cousins also joined the Army.'

'And where are they now?'

'My two cousins became soldiers. They were killed not long after my mother died.'

'I'm sorry,' she said.

He shrugged again. 'We weren't close. Once we joined the Army, I had no time for them.'

She was silent for a few moments, thinking that this man wasn't close to anyone and hadn't been since his mother died. Maybe they were more alike than she'd imagined.

The door opened and she gasped, diving under the blanket. It closed with an abrupt bang and then a heavy silence spread through the room.

'You've done it, then,' came Bastian's voice through the cloth, and she peeked out from the covers to find both Bastian and Mal standing in the room. What were they doing in here? Had they known she was here? Perhaps they were just here to speak to Quin, who, still lying next to her on the bed outside the blanket, had not bothered to cover his naked body, just lay propped up on one side, watching them with a satisfied smirk on his face.

'She came to me,' he said. 'Begged me. Didn't you?'

Lily glanced up at him in apprehension. His voice was different now. Colder. The man who had been so tender with her, gone.

'Yes,' she said, meeting his eyes and was gratified by the shock she saw in them. He would not make her cower or feel ashamed. 'Though he did ask me to beg him,' she continued, her gaze not wavering from his.

Emboldened, she shook the blanket off and got out of the bed, not covering herself. They'd all seen her before, after all. She grabbed the garment she should be wearing tomorrow and pulled it over her head, though it did nothing to hide her nudity.

Without another word, she left the room, though once she closed the door she didn't move, covering her mouth with her hand and wondering if she'd made a foolish mistake by going to Quin.

'What was that about?' she heard Bastian's muffled voice ask.

She didn't hear Quin reply. Mal growled something and the door was flung open. She squealed in surprise at Bastian and he gave her a foreboding look, pulling her back inside.

'Did you forget what happened the last time we found you eavesdropping?'

Lily shook her head. Her earlier courage had fled and she felt the urge to cover herself. But she resisted. She would not show weakness now before them.

She didn't look at Quin. She felt the sting of his betrayal again, worse now, and she didn't understand why she was surprised by it. Though she was also confused by his abrupt indifference. What had she done? He'd turned on her when the other two had arrived. What was it about them that made him change so?

'How did you know she was here?' Quin asked the other two.

Bastian gave Quin a look. 'How could we not?'

Mal started towards her, his eyes roaming freely over the gossamer silk. He met her eyes and she took a step backwards reflexively. She knew he wouldn't hurt her. Not really. But she was still afraid as a doe fears the wolf even when it's not hungry.

'I like this in here,' he murmured, fingering the material at her shoulder. Then his eyes became hard as he turned back to Quin, 'but not out there.'

'This is about tomorrow,' Quin said, running a hand through his hair. 'You aren't angry that I ...'

Mal shrugged, eyeing her again. 'Not angry. We all know the laws.'

Lily shivered, understanding what he meant, that she was fair game now according to the Brothers' rules. She backed towards the door.

Bastian's head swung toward her and he laughed. 'Bit late for shyness. Besides, this includes you, Lily.' His eyes locked on her chest and he licked his lips. She waited for him to pounce, but instead, he looked back at Quin.

'I agree with what Mal says. That dress is dangerous. She cannot wear that tomorrow.'

Quin shook his head. 'What else is she going to wear?

KEPT TO KILL

How else can she get into the house? There are no maids. There are only courtesans and men.'

'It's all right,' she said, looking down at herself and making the decision that needed to be made. 'I will do it.' She looked back at Quin. 'So long as our deal still stands,' she said to him, her tone as cold and level as his had been.

'It stands,' he confirmed and she nodded.

'Very well. I will kill these three men and then I am free of you.' She couldn't meet the others' eyes. This was best. 'All of you.'

She turned and this time no one tried to stop her as she left the room, walking quickly back to hers. She closed the door to her chamber slowly and then leant against it, tears flooding her eyes. She was a fool, she thought, dashing them away. She needed to escape these men, their emotions, their needs, their games. She was not equipped for this turmoil they made her feel.

What had she been thinking, she wondered. What had she imagined she could have with them? She hadn't thought, she realized. She had been seduced by their touches, their gazes, the things she'd never had before. Things she knew now she didn't want, because this path only led to heartbreak. They didn't care for her, she reminded herself. How could they? She was a monster. A killer. The only thing that she was good at was the thing that would get her killed and put on one of those gibbets.

She carefully removed the dress. Didn't want to rip it, she thought bitterly, draping it over the chair. She put her thick nightgown back on, got into the bed, and closed her eyes. But sleep would not come, and all she could think of was the first night in the fortress with Mal. Then, later, with Bastian and him. The things they'd done, the things they'd made her feel. And not just her body; in her heart and in her mind. They were glad that Quin had fucked her, for now they could as well. She was their own private courtesan that they passed around between them, a convenient diversion that no one else had had before. By the time they were finished with her and Quin broke the binding, gods only knew what would be left of her.

Where would she go, she wondered, after all of this was done? Would she travel to the islands? No, there were too many people there. She needed somewhere alone where there'd be no mishaps. She could think of nothing worse than someone accidentally touching her in the street, a child running into her. Her eyes snapped open, heart beating fast. It was bad enough to kill a grown man or woman, but so much worse if she killed a child. She grimaced. Another child, she thought, clenching her fists.

She got out of the bed and, after getting dressed in the peasant clothes that Del had brought her, she slipped out of the safe house into the darkened street. She didn't know this part of the city well, having spent most of her time by the docks, but she knew the general direction she needed to go.

She walked slowly, keeping to the shadows. It would not do for anyone else to notice her. It wasn't against the law for her to be out this late. There was no curfew. But no one else was out. That meant something. And she knew the Brothers did not want her to appear strange or out of place. Considering the fervor that gripped this part of the realm, she had put her black cloak over her peasant clothes too. She could blend in with the darkness more easily as she walked north to the docks.

She knew when she was close. She knew that smell. For a moment, she was transported back to the alleyway, to the abandoned buildings where she and the others had gathered for warmth and safety. *Safety.* She sneered in the darkness. The illusion of safety, perhaps. She breathed in the salty air, the rotten smell of low tide brought in on the breeze pervading her nostrils.

And then she was there; the docks where the ships from all over the realm were moored. The store houses loomed in front of her, gray and stark in the sporadic light from the few lamps that had been lit. Keeping away from their glow, she walked without purpose. This place was different yet the same. She knew that behind these façades there would be children huddled in the dark, hungry and waiting to die just as she had been.

She should leave this place, she thought. She didn't belong here anymore. Gone was the girl that had cowered in these backstreets with her friends. Yet she kept walking, finding the unnamed alley where they'd spent so much of their time. Those places where they had eaten and the shops they'd stolen from. She noticed the baker's on the corner in front of her, still looking the same. Shut up for the night. How many times had they pilfered pies from that window sill? How many times had she and those two thin, freckled boys played and explored the city together?

Lily moved down the alley, her boots not making a sound in the half-dried mud and grime. She found the broken doorway, but she didn't dare go inside, knowing that, at the very least, those who were in there would be afraid. But she stared at it for a very long time, thinking of times long past, wondering what had happened to her friend after Toman had died ... *after she had killed Toman*. She made herself think the truth. She was back here. She had to face what she had done.

What would the men say to that, she wondered. What would the strong, foreboding, immoral Dark Brothers say if she told them she had killed a little boy of barely six winters? How she had watched him bleed from his eyes, shudder in her arms, plead with her to save him. She swallowed a sob.

Of her two friends, one she had killed and the other ... she didn't know. She couldn't remember the last time she'd seen him. But it was before Toman had died, when he'd only just started to feel poorly. Her curse had worked more slowly back then, and Kane had left them to find food or medicine.

But then Toman had died and a man had found her huddled with his body. He hadn't touched her. She learned later that man was Vineri. He had been a high-ranking soldier and he'd been on the lookout for children like her, though she still had no idea how he could have learned of her existence. Before Toman she'd had no curse. It had just appeared one day and then Toman had died while she cuddled him to save him from the cold.

She turned, blinding tears filling her eyes, and went slowly back to the safe house, luckily not seeing anyone and avoiding the lone guards when they walked by. She went back up to her room, took off her clothes, donned her nightgown once more, and sat on the bed. Perhaps it would be better if she did not survive the morrow.

She would kill those three men, and then she would allow herself to be captured, she decided. The city soldiers and the king's laws would take care of the rest. Perhaps then Toman's spirit would be able to rest as well as all the other men she had killed. That thought calmed her, and finally she felt as if she could sleep. Lily closed her eyes. She lay back on the pillow and let herself sink into oblivion.

~

QUIN HADN'T SLEPT WELL. Once Mal and Bastian had left, he had lain on his bed, his eyes wide open, and thought about how he'd let things come to this. When the morning dawned, he got dressed and went downstairs, finding Del sitting in the parlor by herself.

'There you are,' he said. 'I haven't seen you since we got here. Where have you been?'

She looked up from her steaming cup, giving him a small smile. 'I was giving you time before we began. Being the leader of the Army is taking its toll on you, boy. With your unit and your Fourth so ...' she looked out the window, 'fractured, I thought I might give you some time to try and mend your bond.'

Quin sat down heavily. 'Is it so clear to see?'

Del grinned. 'Only because I've known you all your life. I doubt anyone else has noticed. Have you sorted things?'

'If anything, I've made them worse.'

She looked at him sharply. 'You are the Commander and you are the leader of your unit. Gods, boy, you have a Fourth. You must know what you need to do. When your bonds are weak, your unit is weak. You cannot afford that vulnerability.'

'I know that,' he said through clenched teeth.

Del gave him a look but dropped the argument. 'Does the girl's disguise need any alteration?' she asked instead.

'No. It seems to fit just fine ... what little there is of it.'

Del shrugged. 'Does the girl object?' She sounded surprised.

'No, she said she will do what is expected.'

Del stood. 'The unit from the Library will be here as soon as the sun rises over the rooftops. You'll find Drake, Krase, and Vane loyal to the Army, but be cautious. They've been here since they were chosen from the camp children by Greygor. They were educated in the First Scholar's Academy. They're yours, but they're his as well.'

Quin's eyes narrowed at Del. 'What do you mean?'

'I mean, they'll help you as is their duty as Brothers. Just don't tell them anything you wouldn't want getting back to Nixus.'

Quin shook his head. 'He's a fucking librarian.'

Del rolled her eyes back at him. 'He's not just a fucking librarian. The Scholar is a dangerous man, the true power in this city and in the north. He's clever and sly, gets others to do his dirty work for him. And he has power over the unit here. Be cautious,' she said. 'Don't get in Nixus's way and he won't get in yours, for now.'

Quin nodded. He didn't have time to deal with yet more enemies at this moment. If the man wasn't a threat to the Army, then he would leave him well enough alone. 'Perhaps I should have that unit called back to the Army and replaced.'

Del made a face. 'Such a change would draw the sort of attention to the Army that you do not need at the moment. My advice to you is to ensure that this unit understands your authority and sees you as a fair man. They are Brothers still, though they have been far removed from the Army for quite some time. They did their training and the Brothers' trials in the camp after their education at the Academy was complete.'

'I recall,' said Quin. 'It was one of Greygor's ventures.'

'That's right,' his aunt said. 'He wanted Brothers in positions of power here. He was a shrewd man. Greygor knew that the Great Library is the true authority in Kitore, not the palace, whatever the king would have you believe. He takes veiled orders from Nixus as well.'

'We saw the king last night.'

'Indeed? What did that oaf have to say?'

'Nothing you would care to hear, Aunt,' he said in a dry tone.

Del huffed. 'Probably,' she agreed. 'I'll get you some tea.'

She rose and left him in the parlor alone. He looked out the window, making the most of the peace and quiet, for he knew it wouldn't last long.

The air had the warmth of spring in it today, he thought

as Del returned a moment later with a steaming mug identical to her own.

'It's a dark tea,' she said. 'Comes in on the ships from the Islands. You'll like it.'

'Are you all right up here, Del?' he asked her, changing the subject. 'As a caretaker, I mean. If you wanted, I could have you brought back down to the camp.'

Del ruffled his hair, something no one had done in a very long time. 'No, no, my boy. I like it well enough. I've built my life here. The darkness that seeps through the city can't last forever and, hopefully, I'll survive it and live to see a better age. Now, one more bit of advice. Patch up your relationships with your unit. This weakness will not do for the Commander of the Dark Army. It does not lend credence to your position. Greygor's unit hated him, and though they tried to keep it quiet, anyone who saw them together could tell their unit was split.'

Quin said nothing. He knew his aunt was correct. She left him again and he sat in his chair sipping his tea, thinking about how he was going to repair things. In truth, he didn't know if he could after what had happened with Lily last night. He had been afraid that he would call a stop to the mission. He hated that he was sending her behind enemy lines, but there was no other way that he could see. And his loyalty to the Army came first. He hissed a curse when he remembered how his Brothers had looked at him ... how Lily had.

He thought back to last night when he had held Lily in his arms. He hadn't felt such peace in a very long time. He also hadn't had a woman in a very long time. He adjusted himself as he began to harden, thinking of her hot, sweet cunt. The breathy moans she'd made as he had fucked her. He'd meant to go slow. He'd known it was her first time taking a cock. But she seemed so eager that he had not been able to stop himself from having her the way he had imagined; hard, rough; and she had enjoyed it if the noises she had made were anything to go by. The way she shook when she found her release had sent him over the edge as well.

He wished he could see her face as contented as it had been last night when she had lain in his arms, sated. But then he had had to ruin it by pretending that it had meant nothing to him. He swore under his breath once more.

He thought back to how she'd arrived in his room, a walking temptation he couldn't deny. The last thing he'd expected was for her to come to him, to want him. It had been … he hardened further at the mere thought. And then afterwards when they'd talked. He couldn't remember having spoken with a woman about his past ever. But then the others had arrived and it had shattered the little bubble just as he'd realized that he cared for her as much as he did his Brothers – though in a very different way.

How could he possibly make her do the things he was going to ask her to do? How could he be the Commander of the Dark Army if he cared about Lily enough to put her first? If he'd known, he would never have bound her to them in the first place. Never. He had to make her take the deal that he had offered, so he had made her think that she – what they'd done – meant nothing more to him than a dalliance with any woman would have.

Fuck! How could he unbind her? Logistically, he knew how to. There was a book for the Commanders that had these rituals in it back at the camp. He had to do it. Without her, he could mend the ties between his Brothers and they would be united and strong. She would leave and they would go back to their lives. That was how it had to be. It was indeed a mess, but he had to mend the bonds between his Brothers without Lily. He had to.

There was a knock at the door and he saw that the sun

had reached the top of the houses. This would be the Brothers he'd called for.

'Enter.'

Three large men dressed in black trudged through the doorway. Quin tried not to let his astonishment at their statures show, but surprised he was. He had assumed that they would be more *academic* than soldier. They had taken the trials a while ago, after all, and for all intents and purposes, he would have assumed their duties consisted of, well, scholarly pursuits.

But these men were not scholars first and foremost, that was certain. Each man was broad and substantial and clearly spent time in the training rings ... or in the fighting pits from the looks of some of their scars.

They looked hardened despite their learned backgrounds. All were dressed in Brothers' blacks but with a small red stripe on the front of their tunics, he noted, his eyes narrowing on that crimson line, the king's mark and, therefore, the Scholar's. But he said nothing about it, taking Del's advice.

Their leader watched Quin like a hawk with piercing blue eyes, sizing him up, deciding if he was worthy. The man's cropped hair was a deep ginger and he sported a well-trimmed beard of the same hue. There was a small but prominent burn scar high on his cheek in the shape of a five-pointed star.

'Thank you for meeting with me, Brothers.'

The men bowed their heads.

'And you, Commander. I'm Drake,' their leader said. He pointed at the Brother on his left with the long blond hair tied at the nape of his neck. 'Krase and ...' He gestured to the other one. A silver earring dangled from his ear and his black hair was woven in thick strands that went down his back, making him look anything but a learned man. 'This is Vane.'

'Sit,' Quin invited them, and they did so.

A moment later, Jona came, bringing a tray of tea.

'Refreshments?' Quin asked.

They all declined.

'Why are we here?' asked Krase, getting straight to the point.

'Did you ever meet Greygor?' Quin asked him.

'When we were chosen and then at the trials.'

'We heard what he did,' Vane said. 'Old fool.'

He and Krase smirked at each other and Quin's eyes narrowed. These men seemed to have little respect for the authority of the Commander. He hadn't liked Greygor either, but he wondered if the Brothers would be saying the same thing about him when they left the house. He couldn't give a fuck really, but he needed them on his side and he needed their loyalty. As Commander of the Brothers, he should have it by rights, but it seemed he would have to earn it from these Brothers.

'Greygor betrayed us all,' he said, looking at each of them in turn. 'He led many men to their deaths, including my own unit Brother. We put a bolt through his heart.'

The Brothers nodded and he finally saw a small measure of respect in their faces.

'You're here because my unit needs your help,' he admitted. 'Our Fourth—'

'You have a Fourth?' the first one interrupted. They were all looking at each other, suddenly restless.

'Yes. A recent thing.'

'We heard it wasn't …' Vane said, and Drake gave his Brother a pointed look.

'Fourths are rare.' Quin answered his unspoken question.

Again, all three men looked at each other and something passed between them, though to Quin their expressions were indiscernible.

'The Fourth is recognized only once the binding is complete, and ... you have claimed her?' Krase asked.

'I have.' Quin's eyes narrowed. Why was everyone so interested in Lily? 'She'll be here in a moment. You can talk with her if you like.'

'You would allow us to speak to her?' Vane questioned, his jaded tone belying the importance he clearly placed on the answer as he stared intently at Quin, waiting for him to speak.

'You seem capable of speech and so is she,' Quin said dryly, covering his confusion at their odd behavior.

All three fell silent as the door opened and Mal and Bastian entered, Lily trailing behind them.

'Brothers,' Bastian greeted them quietly.

Mal nodded at them and took his customary spot by the wall. Bastian and Lily stood behind Quin. Drake, Krase, and Vane's eyes followed her, though they did not speak to her directly.

'There is a celebration tonight close to the palace. Our Fourth must be in attendance. She's here to kill—'

'We can guess,' Drake interrupted with a sneer. 'But we would perhaps wonder why we weren't given the task.' He looked Lily up and down and snorted. 'How is this girl going to kill any man regardless of how much wine and women he's had?' he asked, his manner mocking.

'You don't know me,' Lily growled from behind Quin in a tone he'd never heard her use before. She was holding her own against these men and he was pleased, proud even.

'It doesn't matter how she's going to do it,' he said to the Brothers. 'She's going in disguised as a courtesan, but she needs to go in later, after the others.'

The three of them looked at each other again, something more passing between them that made Quin wary.

'This is a foolish plan,' said Drake. 'If anyone finds out you have gone against the king's edict, all of our lives will be forfeit.'

Quin stood. 'I'll worry about that. Will you help your Brothers or not?'

'It is our duty as members of the Dark Army,' Drake said after a moment, but he didn't look happy about it. 'You'll receive details of where to be before the celebration begins,' he said to Lily, standing. 'But if you are caught, we will not be able to help you.'

'Understood,' Quin said, looking back at Lily. She nodded once, deliberately not looking at him, which didn't go unnoticed by Krase, who smirked at him.

The Brothers left without another word.

'They have gifts,' Mal muttered after they'd heard the outer door to the house slam closed.

Quin's head shot up as he regarded Mal. 'What can they do?'

'Not sure. Odd unit.'

'Agreed,' Quin said thoughtfully. Hiding a gift wasn't odd outside the Army, but within, Brothers tended to know what their fellows could do. This unit was strangely removed from that life. He would have to deal with them before they turned into a problem as well, he thought, adding it to that ever-increasing list in his mind.

'They may be loyal to the Army, but they have other allegiances as well.' He turned to Lily. 'Are you still of a mind to continue?

'Yes,' she said, not looking at him.

'Good. If you see them tonight, don't let them know about your curse. Mal will bring you the information they send to us later, and we'll show you where you need to go. We will be close by, but this is the closest safe house to where you'll be. You must know your way back here just in case.'

'I know the city well enough.'

Quin nodded and glanced at Mal. 'Do you have sufficient time to get everything together?'

He nodded.

'Good. We'll reconvene here before the sun sets. I will go with you to ensure you get inside without incident,' he said to Lily, and he could have sworn he saw her lip curl in disdain for a moment before her expression closed. 'Mal will be waiting for you when you come out. Bastian and I will be watching the building to ensure we know where you are.'

'Fine,' she said and then, without a backward glance, left the room.

As soon as she was gone, both Mal and Bastian simply stared at where she had been standing.

'She's upset,' Bastian said quietly. Mal nodded in agreement.

'I know,' Quin said, 'but it's for the best.'

Mal practically bared his teeth as he left the room as well. Bastian let out a sigh. 'Best for whom?' he asked quietly before following on Mal's heels, more loyal to Mal than he was to Quin at the moment, Quin suspected.

He put his head in his hands, for once praying to the gods that he would be able to sort out this mess that seemed to be getting worse with each passing moment.

∽

Lily shivered in the dark as she stood next to Quin in the alley. It stank of rotten vegetables and piss, which was an aroma she found familiar and somewhat comforting as odd as that was. It seemed to her they'd been waiting out here for hours, though it hadn't been too long since the sun had set and the revelries had begun.

She could hear sounds of merriment inside, roaring laughter, loud singing. Thoughts of what was going on in there, of what she would be walking into, scared her. She'd accompanied Vineri to celebrations before, but it had only been for show. His guards had always surrounded her so that no one who wasn't supposed to could get close enough to die. Here there'd be no such protections.

She wrapped her arms around herself under her black cloak, beneath which she wore nothing but the disguise that Quin had procured for her. Was she really going to do this? Could she go in there with gods only knew how many people? She looked up at Quin's face when she knew he wouldn't notice, his gaze fixed on the door, waiting for it to open. When it did, his part would be over and hers would just be beginning.

She tried to force all thoughts of uncertainty away. If she didn't, she knew she would become more and more terrified and they'd probably find her hiding in a wardrobe, shaking like a useless little leaf after the carousing was over.

Quin looked down at her for a moment, his gaze unfathomable. She wished she knew what he was thinking. Did he care if this went poorly past her not getting the job done? Was he worried for her or was she as expendable to him as she'd always been?

Perhaps she didn't want to know, she mused, thinking back to when he'd held her in his arms. She'd never felt so safe, so protected. It hadn't lasted long, but she'd treasure that memory for the rest of her life, she thought as she gazed up at the building. However long that might be ...

The door creaked open and her heart felt like it stopped for just a moment in her chest. It was time. She took a deep breath and forced herself to walk forward, ignoring Quin.

As soon as she reached the threshold, a servant who stood on the other side of the door made sure she was inside and, mostly ignoring her, left her standing in the back hall beside the kitchen by herself.

She looked behind her at the door, already shut. She could run. She could still get out of here. As she heard more manly laughter, the clink of glasses and girlish giggles, she wanted to.

No, she had told them she would do it and she would not make herself a liar. She could be free after this was done. Truly free.

She let the cloak drop to the floor, stashed it behind some boxes of refuse, and walked on bare feet towards the sounds of merriment.

Keeping to the shadows wasn't difficult either. There weren't that many candles, and the place was quite dim, bordering on gloomy. She entered one of the main rooms filled with low murmurs and breathy moans. It was a cacophony and, luckily for her, it looked like the attentions of all of the men in the room were engaged with the many beautiful and very naked women. Her eyes widened at the sight of one of them bent backwards, legs spread and being taken by one man while she took another with her mouth.

Lily felt her cheeks heat as she thought about doing that with Bastian and Mal and berated herself. She was here to *kill* three men, not to have imaginings of carnal pleasures with the Brothers. She sashayed across the room, not hurrying, not acting as if she had anywhere to be, all while ensuring no one was within arm's reach of her.

Mal had told her earlier that her targets rarely cavorted with their men. She didn't know who they were, exactly, outside of this building, but the other unit had been able to provide sketches of the men that Mal had made her memorize down to the smallest detail – though little else was known about them save their faces, which she thought a bit odd. Kitore was large, but still a contained place. People couldn't go unnoticed forever here. If any of her unit had thought the same, though, they certainly hadn't spoken to her about it.

She walked past a door as she continued her slow search of the house and heard muted voices from within. Putting her ear against the wood, she tried to discern how many were inside as she went through the plan of the building that Mal had also made her commit to memory. She counted at least two.

Looking around her, she wondered how she could gain entry, sure that there had been another room adjacent to this one with a door joining them together. She went down the corridor to the entrance of the next room, opening it with care and formulating a conceivable lie if she was confronted.

The room was deserted, thank the gods, and the connecting door to the other room was slightly ajar. She padded across the room, not making a noise on the thick woolen carpets that covered the floors. She peered through the door and found three men, who fitted the sketches she'd looked at, sitting at the table. Could this be them already alone? Would it really be this easy?

The men spoke in low voices, two sitting on comfy chairs by the fire while the third paced. Lily took a deep breath. It was now or never, she thought. She might not get a better chance than this.

She stepped into their room, pasting what she hoped was a sultry smile onto her face.

The dark-haired one looked up and frowned. 'The whores are to stay in the main room unless called,' he said, staring at her breasts through the gauze she wore.

'Yes, my lord,' she said, 'but all of the other men seem to be engaged by my friends, and I'm lonely,' she pouted, hoping she sounded plausible.

The blond one grinned. 'Don't send her away. We're almost finished our business anyway.'

Dark-Hair rolled his eyes, yet they still somehow never left her chest. 'We aren't here to dally with whores,' he complained. 'How you can after all that's happened, I—'

'We all deal with grief in our own ways,' the blond one snapped, his smile turning brittle. 'Come here, girl.'

Lily took small steps towards them, her mind screaming at her to run. There was something about these three men. Their gazes were false and something in them was menacing, predatory, but she couldn't figure out what. They seemed like normal men, but she knew somehow that they were not.

Logically, this was no different than being in that pleasure tent in the camp. Although that had been terrifying in its own right, she'd come out of it in one piece. Somehow, this was worse.

She could do this, she told herself as she stood before the blond while the dark-haired ones looked on.

'So you've been yearning for some company, have you?' Blondie asked her, looking her up and down.

She nodded, fluttering her eyelashes at him and pretending shyness that was in fact revulsion.

'I didn't notice you earlier,' the first one muttered.

'I was detained. I came later,' she said, biting her lip as she'd noticed other courtesans doing in the pleasure tent. Drawing from that small experience was the best she could do, however. She had no real idea how paid women acted and no experience of seduction. She stepped a little bit closer, close enough for Blondie to reach her. As soon as she was in his sphere, he pulled her into his lap. But his hands only touched the silky cloth of her dress.

She gasped in his hold, freezing for a second, and his gaze sharpened, eyes narrowing at her.

'Are you new?' he asked.

'Yes,' she pretended to shyly admit. 'It's my first time.'

'That explains it,' he said.

Dark-Hair did not look convinced. 'I'm sure I've seen you before,' he muttered.

'I'm from Kitore,' she replied. 'You may have seen me about.'

Blondie's hands ran down her body and she wished the Brothers were here at this moment. She didn't want any of these men touching her. Almost without thinking, her hand came up to brush against his cheek. He began to smile, but Dark-Hair grabbed her hand with his gloved one before it could touch his friend, wrenching her away and throwing her to the floor.

She cried out as he drew a sword out of nowhere and pointed it at her.

'What's wrong with you?' Blondie yelled, staring at his friend in astonishment.

'We've been waiting so long for them to strike at us, we didn't stay on our guard. She's here to kill us, aren't you, girl?'

Lily cowered as all three loomed over her. How had he known?

'Of course not!' she stammered. 'It's my first time as a courtesan. I'm nervous is all!'

Dark-Hair reached down and she yelped as he grabbed her hair, pulling her to her feet by it.

'Please!' she begged, wondering how she was going to get out of this. Perhaps she could put them at ease and she'd get another chance at them. 'If I was here to kill anyone, I'd have weapons. Surely you can see I have nothing.'

The third one looked her over with a shrewd expression. 'Not if you kill by touch,' he said, raising an eyebrow.

Lily's mouth fell open before she could hide her shock. 'How did you—?'

Dark-Hair and Blondie glanced at their friend.

'Good guess,' Dark-Hair observed.

The third one shrugged. 'I know the history of Kitore. She's not the first oddity the city's wards created to protect it. Doubt she'll be the last.'

The *wards* had made her? Could that be true?

She gasped as all three pairs of eyes that looked back at her turned a deep and bright violet. Her heart thudded in her chest. 'Gods, you're *fae*!'

'Aye,' Dark-Hair said, his countenance darkening.

Lily gaped at them in awe and in fear. She'd never have dreamed she'd see even one of the fearsome males of the Underhill, let alone *three*.

'What shall we do with her?' Blondie asked. 'Kill her and leave her on the Library's steps? Nixus won't miss that.' He grinned evilly and she blanched.

'No,' Dark-Hair said. 'We aren't ready for open conflict. But she will be a message.'

The hand in her hair eased for the barest moment to get a better grip and she broke away from them, dashing through the door into the next room, but Dark-Hair caught her long before she could exit into the hall, his gloved hand closing around her throat. He threw her against the wall with a curse, squeezing her neck tightly.

'Hold still,' he barked.

She couldn't breathe. Her hands clawed at his, but it was no use. He was calm and collected as her knees weakened and she felt her eyes start to grow dim. Her attempts to escape became more and more feeble and, stupidly, her last thought was that she had failed her unit. She had let them down.

Lily woke to the sound of dripping water and the smell of damp, rotten reeds. She could hear the scratching of small animals rustling across the floor. When at last she opened her eyes, she saw she was in a cell.

She shivered. She was lying on a cold stone floor and still

wearing her flimsy disguise. The last thing she remembered was being choked by the dark-haired fae. Where was she now?

There were other cells around her and, although the light was bad, she thought she could make out other prisoners. Most were curled up in the corners of their cells, unmoving.

She heard a faraway clinking of a door and sounds of boots stomping closer. A key clattered in a lock and a door opened in her view. In walked a high-ranking soldier dressed in the king's red whom she didn't recognize. He was flanked by two lesser soldiers and came to stand in front of her cell, watching her, but he didn't speak. He seemed to just be observing her.

'Where am I?' she asked. She assumed it was the king's dungeons, but it couldn't hurt to know for sure. He didn't say a word, simply turned on his heel and left again.

And so Lily sat and waited, wondering when her torture and killing would begin. Surely they must know about her curse. Out of the countless people that had been killed for alleged witchery, they actually had a girl who could do something.

Tears threatened and she tried to hold on to the thoughts that she'd had yesterday, that it was best for her to die in the city where it had all begun. It was fitting, a good thing that she could hurt no one else. But those thoughts weren't as strong as they had been, not now that she was actually here. They didn't make her feel better. Other thoughts were intruding. All she had wanted was to live her life without hurting anyone. Would the Brothers save her? Would they bother? No, she supposed. Quin wouldn't need to do the unbinding ritual if she was already dead. It would be simpler for them. Though of course she had failed to kill those three fae, so he wouldn't do it anyway.

She let a sound of anger escape her. What had that other

fae said? That there had been others like her and she'd been made by the city wards. Perhaps that was how Vineri had known what to look for and why he had taken her from the city so quickly after he'd found her. So he could hide her in the south, in that tower, to add her to his precious Collection. That had always been paramount to him, she recalled, protecting those artifacts.

She was feeling sorry for herself. What had she done to deserve this? She snorted aloud. She'd killed – at others' direction, but she'd still done it. No, she definitely deserved to die here. A tear rolled down her cheek, and she wiped it away.

She noticed that the other prisoners in the cells were getting restless. She could hear the clanking of those who were chained as they moved their limbs. Others were rustling around, and a few moments later, she heard the door open again. A crust of bread was thrust into her cell, along with a small cup of water. She drank the water but left the rest. She was too scared to be hungry.

She wrapped her arms around herself, trying to give herself some modesty, even though none of the prisoners seemed to care. They had their own problems, she supposed.

The third time the door opened, Lily didn't bother to move at all. It was the same man with his two guards and again, he stopped outside.

'Arms behind your back,' he ordered.

She did as he said and the door opened. All three men wore gloves, and not a bit of their skin was showing, save their eyes. Her arms were twisted behind her, and when she cried out in pain, one of them hit her.

'Be silent!'

Her bottom lip wobbled and she bit it hard. She didn't want to show these men the terror that she was feeling. They looked like the types to revel in it.

Her arms were bound and she was walked from the cells and through the door before her. Here there was a staircase of white stone; steps that they began to ascend. She walked with them placidly. They could easily subdue her, after all, and the element of surprise was gone. Judging from their attire, they knew exactly what she was capable of.

When they reached the top of the steps, she blinked as her eyes got used to the sudden brightness. It was day and the sun was shining through large glass windows that lined the high walls.

She stared around in awe. It was a library. *The* Library, she realized. Why was she in the Great Library and not in the king's dungeon, she wondered, becoming more uneasy by the moment.

She was escorted through the stacks, past scrolls and large tomes, past scholars who scratched away on parchments with quills, none of them seeming surprised that a half-naked prisoner was being walked across the main floor.

They reached another set of steps and Lily was pushed up them. She went without a fight, more morbidly curious to see what was at the top than anything. At the end of the staircase, they stepped through a small stone archway that led onto a mezzanine.

It was a large platform in the very middle of the library, high enough for the First Scholar to see anywhere in his little kingdom from this vantage point. And there he sat at a large white marble desk, surrounded by papers and open volumes. He scribbled away as the other scholars had downstairs.

They stood in the middle of the dais in silence, the high-ranking soldier still holding her wrists tightly, his two men behind him. They were made to stand there and wait until the Scholar deigned to notice them.

'This is the one?'

She looked up and saw that the Scholar was staring at her

intently.

'Aye,' the soldier who held her answered. 'Left trussed up on the steps with a note we didn't understand.'

'Who is she? Let me see the note.'

'Don't know, my lord. The missive mentioned an oddity of the wards.' The soldier handed it over and the other man perused it, his eyes flicking back and forth over the page quickly.

The Scholar gave a wave of his hand. 'She's simply one of those *things* that appear sometimes in the slums. Nothing out of the common way, though the last one we had in the dungeon died not long ago, no? She may prove useful. Get rid of that thing she wears.'

Lily tried not to make a sound as her transparent disguise was ripped away, the material tearing like paper. She could do little about the shaking, though, her teeth chattering so hard she thought they might shatter.

The First Scholar approached. He had a short gray beard with smatterings of brown. He wore a tan silk shirt and fine brown trousers of the same material and stylish cropped boots that were in fashion just now, it seemed. Looking at the lines of age on his forehead, she'd estimate him to be approaching fifty.

He looked her over as if she were a rare curiosity, nothing in his face but a calm, somewhat detached interest. After a moment, he went back to his desk and drew on some gloves before stepping closer to her.

'Is she restrained properly?' he asked.

'Yes, my lord.' The soldier's grip on her tightened and made her wince.

The Scholar took her chin and moved her head this way and that as he looked closely at her face. She struggled, but it was fruitless.

'She can't be a courtesan, surely,' he said to the soldier, not taking his eyes from her.

'She was delivered like this, but by …' the soldier lowered his voice to a murmur, 'one of the ones you've been watching. Perhaps they believe *we* sent her.'

The older man's face gave nothing away as he continued his perusal of her flesh, raising her arm and looking intently at the skin of her fingertips.

'Is it just the hands that kill?' he asked conversationally, and it was a long moment before she realized he was speaking directly to her.

'Answer,' the soldier behind her said gruffly and shook her.

'No,' she muttered and left it at that.

The Scholar looked surprised. 'So if one of these men were to touch your face …' he asked.

'He would die,' she answered. There was no point in denying it.

She thought he looked a bit more intrigued. 'Your hair?'

Her brow creased. 'I— I don't know.'

'She's stronger than the others I've examined before,' he said, stepping back and removing his gloves. 'Keep her.'

'In the dungeon, my lord?'

He rubbed his bearded cheek as he considered. 'No, closer. I have some tests I'd like to perform on her. Use *her* old room,' he said – somewhat bitterly. Whoever this other woman was, the First Scholar seemed angry with her.

'Yes, my lord.'

Another soldier appeared at the archway they'd entered from. 'The Brothers you summoned are here, my lord.'

Lily looked up, hoping it would be her unit come to save her somehow, but the three large men who trudged in, though alike in stature to Mal, Bastian, and Quin, were definitely not them. And they weren't dressed in black either. Did Brothers ever not wear their blacks?

She was pulled to the back of the room. The Scholar ordered the man who held her to stay and listen. She kept her head down, watching three sets of feet go past her. Thankfully, no one seemed interested in her or her bared body at all.

'I called you here because I need a job done for me.'

The largest one, their leader it appeared, leveled a look at the man, clearly not intimidated in the least by his authority.

'You must have heard by now that we have quit the Brothers.' He sneered at the Scholar. 'Everyone knows you've got your ears everywhere, Nixus.'

'Yes, I had heard that the second-in-command of the Brothers and his unit had left the Army,' Nixus spat. 'How convenient it must be to be able to cast off such a mantle at will. But the fact is, I have a job and I need Dark Brothers to do it. I need you to retrieve a witch I've heard about in the south. I'll pay you well.'

The three men looked at each other for a moment before the leader answered again. 'The payment is unimportant. We have other plans that don't include trailing after some hapless female,' the leader said in no uncertain terms. 'What of your personal unit? Greygor made you school them for all those years at your academy, give them access to the volumes here for his personal plans in return for your own unit of loyal Brothers.' He grinned insolently. 'Are you afraid that if you let them leave your side, they won't return?'

Lily watched the Scholar's lips thin into a straight line, the only sign that he was angry at the Brother's words. Clearly, he was not used to being spoken to thus.

He let out a huff and waved his hand, dismissing them with the brusque gesture.

The three Brothers turned, each one fighting a smirk, Lily noticed. She didn't lower her eyes quickly enough, though, and their leader's met hers.

He looked surprised for a moment, as if he hadn't noticed her before. His eyes did not travel down her naked body, for which she was thankful. Neither did those of the other two.

As their gazes locked for that moment, she realized there was something familiar about him, but she couldn't place where she had seen him before. She tried to get a second look, but they were gone.

Nixus went back to his desk and began to scribble on his parchments once more, ignoring everyone still on the dais.

Lily was led away, back down the steps and into the main floor of the Library. They went through the orderly rows of books all the way to the back, where it was darker. She was pushed through a doorway that led to a hall at the end of which were more doors. This place was a veritable maze. The soldier opened a door and threw her inside. She heard him locking it behind her with a mumble to the other two soldiers, who laughed as they walked away.

She looked around, finding herself in a small, dingy room with a bed that looked like it hadn't been used for a very long time. A thin layer of dust coated everything, including the floor. Although as she looked down, it seemed as if someone came in here often. There was a sort of trail that looked cleaner than the rest of the stones.

Lily shivered. There was no fire in the grate and it was cold, especially with no clothes on. She pulled one of the blankets off the bed, which, though musty-smelling, was still serviceable, and wrapped it around herself.

Why wasn't she back in the dungeon? She'd thought that she'd be summarily tortured and killed as soon as she was captured, but the Scholar wanted her for something. Tests, he'd said. That didn't sound good at all. He was the most powerful man in Kitore and he had looked at her as if she were a specimen, not even a witch to destroy. She had to get out of this place before he started whatever he was intending.

Looking around the room, she found it was devoid of anything that she could use as a weapon or even as a pick for the lock, though she had no experience with either anyway. Her best bet was for someone to forget about her curse, then she could slip away and back into the city streets. She still knew Kitore well enough to hide herself.

She wondered whose room this had been. It looked like she hadn't lived here in quite some time, whoever she was. Lily sat on the bed and drew her knees up, wondering where Mal, Bastian, and Quin were at the moment. Had they left the city? Were they trying to find another way to kill the fae or had they too been captured? Did they even know that the three men they'd brought her here to kill were fae? She hadn't given anything away about the Brothers, but then they hadn't even asked. They'd simply assumed that the First Scholar had sent her.

She gave a sigh, thinking that there was much more going on here than the Brothers knew. How long would she be imprisoned in this room before someone came and she could try to flee? She'd been content enough to stay in Vineri's tower, but she'd been little more than a half-starved child then. She would not be so malleable now, and she would be no one's instrument. No more. She would rather die.

As it turned out, she didn't have to wait long before the door opened once more and in walked another soldier, one she hadn't seen before, but he looked like a high-ranking guard. She thought perhaps he was bringing food or water, but his hands were empty and something she saw in his face made her jump from the bed and move away from him.

He didn't say a word, his silence alarming her even more as he closed the door with a finality that chilled her to the core.

His cruel eyes never left hers, and she realized she'd been correct in her assessment of him. There was something to fear. He was going to hurt her. But she looked him in the eye, refusing to be cowed as her body shook. He could only beat her, she told herself. He couldn't kill her, because Nixus wanted her for something, and he couldn't rape her unless he wanted to die a painful death – and, if the gloves were any indication, he already knew that.

'You keep those brazen eyes on me as long as you like, witch. In a bit, they'll be too swollen to see much of anything,' he said, pulling his gloves up and then cracking his knuckles.

He didn't bother to cover his head and face as if he knew she had no chance of fighting against him. She cringed as he raised his fist, finding with the first blow that he wouldn't be pulling his punches and knowing that her time here was going to be just as bad as she'd expected it to be in the king's dungeon.

At first, she tried not to give him the satisfaction of making a sound but, by the fifth blow, she had long stopped caring. By the time she was curled up on the floor, unable to move, she'd stopped counting how many times he'd hit her, viciously kicked her, spat on her. She couldn't do much more than gurgle, vaguely wondering why no one had heard her screams. Nixus hadn't wanted her dead, after all.

'Please,' she begged, 'please,' trying once more to make him stop.

He crouched down, looking bored. 'I can pretend,' he drawled, brushing her hair from her cheek gently. 'But I wish you really were her.'

He grabbed her by the hair and hit her head on the stone floor, practically knocking her senseless with a grin on his face that would haunt her nightmares until her dying day – which might be soon after all, she thought as her head lolled.

CHAPTER 12

MAL

He paced up and down the room, not able to sit still. Every time he did, he felt the urge to tear at his own hair, his own skin. They were useless, he, Bastian, and Quin; fucking less than useless.

Bastian sat at the table, a goblet of wine in a shaky hand, and Quin sat on another chair, staring at the wall.

'Need her back,' Mal barked.

'No one comes out of the king's dungeon without his say-so,' Quin said quietly, not looking at his Brothers.

Mal hit the wall with a sound of anger, his fist embedding itself in the soft wood panel and sending pain up his arm, which he ignored. 'You sent her there.'

'And you made that pact with her so that she could leave us,' Bastian chimed in, his gaze unfocused. 'You only wanted her with us for what she could do for you. All you wanted was for her to do your dirty work, fulfil the purpose you set for her.'

'She wanted to leave,' Quin began, his words hollow.

Mal took his knife and stuck it into the table, barely missing Quin's hand, though the desire to sever at least one of his fingers was great. 'Would have stayed with Bastian and me.'

'We don't have the resources here to go against the king,' said Quin, looking Mal in the eye. 'I want to save her as much as you do, but what would you have us do, Brother? Storm the castle with our meager number of three?' Quin snapped.

Bastian got to his feet and threw his goblet at the wall with a yell. 'We cannot just sit here while she's being tortured. They'll know what she is by now.'

'And what is that?' asked Quin.

'Our Fourth,' growled Mal.

They all heard someone pounding on the outer door.

'Who the fuck is this?'

'Probably the king's soldiers come to take us.'

'Fuck,' muttered Mal, grabbing his knife and putting it back on his belt, beginning to pace again.

The door to the room burst open and the floor creaked as Drake stepped into the room.

'What the fuck do you want?' roared Quin.

'Want to know where your Fourth is?' he asked, not bothering with pleasantries.

'We know where she is,' Bastian snapped. 'The king's dungeon.'

'No,' he said. 'She was given to Nixus by the men she failed to kill. Don't know why, but he might well keep her.'

'Keep her for what?' Mal snarled.

Drake looked away. 'His research.'

'So she's in the Library's dungeon?'

'She's in one of the under-rooms at the heart of the Library, and the Scholar has his own forces; loyal men who are his and his alone.'

'Don't forget yourselves.' Mal sneered.

Drake regarded him passively. 'Sometimes loyalty is a

more complex thing than we would like. Commander, we can get your Fourth out, but you must leave the city as soon as we do. You cannot come back. There's little else we can do, but if you do as I say, we can bring her to you.'

'What does Nixus want with her?' Bastian asked, shaking his head.

'What goes on in Kitore and the rest of the north is no one's concern in the south. We have our laws, and the Brothers have theirs.'

'You *are* a Brother.'

The man snorted. 'Perhaps once, but we are what Nixus has made us now, and there is no coming back from that. Be at the docks within the hour, and your Fourth shall be yours once more.'

'What if Nixus catches you?' Quin asked.

The Brother smirked, not deigning to answer, and left them.

Quin stood. 'Pack us up. We leave now.'

Mal didn't need to be told twice. He'd already stuffed everything into their bags that morning.

'She won't want to see you,' Bastian said to Quin. 'You should take the horses and be outside the northern gates. They'll expect us to go south from the docks or via the way we came, so I say we go north as far as we can and then hail a ship off the Strait in a few days' time to go south by sea from there.'

Quin's jaw tightened, but he said nothing. Bastian turned and went with Mal, leaving their packs for Quin to bring.

They both made the short walk to the docks and waited.

'Should never have come here,' Bastian muttered. 'I knew there was something unnatural here, something foul. At least her deal with Quin is void.'

Mal nodded, then frowned. 'Need to make her want us.'

'What do you propose?' Bastian murmured, leaning

against a building, for all intents and purposes looking to any passersby as if he didn't have any cares at all.

Mal shrugged, ostensibly calm but inwardly in turmoil. He had to formulate a plan. Lily was a part of them, a part of him. He didn't know when he'd started to feel such things. Gods knew he never had before. But Lily had worked her way past his defenses, left him vulnerable as a babe where she was concerned. His fists tightened. But when he got his hands on her, he would make her pay for all of this worry she had caused. He didn't blame her for getting caught, but he did blame her for taking Quin's deal, for putting herself at risk for some gold, and the chance – of what? Being alone for the rest of her life? Mal shook his head and Bastian gave him a questioning look.

'We must get her back,' Bastian said, 'and keep her with us no matter the cost.'

Mal nodded.

～

When Lily came to, she was on the floor. She tried to get up, but she couldn't move.

She didn't know how long the man had beaten her for, but it felt as if there was no part of her body that he had left untouched. She coughed, blood dripping to the floor from her mouth. She wasn't sure where it was coming from, but she knew he'd broken some of her ribs as well as one of her arms. She couldn't open her mouth properly, and both her eyes were practically swollen shut.

She started to cry, but when the sobs began to rack her body, she forced them back because it hurt too much. All she could do was lie on the cold stone floor, wishing that she'd never woken up again.

She heard the door being unlocked and couldn't help the

cry of fear that bubbled up from her throat, though she wished she'd been able to hold it in. She didn't want him to know how much she feared him. But if he was coming back, perhaps he would finish what he'd started. She almost hoped he would, she was in so much pain. Lily could never have imagined that he would hurt her so badly when the First Scholar had said he needed her. Would he be punished for what he'd done?

Lily heard someone's sharp intake of breath.

'She's here.'

Looking up from the slit of the eye she could just about see with, she saw the three Brothers she'd met in the safehouse standing over her.

'Does she live?'

'Yes.'

'Nixus didn't order her beaten and he wouldn't have turned a blind eye. He wanted her healthy for his examinations.'

One of them snarled. '*She* was never beaten like this,' another said with a steeliness in his voice that spoke of some inner torment. 'Who did it?'

'It hardly matters now,' the third said. 'Get her up.'

She cried out as she was lifted by a pair of strong arms that settled her gently onto the bed.

'We'll see you to rights, girl.'

'We can't take her like this. Legs broken, her arm. Her jaw. She's coughing up blood, leaking it like bilge water.'

'Heal her,' one of them said in a hushed voice.

'He might find out.'

'What else can we do? The punishment won't be too bad, anyway. He wants us to leave within two days to find that witch he's heard about in the south.'

'Don't know why he's bothering to send us.'

'Does he really think anyone has the power he seeks in

this realm? She's dead. No one could have survived what happened that night, and I'm glad she didn't. The bitch was more trouble than she was worth.'

As she lay on the bed, staring up at them, Lily wondered if they were talking about the same girl whose room this had been.

'Do it now. We told them we'd meet them at the docks soon. We can't even take her to the infirmary like this. And what do you believe the Commander will do when he sees her? He'll call the entire Dark Army to war. We can't let that happen.'

'Very well. Guard the door.'

One of the men put his gloved hand on her forehead.

'Be calm,' he whispered. 'Close your eyes. You'll feel better in a moment.'

Lily felt a warmth spread across her almost immediately. It felt like when she used to put her hand out of her tower window to feel the sun's rays on a warm day, but instead of just on her palm, it was everywhere.

It was only a moment or two later that she was able to open her eyes fully. She looked down at herself in awe as she watched the bruises fade and disappear. She looked back up at him.

'I don't understand,' she said.

The Brother gave her a stony look. 'We all have our curses,' he murmured, turning away.

'Get up,' the other one next to him said. 'We don't have much time.'

'Where are you taking me?' she asked.

'To your unit.'

'You're going to help me escape?'

'We are.'

'Why? Aren't you the Scholar's men?'

None of them answered. A dress was thrown to her.

'Put this on,' she was ordered, and she did as she was told, flinging it over her head.

It was torn and dirty and resembled a sack, but anything was better than being publicly naked a moment longer.

The third one, who was still watching the door, opened it and looked out into the hall.

'Clear. Let's go now.'

She was taken from the room and they moved silently down the hallway to the next door. The third one opened it nonchalantly and went through as if they had every right to be doing what they were doing. Lily heard a low tap on the floor, a signal perhaps that all was clear, because they moved forward again into the stacks. They strode around the perimeter of the library.

They saw no guards, and what few students there were simply gave them curious, fearful glances and were quickly cowed into focusing back on their work by the Brothers' harsh glares.

'Won't they say anything?' she mumbled from between them.

'They know their places,' one of the Brothers said. 'If they know what's good for them, they won't say a word.'

Lily nodded. Clearly there was a hierarchy in this place that she knew nothing about.

'Who are all these people?' she asked

'Students at the academy. They come in here for their studies from the building across the river.'

They walked down the corridor, away from the books. And then they were outdoors on the street, in the sun.

'Thank you,' she said, breathing deeply of the outside air.

The first of them nodded and the second said nothing.

The third snorted. 'Don't thank us yet,' he mumbled. 'Come.'

They walked down the main city road. The sun was high.

And Lily saw that they were walking toward the docks, not to the safe house.

'Where's my unit?' she asked.

None of them answered her.

'Please. We are going to them, aren't we?'

Lily was beginning to panic. What if they were going to put her on a ship? What if she was being taken somewhere else? What if she would never see her unit again? Her hands began to shake until one of them looked over at her, noticed her distress with a frown, and put her out of her misery.

'We are taking you to your unit. They await us by the docks,' he hissed. 'Calm yourself. Foolish woman.'

They were coming to the port from a different direction, but she smelled it all the same once they began to get close.

'Where are they?' she murmured.

'They'll find us,' the leader said. 'We're hardly inconspicuous.'

And then she saw Bastian standing outside on the street. Unable to help herself, she rushed forward, only to be intercepted by Mal, who grabbed her and locked her into a fierce hug. She looked up at him, bewildered and confused but so, so glad that they were there. After what had happened in that room, she just wanted to be held and reminded that it was over. She hugged him back just as hard. He drew away after a moment and Bastian took his place, the large man enveloping her like a soft, warm, but very heavy blanket. She gasped as he squeezed her, putting her arms around his neck and pulling herself closer. She rubbed her cheek against his.

'Are you all right?' he asked.

'I am now,' she said. 'The other unit found me and got me out of there.'

Bastian let her back to the ground and she turned in time to see the three men nod. Their leader handed her a package wrapped in cloth.

'Give this to the Commander,' he said, and she watched as they turned around and walked away as if all of this was a common occurrence.

'Come,' Mal said to her. 'We leave the city now. They'll know you're gone soon. They'll start looking.'

She nodded and they led her along the docks into the streets beyond. When they got to the North Gate, Bastian ordered her to walk behind them.

'You're dressed as a slave,' he said to her. 'Act as one.'

So she walked behind them as he had instructed and the guards at the gate didn't look twice as they left, moving into the open countryside. But when they got to the tree line, Mal and Bastian looked around, their gazes troubled.

'What is it?' she asked, her eyes looking from one to the other.

'The horses are over there, packed and ready for the journey, but Quin isn't with them.'

'Where is he?' she asked.

Mal was looking intently at the ground. 'Taken,' he said, sounding distracted. 'Three, perhaps four.'

'But why didn't they take the horses? Our supplies?' she asked.

'They came for him,' Mal growled. His eyes narrowed at Bastian.

'Who? The Library or the king's men?' Bastian asked.

'Neither. Tracks are Brothers' horses.'

'Drake and his unit couldn't have got here before us. Who else could it be?'

'There was another unit.' Lily spoke up. 'In the Library. The Scholar wanted to hire them to find a woman he'd heard of in the south, but they said no, that they were no longer Brothers.'

Mal's expression turned even grimmer. 'Need to find him quickly.'

'Why? Who are they?' Bastian asked.

'Before your time, Brother,' was all Mal said.

Bastian surveyed the ground himself. 'They've gone east,' he said. 'On foot. They can't be far.'

'I don't understand,' Lily said. 'What do they want with Quin?'

Mal drew his dagger. 'Revenge.'

CHAPTER 13

QUIN

His hands were bound behind his back. There was a black hood over his head. He could hear low, whispered voices, at least three, perhaps four. One was distinctly different from the others. A female.

They were still in the forest. They hadn't taken him back into Kitore, he knew that much. He could hear the rustling of leaves, feel the wind on his back and the crunch of fallen leaves beneath his boots as he was walked forward roughly by whoever it was that had caught him unawares from behind. This wasn't going to end well for him.

He wondered who it was that had him. Was it Drake and his unit? Had they been tricking them all along? Were they truly Nixus's men now? Or was it the king's forces? No, he discounted that quickly. If it was palace soldiers, he'd already be in the king's dungeon.

The First Scholar was the most likely. Quin knew Nixus liked to play games, enjoyed outthinking his opponents and toying with them. Whoever was doing this was trying to keep him on his toes before they killed him, that was certain.

The hood was ripped off. He blinked against the sunlight,

his eyes adjusting quickly, and what he saw surprised him ... and made his heart sink.

'Brother,' he said.

'We are Brothers no more,' Kane growled. 'I told you, Quin, the next time I saw you there would be retribution for what you did to our Fourth.'

Quin looked around, seeing Kane's Brothers, Sorin and Viktor, there as well. And behind them, Lana.

'I did not hurt your Fourth,' Quin growled.

The girl herself seemed unharmed. In truth he was glad to see her alive and well. He had meant no harm to come to her.

'I was trying to save her,' he said through clenched teeth. 'If I had left her wandering the citadel, Greygor would have found her and killed her.'

Sorin strode forward, backhanding him across his cheek hard enough for him to stagger to the side.

'On your knees.'

He was pushed down.

'Firstly, beg for forgiveness from our Fourth,' Kane ordered.

Quin gave his former Brother a hard look, but he turned his eyes to Lana. He did owe her an apology at the very least.

'I regret my involvement, but I did what I did to save you. If I had known you'd be in danger, I'd never have left you so defenseless.'

'Spoken like a true Commander.' Kane sneered.

Lana said nothing. Instead, she turned to Kane.

'Are we finished here?' she asked.

'He must be punished for his crimes.'

'He is the Commander of the Dark Army now,' she hissed. 'It's done. Leave it now, please. Let's just continue on,' she pleaded.

Kane looked back at her with a stony expression, though Quin was astonished when his countenance softened.

'It is our way.'

She rolled her eyes. 'But you are not Brothers any longer.'

'We do not stop truly being Brothers even when we leave the Army,' Kane returned.

She looked at Quin. 'I do not blame you,' she said to Quin directly. 'But I cannot speak for the others.'

Quin gave a nod. 'It is our way,' he echoed, 'but my unit will come for me.'

'It seemed to me they'd abandoned you outside the city gates.' Viktor snorted. 'Not surprising from what we've heard about Mad Mal and the new one who drinks and whores all day and night.'

'They were looking for our Fourth,' Quin shot back, wondering how they knew about Bastian. Kane had met him only once. They were getting news from someone. Who? Was it the same one feeding information to Nixus?

'Your Fourth?' Kane's eyes narrowed. 'Did you capture this hapless woman as well?'

Quin stifled a grin in spite of himself. 'That *is* how it first began.'

He looked at Lana again. Odd that only a few weeks ago, he had been besotted by her. What he had said was true. He had done what he had done to save her, given her some story about his mother making him promise. But really he hadn't been able to get her out of his mind, and he had no idea why.

For the first time, he had put his plans of being Commander away, focusing on someone else. But now, as he watched her, he realized that whatever he had thought he felt before, paled in comparison to how much he cared for Lily. His feelings for her ran much deeper than he had imagined them to before she had been taken from them.

But after all that had happened, she probably hated him. His eyes drifted to the ground.

'I am sorry,' he said, looking back up at Lana. 'I'm glad

you escaped.' He glanced at Kane. 'And I'm glad that you were able to leave the Army with her.'

'It all worked out well for you, didn't it, *Commander*?' he said with a smirk. 'That was the role you always wanted, wasn't it?'

'It was,' Quin said, 'and I am better at it than you ever would have been. I was born for this, and I'm glad that I took it when I could. I would not change it.'

'What good fortune for you, then,' Viktor said.

'What shall we do with him? I assume you have a plan, Brother,' Sorin said.

'I do,' Kane replied, taking a small blade from his belt and putting it to Quin's throat.

'Surely you don't mean to kill me,' he said. 'Your woman is safe.'

'There must be retribution.' But Kane hesitated. 'I told you that when we saw you again, there would be, did I not?'

'You did, but I did not think it would cost me my life,' he muttered. 'You always were dramatic.'

They heard a crunch in the forest and Quin looked up just in time to see Lily, of all people, running into the clearing with an angry scream.

'Get away from him!' she cried.

She was closely followed by Bastian and Mal, who pulled her back, but she had already stopped short.

'You,' Kane said, sounding surprised. 'I saw you in the Library.' An odd look came over his face.

~

WHEN LILY SAW the Brother put a knife to Quin's neck, she scrambled forwards faster than Mal or Bastian could grab her.

'Get away from him!' she cried, but as she got into the

clearing and saw his face, she stopped dead, again met with the strangest feeling of familiarity.

'You,' he said. 'I saw you in the Library. How did you escape?'

Lily didn't answer his question.

'I know you,' she blurted. 'And you know me. I can see it in your face, but how? Who are you?'

Behind him, one of his Brothers rolled his eyes. 'This is a trick, Kane,' he said. 'She seeks to save her unit Brother. That is all.'

'Kane.' She uttered his name softly. 'Kane?'

With a gasp, her hand covered her mouth. She knew him. She remembered him, that boy from her childhood who used to run and play with her, used to help them steal food. The boy who kept her and Toman safe until the end.

She took a step forward and fell to her knees.

'Kane,' she asked. 'Is it really you?'

He looked bewildered, gaping at her in silence. 'I don't know you,' he said at last.

'It's me,' she said. 'Lilith.'

'Lilith is dead,' he said, his voice hard. 'She was killed in the arena. I saw it myself.' His eyes landed on Quin. 'What game is this?'

Tears came to her eyes. He didn't know her. 'That wasn't what happened,' she said, her voice breaking. 'I couldn't find you. I didn't know where you were.'

A wave of grief made her hunch over, her face contorting with the pain of her memories.

'It can't be you,' he said softly. 'Lily?'

A tear ran down her cheek. 'I wanted to find you, to tell you...'

'Tell me what? What happened to you? I saw you slain ...' he said and fell onto his knees in front of her.

'Don't touch me,' she said, reeling back. 'You can't touch me.'

Fresh tears came to her eyes. She'd hoped this day would come so that she could confess, but now that it was here, she wished she could run away from him, from all of them. She knew what she would see in their eyes once she told them what she had done. She had to tell him, all of them.

'I killed him, Kane,' she cried. 'I killed Toman.' She covered her face with her hands. 'I didn't mean to. He was in my arms ... and then he was dead, and after that ... No one can touch me save Quin, Mal, and Bastian. Everyone else dies.'

Kane stared into her eyes, his own glistening with unshed tears.

'You killed Toman?' he asked. 'I thought it was the Collector.'

'He was the one who took me. He said, after Toman, he knew what I was. Whoever you saw die in the arena, it was not us. Vineri took me south that very night and there I stayed—'

'—in Vineri's tower until you and then the Army came,' Quin finished for her.

Kane sat down hard on the ground. 'We were so near to each other,' he said. 'If I had just walked up those tower steps, I would have found you.'

'But you wouldn't have known me,' she said quietly. 'How could you have? I am much changed from the girl you knew.'

She began to cry anew, putting her face back in her hands. She could not bear to look at him, at her unit, sure that she would see in their expressions everything she felt about herself. They now knew the worst thing she had ever done. How could Kane forgive her when she could never forgive herself?

Silence permeated the clearing until Mal finally spoke up from behind her.

'Why did you take our Brother?'

'You know why,' Kane growled, looking around as if only just realizing they had an audience. He stood quickly, his face blanked of all emotion.

Lily stayed where she was, staring at the ground in front of her, feeling as if her heart was breaking all over again.

They were talking around her, arguing. A woman she hadn't noticed stepped forward. She took Kane's arm and pulled him to face her, putting her hands to his face and making him look at her. She murmured something to him that Lily couldn't hear and Kane sighed, closing his eyes and putting his forehead to hers in such an intimate gesture that she was compelled to look away.

'Fuck,' Kane muttered. 'Cut him loose.'

Mal sawed through the ropes around Quin's wrists and he stood, staring at Lily. He didn't say a word.

Bastian stepped forward. 'I believe we've met you, Brother,' he said to Kane, 'but your unit, I have not.'

Kane acquiesced to Bastian's friendliness with a grunt. 'This is Lana, Viktor, and that is Sorin.'

Bastian nodded to them all, turning away with an almost comical grimace as his gaze fell on Lana. Lily had the presence of mind to wonder why, but as Quin and Kane regarded each other and then turned to stare unblinkingly at her, thoughts of anything save Quin and Kane left her.

'How did you escape?' Kane asked her. 'I thought you were a prisoner in the Library. No one gets out of that place unless they go to the king's dungeons.'

'There is a unit of Brothers there,' Lily said, her voice subdued. 'They helped me escape.'

Kane regarded her in silence. 'Why do I think there's more to this story?' he asked, and she remembered how astute he'd been when they were young. No one could lie to him.

She didn't want to tell anyone what had happened in that room, but he didn't press, thank the gods.

'We're traveling through to the Strait,' Quin said. 'You?'

'The Ice Plains,' Kane ground out.

'Very well. I suggest we travel together on the north road until the fork,' he said to Kane. 'Give you and Lily time to catch up.'

The day was bright and sunny with a warmth in the air that spoke of spring looming, though the winds from the far north still held their bite. They all traveled together on the road quietly, the Brothers' eyes on the forest around them so that they could not be easily overrun, though by what, Lily didn't know. All the men seemed to be on high alert.

'What's going on?' she asked Lana, who rode beside her, both of them flanked by Brothers.

'The north road is dangerous,' she murmured.

'Why?'

'Attacks,' Lana answered. 'The further north, the more there are.'

'Attacks from what?' Lily asked, and Lana shrugged.

'No one knows.'

Lily turned her head to look at the other woman. 'Then why are you journeying closer to danger?'

Lana grinned. 'My unit may have left the Army, but they are mercenaries still.'

'Brothers are *not* mercenaries, woman,' Kane said menacingly, moving his horse closer to Lana's. She stuck her tongue out at him and Kane shook his head. 'Imp.'

Lily watched their exchange with fascination. Kane was very different from the boy she remembered, but she was glad to see that he cared for Lana and that she seemed to care for him in return.

Well into the day, they decided to camp at the base of a rocky outcrop to save them from the wind, and that night, as they sat around the fire, Lily listened to the Brothers talk about days with the Army.

She was surprised to find that Quin and Kane had been good friends before Quin had taken Lana, which she still didn't understand his reasons for. Quin rarely did anything without thinking about it first. Did he have feelings for Lana? Lily's belly twisted unpleasantly as she thought on that and she pushed the thoughts away.

Their meal finished, Lily stood to get her pack and bedroll. As she returned to the fire, she was stopped by Kane.

'What happened in the Library, Lily?'

'What do you mean?'

'We have been apart a long time, but I know you, and I see shadows in your eyes now that weren't there when I saw you with Nixus yesterday.'

'I don't want to talk about it,' she said, her heart beginning to thud in her chest. 'It's finished now.' She rubbed her eyes. 'Don't you think there are plenty of past hurts for us to revisit without adding to them?'

He nodded. 'That's true enough, I suppose. I'm sorry about Toman, Lily,' he said. 'I should never have left you both alone that day.'

Lily shook her head. 'It wasn't your fault. There was nothing you could have done,' she said. 'Toman was already dying. Every touch I gave him made it worse. I didn't know. You must believe me, Kane, I would never have hurt him on purpose.' Her voice wavered. 'I loved him. He might as well have been my blood.'

'I loved him too,' he said. 'And I loved you. I still do, Lily. You are my sister. You cannot blame yourself anymore. This wasn't your fault.' He hesitated. 'You aren't the only one with power,' he said softly.

'You?'

'Not the same as yours, but yes, and I've done my share of dark deeds with it.'

Another tear rolled down her cheek as she stood in front of him. 'You'd forgive me?'

He stared into her eyes. 'Look at me, Lily.' She did as he said. 'There's nothing to forgive.'

She let out a sob, wishing she could hug him.

'But I know you don't believe me. Forgive yourself,' he whispered and she nodded. She wasn't sure she ever could. But she would try.

'This is for you,' he said, holding something out to her. 'I think you'll find it useful.'

'What is it?' she asked, looking at a thin metal collar with a small locking clasp with a hole for a key.

'The Collector had it,' he said quietly. 'Did he never put it on you?'

'No. I've never seen it before.'

'Odd,' he said. 'I would have thought Vineri would have kept it on you all the time.'

Was Kane suspicious of her? Did he think she wasn't being truthful, Lily wondered?

'What is it? What does it do?'

'See for yourself.' He held it out to her and she took it gingerly from his bare hand. 'I don't know why I kept it,' he muttered. 'Perhaps it was meant for you.'

She put it around her neck and he took off a chain with a tiny key on it that hung around his neck, giving her that as well.

'Keep them together,' he advised. 'Then you can take it off when you need to.'

Lily was confused. 'I don't understand.'

'Lock it,' he invited her. And she did, looping the chain that held the key around her wrist.

But then he did the unthinkable. He stepped forward and touched her cheek with his hand. She drew back with a gasp, her stomach lurching.

'What have you done, you fool?' she hissed.

'Trust me,' he said with a smile, the smile she remembered from when they were children.

Tears came to her eyes, sure he'd die now as well, just like Toman had.

But he didn't fall. He did not gasp for breath. He didn't bleed from his eyes or keel over dead.

'Your touch won't kill me now,' he said. 'Not now, not within two nights. The collar checks the power you hold.'

'I— I can't believe it,' she said, touching the rigid necklace. 'Will it work with everyone?' Lily asked him in wonder.

'It should. You truly haven't worn one before?'

She shook her head.

'Odd,' he said again.

'Not very,' she replied with a wan smile. 'I was kept in a tower alone, Kane. Vineri ensured that I was too afraid to leave it without him. He knew what I had done to Toman and that I never wanted such a thing to happen again. He would never have given me one of these. He knew that with it, I would find a way to escape. Gods, he didn't even give me shoes unless I was journeying somewhere with him.'

'He made you his assassin,' Kane guessed and she nodded. 'I'm so sorry, Lily. If I'd known...'

She hushed him, tentatively squeezing his hand with hers. Then she hugged him, relishing the feel of him.

'I missed you,' she whispered. 'I wondered so many times what had happened to you, if somehow I had killed you as well. I'm so sorry about everything.'

'I joined the Brothers to get revenge,' he said. 'What could we have done differently?' he asked her, looking over at Lana. 'Everything happened the way that it was meant to.'

He gave Lily a quick brotherly kiss on the forehead before drawing away.

'The collar is my gift to you,' he said. 'Now you needn't worry all the time.'

Lily wiped her misting eyes. 'Thank you, Kane.'

He nodded. 'We will be leaving at first light,' he said. 'But we will see each other again.'

'What are you doing up here?' she asked, wondering if he would tell her.

'Just earning some coin,' he said cryptically. His eye caught Quin's and something passed between them. 'We may even rejoin the Army now that our Fourth is safe. Once we have finished in the Ice Plains. What will you do?'

'I don't know,' she admitted. 'Quin told me he would unbind me from the unit if I killed those men, but …'

Kane glared at Quin, but then gave her a quick grin. 'If you believed they would ever have let you go, you are a fool,' he murmured, turning away and leaving her confused.

She shook her head slightly, not really understanding what he meant. She went back to the fire to sit next to Lana, noticing her staring at Bastian with an odd look on her face.

'Kane says you leave tomorrow,' she said conversationally.

Lana turned to her, nodding with a small smile. 'We'll reach the fork soon. The right will lead us further north to the Ice Plains and the left to the Strait, but I expect we'll see each other again. Kane is very glad to have you back. He cares for you a great deal.' She surveyed the Brothers sitting on the other side of the fire, her gaze training on Bastian again. 'They seem to care for you a great deal as well.'

Lily's cheeks heated. 'I don't think so,' she said quietly.

'They do.' She reached out as her eyes fell on the collar and she took Lily's hand gently, changing the subject. 'I thought Kane might give that to you. I'm glad.' She clasped Lily's hand in hers and then let her go. 'I still find riding all day tiring,' she said with a small smile. 'I'm going to get some rest.'

Lana rose, then seemed to hesitate. 'How long have you known Bastian?' she asked quietly.

'Same as the others. A matter of weeks,' Lily answered, her brow furrowing. 'Why?'

Lana didn't take her eyes from the other woman. 'I don't think he's what he pretends to be,' she muttered and then she was gone, walking quickly away before Lily could ask what she meant.

~

KANE and his unit had left them early, taking the fork in the road that led even further north. Mal didn't speak to any of them. Those outside his unit tended to stay away from Mad Mal, and Sorin, Viktor, and Kane had definitely kept their Fourth, Lana, away from him. He didn't mind. Though he may not feel the urge to kill practically everyone that crossed his path these days, Mal found he still only really cared for the company of his own unit.

He glanced at Lily, who was wearing the collar that Kane had given her. They hadn't spoken much since leaving Kitore either, but when the day was half gone and they arrived at a small stream, they decided to rest the horses for a bit.

He watched as Lily went behind a boulder for some privacy. He followed. Something wasn't right with her. She was happy with the collar. Much of the tension that seemed to always be rolling off her had greatly diminished, but something else was weighing on her mind. He wanted to know what.

She came into view as he moved around the great rock and she startled. Her breeches were down, as she was relieving herself, and he suddenly got another view of the scars on her thighs and he recognized them for what they were.

'*You* did them,' he said, berating himself for not realizing sooner.

'What?' she asked, pulling up her clothes with a scowl. 'Gods, Mal, I was just having a piss.'

'The scars. You cut yourself.'

She laughed off his comments with a shake of her head. 'I have no idea what you're talking about.'

He grabbed her wrist as she turned to leave and her expression turned pleading. 'You don't understand,' she said.

'I do,' he replied, pulling up his own shirt to show her all of his burns.

She stared at the many scars in silence for a long time. 'How many?' she finally asked.

He shrugged. 'Three hundred. Stopped counting. You?'

'Forty-four. But I'll never have to do any again,' she said, touching the collar around her neck.

'Even if you kill …' He shook his head. 'The penance is paid with the guilt you carry. I marked myself because I felt none. If you want to hurt, I'll do it, but not like that. Never do *that* again. If I see any more marks appear, I'll take my belt to your arse myself,' he said harshly.

He felt her shudder in his arms. He combed her hair back with his hands and pulled it slightly, making her gasp.

'Want to learn to shoot?' he asked, brandishing his bow.

'Yes,' she said with a shy smile.

He gave it to her and showed her how to pull it, to nock the arrow, to hold it properly with her two fingers to keep the arrow level, and to let it loose. He demonstrated to her the correct technique, shooting a bolt into a tree thirty paces in front of them.

'Your turn,' he said.

She did as he did, and he helped correct her stance. She

let the arrow loose and it flew into a thicket past the tree. She stared at the tree in such consternation that he flicked her nose.

'Takes time. Practice.'

She pulled the bow for her next shot and he put his hand into her breeches, cupping her intimately.

She turned on him. 'I cannot be expected to make this shot with you doing that,' she admonished as he played with her gently.

'Learn to focus,' he chided back.

He took the bow from her hand and set it on the ground. The arrow he kept in his hand. He heard the others still just on the other side of the boulder and smirked. They must know what he was doing.

'Hands over your head,' he said, and she did as he told her. Taking her breeches back down to her ankles, he pushed her back against the boulder so that he could take them off completely.

'Your tunic,' he said, watching her fumble with the clasp, but she took it off, standing in front of him in just her thin undershirt. He could see her chemise underneath.

'The rest of it,' he growled and watched a tremor take her.

'But it's cold.'

'I'll warm you,' he promised. He drew the shirt and chemise over her head. When she was naked and shivering in front of him, he held the arrow by its shaft and drew the feather fletching over her breast. She gasped as it cut her and he grinned as he licked the tiny trail of raw skin it had left in its wake. He did it again and she shuddered, not making a sound as he cut a path in quick flicks down past her navel. His tongue traveled along those as well.

'You like that,' he whispered against her stomach, kissing her navel and laving down to her mound. He pushed her back against the boulder and gripped her thighs, lifting her legs to put them over his shoulders.

His tongue delved deeply into her and she arched her back with a cry, grabbing his hair and pulling it, pulling him to where she wanted his tongue. He smiled as he licked her and for once did not tease her, giving her what she wanted quickly. She cried out, biting her knuckles to muffle the sound as if the others wouldn't know.

He'd noticed Quin in his periphery some time ago, watching from the tree line so that she didn't know he was there, his gaze hungry. Mal had decided to give his Brother a show. They needed Quin to admit that he wanted Lily as much as he and Bastian did. That was his plan.

It was the only way he could think of so that Quin would not acquiesce to her wishes. Now that she had that fucking collar, she could easily leave them if she could make Quin unbind her. A part of him knew it would be for the best, but as he had already told her, he was not a good man.

He made her cry out again and brought her to her peak, pretending that Quin was not staring at them wishing that he was tasting her instead.

When he finally let Lily down. Quin was gone. Mal met her eyes with a chuckle and wiped his mouth with the back of his hand. He kissed her lips hard.

'Going to fuck you later,' he vowed, leaning in to whisper in her ear, 'and let the others watch.'

He heard her sharp intake of breath. 'Both of them?'

'Yes,' he promised darkly, helping her on with her clothes.

When they emerged from behind the boulder, Bastian gave him and Lily a slow look. Quin was nowhere to be seen. Bastian flicked his head into the trees.

'He's gone ahead,' he said, with a knowing chuckle.

Bastian knew what Mal was doing, and if Mal knew his Brother, Bastian would be doing the same before the week was out and they caught their southbound ship from the Strait. By then, they'd be well on their way to breaking Quin, and his notions of unbinding Lily from their unit would be crushed once and for all.

There was no way they were going to let her go without a fight even if she wanted to leave them. Mal and Bastian would ensure that she didn't by any means. By the time they got back down to their camp, breaking the bond would be the furthest thing from Quin's mind ... and hers.

CHAPTER 14

BASTIAN

Their journey that day was monotonous, which, considering they hadn't seen another living soul since Kane's unit had left them, was welcome.

Bastian, for one, was glad to see the back of the other unit. Lana recognized him and she had tried to speak to him about seeing him in the God Realm all those weeks ago. He'd pretended ignorance, told her she must be confused, that she had mistaken him for someone else, but he knew she was suspicious and he still wasn't ready to tell his unit the truth. He thought she might have said something to Lily though as well. Riding next to him, she kept giving him side-long glances when she thought he wouldn't notice. How much time did he have before his secrets were forced from him?

As they traveled, there was a pervading feeling that they were on the cusp of something, that this was some sort of limbo and at any moment they would be thrust into the middle of a battle or some other perilous event.

By unspoken agreement, Bastian, Mal, Quin, and even Lily kept their eyes on the trees. Every rustle made Bastian tense. He wished they hadn't been forced further north, but it was the only way to get south again. He hadn't heard much in Kitore about what was happening up here, and that worried him. There were always stories, tales, rumors, yet all he'd been able to glean was that of the few who'd traveled this way, none had returned.

They made camp by the roadside in the evening, deciding that it was too dangerous to venture into the forest in the dark. Gods only knew what lurked. So they made do with hard biscuits instead of hunting for meat.

Thankfully, Mal had resupplied them from the cache in Kitore, so they weren't lacking in necessities. They huddled closely by the fire, and, although Bastian had heard Mal telling Lily all of the salacious delights that he had planned for her earlier, a somber mood had settled over all of them and it did not lend itself to carnal diversions. The most they would be doing tonight would be sleeping, he suspected.

Instead, he sat next to Lily, putting his arm around her. She tensed for a moment before leaning into him. She enjoyed a cuddle, he knew, after all those years without. So did he, in point of fact. On the Mount, the gods were always a tactile lot, embracing each other, touching, snuggling, fucking. But here it was different. He missed that about the Mount. He even missed some of the other gods, which he wouldn't have imagined possible, having spent so long in their company.

In the flickering light of the fire, he unrolled his bed of blankets and put Lily's next to his. She didn't say a word, simply climbed in next to him and closed her eyes. He settled down for the night. Mal would take first watch. He pulled Lily closer, put his arms around her, and heard her sigh contentedly.

The next Bastian knew was a sharp pain through his skull. And then nothing.

The first he realized that anything was amiss was an all-around feeling; a smell, an aura; and when he opened his eyes, he knew already that he was no longer in the Mortal Realm but on the Mount. He looked around, finding himself in the old throne room. This was where everyone appeared *or reappeared.* He saw Magnus lounging on one of the daises. His friend looked surprised to see him.

'Thought you were off living a mortal life,' he said with a roll of his eyes.

Bastian shrugged. 'I was. Where the fuck is my body?'

Magnus looked at him as if he were a fool. 'Dead, probably. How else would you have got here?' He gave a chuckle. 'Unless you found a witch to fuck you with one of those stone cocks.'

Dead. What if Lily, Mal, and Quin were also …? His heart began to quicken. He had to get back to them. Now.

'Where's Gaila?' Bastian asked, beginning to ascend the white steps to find her. She was the only one of them who could do it.

'You haven't heard? No, of course, you wouldn't have … Gone.'

Bastian stopped in his tracks? 'Gone? Where? She's practically trapped here, Magnus. She can't fucking *go* anywhere we cannot find her.'

Magnus looked uncertain for the first time. 'We don't know. She's not on the Mount; she's not in the small realms she's permitted in. She's just … gone.'

Bastian left his friend, making his way through the many rooms of the Mount, feeling the familiarity, seeing those he'd known for so long and yet wishing he was back in Lily's arms. He didn't belong here anymore. Even in the short time he'd been away, he had changed.

He heard Magnus laughing in his wake. 'Where are you going so quickly? All you have is time.'

He rolled his eyes. Had he truly been the same – without focus, without any sense of urgency?

He took the portal to Gaila's Realm and found it open and dark, which didn't bode well. It was always locked, whether she was in residence or not. He walked into her bower. Her window to the outside was blank, showing nothing.

Surveying the rooms, he saw nothing out of place. It was as Magnus had said; she was just gone. On his way back out, he spied a box on the table. He'd been in her chambers often enough to know that he'd never seen it before. It was new.

He opened it carefully, a small spark of power showing that he was the only one who could have. She'd left it for him. Inside was a small vial of liquid and a note written in the old script.

'Idiot. I knew you'd not last a season in the Mortal Realm.'

Bastian barked a laugh. He could practically hear her caustic tone, but he frowned as he read the rest of her message.

'They're coming for me. By the time you're back, I'll be gone. Use the vial to get back to the Mortal Realm. Don't be foolish enough to die again, or you'll be stuck on the Mount without a body.'

Bastian sat down hard on one of her ridiculously plush chairs. He looked again at her blank window. It didn't even flicker. Her magick was no longer here either.

He examined the vial she'd left. Using his fingernail, he picked off the wax seal and drank it down in one. Gaila would turn up soon. She had to. She wasn't dead. She couldn't be. She was the Goddess, the first of them. He frowned. They couldn't really have got to her here ... could they?

Lily wept quietly on her horse, Mal and Quin riding on either side of her. It had been two days. Two days since that thing had come into their camp and killed Bastian while the others slept.

Mal blamed himself. He was on watch yet hadn't seen anything. Quin hadn't either. But Lily had.

With Bastian's scream into the night, she had woken to see a thing sucking the life from him. Bastian had told her before that he could see her power as a dark smoke around her. She imagined that that was what it looked like; a smoky, nasty, faceless thing. A malevolent mist. Was it what was inside of her, she wondered? The awful thing that had killed a man she loved?

She'd fumbled with the key to the collar, wishing she had practiced with it so she was faster at taking it off. When it finally fell to the ground, she tried to touch the thing, to kill it. But her hand met only air.

Why Bastian? Why not her? She had been right next to him. But it hadn't touched her.

Then, as Bastian had gone gray and cold, the thing had turned solid and black, sinewy and thin. Its arms and legs long and wiry. Its face a hole with no eyes, just a maw. She threw herself at it in anger. And, oddly, the thing without a face had looked surprised somehow before it gave an unearthly screech and exploded into nothing.

She clawed her way back to Bastian, tears blurring her vision. But he was dead. She gave a wail and hugged him to her, looking up to see Quin staring at them with the ghost of an expression of sorrow on his face.

Mal fell to his knees next to her, stroking Bastian's hair.

'I couldn't see anything there,' he whispered. 'I don't understand ... How could you see it and we couldn't?'

Now she listened to the thud of the horses' feet as they

made their way to the Strait to finally get a ship down south. She should leave them as soon as they got to the camp, make Quin unbind her. She told herself she should put all of this behind her. But as she looked at Mal and even Quin in their grief, she didn't know how she could.

'What was that thing?' she whispered. Quin's hand settled over hers where she gripped the reins.

'There are many creatures lurking in the Dark Realms,' he said quietly. 'I doubt it even has a name here.'

'Why couldn't you see it and I could?'

He shook his head. 'I don't know, but if those fae were right and you were made by Kitore itself to protect it, I suppose it would stand to reason that you would be able to see the city's ememies.'

They came upon a village. It was silent and still. Doors hung open. Belongings were strewn about, trampled in the dirt. It was deserted.

'The realm is dying,' Mal said. Neither she nor Quin spoke.

Lily spied something on the road some paces away that reminded her of a dog or a wolf. But it wasn't one.

'I can see that thing,' Quin muttered and Mal nodded as he stared at it.

It turned to look at them, its grotesque face full of black eyes and razor-sharp teeth. It let out a screech not unlike the thing that had killed Bastian, and Lily cringed at the sound. Without hesitation, Mal shot a bolt into its chest and it fell over dead.

'We need to get to the Strait,' Quin murmured.

They rode for the rest of the day and into the night. It wasn't safe to stop. They didn't see another living soul on the road. But they did see bundles of rags, bones, and not just humans, but deer, boar, squirrels. They'd heard no birds in days. It was as if every creature in the whole of the north past Kitore was dead.

'How long until we reach the Strait?' Lily asked.

Quin didn't take his eyes off the roads, always scanning for movement.

'Today,' he said. 'Whether we'll be able to get a ship from there is another matter,' he muttered.

'You don't think there will be any?'

He gave a snort. 'I think everyone's dead.'

'We take a skiff,' Mal said.

'And what? Sail around the coast as far as we can get?' Quin shook his head. 'We won't get far enough. We can't stop in Kitore. We'll be noticed and thrown into the king's dungeon before you can blink. The seas are too treacherous after that. We'll be dashed to bits and drowned. And that's if one of those fucking Dark Realm *things* doesn't sink us first.'

Lily gave a cry as she saw a figure standing in the road in front of them. It couldn't be ...

'Bastian?' she whispered, putting her hands over her mouth in shock. It looked exactly like him.

The other two stopped bickering and stared at him.

'A trick,' Mal growled, drawing his bow.

The man in front of them threw his hands up. 'Wait! Wait. It's me, Bastian.'

'You're dead,' Quin snarled. 'You are not our Brother.'

'I am! I promise you I am.'

It looked like him. It sounded like him. Lily slid down from her horse, took off the collar carefully, and approached him despite the others calling her back.

'Is it really you?' she asked, standing in front of him.

'It's me,' he said. 'You panicked in that tiny boat after the ship went down because the world is so big. You hate having the power that you do. You love it when Mal and I fuck in front of you.'

Lily's cheeks heated. That was definitely something Bastian would say. 'If you're not Bastian, you'll die if I touch you,' she said.

He shrugged and held out his hand. Lily stepped forward and touched it quickly, dancing out of his reach again. He didn't seem affected.

'You were dead,' she whispered, tears coming to her eyes. 'We burned you on a pyre.'

Bastian winced, looking sheepish. 'I— there's something you should know ... about me. That all of you should know,' he said, his apologetic eyes falling on Mal, who was now next to her. 'I should have told you before, but ... I didn't know how.' He looked away. 'I'm a god,' he whispered.

~

QUIN WAS STILL REELING that afternoon. He could scarcely believe what Bastian had told them. But it had to be true. He'd seen Bastian's corpse, burned it himself, yet here he was, healthy as he ever had been, sitting on his horse and cuddling with Lily.

'Strait isn't far,' he said, keeping an eye on the horizon.

Bastian was keeping an eye out on one side of the forest and Mal, the other, Lily doing her part as well. How long before they were attacked again? As far as he could tell, Dark Realm beasts had overrun the lands further north than Kitore. How none of them had known this, he didn't know. It should be common knowledge.

They approached the coast, where, if they had good fortune, there would be a ship in the bay that they could signal to. It was raining and the clouds had rolled in quickly this morning. He huddled down on his horse for warmth.

'There it is.' Mal pointed and they saw the long sturdy

jetty. It looked abandoned, its wardens either dead or fled. 'There's a ship.'

'Thank the gods,' Quin said under his breath.

Quin dismounted and went into the small shack located by the side of the jetty. The wind whipped, snatching the door from him and slamming it into the wooden wall with a crash. He found a torch and lit it, putting it on the end of the pier and hoping it would last long enough for the ship to see it and send a boat for them.

Luck, it seemed, was in their favor, because soon he saw a fire lit on the port side. The mist was rolling in now too, so he could hardly see it. They stood hunched on the jetty, hearing the howling of the wind … and other noises approaching too.

Quin and the others drew their weapons, watching the beach.

'Let us know if anything approaches,' he called to Lily specifically as she was the only one of them who had seen both the dog creature Mal had killed in that dead village as well as the thing that had slain Bastian.

She nodded.

They heard the lapping of a boat's oars and a small skiff appeared out of the gloomy haze just as Lily called out, pointing to the wood planks they were standing on.

'There's something over there.' She turned to Quin, horror pervading her countenance. 'It's under the quay!'

'Fuck! Get to the edge,' he said, turning his gaze to the seas, so oddly calm considering what was happening on the land. 'Hurry! We'll pay double if you get us all on your ship safely,' he yelled.

'I see it as well,' Bastian yelled. 'It's coming!'

As soon as the boat was close, they climbed aboard, Lily first, followed by Mal and Bastian and, finally, Quin.

'It's almost upon you,' Lily screamed as he jumped, crashing into Mal, who caught him before his face struck the hull of the small boat.

'Where is it now?' Mal asked.

'It paces the end of the dock. It looks angry. It can't come in the water,' Bastian said, sounding relieved.

'How is it that you can see it when Mal and I can't, Brother?' Quin asked, putting his hand on Bastian's shoulder.

Bastian had the audacity to smirk, pointing at his own chest with his thumb. 'God,' he muttered.

They sat in the boat, cowering together while catching their breath. Quin continually scanned the waters around them. He glanced at Lily, her face pale and drawn, and, for the first time, he was truly afraid. He couldn't protect his unit; he couldn't protect her against enemies he couldn't even see. How could he keep her with the Army knowing that she wasn't safe with them? Better she go as far south as possible, perhaps even to the Islands. He had to unbind her from them. He had to free her from the Brothers.

The fog was thick as the outline of a large ship came into view. They climbed aboard, Quin thanking the gods they were alive. He hadn't voiced his fears to the others, but there had been times he'd thought they would all die out in the forests, becoming just more piles of bones like the ones they'd found littering the roads.

He couldn't understand why no one knew what was happening. Why was no one in Kitore talking about it? They must know.

A man on the deck approached them.

'I'm the captain,' he said with a flourish. 'Where do you come from?'

'Kitore,' Mal ground out menacingly, causing the man to take an abrupt step back.

Quin put his hand on Mal's shoulder and gave it a squeeze, a silent command to calm down.

'We journeyed from Kitore.'

The captain looked surprised. 'No one's come from that city in a long while, not this way.'

'Do you have news from the Ice Plains?'

The captain grimaced. 'Nothing good. The portals through to the Underhill collapsed, they say. Some of the poor blighters got out before the rest were sealed off. Went to Kitore for help, I heard, but that's all I know.' He shook his head. 'Don't know what's happening in this realm.'

'Do you have any cabins?' Bastian asked, changing the subject.

'Aye, if you can share. I'll have one of the men show you down. There's a galley.' The captain paused, his eyes narrowing as if it had only just entered his mind that they might be paupers. His demeanor suggested that they'd be cast over the side if they were. 'If you can pay.'

'We can,' Quin said, drawing out a jingling pouch and handing it to the captain.

A sailor approached and took them down a ladder and through a hallway to a smaller stately room that had two small beds, a table, and a couple of chairs.

'You'll have to share,' he grumbled. 'There's wine there. Go to the galley for your evening meal.'

Quin nodded and the men left. All four of them threw their bags down and heaved a collective sigh of relief, Lily and Bastian sitting down heavily on one of the beds while the other two sat on the chairs by a small table.

'I don't want to count my chickens,' Bastian said, 'but it looks like we got out of there alive.'

Quin gave him a look. 'I've never heard of a God wanting to live as a mortal. Why did you come to this realm?'

Bastian grimaced. 'I'd been on the Mount a long time.'

Then he glanced at Lily. 'It's not unusual for gods to decide to live mortal lives where I come from.'

'Why did you come back?' Lily asked, her eyes searching.

'There's nothing on the Mount for me now,' he said, taking her hand. 'There are things I value more here.' He turned to Quin. 'How long before we get back to the Westport,' he asked, 'assuming we aren't slain before we get there?'

'Five days. The currents and the winds are in our favor,' Quin replied, and Bastian nodded, lying down on the bed.

'I'm going to rest. Coming back from the dead is tiring work,' he stated airily, drawing Lily down into his arms and holding her close. She let him and closed her eyes, clearly as fatigued as Bastian was.

Quin sat in the chair, leaning back in it and trying to find his calm. After days on high alert, he was finding it difficult. Mal disappeared out of the room, mumbling something about food. Bastian and Lily seemed to have fallen asleep, the solitude giving Quin time to think on their situation.

He didn't know what Lily was feeling now. Would she ask him to unbind her when they got back to the camp? Would Mal and Bastian let her leave if she wished it? Would that even be safest for her?

And what of Bastian? It was clear that Lily was one of his main reasons for returning to their realm. Would he seek to go with her if she decided to leave them? Such a thing was almost always impossible. A Brother was a Brother. For life. But Bastian was a god. He could do as he liked, Quin supposed. He frowned. Full units could leave if they wished and the Commander gave his blessing. Some had done so in Greygor's time; settled down and become land-owning freefolk. If Lily wanted to leave and the other two did as well, would he give up the Army for her? Could he?

It was clear that there was much more going on now than just the portal wards failing. That was just the beginning and

Quin couldn't help but think on the original purpose of the Dark Army. Could it be that the wards had failed before? Or, perhaps, that they had not existed once?

He'd studied all of the old tomes in the Brothers' archives in preparation for becoming Commander, and the oldest texts didn't mention the wards at all. Maybe there hadn't been any. That would explain why the Dark Army had come to be, and why they had not been needed to protect the Realms in so long; why they were now mercenaries instead of sentinels.

But there were other questions as well. If all the portals further north were gone, where were the Dark Realm beasts coming from? A new portal hadn't opened in many, many years. Could it be that one had been birthed somewhere in the northern wilds?

Mal returned a moment later.

'Heard some of the sailors,' he said quietly, so as not to wake Bastian and Lily, who seemed so calm on the bed together. 'The Underhill was overrun. Portals collapsed. Many fae died fighting. Ones that escaped went to Kitore.'

'Where they were murdered,' Quin finished.

Mal nodded.

'All those corpses hanging on the northern wall weren't members of the city,' he said. 'They were fae refugees.'

'Can't tell a fae corpse from human,' Mal said quietly.

'The Underhill has always been under Kitore's rule. Why kill the ones who came looking for sanctuary?'

'Lily said that the men we sent her to kill were fae as well,' Quin said.

Mal looked at him sharply. 'We did someone's dirty work.'

'Aye,' said Quin. 'We've been played false. The fae and the Army have never been at odds before, and they wouldn't be plotting against us now. Someone has made the Army do their job for them, hoping for us to be caught. Two birds …' He frowned. 'We've a betrayer in the camp.'

'Maeve,' Mal muttered. At Quin's expression, he drew himself up. 'She was gone for a long time. Never retook the trials.'

Quin let out a slow breath. Could it be Maeve? He had lent her power when they left for the north. She could have used that to her advantage. 'She has her problems with the way the Army and the camp works, but I can't see her betraying Callan, Jax, and Seth.'

Mal shrugged. 'Lily say anything more?'

'No, and nothing about her time in the Library. She will not speak of it. It's as if … She was unharmed when Drake brought her to you?'

Mal's gaze became unfocused. 'That I could see.'

'And yet it feels as if she suffered some great horror. We need to get it out of her. And we don't have time to wait if what she's keeping back is important information that we'll need.'

'Can get it out of her.' Mal didn't look happy with the prospect, though.

They both heard Lily make a small noise and turned to look at her.

'Dreaming,' Mal said.

'Not a good dream,' Quin added, watching how her eyes moved quickly beneath her lids, how her hands clenched and unclenched and her legs jerked. 'Wake her.'

Mal went over to her and bent down, shaking her gently to wake her. Her eyes opened on a gasp as she looked around the room with frightened eyes.

'You're safe,' Quin said as Mal stroked her face. 'But it's time you told us what happened to you in the Great Library.'

Her lips tightened into a thin line. 'Nothing,' she said.

Mal pulled her gently to her feet and Quin saw that Bastian was awake now as well.

Lily looked away. 'I don't want to speak of it,' she declared.

'It might be pertinent.'

'It's not,' she said, her expression mulish.

Mal made a noise of anger and she flinched.

'You can hurt me if you want,' she said, 'but it won't make me tell you.'

Mal spun back to her, a look of surprise on his face. 'Would never harm *you*, not like that,' he ground out, looking hurt. Her face softened and she touched his stubbled jaw.

'I know,' she said quietly, taking a shuddering breath. 'Something did happen in the Library, but …' She put her head in her hands with a self-deprecating laugh. 'Gods, I don't think you'll even believe me.'

Quin went to her. 'We will,' he said firmly. 'There should be no secrets between us. We are a unit, after all.'

He watched her face to see if she would give anything away about what had happened, but she had learned much since she'd left that tower. She was a closed book now when she wanted to be.

'Please give me until we reach the Westport. I give you my word that I'll tell you what you want to know by then.'

THEY'D BEEN on the ship for only three days when they passed Kitore and sailed around the rocky cliffs. After that, the sea had turned rough and Lily had not enjoyed the journey, her belly rolling with every pitch of the boat. She'd found the book in her pack that Drake had given her. Quin had told her to read it first to keep her mind occupied during the voyage, for which she was thankful.

The Brothers were standoffish and she knew it was because they wanted to know what had happened in the Library. She would need to tell them, but every time she thought on it, she felt so ill, she was afraid she would retch.

Quin had also told her that, if she wished it, he would unbind her from the unit and give her the means to be free from them regardless of the deal they'd made in Kitore. They wanted to know if she'd yet made a decision, if she would stay with the unit or if she would make Quin unbind her. In truth, she still didn't have an answer. She fingered the collar around her neck. She could go anywhere she wanted. She could do anything. As long as she kept this on her, she could live a normal life without towers and closed doors. Without being alone.

She thought back to the book, which had turned out to be an account of some long-dead Commander of the Army. She found it very interesting, though the Brother who'd written it had clearly been a madman. It had started out normal enough, with descriptions and thoughts of days' events, but gradually, the pen's scratchings seemed to get more scrawling. There were sketches of Dark Realm creatures that plagued him in his dreams, pages and pages about nightmares and rantings about portals that made no sense. She had no idea why Drake had wanted Quin to have it.

She approached said Brother on the deck and stood next to him. He looked down at her with an almost fond expression.

'What is it?' he asked.

'It's the book. I've read it from cover to cover and I don't understand why it's important.'

Quin looked out towards the horizon. 'If Drake wanted me to have it, he had a motive even if it's not readily apparent. That man's no fool. He knows more than he let on, and he's trying to tell me something without saying the words. Is that all you came to talk about?'

'I'm bored,' she blurted. That wasn't what she'd meant to say to him, but she didn't know what to say, in truth.

'Come,' he said, not looking at her. He took her hand and led her below decks.

Lily followed him back down to their small room, finding Bastian and Mal already there, both just in their breeches. They'd been waiting for her, she realized, looking back at Quin, who was regarding her strangely. He seemed to know what she wanted, but he was going to make her say it aloud, she realized.

She stared at them, feeling shy and wondering how best to approach them. Besides cuddles from Bastian, none of them had touched her since Mal had in the forest, and she wasn't sure why, but it was making her feel tense and anxious.

She removed her tunic and her boots and found when she looked up that they were watching her with curious interest.

'I—' she began. 'I want—' She looked away, her cheeks heating, and Bastian gave her a slow smile.

'Come,' he commanded, and she walked to him. 'I know what you want, and I would give it to you, but it comes at a price.'

Lily bit her lip and nodded, at this moment feeling as if she'd do anything to feel his hands on her.

'What is the price?' she breathed.

'You tell us what happened in the Library.'

Lily grimaced and turned away.

'That's the price,' he said. 'If you don't want to pay it, it's up to you.'

She rolled her eyes and gave a small growl. 'You told me I could have until the Westport.'

'Changed our minds,' Mal said.

'No,' she said, feeling angry and annoyed. She turned to leave the room, but Quin blocked her way. She watched him turn the key in the lock and take it out, stowing it at his belt.

'You cannot keep me here,' she said, but his expression told her that they could and would.

She sat petulantly in the chair, her eyes widening as she noticed Bastian approach Mal, his gaze not straying from her.

Mal grinned, quirking a brow as Bastian took his hand and pressed it to the bulge in his breeches.

'Certain you don't want to be here?' Mal asked her, his gaze rolling over her as he palmed Bastian through his clothes.

Bastian looked uncertain for a moment, pulling away from Mal slightly.

'Have you ... are you ...? Now that you know what I am ...'

Mal took Bastian's face in his hands and kissed him full on the lips.

'You are a member of my unit,' he said, unbuttoning Bastian's breeches and taking hold of his cock, moving his hand over him.

Bastian looked relieved. 'I thought that perhaps ...'

'You thought wrong,' Mal murmured, nuzzling his neck and giving him a bite that had Bastian yelping.

They turned to look at Lily, who was already wishing that she was between them. Quin removed his own tunic and shirt, the broadness of him, of all of them, making Lily's mouth go dry.

But none of them touched her. She made a noise of frustration. She knew what they were doing.

'Fine,' she hissed. 'You want to know what happened? The fae caught me, knocked me out. When I woke, I was,' she swallowed hard, 'I was in a dungeon. They took me to the

First Scholar. He examined me, said he wanted to keep me for something. I was taken to a room and then one of his … guards came. He had gloves on.' She looked down at the floor. 'He beat me,' she said. 'Kicked me. Spat on me. It went on for … so long … By the time he was finished, I couldn't move my legs. I was coughing up blood. My ribs were broken. I couldn't breathe. There was so much pain.'

She looked up to gauge their reactions. All three stared with open mouths, their fury a sight to behold.

'B-but … no injuries,' Mal stuttered.

'Drake's unit found me. One of them healed me,' she explained. 'It was quick and painless and then I was fine, but I can't stop thinking about what that monster did, the blows he rained down on me. I could do nothing to stop him.'

A tear rolled down her cheek and she brushed it away angrily. 'I see him when I close my eyes. In my dreams.'

Quin put his hands back on her shoulders, drawing her backwards towards him gently.

'It wasn't the first time he had done that to a woman in that very room. He told me about the things he'd done before while he did them to me,' she continued. 'That makes it worse. I wish I could have killed him. But I couldn't.'

Quin hushed her. 'It's done now.'

Mal came forward and brushed his fingers over her face. 'Will give you revenge.'

She shook her head. 'I just want to make sure that he can never do that to a woman ever again. He loved what he did. He loved my cries, my begging. What you did with your belt was the worst beating I'd ever had,' she said, looking back at Quin, 'but it was nothing compared to what he did.'

Quin met her eyes and tilted her head back. He kissed her gently on her lips. 'We'll make sure he dies for it,' he promised.

He unbuttoned her breeches and eased them down her

thighs, pushing her back into the chair so that he could take them off. Sitting in just her chemise, she stared up at Quin's shirtless form, taking him in. She needed him. Them.

He put two fingers under her chin, raising her up to standing once more and turning her to face the others. He kissed her neck while the others watched, his hands running up and down her body, making her shiver and shake and want.

He drew her chemise over her head, baring her to them before picking her up and gently laying her on the bed.

Bastian and Mal were in the background, kissing each other. He rolled his eyes at them, spreading her legs wide and looking down at her slit.

'I saw what Mal did in the forest,' he admitted, opening her thighs even further. 'How I wished it was me tasting you.'

His head descended and she moaned as he licked her, two of his thick fingers entering her at the same time, making her gasp and lift her hips from the bed.

A now naked Bastian joined them, taking her breasts in his hands and kneading them. He groaned as Mal began to fuck him from behind, bending down to suck on her nipples as Mal thrust into him.

Bastian bit her gently, making her squirm as Quin eased himself inside her channel and began to fuck her slowly. She whimpered and pleaded for more, but he refused to quicken his pace.

He reversed their positions so that she was atop him, grinning at her surprised expression. 'It can be done many ways,' he said with a gleam in his eye.

Mal came quickly, letting out a guttural cry as he finished and Bastian stood, his cock still hard. She leaned over and took it in her mouth as Quin held her hips and began to move her up and down, his staff pistoning in and out of her in such a way that she began to shudder and gasp at the delicious prickles that built within.

Bastian was content to let her mouth work him as he watched Quin taking her, pinching her nipples hard and making her squirm. Then Mal was behind her and she took in a deep breath as she felt his hand caressing her arse. She heard him spit and then a finger was inside her back passage, and she cried out, almost not able to breathe. The sensations were too much to bear!

He was gentle as he eased in and out and, with his other hand, pulled Bastian– and Bastian's cock– away from her.

Bastian grasped Mal's hair and pushed his staff into Mal's open mouth just as Lily reached her peak, throwing her head back and screaming loudly as Quin thrust into her spasming channel and Mal's finger kept its pace in her other one. She tightened around Quin's cock and he found his release without warning, gripping her tightly and plunging into her hard and deep.

A moment later, Bastian let out a groan too as Mal swallowed his seed. Bastian pulled him up and kissed him with a sound of contentment that Mal mirrored immediately.

All of them finally sated, Quin took Lily in his arms and she curled up next to him, Bastian on her other side, while Mal got dressed and left to find them food and drink.

Lily closed her eyes and let herself drift, feeling as if a weight had been lifted from her now that she had told them what had happened in the Library. She didn't know what she expected from the Brothers, but it wasn't the kindness that she had seen in all of their eyes, even Mal's. It made her wonder if perhaps she *could* make a life with them. She loved them, after all, and she was beginning to understand that they did really care for her as well.

Notwithstanding the Brothers' promises, Lily knew enough to realize that she wouldn't be readily able to forget what had happened to her, however. She wasn't a vengeful person, but she founded she wanted to see that monster who'd beaten her get his comeuppance. If the opportunity presented itself, she wouldn't ignore it. Knowing that the Brothers understood that, did give her some measure of comfort.

~

They arrived back at the camp a few days later, the ship's journey dull and painfully boring, thank the gods. Once they reached the Westport, they traveled straight to the camp, finding it in its usual orderly fashion in the same place they'd left it, though Vineri's fortress was now stripped bare and half demolished.

Quin took Lily directly to his tent, noticing at once that the great desk was now tidy, the piles of haphazard papers gone. There were but a few pieces for him to deal with. Despite his suspicions, Maeve was a good steward, he noted.

Lily went to the table, always stocked with food, and piled a plate high, much to his amusement, as soon as they got inside. Seeing his gaze, she grinned sheepishly, her cheeks reddening as he sat at his desk and looked over what Maeve had left him about the goings-on while he'd been away. Thanks to her succinct notes, it didn't take him long to catch up.

Lily unpacked the bags, putting the book from Drake on his desk. He sighed as he stared at it; the diary of a man who had gone mad in his quest to understand their realms, rambling about the fae, portals, wards. It was interesting, granted, but he still didn't understand Drake's reasons for giving it to him save that the wards were mentioned, perhaps for the first time. He'd never read anything about them in the other archival tomes from before the man's time, after all.

Quin had decided what he would do. Perhaps *that* had been Drake's aim all along. It would be a hard sell to the Army, but after the devastation he'd seen in the north that would inevitably sweep across the whole of their realm, there was no alternative. The Army of the Dark Brothers had been created for a task, and they must perform it again or there would be nothing left for anyone.

The boy appeared in the tent with a note. Quin took it from him, looked it over, and stood immediately.

'What is it?' Lily asked.

'It's Maeve. She was attacked last night,' he said, reading the note again as he strode from his tent, Lily following closely behind him.

He went down the two rows it took to get to the tent Maeve shared with Jax, Callan, and Seth and rang the bell outside.

Seth appeared at the door.

'Where is she? What happened?'

'We know little more than I put in the note. She has not woken since she was found yesterday in your tent.'

Quin's eyes narrowed as he went in, finding Maeve on the bed unmoving, Jax and Callan sitting on either side of her, each clutching one of her hands. The side of her face was bruised. Someone had hit her with something heavy.

'Who did this?' Callan looked up at Quin. 'Who the fuck did this to our Fourth?'

'Has anyone seen Morden?' Quin asked grimly.

'Morden?' Jax scoffed. 'Morden is weak. Pathetic. He couldn't even pass the trials to become a Brother.'

'But has anyone seen him?' Quin ground out.

'Not for days.'

'Get the word through the camp. Morden is to be found and brought to me. He can't have gotten far,' Quin called, walking from the tent.

Greygor's steward was the only other person who could have done this. And he would have had all of the information that was disclosed to their enemies as well. It had not sat well with him thinking it was Maeve. She was a straightforward woman. Subterfuge? Cloak and dagger? That wasn't what he would expect from her. If she had a problem, she would come at him head-on.

Quin was a fool for not having considered Morden before, but he was such a pathetic worm. He was never at the forefront of Quin's mind, if he was honest.

~

LILY AND QUIN returned to the tent and it wasn't long before a short yet haughty man was brought in. Morden, she presumed. He looked at Lily with disdain before Quin rose from the desk and hit him hard.

He stumbled back.

'Did you attack Maeve?' Quin thundered.

'She— she was betraying the Brothers! I saw her writing a missive to the Great Library. She gloated to me that you had given her the power of the Commander and that she would use it how she saw fit. She received monies from the king for information on Brothers' movements, on the inner workings of the camp. I sought to save us all!'

'You fucking liar,' Quin spat.

'I speak the truth,' Morden insisted. 'The *woman*—'

'—is not your concern,' Quin said.

A soldier in gray entered the tent and put a bag on Quin's desk. 'This was found hidden under his tent. It's full of gold, Commander.'

'Aye,' Quin said, 'payments for Dark Brothers' secrets. Did you attack Maeve because she found you out? You might as well tell the truth. You'll die either way.'

Two of Maeve's unit came into the tent. 'Maeve is awake,' Callan said. 'You can guess her story. We've come for him ... as is our right.'

Quin waved a hand. 'He's yours. Get what you can out of him. I want to know who he's been spilling secrets to and exactly who he's told what. Do what you like with him after you get what I need.'

'No!' he squealed. 'I'll not die for what I did to that bitch. She deserved it!' He began to struggle in Callan's grip. 'If you give me to them, I'll tell them nothing! But let me live, let me go, and I'll give you everything you want to know.'

Quin's lip curled up into a sneer. 'Get him out of my sight.'

'No! No!' The man was dragged away, his screams growing dim as he was taken.

'What will they do to him?' Lily asked.

'You don't want to know,' Quin said solemnly, staring at the closed tent flaps.

Later that day, Lily lay on the great bed that now stood in the tent. Where Quin had procured it from, she didn't know, but it was large enough for at least three of them to share comfortably.

Though she thought that Quin was being presumptuous in assuming that she would stay, she had decided that she would. She just hadn't told them yet. She grinned. Perhaps she didn't need to.

Mal and Bastian both moved their belongings in with Quin's; he'd ordered his men to make his tent larger to accommodate them all. It now boasted a second small room for sleeping that had been added in record time by soldiers, who looked at her curiously but didn't speak to her.

She frowned as she watched Quin working at the desk. He was worried about what was happening in the north, with the wards and portals. They all were, but she couldn't help but think, after what Bastian had told her about the Mount, about that goddess disappearing, that there was something more happening that they didn't understand.

Quin had decided that the Army would become the sentinels of the realms that they had always been before when they were needed. Perhaps that was all they could do, fight the encroaching darkness as best they could from their tiny corner of the many realms that existed.

She could also help in some way, she thought with a smile, quietly disrobing before wandering through the tent to where Quin sat, deep in thought. She knew that Mal and Bastian were watching her from the table where they were sharing a meal, so she took her time, letting them see her.

Quin didn't look up from what he was doing until she sat in front of him, plonking her bare arse on the desk. He took her in, leaning back.

'I have work to do,' he murmured, though his gaze began to heat.

'It'll still be there tomorrow,' she said, taking hold of his tunic and drawing him closer, playing the practiced courtesan even as she tried to control her quickening breaths.

'Will you?'

She looked into his eyes. This was the first time he'd asked her directly if she was going to stay with them. She glanced at the others, finding them silent and waiting with bated breath for the answer she would give Quin.

He took her hands in a sudden motion. 'If you wish it, we can leave. All of us. Tonight.'

Lily's breath caught. 'You'd leave the Army? Give up being Commander? For me?'

'For you. For me.' Quin glanced up at the others. 'For all of us.'

Tears came to her eyes as she held his gaze. She knew how important being Commander was to him, how hard he'd worked all his life for it. It was his purpose. At least for now.

She turned back to him and put her hands on either side of his face. 'No,' she whispered. 'We can't leave. In truth, I don't want to. I want to fight this darkness with you. I want to make sure it doesn't consume us all. I'm your Fourth and we're a part of the Army.'

Her lips descended on his and it took him a moment to respond. When he did, however, it was with a growl of contentment and he grabbed her, squeezing her to him as he lifted her up, wrapping her legs around him. He carried her to the great bed and put her down, making her watch as he took off his belt and pulled it taut, mimicking what he'd done in the forest.

She tensed uncertainly. 'You're not going to …'

'Punish you for making me wait for your answer?' he growled. Then he grinned, throwing the belt to the ground as the others came to stand next to him, looking down at her on the bed, their gazes roving over her, their eyes promising dark pleasures that made her shudder in anticipation.

'Perhaps a little, but I think you'll enjoy it.'

The End

If you enjoyed this book, it would be amazing if you were able to leave a review on Amazon.

Reviews are so, so helpful to authors (especially new ones like me!) to get us noticed and, I'm not gonna lie, I love reading them!

Also, keep reading for the exclusive first chapter of *Caught to Conjure,* Book 4 in the Dark Brothers series!

. . .

THANKS FOR READING! Not ready to leave Lily and her Brothers? Join my mailing list and receive an exclusive epilogue to find out what happens after Quin changes the Army's purpose!

Use the URL below for your exclusive bonus scene:
https://BookHip.com/VKPJRCX

JOIN MY MAILING LIST

Sign up to my newsletter and receive an exclusive epilogue to find out what happens with Lily and her Brothers next!

Members also receive exclusive content, free books, access to giveaways and contests as well as the latest information on new books and projects that I'm working on!

Use the URL below:
https://BookHip.com/VKPJRCX

It's completely free to sign up, you will never be spammed by me and it's very easy to unsubscribe.

AND keep reading for an exclusive sneak preview of Caught to Conjure, Book 4 of the Dark Brothers Series.

CAUGHT TO CONJURE (SNEAK PREVIEW)

A powerful witch who escaped a life of cruelty. Three Dark Brothers who have a score to settle with her. Will they band together to stop the destruction of their world, or is their hatred of each other stronger than any love?

Pre-order Caught to Conjure (Release date 2021) at www.kyraalessy.com/caught2conjure

Vie

Someone was coming. She'd been feeling it for days; an odd change – perhaps in the wind. It wasn't strange for her to get these funny little wisps of foresight. Vivienne was a witch after all. But with this one came with a definite feeling of dread that kept her up in the night, made her startle at shadows, and, at the moment, it was setting her on edge as she moved around her small cottage making tinctures and healing potions for the various people who came for her services.

Vie put down the bottle of oil she was mixing with an infusion of flowers and herbs with a sigh. She couldn't concentrate and that usually meant something was imminent.

With a calm borne of the many, many times she'd had to hide from those who'd wish her harm before, she gathered her most prized possessions; the ancient tomes that were irreplaceable, and some of the artefacts she'd acquired that were useful in rituals. She stowed everything safely under the floor, covering them with a stone before replacing the floorboards. At least if anything happened to the house, they would be safe there. They were just about the only possessions she had brought with her, dragging them all the way from the north, and she wasn't about to let anything happen to them.

She glanced around, wondering if she was forgetting anything. Was there anything else that she needed to save? But, as she surveyed the rest of the small room and behind the curtain where her bed was, from the herbs she'd gathered herself to the glass vials of potions on the shelves she'd built herself, all of it was easily replaceable, hard work she could perform again.

It wouldn't be hard to start afresh somewhere else. She had planned for this, after all. It was why she donned the mask of the crone whenever she did business with the folk here and why she also had another disguise of a widow. The rituals and spells required to be able to change one's appearance into another's at will were complex, time consuming and challenging, so she'd only done it twice, only had two different faces. But it meant that she was well-known in the village as a completely different person; a young widow named Marla who was more or less respected.

No one knew she was a witch. The Crone could disappear and, as Marla, she could live in the village until the end of the summer with none the wiser. She'd decide, after a sufficient amount of time had passed, to visit some nonexistent relatives elsewhere and simply never return. Vie would set up somewhere else – as the crone of course. She had a small cache of coins saved and, of course, she reminded herself, she'd known she'd have to leave one day.

Taking one last look around, she frowned at the unexpected rush of loss. She had been happy here in this place by the southern coast and she'd enjoyed helping the people even if they did view her with suspicion and dislike.

She closed the door gently and left her small house, the hearth still warm, taking nothing with her save a sachet for protection that she shoved into a hidden pocket in her brown woolen dress.

Walking quietly into the thicket close by, she waited to see who would come, morbid curiosity taking over. Who from the village would it be, she wondered. Marcus, the Smithy? He'd always been vocal about anyone who seemed different having spent some time in the north, where the fear of magick was rampant. Or would it be Silva, the seamstress who had a shop in the little town close by. She'd made no secret of her distaste for anything 'Dark Realm and conjuring', going so far as to forbid those in her tight knit circle from visiting the Crone. What the woman didn't know was that all her friends still did, wanting their potions and balms.

Vivienne knew who in the village couldn't conceive, which ones hated their husbands or their wives. Some came wanting potions for curses or poisons for killing. She had the skill of course, but she'd never wanted to hurt anyone. It just wasn't in her nature to wish anyone harm. So when those villagers did come, she usually gave them something to make them see the destructive path they were on instead.

Hearing voices in the distance, she ducked down. Here they came in the full daylight with their *torches and pitchforks*. She was one, lone woman. She rolled her eyes. Ridiculous.

Sure enough, as they rounded the bend of the little dirt track, she saw the Blacksmith was in front, several other men and women following, anger in their countenances. She frowned. Something must have happened. There was no reason to come for the witch unless some disaster had befallen the area. No one was ill in the village at the moment. There were no storms imminent. By all accounts, everything seemed fine.

'Come out, witch!' the Blacksmith bellowed, making her shiver in spite of herself. It didn't matter how many times the animosity was directed at her, it never got any easier to take. Gods she'd probably burst into tears later when she thought on this afternoon.

Thank the Gods she hadn't been caught unawares and wasn't still in there. By the way the people were riled up, she'd be burning on a pyre by supper.

She took a deep breath and reminded herself that she had nothing to fear now even if they caught her watching. She had already changed into her widow's face and had donned the clothes of her disguise. No one would know who she really was now. And she had nothing on her person that could tie her to this place. If anyone saw her, they just imagine she was part of the group. Yet still, she hid. Watching. Why? She didn't want to see her little house burned. She loved it. She loved everything about it. It represented her freedom, her dignity, her life that she'd carved out for herself against the odds. She didn't want to see it aflame, but she could not look away.

'We'll smoke her out,' the blacksmith yelled, throwing his

torch up onto the thatched roof. The dry grasses caught immediately and she found her eyes filling with tears. It was so foolish, she thought. She'd known this day would come and yet the sting of it was almost too much to bear, so much so that she almost missed the soldiers that stood behind the small crowd that had gathered.

Vie's heart almost stopped in her chest, her stomach clenching in fear and dread, as she looked each man over, feeling marginally better when she saw that none of them was familiar to her. She knew those uniforms though; the red and black of the Great Library of Kitore, of its Academy, of the Great Scholar Nixus himself; the real power in the Capital and a man she never wanted to see again. He haunted her nightmares and her darkest imaginings. She'd spent two years so desperately trying to be free of him, but her mind always dragged her back to that place where she had spent her youth. She stumbled back, finally looking away. She fled down the path, away from the crackling of the fire.

It wouldn't take long to get to the small house she had taken not far away there. Perhaps there she would feel safer. No one would know her, after all. She walked down the path at a normal pace though her body was screaming at her to run as far from the soldiers as she could get. The dense forest around her suddenly felt threatening as she hurried along while trying to pretend she wasn't in fact fleeing for her life. So engrossed was she in her fears that, at first, she didn't notice the three men who stepped into her path until they were practically looming in front of her.

Too late to turn around. She stopped dead in her tracks. It couldn't be them. Not them. She pasted a pleasant smile on her face, her palms beginning to sweat.

'Afternoon,' she said brightly, beginning to walk once more, hoping she wouldn't give herself away.

She intended to pass them by, knowing that they

KEPT TO KILL

wouldn't see anything amiss in her countenance. She knew how to keep her feelings and thoughts to herself. The lessons had been hard, but she had learned them.

She made to go by the leader, Drake, his eyes still as piercing blue as she remembered and that deep copper hair she'd admired from afar ... he kept a short beard now, she noticed. As methodical as he was, he probably trimmed it every morning without fail. His arm shot out, stopping her from taking another step.

Outwardly, nothing gave her away. She looked up at him innocently, acted as if she'd never seen them before and had no idea they were very dangerous men.

'Who are you?' he asked, the low timber of his voice reminding her of a time she rarely let herself think about now.

Vie let her brow wrinkle in confusion.

'My name is Marla,' she said, drawing back a step as any woman might do when confronted by three large men such as them.

'No games, witch. We don't have the time,' the man said tiredly, his eyes rolling.

Vie remembered that too. She hated that expression, that tone, always so *bored* with her misery as if it inconvenienced *him* somehow. Her jaw tightened.

'There's a crone who lives in the forest that way.' She pointed and then gave him a patient smile. 'As you can see, I'm plainly not she. Please let me pass. I must get home.'

She took a step forward and saw him look at his Brother, Vane, who sneered at her with a nod of his head.

'Take her,' Drake ordered said and she found her arms in the grip of the other two.

Krase's was the most punishing, which was ironic considering he was the one that could heal. Perhaps that was why he was more heavy-handed, she thought, because he knew he could just take the pain away when – if – he felt like it.

The other one, Vane, was gentler in his hold. He was the one she would work on first. She whispered words, an inaudible incantation. One of many she knew from memory that would make touching her cause him pain. Vane swore, his hand leaving her as he stared in incredulity and then she directed it towards Krase.

He growled low, looking at Drake.

'She's conjuring,' he said through gritted teeth as he resisted the pain.

She pulled away from him, trying to loosen his grip without magick, but he clamped down tighter.

She let out a sound of anguish as Drake pulled pink vial from the pouch at his belt. The sight of it made her head spin, terror taking over immediately. He didn't give her a chance to stop what she was doing. He simply threw it at her feet where it smashed in the dirt, vapors filling the air around her.

She coughed and spluttered, letting out a wail that was cut off right in the middle. As the potion worked its tainted magick on her, she was plunged head-long into her memories, transported back to the Great Library, back to the Academy eight years before on that very first day she'd met them.

~

8 years prior

So, what do you say, girl?' Nixus, the First Scholar asked her, smiling kindly.

Vivienne gaped at him, shivering as she pulled the woolen blanket he'd given her close. She knew what she should say. She'd been on the streets just long enough to see the crueler sides of men. She couldn't trust anyone. But it was snowing outside and, as the winter had rolled in, she'd quickly realised why so many didn't last long on the streets of Kitore. It was just too cold out there to survive.

She glanced up from the high stone platform that rose up from the main library floor under the massive vaulted ceiling of the Great Library. They were surrounded by great stone columns and row after row of books, more than she'd ever known existed.

At her silence, he continued, 'How long have you been carrying messages for us? A few weeks now?'

She nodded.

'And before that, when your mam was alive you lived with her?'

Again, Vivienne nodded.

'You know the streets are no place for you,' he tutted. 'Your mam wouldn't have wanted that for you.'

He was right. Mama had thought she had time to work off the debts Da had left her with. Her death had been sudden. She'd had no idea Vivienne would end up destitute, never prepared her for such a thing. Without her gifts, Vivienne wouldn't have lasted two days. Even now, they were numbered. She knew what happened to girls who reached a certain age. She'd successfully stayed out of their clutches for some weeks, but soon, one of the gangs would make her join them. After that, Gods only knew what she'd be forced to do. And what if someone found out about her gifts?

It was already getting difficult to explain away the phantom winds or the fact that the stones the baker had let her warm in his oven to take back to her little corner of the derelict building she lived in hadn't cooled for days.

She made up her mind in that moment. She couldn't afford to give a fuck why he wanted to take her in. She knew her da had worked for the Library before he'd been slain in a tavern brawl two summers before. He'd always spoken of Nixus as an honorable man. That would have to be enough.

'I'll go to the Academy?' she asked him softly.

He nodded with a gentle smile that made his eyes crinkle. 'Yes, you'll attend my academy. All those I take in must learn.'

'There are others?'

'Only one at the moment. You'll have a room here in the Library itself, but the Academy is just across the river. You'll be clothed and fed and, eventually, you'll assist me with my research if you work hard.'

She looked up at him. 'All right.'

Putting a hand on her shoulder, he gave it a reassuring squeeze. 'I'll have you shown to your room,' he said as the door to his mezzanine opened and three older boys trudged in. 'Perfect timing. This is Vivienne. She will be joining us here in the Library. Vivienne, this is Drake, Vane and Krase. They attend the Academy as well, though they're slightly ahead of you in years. Take her to the end chamber,' he ordered, summarily dismissing them all.

Still clutching her blanket, she surveyed them. Each one simply stared at her in open animosity that made her cant her head. They didn't even know her and yet they already didn't like her. All three filed out, the one called Drake gesturing impatiently for her to follow them, which she did. They led her down the steps and across the Library floor, passed tables where other students at the Academy worked in silence.

She caught sight of another boy, staring at her from the stacks, pure hatred in his eyes as well and she frowned. Why did no one seem to want her here? Was it because she was from peasant stock? The Academy was where all the wealthy families in the north and further afield sent their precious children, after all. She was clearly not going to be housed with them as the dormitories were inside the Academy itself, just across the river. Not that she cared. Just being out of the cold was enough.

Her heart began to thud in her chest as she watched him smile nastily at her. After her time on the streets, she was afraid of boys like him. She would readily admit that to herself. But surely nothing bad could happen to her while she was under the care of the First Scholar.

The three boys walked tin front of her. One of them glanced back at her and murmured something. The other two snickered and she looked down at the floor self-consciously.

They turned down a hallway and plodded down some steps. There were three doors. They stopped outside one and Krase gestured with his head. 'That's you, witch.'

She blinked at him. He couldn't know ... could he?

'Give me your blanket,' Vane sneered.

Vivienne took a step backwards. 'Get your own,' she whispered, more quietly than she'd wanted to. Gods, she'd never have made it on the streets, she thought as she looked up at his scornful face.

His hand darted out and ripped it from her. She let it go, more out of surprise than anything else.

Each one looked her up and down with disdain and her cheeks burned at their perusal of the ragged, dirty dress she wore.

The third one, Krase, leaned in towards her. 'Word of advice, Witch. Do as you're told here.'

And then all three of them pushed by her, strolling down the hall as if they owned it. Her hand pressed against her racing heart and she swallowed down her fear and anger, reminding herself that this was better than the corner of the derelict building by the river that she'd been living in.

She opened the door to a small, sparse and windowless room. A single candle burned on a small, table beside a narrow bed. She smiled. Despite the company, this was infinitely better than the streets.

Read the next dark adventure in this amazing series today!
More info at www.kyraalessy.com/caught2conjure

ACKNOWLEDGEMENTS

A special thanks to everyone who's been reading my books so far. Your support is what keeps me writing!

Without your feedback and comments, I would probably have quit by now!

Thanks so much to all of you!

ABOUT THE AUTHOR

Kyra was almost 20 when she read her first romance. From Norsemen to Regency and Romcom to Dubcon, tales of love and adventure filled a void in her she didn't know existed. She's always been a writer, but its only now that she's started to tell stories in the genre she loves most.

She LOVES interacting with her readers so please join us in the Portal to the Dark Realm, Kyra's private Facebook group, because she is literally ALWAYS online unless she's asleep – much to her husband's annoyance!

Take a look at her website for info on how to stay updated on release dates, exclusive content and other general awesomeness from the Dark Brothers' world – where the road to happily ever after might be rough, but its well worth the journey!

- facebook.com/kyraalessy
- twitter.com/evylempryss
- instagram.com/kyraalessy
- goodreads.com/evylempryss